T0194346

Other works by Daniel B. Hunt:

(Science Fiction)
The Eclipsing of Sirus C: A Dryden Universe Novel

(Fiction)
Stories of the Midnight Sun

(Poetry)
The Modern Day Poet
North Wind Muse

ORIGINS

A Dryden Universe Collection

DANIEL B. HUNT

ORIGINS
A DRYDEN UNIVERSE COLLECTION

iUniverse books may be ordered through booksellers or by contacting:

iUniverse
1663 Liberty Drive
Bloomington, IN 47403
www.iuniverse.com
1-800-Authors (1-800-288-4677)

ISBN: 978-1-4917-8906-3 (sc)
ISBN: 978-1-4917-8907-0 (hc)
ISBN: 978-1-4917-8908-7 (e)

Library of Congress Control Number: 2016902472

Print information available on the last page.

iUniverse rev. date: 02/26/2016

For my daughters, Mykenzie, Lindsey, and Ona. All corners of the world and the vast distances of space cannot hold the love I feel for you.

For Theresa, because dreams should be big.

And for Jordan, the apple of her father's eyes.

Contents

Acknowledgments

Joel Stottlemire had a crazy idea: create a science-fictional universe that artists could freely use and jointly promote using Creative Commons licensing. He called it an experiment—The Dryden Experiment. Joel and author John Berg initially developed the Dryden Universe and established the framework for the stories in this collection. Their creative effort not only provided me with a rich fabric to explore but also provided many other artists with an opportunity to showcase their talents in a welcoming and warm environment. I am very grateful to both of them for their encouragement. They challenged me to tell interesting tales of people who find themselves in extraordinary locations while dealing with human weaknesses and desires. I look forward to my next explorations in this wonderful world born of their imagination and their love for this craft of storytelling.

There are a plethora of other people who have contributed to my writing and education over the years: Mrs. Pick and Mrs. Carolyn Doty, creative writing teachers who are sadly no longer with us but whose influence I feel every day; the talented Gavin Revitt, who took to my stories like a duck to water and created many wonderful illustrations based upon them, and who, incidentally, is responsible for the stunning cover art; my peers and role models in the infantry; my colleagues in Germany, Bulgaria, the Sudan, Greece, and Azerbaijan who welcomed me into their lives and taught me about differences in our societies while concurrently reminding me of our shared humanity; and my family and friends who never lost faith in me when, like most people, I floundered. Most especially, I thank my daughters, Mykenzie, Lindsey, and Ona, for bringing the world to life and reminding me of the wonders of the universe. And of course Elnara, who has given me a second chance at happiness, for which I am eternally grateful.

Finally, I thank my fans for their support and kind words. Hearing you talk about your love for science fiction and fantasy and your excitement about the Dryden Universe reminds me why I started writing. We are kindred souls. I hope you enjoy these stories and that you fulfill all of your dreams.

Daniel B. Hunt
Fairview Heights, IL
September 2015

THRESHOLD

MASTER SERGEANT Sayer Kade stood in the open airlock, his breath ragged in his ears, as he waited for the signal to jump. The *Ark Royal* moved silently above the asteroid where Terra Corp's mining station sat silently, several hundred meters below. The *Ark Royal* had not been attacked as it framed within system and began its short cruise to the asteroid. The asteroid was gray as cremated flesh, yet on the tall spires that stood near several habitable factory domes, red and green lights occasionally blinked into the darkness. The mining station was strangely quiet. *Ark Royal's* Captain Donovan Cole's communication attempts had gone unanswered. The rioting workers who had taken over the station were absolutely silent. Nothing moved.

The stillness did not sit well with Kade. Early in his career, he had been on several similar missions. Mining stations were tough on people, and after a while the employees started getting ideas about equality and shared ownership. Demands were made and denied, and force was applied. The workers redacted, and the operation started again while Terra Corp slowly began shipping out the troublemakers and shipped the remaining staff to other stations over time. It was not something Kade's elite unit typically handled. But here they were. It was abnormal.

It always came down to this, Sergeant Kade knew. He looked down as the shadow of the *Ark Royal* flicked across the asteroid below. The ship's shadow was tiny against the rocky ground. It looked like a weak, helpless bird slipping across the alien terrain. Sergeant Kade steadied his beating heart.

All the fancy technology, standoff lasers, Gatling guns, torpedoes, banks of rail guns, and fleets of fast attack ships and battle cruisers could do only so much. At the end of the day, it was the soldier that had to do the dirty work. The recruiting stations didn't tell you about dry mouth, sweaty palms, tunnel vision, body shakes, or the smell of men pissing and shitting themselves. That knowledge came later. No. When you first joined up, it was all flashy tech, comrades in arms, and martial music. They convinced you that you were unstoppable. The first time you took Juice, those tiny nubots infused the body, rebuilding muscle tissue until you were a lean thoroughbred. The nubots, little nucleic acid robots gen'd up in some septic free-fall laboratory owned by Lin Corp or Terra Corp, made new recruits feel invincible. Young, strong, and chalked up on Stem, they were roaring to go. It was this false sense of strength that allowed newbies to rush headlong into combat where, for the first time, they met men like Sergeant Sayer Kade. He was a brute. Augmented, rebuilt, tweaked, and charged, like all the special soldiers of the elite Geist Marines, he was preterhuman.

Of course, Sergeant Kade had been a newbie once. Hell, they had fallen like flies. His company had dwindled and faded until only fifty of the original 120 were alive or not wrapped in some medical tube with boiled brains or emotional and physical scars so deep that their bodies refused to function.

When the executives in Terra Corp reassigned Sergeant Kade and his surviving comrades-in-arms to other units, Sergeant Kade was dismayed. The people he had come to trust, come to love, were strewn about the systems like so many pieces of meat. The move had stripped him of his military family. It was too much. He could not go on as if everything was normal. He did not want to invest any more of his emotions in another group of marines. He had to do something different.

If Sergeant Kade was going to continue fighting these dirty little battles in distant places, he was going to be one of the best. And he was going to fight next to others of a like ilk. So he took the test, volunteered, and signed away his life with no chance of parole short of death to join the Geist Marines. Dead or should be dead—that was the new retirement plan.

Juice was nothing to the stuff they had fed into Kade's bloodstream. It was not a particularly pleasant experience either. Sergeant Kade had burned, his flesh crawling, his mind shrieking as nubots and nanobots coursed through his body, destroying, rebuilding, shaping, and warping. The eyes—he shuddered. That had been the worst. The doctors and technicians had strapped Kade's arms down to prevent him from ripping his own eyes out of his skull as the horrid micro machines swarmed over his retinas and dove through his pupils. His eyes had bled, yet the terrible machines captured the blood and used it as building blocks for his new eyes.

Now Sergeant Kade could see in the dark; his vision was perfect. He was strong, physically powerful; his bones, muscles, and sinews were augmented to three times the strength of a typical man. His nervous system was enhanced, and his reflexes were razor sharp. Like all the other Geist Marines, Kade's lung capacity was improved, and floods of bots that floated in his blood stream were standing ready to repair injuries and stave off death. So much money had been spent on Sergeant Kade's augmentations that a fifth of the price would have kept a family of four in comfortable living for a few decades. The amount of money Terra Corp had invested in the other eight members of his squad was mind-boggling. That was why this mission made no sense. Sure the mining facility was one of the most valuable in Terra Corp's collection. It was full of precious metals and minerals and had a huge supply of the raw materials used to produce insanity crystals, but sending in the Heavies—slang used to describe the ultraexpensive Geist Marines—was overkill. Mass overkill. For this particular rock, Terra Corp could have easily sent in a couple of cruisers and a battleship, dropped a few companies of regular marines, and swept the workers on the station back into the Dark Ages in a matter of a day or two. Why had they sent in Kade's unit? What was so special, or so dangerous, about this particular rock?

There was another reason Kade had slipped into this life of dirty battles on strange worlds. The thought rose unbidden into Kade's mind before he could suppress it. Her memory was a dark shadow against his soul. Dark eyes, dark hair, and a darker heart. She knew nothing of loyalty or of the greater call of service to the human race. Her universe revolved around the tiny sun of her tiny self. She wanted, he knew. She wanted and wanted but never even considered the cost. Someone had to pay for her little life in her little house on her little planet with her little new boyfriends and social circles. The worst for Kade was not the hidden affairs and constant lies that ended the marriage but rather the extreme betrayal and total disregard and lack of appreciation for his efforts to support her corporeal demands. In the end, Kade had been willing to meet her halfway, but for her, Kade was not even worth the miniscule effort of a video call. She wanted. She ate people like a black hole, capturing them with her grace but then stripping them of everything to feed her need before casting their husks carelessly out into the darkness. He knew he was better off without her. But that didn't help at all.

"Wish we'd get on with it," the raspy voice of Sergeant Stratton rippled in Sergeant Kade's helmet. Sergeant Stratton had lost his vocal cords in a rather nasty little battle on Aldor Prime in the system of the same name. The techs had replaced his cords, but something had gone wrong with the procedure, leaving Stratton's voice gruff and ragged. He had also lost his right arm at the elbow, which had been replaced by a cybernetic model. Stratton claimed that he could feel the titanium of the prosthetic burning the stump of his living bone whenever the air was cold, but Sergeant Kade wondered about the claim. He thought Stratton just enjoyed bitching.

"We'll be jumping soon enough," Kade replied. "Make sure your guys stay with the packs." The packs contained advanced robots, like Sentinels and Scouts Mark IIs. They would give the Geists the edge in any small-unit battles, but the packs were a double-edged sword. If they fell into the wrong hands, they would cause the Geists considerable problems.

"Is everyone hooked in?" he asked.

"You're the last, boss."

Sergeant Kade pulled himself away from the open hatch and shuffled back toward the waiting squad. The jump master, a too-young lieutenant whose name Kade could not recall, helped Kade struggle into his jump chute. The full-body contraption normally would have been a considerable weight, except for now, on the decompressurized deck in free fall, it was just a bulky nuisance. Hooked into the rectangular jump chute, or JC, Kade shuffled forward toward the open portal once again. The JC propulsion unit would allow his squad to float through space to the asteroid below. In it were Kade's weapons, meals, water, and other support items as well.

"Communication and tactical satellite pods launched," a flat voice announced over the general communications net.

"Here we go," the lieutenant said, though he was not going anywhere.

Sergeant Kade shuffled into the open doorway and leaned out into space. The asteroid was directly below him. He felt, as he always did on these types of jumps, as if he were at the top of a deep well and—for some damn reason he could not fully understand—was preparing to leap to his death. It felt like a type of suicide.

The light inside the jump deck changed from red to green, and Kade heard the command, "Jump." He squatted down and pushed himself out of the doorway into space, keeping his arms against his body. And he began to fall, floating at first under the impetus of his jump, but then he felt gears in the JC churn, and soon the propulsion unit was pushing him faster and faster toward the gray asteroid. The unit's computer was on a set trajectory. It would keep Kade and the other eight members of his squad pointed headfirst toward their destination until the last possible moment, before rotating them for a soft landing.

Sergeant Kade hoped the miners didn't have Sheet Lasers. Those things could cook a man in a matter of minutes. But as he fell, everything remained quiet—a mystery.

The commander of the *Ark Royal*, Captain Donovan Cole, watched the nine blips descend toward the asteroid and Echo Mine. Light flared silently from the marines' JCs. The navy mockingly called the small propulsion and battle support units "jackasses." Who the hell knew why? Red T-lines, lines of trajectory, indicated the squad's anticipated path. Captain Cole knew where the marines were going. The lines flicked off and on in an irritating way. Some Terra Corp techie had received some bonus for that little unnecessary detail in the tactical computer's programming. Captain Cole was sure of that.

God, the lines were irritants.

He shook himself and focused on the mission.

Captain Cole's eyes shifted to the larger tactical display. The communication and tactical satellites were in position above the asteroid. With them, *Ark Royal* would be able to maintain communications with the marines while providing them with robotic air support. For *Ark Royal* was moving away from the edge of the asteroid belt where Echo Mine lay like a sour taste in the captain's mouth. He would move the vessel to the outside of the ring where there was space to maneuver and where he could put the ship at a defensive distance from the rock. His secret orders had been somewhat cryptic.

"Expect strong resistance," it had read. From what? It was just a mining and production station, and there were no other ships in the area. Why was the head shed in Terra Corps' military arm, known as the Defender's Division, so concerned about this particular rock?

"Execute ship's maneuver," he ordered.

It did not take a large crew to control the *Ark Royal*. The command room was cramped and barely allowed for the six stations: Propulsion, Weapons, Communications, Sensors, Internals, and Tactical. The *Ark Royal's* remaining crew members were manning stations that were "quadrified." The vessel was split into four distinct and separately sealed compartments that allowed for full spherical arcs of fire. The ship could fire in 360 degrees. However, in the center of the ship, facing toward the bow were the *Ark Royal's* torpedo bay and three main rail guns. The placement of these items in the center of the ship had more of a psychological reason than a practical one. For humans, it was easier to point the ship either at or away from an enemy—fire or run. It was all relative to the command room's perception of the bow. In a fix, Captain Cole could just point *Ark Royal* at an enemy ship and blaze away with the ship's main rail guns or find an empty space between enemy ships and jump to safety.

"Sir, engines engaged. Moving toward our defensive position," Lieutenant Colette Giggatelli replied. She was studiously examining the control console as she maneuvered *Ark Royal* away from the asteroid.

"Ensign Naidoo," Captain Cole said as he took his command seat. "Begin launching the Ripplers as we planned. I want them about point five AU out. I don't want some ship jumping in right on top of us; I want to keep them from using their frame drives and hitting us hard before we have time to react."

"Yes, sir," Ensign Naidoo replied from Tactical. Redman Naidoo was the youngest and least experienced member of the command crew. He had only recently joined the ship during their last port call on Earth. His file gave him good academic marks, and he was technically quite proficient. Tactical was always the first position new officers held on ships. Running tactical was the nearest thing to the computer-generated scenarios one had in training. The ensign's job was to help the computer better protect the ship. Running

7

tactical was almost like playing a video game. Still, Captain Cole would have to keep an eye on him.

"Launching now, sir."

The captain watched. Eight Ripplers appeared on the tactical display as they shot out of *Ark Royal* toward their preprogrammed positions. The Ripplers would form an arc around *Ark Royal*. Ripplers allowed the defending ship time to react. If they detected an incoming ship, the Rippler would detonate, creating a Flat Spot. Flat Spots prevented ships from using faster-than-light frame drives. Enemy commanders could therefore only maneuver at slower-than-light or in-system speeds. That would make them vulnerable while providing an opportunity for *Ark Royal* to retreat should it be necessary. Of course, as the captain knew, it was a two-way street. Once activated, the Ripplers would cut off escape vectors too. They could, if not carefully placed, trap *Ark Royal* against the asteroid belt. So in the tactical plan he, Ensign Naidoo, and Cole's second in command, Lieutenant Commander Kory Spade, had devised, they had left a couple of gaps. And Ensign Naidoo had those gaps preprogrammed in the navigation computer for a fast exit.

"The repair bots are all out too, sir. And the platoon of marines are deployed in their suits in decompression bays near the hull of the ship in case someone tries to board us."

"Thank you, Commander Spade," the captain replied. "Anything from Echo Mine?"

"No, sir," Junior Lieutenant Kapana answered from Sensors. "No movement at all." JL Kapana had a deep baritone voice. It resonated pleasantly in the command room. In his former life, he had been a member of an amateur singing group and a minor thespian on his home world of Eibsee Major 95128. Captain Cole noticed that the double *s* sound normally associated with the accent from Eibsee Major 95128 and its sister habitable worlds 4277 and 3522 was missing from Kapana's speech. JL Kapana's accent only came out when he was stressed or extremely tired.

"Keep an eye on them, Kapana.

"I am going to make a ship-wide announcement," the captain continued. "As distasteful as it has been for me, I was ordered not to tell the crew or the Geist Marines this part of our orders until we were in our final defensive positions. Commo, make sure Sergeant Kade and his marines can hear me too. So listen up. I'll make the announcement first in full, and then when I am off the net, you can ask me any questions you might have. Understand?" The captain looked around at his crew. They nodded or smiled, indicating their understanding.

"Good. Here goes."

Captain Cole toggled a switch on his communicator. "Attention. Attention. This is Captain Cole. *Ark Royal* is now taking up defensive positions before the mining station called Echo Mine in the Selee system. This is a for-record order.

"The Defender's Division has advised me that we should expect heavy resistance of an unknown nature. All defensive stations are to be permanently manned until further order. Subunit commanders are ordered to rotate crews through their positions in full battle gear. All crew will remain at level three when on rest periods—battle gear on, helmet off. As of now, *Ark Royal* is going to inactive sensors. Sensors around Echo Mine will remain active. Priority of communication remains with our marines landing on the asteroid. Lieutenant Leforce to the bridge and relieve Commander Spade. Commander Spade will lead us on second shift. Let's stay alert and stay alive. That is all. Captain Cole out."

"Was there nothing more, Don?" Kory Spade asked in a light voice.

"No." The captain shook his head and raised his eyebrows in shared frustration.

Nobody else had any questions.

"Goddamn crap!" the voice of Sergeant Kade spit over the command net. But the sergeant did not elaborate.

"He's about as happy with the lack of clarity in the original orders as I guess you can be." Commander Spade laughed softly.

"Any idea of what resistance the knuckleheads are expecting us to face?"

"No. No." Captain Cole was not sure he appreciated Sergeant Kade's tone. He ignored it. The man had a right to be upset. He was about to land on the damn rock. Not the best time to be told that HQ expected a real shooting war. And the man had damn little support. He and his folks were going in blind.

"All right then," Commander Spade said, taking a step toward the command room's portal. "I'll see if I can get some rest."

"Thanks, Kory. It is what it is." Captain Cole liked his second in command. They had served once together, briefly, as staff officers in the planning division. A boring but informative job, it had given them time to get acquainted with each other and each other's families.

Commander Spade departed, and an excited and determined Lieutenant Leforce took his place. A good man. Leforce. Solid. But he lacked imagination.

The *Ark Royal* finished its maneuvering and rested like a watchdog at the edge of the asteroid belt. With the Ripplers in place to their front and the wall of asteroids to their rear, the crew of the *Ark Royal* settled down on the edge of a razor and waited. In the dark universe, the distant star burned, the gas giants moved, and nine Geist Marines cursed as they dropped toward what might be a hell of a reception.

Resistance of an unknown nature! Sergeant Kade cursed as his squad shot downward, headfirst, toward Echo Mine. All eight squad members flooded the squad's tactical net with their own oaths, and Kade snapped them back to silence. There was nothing they could do about it now anyway. The nine of them were committed. At least he knew that the bots would be deployed, and everyone would be on their toes the instant they touched down. He just hoped they made it that far.

The surface of the oblong asteroid was gray and pockmarked with craters of varying sizes. The lower extremity of the asteroid was dark with shadow, but the sun-side was bright with the reflected light of the system's star. As Sergeant Kade descended, his eyes were drawn to the five domes of Echo Mine. He knew from his briefing material that the mine was less than twenty standard years old. Four of the five domes were arranged at each corner of a square. In the center, connected by transit tunnels, a larger dome loomed. The center dome was the operational dome and was positioned over the mineshaft. It was the main production facility that processed raw ores and the ingredients used to make insanity crystals. Two of the smaller domes were for habitation, one was a workshop and equipment dome, and the last was the Microgravity Materials Lab where the insanity crystals were grown. The lab dome was unpressurized. The extremely low gravity and atmosphere of the asteroid allowed for exceptionally pure crystal growth in powerful magnetic cylinders. The near vacuum allowed for the combining of material on an atomic level and the layering and creation of extremely versatile crystals. Besides highly coveted and profitable insanity crystals, the lab also produced high-quality solar cells, transistors, and other exotic components.

Sergeant Kade thought the buildings looked like the dots of the number five on a six-sided die. But instead of the normal red or blue of a die, the domes were as gray as the surrounding terrain. The mine was nestled beneath a smothering cliff in an area that resembled a question mark. That left the mine surrounded on three sides by a ragged rock wall, while before it a wide plain of basaltic crust expanded in an area named Calico Flats. Large and small boulders were strewn across the asteroid's surface; they reminded Sergeant Kade of a giant graveyard.

The two control towers near the center dome rose several hundred meters into the air. Red and green lights blinked on their pinnacled tops. The tower to the three o'clock position was Alpha Tower. It was the main control tower for the mining operations. From there, Kade knew, operators controlled robotic mining equipment and monitored the mine's processing plant. Bravo Tower, at the six o'clock position, served three purposes: it monitored the domes' life support system to include the small fusion power plant, it was the landing zone's control tower, and it monitored space for any threats. Being in an asteroid belt meant smaller objects constantly bombarded the asteroid.

Sergeant Kade looked from the mine to the top of the cliff wall, at twelve o'clock from the mine, and found what he was expecting. A series of solar-concentrating mirrors that focused light from the system's star was perched near the cliff's edge. A small building, square and flat and barely discernable from this distance, was smudged near the array. The array captured and concentrated light, which was then enhanced by the fusion generator and argon gas. The amplified light was then directed at a threatening asteroid. The laser would heat the surface on the incoming asteroid, causing its surface to vent, creating spouts of debris, which were ejected into space. The force of that ejection caused a rocket-like effect that pushed the asteroid in a set direction. It was quite clever. Additionally, the array could pulse a strong beam at smaller objects too, destroying them. Unfortunately, the device could also be used to fire at the Geist Marines as they descended toward the surface.

Sergeant Kade had personally programmed one of the two defensive satellites launched by the *Ark Royal* to target the array. One hint of movement, and a twenty-foot long, inert tungsten pole would be shot down to the surface at Mach ten. When the tungsten device hit the array, it would release kinetic energy equivalent to five tons of TNT. That, he thought, would be the end of the array. And Sergeant Kade liked kinetic bombardments because there was no release of radiation. It was clean and therefore posed no residual threat.

Kade was tempted for a moment to knock the array out now, but he decided against it. Before any operator could position the array to hit the Geist Marines, it would be destroyed. And who knows?

The array was there for a reason. What if they needed it to protect the mine from an incoming meteor?

At the five o'clock position from the mine, Sergeant Kade could make out the flat landing pad used to shuttle processed ore and crystals to space. Oddly, not a single shuttlecraft was visible on its surface. It was there, at the landing pad, that he and his marines would touch down. While doing so meant they would have to hoof it to the mine, which was a good two kilometers away, it provided the best initial fields of fire. It was also under a slight rise in the terrain that ran like a hump all along the open face of the mine. Once on the ground, the marines could move laterally along the entire mining station's front, thus allowing for a tactical approach. Hidden in this way from direct sight, the location also protected them from direct-fire weapons.

"Rotating for final approach," he announced over the tactical net. The JC units pushed propellant out, and Kade began to rotate. The squad was now parallel to the top of the cliff as the JC units slowed their fall. There was no sign of activity below.

The Geist Marines landed softly on the ground. The JC units automatically detached from their backs and slid behind them.

It was only a few moments before the marines had extracted their personal weapons. Most of them carried KNR flechette rifles. The rifles fired iron needles at ultra-high velocity with very little recoil. Since the projectiles were small, each rifle carried high-capacity cartridges that were easily exchanged, allowing for significant firepower. Two of the marines carried Ram 592s with their laser-guided smart munitions. Point the weapon in the general direction of the target, squeeze the trigger, and the supersonic munitions flared like a tiny, bullet-sized missile toward the target, adjusting its flight trajectory as it went. The 592s could not carry as many rounds, nor did they fire at a high rate of speed, but they almost never missed.

While the marines were moving into a tactical defensive circle, their JC units grew legs and rose, like dogs, from the landing pad. They were programmed to trail the marines, carrying their supplies.

A bright light flared above, and Sergeant Kade glanced up through the glass arc of his helmet. The two combat packs were touching down in the center of the perimeter. Corporals Yeaw and Mardick quickly moved to them and began activating the two Sentinels and launched the Scouts Mark IIs. The Scouts were four feet from front to rear and resembled spiders, though they only had four appendages apiece. They were sensor heavy and provided close air support for the marines. They were soon buzzing over the hasty perimeter in an ever-widening circle as they spun out and up, searching for an enemy. Sergeant Kade opened two small video windows in the faceplate of his helmet to get a close-up of the terrain as seen by the Mark IIs. The landscape was dried, cracked, and silent. The Mark IIs' sensors detected no body heat signatures. The winding, gravel road that connected the landing pad to Echo Mine looked long unused, and in the distance, Alpha and Bravo Towers seemed disembodied and unaware.

"Mardick, send your Mark II toward the mine," Sergeant Kade ordered.

Kade dropped to a knee in the center of the perimeter as the two Sentinels, churning gears, fully extended. The robots had bulbous sensors for a head and moved on a tripod of tracked limbs. Dark, double barrels of the robot's pulse rifles rotated upward and pointed out. The Sentinels were also capable, he knew, of short hops or flights that allowed them to get over difficult terrain. "Keep the other one in over-watch, Yeaw. I want to know if anything moves."

"Aye—right, Sarge," the two answered in unison as the Mark IIs moved to fulfill their assigned tasks.

"Stratton, Dixon," Kade called to his team leaders. "Let's talk. Everyone else, stay alert."

Sergeants Eric Stratton and Steven Dixon walked to the center of the small perimeter and took a knee next to Kade. They each pulled a small communication interface wire from the side of their armored space suit. Kneeling in the triangular pattern they so readily fell into, they each reached to their left and plugged their cable into their neighbor's com-jack. This created a private communication loop and allowed them to discuss their next move without anyone eavesdropping.

"What-da-ya think?" Master Sergeant Kade asked. The light of the system's sun reflected against the polarized faceplates of his team leaders. He could not see their faces. It gave the other two men an inhuman look.

"Send the dogs out first," Sergeant Stratton's rasping voice replied. "Just in case the roadway is mined. Spread out; move slow. See what happens." The JC units were often referred to as dogs once they took on the role of personal equipment carriers. While they had not been designed as mine sweepers, troops often used them in that fashion. Better to send the JC units out front and follow in their footsteps than leave the dogs to trail behind, as had originally been intended by their designers, and have the troops activate a mine.

"Dixon?"

"Yeah, Sarge. Sounds good to me. Spread out in a wedge, but I suggest we avoid the road; move up the berm to our left and have the two Sentinels centered on each side, a little back from the line. Standard stuff."

"Okay." Sergeant Kade glanced at his faceplate display. Corporal Mardick's Mark II was a quarter of a klick down the road. Corporal Mardick focused the unit's high-definition camera on the silent mine. "But I want Fox and Eyre to pull a drag position. I want their 592s back of the line. I don't want them caught in the heat of initial contact so we can take advantage of the 592s accuracy. Let them snipe the enemy and keep an eye on our six."

"Two wedges in parallel then?" Dixon asked.

"Right. Alpha team on the left. Bravo on the right. I'll fill the center gap. Sentinels on the inside of each wedge with the 592s in drag. We'll follow the berm about four hundred meters or so before turning toward the mine. When we reach the lip of the berm, we'll stop and assess. Then it's out in the open and a bold, slow approach, bounding by teams. Keep your distances. I want everyone wide apart. There is no telling what will happen. And we'll fall back here for a stand if necessary. But I want to push forward through any resistance. Call in fire support from the orbiters and the Mark IIs. Got it?"

"Yep," Sergeant Stratton replied. "God, I hate walking."

"Dixon?"

"Sorry, I was nodding my head," he laughed. "Forgot you couldn't see me."

"I'll contact the *Ark Royal* and advise them of the situation. We'll move in five," Sergeant Kade finished as he dismissed his team leaders.

The three unplugged their communication lines, and the two junior sergeants moved back to brief their teams. Sergeant Kade called the *Ark Royal* and concisely explained their course of action to Captain Cole. He then used the retina tracking response system in his faceplate to virtually predesignate targets along his planned avenue of approach. At the same time, he pushed the graphic to the squad. One of the advantages of having four satellites in orbit was the use of triangulation to create a makeshift global positioning system tuned specifically to the marine's frequency. The entire squad could track the squads movement along the digital graphic Kade had just pushed as the squad crept forward toward Echo Mine.

A few moments later, the squad was up and plodding in formation along the bottom of the berm. The dogs were out front a hundred meters as the men and Sentinels trudged in the loose dust of the asteroid's surface. The marines held their rifles at the ready. As they maneuvered, they keyed off Sergeant Kade's position. After a short pause at the lip of the berm where a quick visual reconnaissance was made, the squad moved up and stepped into the open plain of Calico Flats. The road to the LZ on their right flank, they angled toward dome two. It was a living quarters dome at the nine o'clock position. But halfway across the plain, Sergeant Kade turned the squad forty degrees back toward the main dome. This gave them an expansive field of fire as they crept silently toward the tomblike structure. Their passage kicked up a small cloud of dust that, due to the weak gravity, hovered about them in a thin veil. Finally, after an hour of silent movement, they found themselves directly facing the main dome, with numbers one and two domes to their respective right and left.

"There," Corporal Ryes, the man on the far left said, raising his KNR-FL toward a jagged tear in the side of dome two. "There are scorch marks on the habitation dome, just under the shadow line. Looks like laser marks and a small debris field."

Kade took a hard look in the direction the corporal was pointing. It took him a minute to see what the other man had seen. It was indeed a hole in the side of the dome, with long burn marks along the outside wall. Scattered about the ground before the hole were pieces of the building. The ground was scuffed, and now that he was looking, Kade saw a multitude of boot prints and wheeled and tracked vehicle marks mixed helter-skelter all along the area.

"Over here too." This from Jehu Eyre, who was using the targeting scope of his R-592 for a close-up view of dome one.

"What do you make of it, Sarge?" Dixon asked. He motioned with his hand, and his fire team all sunk to a knee.

"Looks like a fight to me," Sergeant Kade replied. "Let's get the—"

"Door to the main dome just moved a crack," Corporal Shea Alexander announced. She swiveled her position and raised her flechette rifle toward the center dome.

"Weapons tight," Kade ordered. He didn't want anyone firing until they had a chance to see who was on the other side of the door to the larger operational dome.

Just then the garage door slid to the side, providing just enough room for a petite figure to emerge. The figure wore a standard spacesuit. The TC monogram and planet Earth insignia of Terra

Corp was emblazoned on the shoulder of the suit. The word *Echo* was shaded in an emblematic circle on the suit's chest. The figure tentatively approached the marines, stopping two hundred meters before the squad. The right side of the figure was in shadow, but the sun illuminated the person's left side. In the figure's left hand, Kade could see, was a small pistol of some sort. It was held closely with the barrel pointed down. A feminine voice suddenly erupted from external speakers in the spacesuit.

"Are you the cavalry?" The voice was soft yet sarcastic. Kade could not see the face behind the voice.

"And you are?" Kade replied, switching his external speakers on as well.

He heard the figure sigh, and the woman stowed the pistol in a leg holster on her left thigh. "Theresa Sloan, foreman of Echo Mine. And you are?" she mimicked.

"Sergeant Sayer Kade, Geist Marines."

"Ah," Theresa said. Kade thought he heard a wry smile in her voice. "The Heavies. Well, that is something. Where are the others?"

"Others?"

"Yes. You know. The rest of the marines."

"You were expecting more?"

"Of a rescue party? Damn straight. Half my people are dead. We're hunkered down in the main shaft for the moment, but who the hell knows when those … things will figure out how to get through the dome. It's all been a bloody mess! I'm tired. I haven't bathed in weeks. And I sure as hell expect Terra Corp to send in real reinforcements, not just junked-up Heavies." She shuddered angrily.

"Look, Miss Sloan." Kade stood up and pointed his weapon at the ground in a nonthreatening manner. "We're here now. Can we get out of the open, and maybe you can explain to me what has been going on?"

"Sure." Theresa looked left and right, then turned about and started making her way slowly toward the partially open garage door.

"Aaron," she broadcasted in the open. "It's all right. They're Geist Marines."

"Oh thank God!" a man's smooth tenor voice replied as a second figure wearing a spacesuit emerged from the dome and the garage door began to fully open. "Anne, David, did you hear? It's the marines."

"God bless—'bout time," a cacophony of voices responded.

"Stratton, keep Alpha team out here. Set up a perimeter. Both Sentinels remain; Bravo with me." Kade moved toward the now-open garage bay. Beyond the large portal, Kade could see multiple vehicles and the small waiting party of four. They all carried some type of small arms, and Kade could tell, even through their suits from their body language, they were exhausted.

"We have the outside fully monitored," Theresa stated. "We tracked your progress all the way from the LZ. It would be safer for everyone to come inside," she added.

Kade considered. "All right. Dogs inside. Sentinels outside. Everyone in. Keep the Mark IIs up and about." He directed his next comments to Miss Sloan. "I don't like surprises."

"Believe me," she sighed. "We've had all the surprises we could ever want in a lifetime. Come on. We can pressurize the dome again once you are in and get to know each other."

The four miners moved back into the bay, and Kade followed. Soon he and his squad were inside, the dome was at normal pressure, and the group of marines and miners were lounging around a large, rectangular table, sharing a cup of steamed coffee.

"They came a little over a month ago. Hit us hard," Theresa was saying. She was a comely woman in her early forties with shoulder-length blond hair and eyes that changed from green to gray as she turned her head and the dim phosphorescent light refracted from her pupils.

"They, who?" Sergeant Kade asked.

"Don't know," the mine's medical doctor, David McCall, answered. He was average build and height, and his left arm was in a sling. He looked gaunt. Hell, Kade thought, they all did.

"Didn't they have uniforms?" Corporal Alexander asked. Like the others, her helmet was removed. But instead of the typical short hair of the other marines, Alexander had a plush wave of brown hair that went down past her shoulders. She was leaning back in her chair with her feet propped up on the table. Somehow she was able to put her feet up without making it awkward or insulting. It didn't hurt that her face was chiseled, smooth, with clean lines and high cheekbones.

"Lin Corp?" Corporal Fox jumped in. Everyone always wanted to blame Lin Corp.

"You don't understand," Aaron Noble, one of the machine operators for Echo Mine, answered. He sat across from Sergeant Kade, next to his wife, a deep brunette with a short bob cut. "They're not human."

"To be precise, what he means," Theresa interjected, "is that the things that attacked us are not human. Humanoid. Yes. Human. No way. They are aliens."

Alien? Sergeant Kade thought. Outside of the elusive Technoprey that resided on a gas giant on the outer edge of the universe, not a single other highly evolved, intelligent life form had been discovered on the thousands of worlds humans had explored or the hundreds of their inhabited worlds. While there were plenty of lower life forms, and even those at the top of their local food pyramid, the universe had been found to be surprisingly devoid of higher life forms on par with humans.

"Why do you say they are aliens?" Kade asked. "Are you sure they are not just augmented humans, pirates, or some new kind of attack force from one of the main corporations?"

Theresa Sloan paused, her hand half-raising a cup of coffee to her lips. She studied Sergeant Kade briefly, shook her head, and placed her cup back on the table. "We had two of them—their bodies—for a while. Doctor?"

"That's right," Dr. McCall said. "The creatures are bipedal and have two arms. They are symmetrically similar to human beings. They are a little shorter ... thicker bodies and quite powerful. Their skin is leathery, and their facial features are a bit sunken. Their blood is not red, and from what I could tell with a brief examination, they may be methane and nitrogen breathers. Mostly nitrogen," he added.

"The little bastards bleed," Anne Noble said harshly. "But the doc's right; their blood ain't red. I hit 'em with my pulse gun. Blew one's whole frik'n head off. Bastard."

"A little testy?" Sergeant Stratton piped in, his voice amused. "Marine?"

Anne Noble shifted in her seat, her eyes intense and hard. "Fifth Corps, back in the day. Been out now for ten years."

"Good unit," Stratton offered.

"Yep. The best."

Kade didn't know about that, but it was nice to hear a semiprofessional validate what the other miners were saying.

"Three or four ships leapt in system a month ago," Sloan continued. "They were on us before we really knew what was happening. Frank, John, Victoria, and Susan were all caught out in the open, moving processed ore and crystals to a lander for shipment back to Terra Corp. An otherwise normal day, and suddenly all hell breaks loose. I managed to get a message pony launched to Terra Corp. Since then, it's been a series of clashes. They got," she waved her hand, "into the outer domes. Those domes aren't constructed as solidly as the central factory dome. So we camped out here—those of us who are left. We try not to go out. They try to get in. Thank God you arrived before they figured out how to penetrate this dome's walls."

Kade sat up suddenly. He had a sinking feeling. "You're still fighting them?"

"Every night," Theresa confirmed.

Kade looked at Sergeants Stratton and Dixon. They had all had the same alarming thought.

Kade stood up. "Kade to *Ark Royal*." His voice was flush. "Kade to *Ark Royal*!"

"*Ark Royal*," a voice floated out of the electromagnetic ether.

"It's an ambush," Kade warned. "It's an ambush. Protect yourselves!"

Just then, Fergus Yeaw announced, "Mark IIs—movement outside. Both Sentinels have activated targeting computers."

"Gear up," Kade ordered. *Damn miners*, he thought. They could have told them with the first breath that the mine was still being attacked. He looked at Miss Sloan accusingly.

"Of course it's an ambush," she said darkly. "What the hell did you expect? Didn't you get the message drone?"

Outside, the sound of muted, automated gunfire erupted. The dome shook as an explosion occurred on its surface. The marines scrambled back into their full gear as first one and then the other Mark IIs were put out of commission. The Sentinels increased their fire, but after a few minutes, they fell silent too.

"They're early," Theresa said stonily.

Sergeant Kade deployed his troops in the vehicle bay. An incessant pounding began at the bay doors, followed by a hissing noise. They were cutting through the walls.

"Back. Back!" he ordered. Standing in an open vehicle bay was not a defendable position. His squad started moving backward, step after step, toward the center of the operational dome and the entrance to the underground mine. Kade noticed in his tactical display that the communications and defensive satellites were no longer responding from orbit.

"*Ark Royal. Ark Royal*," he tried. But the ship was not responding.

Damn. Damn. He fell back to the mine shaft behind the others as the metal of the dome screamed.

And they had been drinking coffee!

Whatever they are, they're getting through, he thought.

"Fire!" Captain Cole yelled as the ship shook again under the impact of the strange particle gun that the three attacking ships favored. "It's an ambush," Sergeant Kade's voice blared over the communication net. "It's an ambush. Protect yourselves!"

No shit, Captain Cole thought grimly as the lights on the ship blinked and the *Ark Royal* shimmied. He was gritting and grinding his teeth.

The three triangular-shaped vessels had appeared out of framed space just beyond the asteroid belt. The auto-detonating Ripplers had snatched two of them, but the third ship had attacked through one of the grooves between the devices. There had been barely any time to react before the strange ship roared across the front of *Ark Royal* with a barrage of lasers, a pulse weapon of some sort, a multitude of tiny explosive rockets, and that damn particle gun. So far, the hull's armor had weathered the beating, but the captain was not sure they could take another raking from those guns.

Ark Royal had responded in kind. Two salvos from the port-side guns initially answered, and a rapid turn of *Ark Royal* toward the foremost attacking ship had allowed the captain to bring his three main guns to bear. Three huge, steel bolts shot out of the main rail guns, raking the side of the alien ship as it attempted to swing back around for another run. The rail guns had caused a section of the attacker's ship to go dark. It was venting gas and debris into space. Captain Cole was not sure what that meant as far as significant damage to the enemy ship, but it couldn't be good for them.

"Sssir," Junior Lieutenant Kapana said from his post at Sensors, his voice tight as he fought to control the adrenaline rushing through his body, "the other two shipsss are maneuvering out of the Rippler effect. They will be out of the flat spotsss in fifteen minutes. They were both on the edge of the Rippler's effective range."

More good news, Captain Cole thought dourly. He had to defeat this first ship before the other two broke free and were able to use their faster-than-light drives. "Load the tubes with Nebula torpedoes, Ensign Pennington. We're burning down the farm. Use a widespread pattern. We're going to hit them with everything we have and then make a dash for it. Barlow," he barked. "Warn the Geist Marines we are leaving. Tell them to hunker down. We'll be back. Lieutenant Giggatelli."

"Yes, sir."

"When I tell you, get us through a Rippler gap—the further away from those ships the better."

"The two enemy ships in the Rippler fields are firing at us, sir," JL Kapana warned.

The *Ark Royal* began a hard turn to position itself directly behind the engines of the nearer attacking ship. It was well understood that where a ship exhaled propellant, there was little room for weapons. The stern was the typical weak spot for all interstellar ships. The enemy ship, in contrast, was beginning to spin along its center of gravity like a car rotating around its heavier engine block in a controlled skid, in an attempt to keep *Ark Royal* from gaining the advantageous position. All enemy ships were firing again, and once again *Ark Royal* let loose from four sets of forward guns. Argon and crystal-enhanced laser light burned across space toward the enemy ship. The *Ark Royal* was firing both green and red laser weapons while the enemy was using a blue laser, likely kicked through barium crystals. Terra Corp had found barium-based lasers less powerful than their counterparts, but they seemed to be doing a number on the front of *Ark Royal*.

"Sir, we have decompression in the forward weapons bay, upper quadrant. No report yet from inside the bay," Lieutenant Crispin Leforce offered.

"Weapons from the bay still firing," Ensign Pennington added. Her hands were flying across her control panel.

"Someone is alive up there," the captain said. "Good. Get Kory to the damage control crews. Tell the commander that it's his show." The captain looked at the tactical display. A multitude of rockets had been fired from the two enemy ships trapped by the Ripplers. *There must be over a hundred of the things*, he thought. Once the rockets punched through the Rippler field, they would blanket the area where the *Ark Royal* sailed. The *Ark Royal* would be surrounded in a sea of destruction with no way out. It was time to go.

"Pennington?" The captain drew her name impatiently out with an edge in his voice. "Are the Nebulas in the chute?"

"They are being armed now, sir," she replied. She rotated in her chair and looked at the captain. "A minute?"

"Sir, I've calculated the best evasion course," Ensign Naidoo at Tactical said.

"Got it," Colette Giggatelli replied as her hands dashed over her keyboard. "We are ready when you are, Captain."

"Pennington?"

"Yes, sir. I mean ... we are ready, sir. All main guns ready."

"Wait for it ... Wait for it ..." the captain said. He could feel the tension rise. His heart beat so hard in his chest he wondered how it did not explode from his body. "When they turn broadside, Pennington." He gave targeting guidance. "Lead them a bit."

The command room fell silent. If it weren't for the constant feedback from crews firing their weapons or trying to staunch the damage to *Ark Royal's* forward bay, the room would have been tomblike. The enemy ship suddenly skidded to port and, as if following an unheard command, Lieutenant Giggatelli pushed the frame drive to maximum while Ensign Naidoo yelled, "Now, sir!"

Ark Royal lurched forward.

"Fire!"

Ensign Pennington fired, and the rail guns belched while a cluster of Nebula torpedoes shot into space, their frame drives activating. They spread quickly out and dove mercilessly toward the enemy. But there was no time for gawking.

"Get us out of here!" the captain roared. He saw the danger. The enemy's rockets had crossed the threshold of the Rippler, and as they did so, they flicked into folded space. The first rockets were already appearing around the *Ark Royal*, exploding and causing the ship to rumble and strain. They were lucky not to have already been hit.

"Brace! Brace! Brace!" Lieutenant Giggatelli yelled over the ship's intercom as she executed the flight plan devised by Ensign Naidoo.

The nose of *Ark Royal* twisted downward as the rear of the ship spun 180 degrees. Everything not otherwise tied down flew across the room, and people were jerked in their chairs. Captain Cole had never heard metal scream before, but the whole ship seemed to emit an ear-bleeding screech that made the bones in his body ache. He looked incredulously over at Ensign Naidoo and noticed the young man had his eyes closed. *What the hell type of maneuver is this?* Captain Cole wondered. How the ship was going to manage it without being ripped to shreds was beyond his comprehension. *Parts of the ship must be pulling over fourteen gees! That amount of force can kill people.* As *Ark Royal* flipped head over heel, the engines bloomed, and they began skipping out of system as rapidly as possible.

Ark Royal steadied, and the amount of gees returned to normal. The captain felt a trickle of blood under his nose. "Jesus, Joseph, and Mary! Mr. Naidoo! What in the heavens was that?"

"I …"

"Not now! Later. Status?"

"We raked the enemy ship. They appear listless. The other two ships have stopped engaging us and are adjusting their courses toward their injured sister ship. We're gaining daylight between us," JL Kapana said from Sensors.

"Damage to the forward bay is manageable. Casualty reports coming in now," Lieutenant Leforce added from Internals. "Commander Spade is moving people to the health unit. He reports a handful dead and maybe a dozen or so seriously wounded. The rest … minor scrapes and burns."

"Have they sealed the breach?"

"Not yet, sir. Commander Spade estimates there are several hours of work. And he'll have to get a crew on the hull to weld in plates."

"Okay. Could be worse. Coms?"

"Recording broadcasts from the three enemy ships, sir. We will download them back at Fleet headquarters for analysis. Sir?" Ensign Barlow asked. He cocked his head to the side like he was wont to do when unsure of himself. "Permission to launch a stealth drone? The Geist Marines ..." He left the rest unsaid.

"Wait a bit, Ensign. Good idea. But let's get some more space and then launch it into the belt. It can pick its way back to Echo Mine hidden in the rocks. Laura."

"Sir?"

"Outfit it with communications, basic sensors, and then pack it with as many aerial support munitions as you can. Oh, attach a combat resupply pack to it too. I hate to abandon them. Who knows? The Geist Marines might get lucky."

"Yes, sir."

"We lost two of the forward ARG-L35s, sir," Pennington said from Weapons. "All K-90s are operational."

"Thank you." The captain took a deep, steadying breath. He looked up at the tactical display. The enemy ships—whoever they were—had indeed reached the edge of the Ripplers and had begun a rapid transit to their injured comrade. For now, *Ark Royal* was forgotten. That was fine by him. It had been a rather close call.

Run deep. On Earth in the old saltwater navy, submarines dove into deep waters in a bid to keep the circling hawks above from seeing their shadows under the waves. It made dropping depth charges on submarines problematic. The sea is wide and wild. It was an old adage and sounded to Captain Cole like sage advice. And in the deepness of an endless universe, he could run deep. Very deep indeed.

As *Ark Royal* skipped along, the solar wind at its back, they left Selee's inner solar system and headed toward the Oort Cloud of Sol system. Captain Cole ordered *Ark Royal* to the large naval base on 90377 Sedna, a trans-Neptunian object in the Sol system. Once thought to be a mass of water, methane, and tholin heteropolymer formed by the interaction of methane and ethane, infrared radiation, and gravity, it turned out to be a dwarf planet. Tucked within the Oort cloud, it was a perfect place for Terra Corp's premier naval base.

It took Sedna over eleven thousand years to orbit the sun in an elongated arc, and it never got closer than 76 AU of its mother star. Strangely, it was a large concentration of organic material that gave the dwarf planet its deep red colors. In addition, the dwarf had two oceans of liquid water and several large lakes. Freestanding water was made possible by orbiting solar concentrators that beamed heat down to the planet where it warmed the atmosphere. Some of the power was collected at power stations, which then fed Sedna's power demands. And Captain Cole made his domed home on the coast of the southern ocean, on the cold rocky beach where his children played under the distant spark of the beacon sun. He suddenly longed for a moment with his wife under Sedna's three moons: Cynthia, Selene, and Diana. They were three guardians in the night's sky. By them he rocked his two boys and his daughter to sleep. By them he made love to his wife.

To Callirrhoe Station, he thought. *To home.*

But as the *Ark Royal* healed and cremated and stored its dead, he knew in his heart that there would be no rest when he returned home. He would kiss his kids, kiss his wife, and return to the distant outpost on the edge of known human space to save or bury those he had left behind. He cast a prayer to the three watchful sisters of Sedna to send their luminous glow to the marines and guide them home.

Home. Home. Home. Where his children were dreaming.

There was a rush of wind and a sudden pull that threatened to sweep Sergeant Kade and his marines from their feet. The dome wall gave in a large explosion, and the operational dome began rapid decompression. Alarm klaxons rang; people cursed. Through the dread mist of dust and debris, around the large industrial vehicles parked in the bay, Kade's enhanced vision saw movement in the infrared. He picked out humanoid shapes pushing their way into the gap and fanning out. They did not have the heat signatures of human beings. Their heat was generated lower in the torso and then again in the head. They did not move with a human gait but rather seemed to shift their hips from side to side as spindly legs bent in three places with each stride. Yet Kade felt no fear. Fear was for later, when the air was still and there was time to think. He took a series of steadying breaths and raised his rifle. He didn't remember pulling the trigger, but a torrent of flechette rounds exploded from him and from his squad as they fell back, back to the deep mine shafts. The enemy returned fire, but they didn't seem to know the Geist Marines' exact position. The aliens moved haphazardly and tentatively into the vehicle bay as if indecision was their guidepost.

"Down here. This way!" Theresa Sloan called as she faded further into the interior of the dome, past processing structures with their belts, pipes, and machines used to prepare the raw ores for shipment. She was leading them toward the main corridor, out of the open section of the central bay. Like all mining facilities in space, Echo Mine was honeycombed with decompression doors and failsafe devices.

The doctor and the two miners, Aaron and Anne Noble, led the retreat. It was obvious to Sergeant Kade, even as he was engaged with the enemy, that the four miners had rehearsed this many times before. They had always anticipated the dome being breached.

Kade almost tripped on his JC unit as he backed rapidly, firing his weapon at the darting shapes that now flowed uninhibited into the dome from outside. He had forgotten about the dogs. He quickly called up the dog's programming menu on the inside of his faceplate and identified the heat signature of the attacking aliens. Kade then ordered the dog to defend. An ARG-P5 rotated out of the robot's back and swiveled, the black barrel moving like an electronic eye. Then the dog began to fire in rapid succession, and soon the other eight dogs joined its fire. Nine marines and nine dogs poured defensive fire into the advancing foe, and for a moment the aliens lost their momentum as they sought cover, returned fire, or died.

A sudden movement caught at the edge of Kade's vision. It was enough of a warning. He twisted at the last moment as two of the aliens appeared on his flank at close range and fired at him. The first round ricocheted off his armored suit after scoring a glancing blow near his abdomen. The second and third rounds missed completely as, with an instinct born of years of training and physical enhancements, Kade rushed into the two aliens and began pummeling them with the front and butt of his rifle. He smashed down into one of the creature's faceplate with a side swing while reaching out unconsciously with his left foot toward the other and sweeping the thing off its feet. While they were fast, Kade's enhanced nervous system and strengthened sinews were more than the aliens could handle. Sergeant Kade was in his element. He was angry. As the first creature's face crumbled beneath Kade's rapid blows, the other tried unsuccessfully to scramble away by crawling backward against the hard plastaform floors. Kade was on it in a moment. Releasing his rifle that had become lodged within the first creature's faceplate, he grabbed the second alien's arm and snapped it with a vicious jerk. This shocked the creature, and in that moment, Kade pinned it to the ground with his right foot, drew his pistol from a leg holster, and shot the creature through the head. He then spun and shot a third creature that had emerged out of the chaos, directly in the chest, and its body thumped to the floor as well. Sergeant Kade bent down and extracted the end of his rifle from his first victim and was firing into the mêlée in a matter of a few seconds.

"Retrograde by bound." Sergeant Kade issued the order through the tactical net. "Alpha, support. Bravo, fall back." It was a military maneuver that would allow half of his unit to fall back while the other half continued to fire upon the enemy. Cover by fire—and old and well-worn military mantle.

"Alpha, set," Sergeant Stratton rasped.

"Bravo, moving," Sergeant Dixon replied.

The choreographed maneuver continued for a couple minutes as the squad followed the retreating miners ever deeper into the dome. Soon small explosions began erupting to Sergeant Kade's left and right as the aliens began using some type of explosive projectile. The squad responded in turn, launching sixty-millimeter explosive, smart rounds from the bottoms of their rifles. While they only had six rounds apiece, the answering salvo was a rapid fifty-four rounds combined. Pieces of equipment blew apart, and concussion waves danced in the hanger like raindrops in a pond. Once or twice Kade was blown from his feet, but none of the deadly shrapnel pierced his suit.

Then Kade heard something, and a machine appeared in the smoke and dust off to his right. The air hissed, and a blare of energy ripped forward from it toward Bravo team. The life beacon for Corporal Mardick vanished from Kade's tactical display, and there was a large explosion as the beam impacted a dump truck. The front of the dump truck was blown apart, and the air was filled with falling shards of metal.

"Mardick is down," Dixon called.

"Can you get to him?"

"What piece of him?" Sergeant Dixon asked. "Mardick has been blown apart. He's dead."

"Concentrate all fire on that thing!" Kade ordered. But the order had been unnecessary. Everyone poured fire into the robotic vehicle that had attacked them. But the thing's armor was significant, and it shook the attack off like a horse switching its tail to chase off flies. Sergeant Kade could feel the tide turning once again as the enemy fire began to build. Not only were the alien attackers not taking as much direct fire, but their confidence had returned, and now the marines were getting hell.

"All dogs support," he barked. "Rapid retreat." The alien robot vehicle had fired again, and this time one of the JC units was vaporized.

The order given, the dogs stood their ground while the marines beat a hasty retreat toward the rear. Through the dust and noise, Sergeant Kade made out the petite frame of Theresa Sloan. She was standing by a heavy airlock door and motioning the marines through. The marines were now masking each other, and the volume of fire from them had consequently fallen. Corporal Eyre and Fox were standing to either side of the door with their 592s, sending well-aimed shots at the aliens. The tiny smart munitions whizzed uncomfortably past Sergeant Kade and hit the creatures again and again.

"Get the dogs in!" Sergeant Stratton ordered, and now the dogs loped back toward the airlock door.

Sergeant Kade popped a cartridge out of his rifle and loaded a new one. He dropped to a knee fifty yards in front of the open airlock as the dogs raced by, still firing their weapons over their backs at the now-advancing aliens.

"We have them!" Sergeant Stratton called through the tactical net. "Come on!"

Sergeant Kade fired a final burst as Eyre and Fox slipped through the door. When Kade stepped through the door, he saw that the marines had continued to fall back down a long corridor hewn out of the living rock of the asteroid. While the corridor was wide enough for a dump truck and other big equipment, it was also a potential tunnel of death. If the aliens caught them in that confined space, the marines would be eaten alive.

Kade turned and grabbed Sloan by the waist. He planned to carry her rapidly down the corridor. But she slipped out of his grasp and pushed the heavy airlock door closed. Just before she sealed it, she paused to take a final look at the burning bay and attacking aliens. It was an odd, unhurried, and defiant gesture. But soon she had the airlock secured, and she turned toward Kade.

"Those doors are a mix of titanium, platinum, and steel. They are designed to protect the dome from an underground explosion and also act as a bank vault to protect the ores and processed insanity crystals. We store the completed crystals in a vaulted room down to the left until we can ship them. It'll take those things a while to get through," she said. Her voice was calm and contemplative.

"But there are only a few additional doors down the corridor. Once we are out of it, we are in the heart of the mine."

"Just a warren of mine shafts?" Kade asked. He stood relaxed, breathing deeply.

"Yep."

"Well," he said. "They'll have to find us then." He turned and began a leisurely walk down the corridor. It was strangely silent. "Come on."

Sergeant Kade and Foreman Sloan took their time walking deep into the heart of Echo Mine. Both in their spacesuits, he towered above her lithe body. They walked past a bulletin board for employees. Beneath a large sign that declared the number of safe days at the mine without an accident, the number 421 had been scratched out and replaced by a roughly written zero.

Stratton, Sergeant Kade thought sardonically. Only Stratton would stop long enough to scratch in a zero. That man had a strange sense of humor.

How long could they hold out? Sergeant Kade wondered. How long before Terra Corp sent reinforcements? Would they even send them? He didn't like the idea of spending the rest of a short, uncomfortable life in a subterranean world being hunted by alien soldiers and killer robots. What Kade could use was some good news. Anything. Anything at all.

The fleet admiral was a staunch man. Just under six feet tall, he stood with both hands on the large conference room table, studying photos of the alien spacecraft. A model of Selee system floated in three dimensions in the center of the table as his staff officers considered the records from *Ark Royal*. The ship's captain was here as well. He was standing stiffly near a marine general who had the obvious opinion that Captain Cole had deserted the Geist Marines and condemned them to a lonely grave. Admiral Rakesh Mehra, an ethnic Indian from the old subcontinent of Earth, was not so harsh with his criticism. The captain's fortuitous return had resulted in a bonanza of intelligence about the capabilities of the alien force. And, he sighed as he looked about the eager and worried faces around the table, the admiral and the executives at Terra Corp and the government folks had sent *Ark Royal* and the Geist Marines to Echo Mine knowing that it was a probable trap. They had not wanted to risk a larger force before they had an idea of what the alien technology was like. Yet while the *Ark Royal* was engaged in its battle, the navy had assembled a fleet of warships here at Callirrhoe Station. They were therefore as prepared as they could be for a counter assault. It was not Captain Cole's fault. He and the Geist Marines had been used for a strategic purpose.

"We are ready, sir," Fleet Admiral Mehra's aide-de-camp whispered to the admiral.

The whole group had been strangely quiet. Admiral Mehra cleared his throat. Everyone around the table froze, and the few whispered conversations ceased.

"To answer your question, Vice Admiral Crow," Fleet Admiral Mehra continued an earlier conversation into the sudden quiet, "the race has been named the Khajuraho after an ancient Hindu god, a son of Shiva and Parvati. He was a god of war and education. A builder and a destroyer. And we have to call them something other than Race X. Scientists … have no imagination." That drew a laugh from the assembled officers.

"Gentlemen. Ladies. Captain Cole," the admiral highlighted the captain's presence in a way of affirmative recognition. "We have been able to make some calculations about the Khajuraho's ships and weapons. Thanks to the captain." He nodded his head to Captain Cole.

"Thank you, sir."

"Not at all, Captain." Fleet Admiral Mehra glanced around the table. His eyes lingered on the marine general, General Grant Gaspar. The man was graying at the temples and was as harsh as a desert sun. General Gaspar retained his opinion and composure and gave the admiral a tight smile.

"Yes. Well. Let's see that last bit again," the admiral said, waving his hand nonchalantly toward his aide.

"Yes, sir." His aide-de-camp pressed a digital control on the tabletop, and the three-dimensional display adjusted. It showed the *Ark Royal* engaging the first alien ship at close quarters as the other two alien vessels were still trapped in the Rippler's grasp.

"Tell me, Captain," the admiral said curiously. "About this maneuver."

The digital *Ark Royal* fired all weapons as around it rockets began to flick in from framed space and explode around it. Suddenly the *Ark Royal* pivoted on its bow, the whole ship whipping topsy-turvy, head over heel in an amazing 180-degree arc. Debris was ejected from *Ark Royal*, and it vented dark smoke from a puncture wound in its upper, forward weapons bay. The *Ark Royal's* engines blared to life, and the ship darted away in an improbable direction. It was an amazing feat of piloting. The admiral had not known a ship was capable of that type of maneuver. After many iterations of simulations, it had been decided that the move was a stroke of genius, and had the *Ark Royal* not taken it, the ship would have likely been destroyed by the barrage of rockets launched from the two alien ships trapped in the Rippler effect.

"Yes, well," the captain mumbled. This drew another round of refrained laughter from the assemblage. "As I have explained, Sir, Ensign Naidoo—Redmond Naidoo—he … well, he says he calculated all the options and this … er—steermanship?—was the best solution. He is eager. A bit odd. But a fine young officer."

"I'll say." The admiral laughed. It was a fresh and natural sound. "I do hope you spoke sternly with him. And put him in for an award?"

"Of course, sir." The captain smiled and looked a bit embarrassed.

"Good. Good. Now, everyone, down to business."

"We have to go back," General Gaspar interjected.

Fleet Admiral Mehra sighed. "Of course, General. That is why we are here and why the fleet has assembled. And, may I add ..." He took a moment to acknowledge the staff from Lin Corp and Syrch Corp. The two rival corporations had sent ships for the return mission as well. Not only was the discovery of a hostile alien life form a concern for all humanity, the admiral thought sardonically, the Khajuraho were also a potential wealth of new technology and new markets. Nothing like fear and greed to bring people together, he mused.

"Thank you, Admirals Molouf and Oduya." Admiral Molouf had a good reputation as a strategic planner, and Oduya, proud of his ancient, African warrior heritage, was known to be solid and steadfast. As much as he distrusted their ultimate goals, Admiral Mehra was pleased to see them aboard for this specific mission.

The admirals nodded in return.

"I think we have agreed, in principle, to our course of action," Fleet Admiral Mehra continued. "Admiral Oduya will lead the counterstroke. General Gaspar will land with his forces on the asteroid and secure Echo Mine and ... recover our marines and the civilian employees of Terra Corp. Admiral Molouf will be in near reserve. He will set up a blockade of the system and has the primary mission of tagging one of the alien ships so we can track it back to its home world. I will have the remainder of the fleet just outside Selee system, and if we can discover the alien's home, we will combine our forces there in overwhelming force. At that point, hopefully short of full-scale war, Ambassador Weir—Ambassador," he acknowledged the thin man who had settled demandingly in a chair opposite Fleet Admiral Mehra. "Ambassador Weir will lead a delegation to the alien world, and we'll hope we can settle our differences politically. After all, we all like a good trade agreement."

The group laughed.

"We will be leaving in forty-eight hours," the fleet admiral continued. "Unfortunately for Captain Cole, we cannot bring the *Ark Royal* with us, as it needs some repairs and refitting. It will be in dock for a few months. But, Captain, you will join me aboard the flagship *Monarch*. You are, at least for now, a member of my personal staff. The rest of you will report to your ships in twenty-four hours. Admiral Molouf will work out the red team plans." Fleet Admiral Mehra looked directly at Ambassador Weir. "A red team will assume the role of enemy forces. They will plan for their defense and play the enemy during combat simulations. It will help us develop and evaluate the details of our plan as we head back to Echo Mine."

The ambassador smiled. Admiral Mehra did not know if the ambassador understood this, already knew this, or just didn't care. But Admiral Mehra had promised Terra Corp he would play nice with the government types.

"Okay, then, no questions?" The room was silent. They had already gone over the initial assignments and plans. This was just the formal meeting to cement the orders officially. "To your ships then," the admiral said. He straightened up and looked across the table at Captain Cole. The young captain did not look very pleased.

"Stay for a moment, Captain Cole," he said. "Everyone else, dismissed."

The officers began to ply their way out of the briefing room. Fleet Admiral Mehra watched them go. After a few minutes, he, his aide-de-camp, and Captain Cole were the only ones left in the room.

"Can you step outside, Jimmy?" the admiral asked his aide.

"Sir." His aide saluted sharply and stepped outside the door. Admiral Mehra knew his aide would keep others out of the room.

"Come. Sit down, Captain."

"Thank you, sir."

"Sorry to do that to you, Donovan. I am not stripping you of your ship. You will get her back. But you and I know that it needs work, and while I can spare your XO, you I can't." The two men sat down, and Admiral Mehra leaned forward toward the captain like a fellow conspirator.

"How is your family?" the admiral asked.

"Fine, sir. Thank you for asking."

"You have a house here on Sedna?"

"Yes. A small dome by the shore—the southern ocean."

"And your kids? How are they? Did they miss you?"

Captain Cole smiled. "They were waiting for me at the spaceport when I arrived back on Sedna. They were just outside of the passenger tube, jumping up and down. Romia, my wife, was there too. And ... you know how it is, sir."

"Yes. Yes. I do. I am sorry, Captain, that I have to take you from them so soon. But you have combat experience against the Khajuraho. And you've had some time to get a feel for Selee system, and you know the sergeant in charge of the Geist Marines. Your advice will be invaluable to me."

"Yes, sir." Captain Cole replied dutifully. "I just ... I wish I were taking *Ark Royal* back as part of the battle fleet."

The admiral sat up straight. "She'll be here when you get back, but I understand. Right now, go say good-bye to your family. Get aboard *Monarch* before she departs. That is all I ask."

"Yes, sir."

"Okay. Dismissed, Captain."

Captain Cole stood up and offered a salute. The admiral returned it, and Captain Cole began to leave.

"Oh, and, Captain."

"Sir?" He turned back to the admiral.

"You did well."

Captain Cole stood still for a moment. "Thank you, sir. I will pass the compliment to my crew. They will appreciate it."

"Yes. You do that, with my blessing. Good night, Captain."

"Good night, sir."

Long after the other officers had left the briefing room, Admiral Mehra studied the battle footage and the computer-generated recreation. He felt a deep unease. It had been a long time since two cultures had met and clashed. In Earth history, such a meeting normally resulted in the less technologically advanced civilization being nearly wiped out. In the Americas, after the Spanish landed there in the fifteenth century, the Native Americans suffered from European diseases that killed over 90 percent of the native population. Those that survived were enslaved or butchered while their ancient and proud civilizations were cast to rubble and dust. Though the navy knew very little of the Khajuraho, the Khajuraho's very existence suggested to the admiral that the Khajuraho were winners. Like humans, they too survived an evolutionary process and emerged as apex predators. They were at the top of the food chain. As a race, the Khajuraho didn't know how to lose. Winning, survival, these things were imbedded in their DNA.

We will have to be stronger, the admiral thought. He had to not only defeat them but crush them. They had to shake the Khajuraho's very sense of their place in the universe, with their own god, and make them fear the shadow of man. *We will eat*—the admiral knew—*or be eaten. It is the way of life.* And Admiral Mehra had no intention of being anyone's, or anything's, dinner.

Fleet Admiral Mehra stood up and walked purposefully out of the briefing room. He felt both the hunter and the hunted. But he was not afraid.

The aliens were making their way down the narrow corridor in Echo Mine. The creatures had long ago turned off the life support system in an effort to smoke the marines and miners out of their hiding. But even the noxious gas the aliens had pumped into the miles of deep-seated shafts had not managed to flush their prey. With the JC dogs, their spacesuits, and supplies that Theresa Sloan had had the forethought of stashing in anticipation of their reclusive life, the small group had managed to survive. It was not a comfortable life, and remaining perpetually in their pressurized suits was mindboggling and frustrating. But they clung on. And as Sergeant Kade's father had always told him, living was half the battle. Not only did they eke out a miserable life, but they turned their frustration outward. In the two months since the *Ark Royal* had fled and abandoned them, the Geist Marines had been a small yet bloody thorn in the alien's otherworldly feet. Time and again, the marines had ambushed the creatures as the aliens, seemingly intent upon stripping the mine as much as possible, moved along the miles of shadowy tunnels.

The marines' guerilla war was not without its price. It had cost the marines two of their number and half of their robotic dogs. Corporal Reyes and Yeaw were dead. Reyes had been shot by several of the aliens in one of the earlier fights before the marines had really gotten a feel for the creatures' military capabilities and limitations. The marines had been lucky to recover Reyes's body. They had not been so lucky with Yeaw. Yeaw had been crushed when the ceiling was blown apart by one of the alien's mobile robots. A huge section of the mine crashed down upon his head. Sergeant Kade was pretty sure that the aliens had dug the corporal's mangled body out from beneath the ton or more of rock that filled the passageway. The aliens had remained in the area of the collapse, in force, for quite a while. And they had brought heavy excavating equipment. Kade imagined Yeaw's body on a dissecting table beneath jaundiced lights. It was an uncomfortable thought.

The ambush Sergeant Kade had set up was nearing execution as the aliens, about a dozen of them, moved down the corridor. The marines were spread along two elongated corridors off the main, giving them a good field of concentrated fire while providing three separate routes to flee. The plan was to fire all weapons for a mad minute, kill as many of the aliens as possible, grab a prisoner, and then duck back into the darkness, rendezvousing in a predetermined location. Once at the rendezvous point, the marines would hastily reload and redistribute critical equipment before falling back to their main defensive position.

The main defensive position was in a wide storage chamber with two doorways. The primary tunnel leading to the space was one of the newer ones and lay deep within the mine. The other tunnel, freshly excavated by the Nobles—the married miners—led upward at a steep angle and terminated below the solar concentrating mirrors that loomed above Echo Mine on the plateau above the station. The new tunnel did not intersect with any of the preexisting tunnels, and it was highly unlikely the aliens would, even reading the station's records, know it was there. One way in and one way out. *Keep it simple*, Master Sergeant Kade thought.

What they would do in the event they had to use the escape tunnel and reached the surface—well, that was a course of action Sergeant Kade was still working on.

Sergeant Stratton and Corporal Clancy along with the remaining four dogs were at the main defensive position now. They were helping Theresa Sloan and Aaron and Anne Noble reinforce the place. Doctor David McCall was there too. Doctor McCall tried to help, but with one arm in a sling and his skills in construction severely limited, he was not of much use. To keep the man busy, Kade had given the doctor the task of preparing a first aid station. That had been a mistake. The doctor had insisted that the station be pressurized. How else, the doctor had argued, was he supposed to treat a patient? The doctor couldn't reach inside a person's pressure suit. And that meant he needed the skills of Aaron and Anne Maria Noble. The construction of the aid station therefore took away from work on the defense. But it kept the doctor busy. Kade knew that idleness was problematic for people under threat of attack. Doctor McCall was no different from anyone else. He needed his distractions, or the stress of their situation would find other, much less productive outlets.

The defense was already a concentric ring of fighting positions that had been dug using a backhoe and other mining equipment into the hard ground. Theresa had found the preparations difficult, as the digging revealed a vein of precious carbonates of good quality. It was enough to grow a couple vats of insanity crystals with a market value that could make them all wealthy. But there was no time to harvest the carbonates. Instead, after a curse and a small, frustrated dance, Theresa sighed, the equipment roared, and the carbonates were crushed as the fighting positions were completed. Now the five of them were finishing connecting trenches between each position so that defenders would not have to fall back or move from fighting position to fighting position while being exposed on the surface. The last job was to connect all the positions, including the shallower ones made for the remaining robotic dogs, to the escape tunnel. The whole structure looked like half of a wagon wheel, with the spokes of the wheel terminating at a bunker positioned right before the opening of the escape route. The defense was supposed to be done by the time Sergeant Kade, Sergeant Dixon, and Corporals Alexander and Eyre returned.

No. No. Something is not right, Sergeant Kade thought as he watched the aliens move down the corridor. There was something about the aliens' lanky movement that was unexpected. It was cautious. Deliberate. Their three-jointed legs clacked oddly down the rocky surface as faces hidden behind inhuman-looking faceplates that reflected glare from the lighting they carried seemed attentive. It was as if they were anticipating an attack.

And this didn't sit well with Sergeant Kade.

The marines had not operated in this quadrant or level of the mine before. The idea was to make the aliens think the marines were limiting their operations to certain areas of the mine, thus lulling the aliens into a lackadaisical approach elsewhere. The marines hoped to use this illusion of safety to surprise and capture a live alien or two for questioning. Yet that was not what Kade was now seeing. The aliens slipped silently forward, weapons at the ready, and Kade got the distinct feeling the aliens were peering expectantly forward.

"Fall back," Sergeant Kade ordered quietly into the tactical net. If he had had an option, he would not have used the radio at all. But here, hidden in the dark, there was no other way to effectively give an order. If Kade had given the retreat hand-and-arm signal, nobody would have seen it.

The four marines began moving away from the ambush position. Two moved left, and two moved right. Suddenly the approaching aliens rushed forward and began firing down the tunnel toward the marines. The marines returned fire, and Sergeant Kade triggered the explosive devices the marines had hidden along the kill zone. Unfortunately, the aliens had stopped before the kill zone, and the bulk of the explosive ineffectually rang in the noxious atmosphere of the mine.

"They knew we were here, somehow," he yelled as he fired and an alien shuddered. "Back. Back!"

Just then the ceiling of the tunnel gave an ominous convulsion, and part of the roof collapsed only a few dozen feet from where Sergeant Kade and Corporal Alexander were exchanging gunfire with the aliens. From out of the hole emerged four spindly, metallic arms that pulled a malignant torso from beyond the ceiling into the tunnel. The robot had a peculiar set of sensors that resembled vindictive eyes. As Sergeant Kade and Corporal Alexander fired into the thing, a fang-like pair of slick barrels emerged near the robot's sensors, and a sudden burst of blue laser leapt forward smashing into the corporal with insidious violence. The corporal's body was flung back into the hard rock of the wall as a burst of blood exploded on the inside of Alexander's faceplate. She lay unmoving on the ground. The robot-creature swiveled its weapons and eyes toward Sergeant Kade. The Geist Marine rapidly fired three sixty-millimeter smart rounds at the robot. The rounds exploded on contact, and the concussion blew the robot off the ceiling. It landed with a crash to the floor.

Sergeant Kade did not wait to measure the effect of the explosions upon the thing. He slung Alexander's body over his shoulder and, firing one-handed, hurried out of the line of fire. Soon he was not firing at all. He was dashing down the dark corridors, using the infrared light from his helmet to rapidly pick his way away from the ambush site. He could hear metal scrape and rasp behind him. He hoped Dixon and Eyre had made it out. If they could all get past the motion-detection devices they had put in each escape tunnel, they had a chance. The IR-10 actuators were connected to significant amounts of explosives. The movement of the marines past the IR-10s would activate the devices. After that, the next movement down the tunnel would trigger the explosives, which were strong enough to tear down the ceiling and walls. It would surely kill anything within fifty feet.

Run, Sergeant Kade urged. His heart beat furiously as his legs pumped and his eyes strained. *Turn left, one.* He counted. *Turn left, two.* One turn to the right, he knew, and he would activate his IR-10. Then he just had to make it down the corridor to his last turn. At that point, he would be relatively safe. And though Sergeant Kade had augmented strength, lugging Corporal Alexander's dead weight, along with all of her equipment, was wearing Kade out. He couldn't continue sprinting in the dark like this forever.

Thank God they were on a low-g asteroid. Kade was not sure how severely she had been injured, but there was a chance the bots could save her. He would not leave her. So he adjusted her still form on his shoulders and pushed on.

He dashed past the IR-10 actuator with a great sense of relief. Now he began picking his way deeper into the mine, following a digital map and route projected against his internal faceplate. He didn't dare make a voice-radio call to alert the defensive position that something had gone wrong. Instead he activated a burst of communication that lasted no more than a second. If the others at the defensive position picked it up, they would know something was wrong, and maybe they would be ready. If the aliens had managed to find Sergeant Kade's' ambush site, there was no reason to believe they did not have the capability to find the defensive position as well. Had they used some type of ground-penetrating radar? He wondered. Or had they rigged the mine with their own hidden motion devices?

Whichever it was, or if it were some completely new technology, Kade knew it was time to go. They would have to leave the mine and try to survive in the open on the face of the asteroid. Once exposed in that way, Kade did not have much confidence they would live very long.

The ground shook behind him, and the gangrenous air reverberated. A cloud of dust billowed out from the tunnel behind him. The force of it knocked Sergeant Kade to the ground, where he bounced along the hard rock several times. He was surprised that he managed to keep hold of Corporal Alexander. Kade rose to one knee and shifted her weight once again before standing. With all the dust in the air, it was extremely difficult to see as the particulate flecks reflected his infrared light in a thousand-thousand directions. It was similar to the blinding effect of turning on a ground vehicle's high beams in a thick fog; only here he did not have indirect lighting that would make navigation along the pitch-dark tunnel possible. With no other option, he dimmed the light almost as far as it could go. Letting his rifle swing and bounce against his chest as he moved, he put his right hand on the wall and began following rough stone blindly.

Did it matter to him at all? The thought popped oddly into his mind. Why his wife's infidelities suddenly jumped out of the fogged darkness he didn't know. The anger and sense of loss he had felt at those revelations, all those years ago, rose fresh and raw in his heart. His eyes burned as the welling of emotion threatened him once again. Sergeant Kade pushed on and struggled to suppress the feelings. But they had a grip on him, and as he stumbled in the darkness, he could hear her voice again, harsh, shrill, telling him he was not the man she had hoped he would become. When had he ever asked her to become something she was not? He had been happy to have her because of who she was, not because of who she might one day be. But that had not been her way. She had wanted Kade to change, to become something she imagined in a frenzied dream but that had no basis in reality.

Kade was gruff, like stone, but he was loyal to the point of fault, and his feelings, though often concealed behind the trappings of his profession, were vast wells in his soul. She had never seen that. She couldn't. Her eyes were always turned to the lesser things in life that hovered on the surface, the mundane. She had no sense of the wider universe. Unlike Kade, she sought an insignificant life and dreamed of simple grazing like myotonic goats. Any shock made her collapse in an unconscious heap, and if she awoke, she would contentedly continue grazing in a mindless way. It was crazy. She was a victim of the universe. But Kade was not a goat. He was no victim. He was a watchdog, fierce and proud, and he faced the universe with determination. Had it been simply that all along? He wondered.

Had she been so afraid of the vastness of the universe, with its wild unpredictability, that her spirit had finally broken? Was she hiding from Kade or from life? It was the same old question, wrapped here in the subterranean vault Kade suspected would be his grave, that haunted him.

He had loved her; that he knew. But he had come to learn that she had never loved him. He had been a rock in a storm when she needed it. And in return, she had made him feel as if the universe were not just an empty void, that there was some meaning to the struggle besides taking the next step, swallowing the next breath, and breeding like an amoeba in a petri dish. She had sheltered in his shadow but had never been able to join, committed in spirit and heart, her life to his. She was, he finally knew, incapable of it. His life before, with her, had been a lie from the start. And it had left Sergeant Kade cool and aloof. He was a machine. Dangerous and hidden in the gray places of the universe. And where he tread, death followed.

It took a fumbling while for Sergeant Kade to maneuver over the rocky passageway and out of the haze of dust. His shoulder hurt.

Once clear of the smoke and dust, he stopped and laid Corporal Alexander on the ground, checking her vital signs. Her pulse was weak but steady, and the blood that had exploded on the inside of her faceplate was gone. It was not dried to the faceplate, but rather the army of nanobots and nubots had been steadily working. Blood was a biological building block, and the infinitesimal bots were using it to reconstruct Alexander's body. The corporal was still unconscious, which was a good thing. Nobody said the bots work was painless. Kade shuddered. He had been seriously injured on numerous occasions, and the work of the bots always felt like a million ants were crawling in his body, eating away at him while he writhed in helpless agony. If he could get Alexander back to the doctor in time, he might be able to sedate her and keep her blissfully unaware of the terrible work being done within her.

He took a moment to stretch his back and reload his KNR-FL flechette rifle before picking the woman up and slinging her once again over his shoulder. In this awkward way, he made his winding way back to the defensive position where he found Dixon and Eyre and the others waiting for him. The marines were manning the foxholes. Theresa Sloan and Doctor McCall appeared out of the main bunker in the rear of the defense and rushed to help Kade with Corporal Alexander.

"She's alive," he managed as they accepted her weight from him.

"Help me get her to the medical station," the doctor said as he began running diagnostics on the injured woman. With one arm in a sling, the doctor could not carry her himself. He electronically patched into her spacesuit and used the vitals monitored by the suit to get a better idea of Alexander's medical condition.

"What happened?" Theresa asked breathlessly as the three of them carried Corporal Alexander to the makeshift airlock of the medical station. "Dixon said they were on to you. How?"

"Who knows," Sergeant Kade replied. They managed to get Alexander on to a gurney and into the airlock, cycling it closed as the doctor disappeared inside, leaving Sergeant Kade and Theresa

Sloan outside. "It doesn't matter. What matters now is that we can expect them to come after us here."

Theresa looked at their defenses. "A few hours ago, I thought our defenses were strong, significant, a subterranean fortress. Now I'm not so sure. What do we do?" she asked. She tried, unsuccessfully, to keep the fear out of her voice.

"Stratton? Dixon? Give me a moment, gentleman," Kade called over the tactical net. "Let's go back into the bunker and talk this over a bit, Theresa. The doc is busy; the other marines and the dogs will watch the perimeter. Are the Nobles in the bunker too?"

"Yes," she answered as the two of them began walking toward the bunker. It was a great gray rock and sand mass at the rear of the chamber. Behind them, Sergeants Stratton and Dixon detached themselves from the perimeter and slipped behind Sergeant Kade and Theresa like muted shadows.

Sergeant Kade waited until everyone was situated. It was a close fit. He noticed that the firing port had been raised so that fire coming from the bunker would fly harmlessly over the heads of those in the outer perimeter. He was happy to see that Alpha team had not been idle while he and Bravo team had been out on their failed adventure. He sat heavily on one of the chairs they had confiscated from some office nook in the vast mine. God, he wanted to take his helmet off and have a real cup of coffee. Instead he pulled his drinking tube attachment out of the top left side of his suite, near his collarbone, and stuck one end of it into one of the available water sources. His mouth was parched. And his hands were a bit shaky. It happened more and more—the physiological aftereffects of battle. But it did not concern him. The blurry eyes, shaking muscles, and lack of fine motors kills were old friends. He figured he would start worrying when he no longer suffered these little inconveniences of his body.

Sergeants Stratton and Dixon were the last to arrive. The whole group, the two sergeants, the married miners Aaron and Anne Maria Noble, and Theresa Sloan sat in a close, cramped circle. They all jacked into a small, central communicator system so they could have a conversation without broadcasting a signal.

"It's just like Shea to sleep through all the excitement," Sergeant Eric Stratton hissed with his damaged vocal chords. He laughed gruffly. He paused in silence for a moment. Sergeant Kade heard the other man sigh. Like everyone else, Stratton was tired. "What's next, boss?"

"Well …" Master Sergeant Kade considered for a moment. He didn't want the others to know how little time he had spent planning their move if they were attacked here. He had hoped the position was deep enough underground that the aliens would leave them alone. Once it had been set up, it had been Kade's intention to end his little personal guerilla war and hunker down for the inevitable counterattack by the navy and marines. It would have been a nice, self-imposed prison. But now he hoped it would last them long enough for them to move vital supplies to the surface through the escape tunnel.

"We have to leave," he said. "We can take a lot of them with us when they come, but it will only be a matter of time before they get tired of playing with us and just blow the whole chamber down on our heads."

"You think they'll do that, boss?" Sergeant Stratton's voice was full of concern, and, rather surprisingly, there was an undercurrent of fear in the veteran's voice. "I'd prefer that than … well … you know."

"No," Theresa interrupted. "We don't know."

"Yes, Sergeant Stratton," Aaron Noble added. "What do you mean? What is worse than being buried under tons of rock?" Being buried alive was a common fear of miners.

Sergeant Kade smiled though nobody could see him. He wished he could clearly see everyone else's faces too, but they were half-hidden in the depth of their faceplates. "What did we want with a captive alien?" he asked rhetorically. They all knew. They wanted a live one to question and to use as a guinea pig. The only way to learn about their enemy was to have one of the aliens in their unforgiving grasp. Biology, psychology, the strengths and weaknesses of the aliens would slowly be revealed under the edge of experimentation.

"Oh," Aaron said sullenly. "I hadn't thought about that."

"Well, it won't come down to that. Will it, Sergeant Kade?" Theresa interjected.

"Let's hope not. Dixon."

Sergeant Steven Dixon sat up. He had been slumping. "Yeah, Sayer?"

"You only have Eyre left. I want you to send him up to the top to secure it. We'll move critical supplies up there—the Nobles and Miss Sloan. The rest of us will hold the line."

"That will leave us a bit short," Dixon stated.

"I can help," Anne Maria Noble said into the silence. "I was a marine once. I can still handle a flechette rifle."

"Anne," Aaron worriedly said. "That was a long time ago."

She put a comforting hand on Aaron's leg. "I don't have to carry a couple hundred pounds or run ten klicks. I have to sit on my backside and shoot ducks from one of these fancy duck blinds. You know we can't all fit in that little tunnel all at once with moving equipment. It will be wasted labor. I can help, honey. We are all in this together."

There was a moment of silence as Aaron held his wife's hand and looked at her with eyes suddenly old and frightened. "Anne," was all he managed.

"Thank you, Marine. We can use the help." Sergeant Kade took a short drink and put the cap back on the bottle of water and put his drinking tube away. "You'll work with Sergeant Dixon. Steve?"

"Fine. Thanks," the sergeant replied.

"So it's up to the top—and then?" Sergeant Stratton brought the subject back around to topic.

"We'll find a place to hide out, and we'll wait for reinforcements."

"Not that complicated, is it?" Sergeant Stratton laughed harshly.

"Nope."

"So, let me get this right," Theresa said. "We are going to leave the mine and find someplace on the surface to hide? What if we can't find a place to hide? What if help doesn't come? What if we run out of food or can't recycle water any longer?"

"We'll work something out," Sergeant Kade replied. "But I am open to any suggestions. Anyone else got an idea?"

"We'll be slaughtered down here if they come in force—which they will," Sergeant Stratton said bluntly. "Oh, we'll take a slew of them with us, but in the end, staying here under constant attack is just a slow form of suicide."

"Nice." Theresa's voice was tight. She stood up with her hands on her hips, and for a moment Sergeant Kade thought she would walk away. Instead, she seemed to get a grip on their situation, and she sat back down. "Okay, out on the surface. We can do that. We should start moving supplies soon."

"Is now soon enough?" Aaron Noble replied. "The quicker we can get our stuff out of the mine, the faster Anne will get off the firing line."

"That sounds great," Sergeant Kade replied. "Now, we have work to do, and I want to check on Corporal Alexander. Thank you."

The group unhooked their communication cables and filtered out to their duties. Sergeant Kade sat in the brooding bunker, gathering his thoughts. He wondered if Terra Corp and the marines would really come back. They had been gone a long time, and maybe Echo Mine was not as valuable as Kade had thought. Maybe they would all die there or end up as experiments in some septic alien lab. They were dark thoughts.

Sergeant Kade stood up and pushed himself to action. He picked up his rifle and stepped out of the bunker, moving toward the medical station. The only thing he knew for sure was that the pressure was building. There would be a battle soon, and the odds were stacked against him.

Maybe it was the end. But it would be his end. And he was where he wanted to be, with his soldiers, living a soldier's day.

A gear rotated on the sleek body of the stealth probe as it peered from its concealed position out at its surveillance target. The probe's structure was black and irregular. To a casual observer it would appear to be just another of the millions of tiny objects floating in Selee's asteroid belt. It saw the alien ships moving to and fro as ground-to-air transports brought ore and pilfered crystals from Echo Mine to a waiting cargo ship. The probe's computer identified the ships as UNK-1, UNK-2, UNK-3, and UNK-4. They were floating peacefully in a defensive ring around the asteroid where Echo Mine lay like a scar upon the primordial landscape. There had been no signal from the asteroid telling the probe what to do. So its digital mind churned, recorded, and waited.

Into the silence of its lonely vigil, a burst transmission skimmed across its antenna. A quantum encoded message dug itself into the computer's brain, and without forethought, an answering message burst forth from the probe along a narrow beam, out past the asteroid belt, past the system's planets and into the deepness of space. Its return message was an affirmation of orders. It understood. Roused, it focused its infrared and spotting scopes at the ships hovering around the asteroid, relaying images and readings into deep space. It ran diagnostics on its armaments and propulsion system. The probe considered and weighed its options and then emitted an unnoticeably minute amount of gas from its side. It was enough of a push to get the probe moving once again. It slipped out of the shadow of a large asteroid and joined a group of smaller ones that were moving across the face of the belt in the general direction of the mining station.

Mission understood, it signaled back. *Executing.*

Captain Cole looked at the tactical display in the admiral's command center. The fleet was moving out to their attack positions. The admiral's flagship, *Monarch*, was surrounded by its sister ships: *Avenger, Eos, Nornen, Rover, Skipjack,* and their assault ship the *Warbler*. The *Monarch*, a capital class battleship, lorded over the two heavy cruisers, two destroyers, the frigate, and the assault ship as they maneuvered on station just outside of Selee system. Admiral Molouf's blockade group, the heavy cruiser *Scorpion*, the cruiser *Valor*, and the destroyer *Lightning* were moving to their position in an elliptical arc a few AU out from Echo Mine. Their mission was to intercept any enemy ship trying to depart the system.

The time for stealth was over, Captain Cole knew. It was time for shock and awe.

The seven-ship attack group, led by Admiral Oduya, was away, speeding toward Echo Mine as rapidly as their framing drives could manage. The attack group's main power lay in the state-of-the-art battle cruiser *Natsek*. It, like the destroyer *Chung Mu*, belonged to Syrch Corp. They were accompanied by the heavy cruiser *Avalanche*, the *Alliance*—a destroyer, the cruiser *Fiske*, and the two ships that made up General Gaspar's asteroid assault force: the frigate *Ailanthus* and the assault ship *Grampus*. Their encoded transponders helped the *Monarch* keep track of them as they bound forward. Also on the tactical display were four enemy ships. Three of them were off station in the approximate location that *Ark Royal* had taken up two months before, their backs to the asteroid belt and their guns concentrated forward to open space. A fourth ship, most likely a supply ship of some sort, Captain Cole thought, was within close operational range of Echo Mine. The Khajurahian ship rode in the asteroid's sky with apparently no care in the world. That was a good sign.

"Captain Cole." Fleet Admiral Mehra strode up behind him. The man moved to the captain's left and looked down at the display. "Are you ready to see how well this plan works? Funny things, plans. We spend all that time working out every detail only to have it thrown out the door the instant we begin to execute it. The outcome is now part skill, part luck, and part momentum." The admiral put both hands on the display table. "Do you wish you were going in with them, Captain?"

"Yes," he said. "No," Captain Cole added. "It's complicated."

The admiral smiled. "Yes, it can be. But we may get into the action. There is no telling what type of weapons these ships," he waved his hands at the three enemy ships that were apparent warships, "have that we know nothing about. Let's hope they don't surprise us with some type of super weapon."

Captain Cole looked at the admiral and realized that inside the man's calm exterior, the admiral was worried. "It's a good plan," the captain offered.

"Yes, it is. And now we get to watch the opening moves like we were watching a video program on channel one."

Suddenly the Khajurahian supply ship blinked on the display table, and the rotund thing listed as if something had pushed the starboard side of the ship down toward the asteroid. *The stealth probe's suicide attack*, the captain thought. *It is now or never.* At that moment, Admiral Oduya's attack force framed into system and quickly closed to within striking distance of the three enemy ships. The telltale signs of Rippler torpedoes raced out of the forward ships, the cruisers *Avalanche* and *Alliance*. Captain Cole found he was holding his breath. One of the enemy ships managed to maneuver away from the incoming Ripplers, but the other was caught in the sudden golden glare of Kirlov radiation that crippled the enemy ship's framing drive. The enemy apparently hadn't realized that these devices, Ripplers, were portable and could be fired on the move. It was the first critical mistake of the engagement. The mostly immobile alien ship continued to fire its blue laser weapon at the human's fleet, but sensing weakness, space was suddenly filled with concentrated fire from all but one of the attacking warships.

A barrage of lasers, pulsars, rockets, torpedoes and rail-gun fire whipped toward the trapped ship as it helplessly attempted to outmaneuver the incoming attack using ion drives. It was a futile effort. The laser and pulsar fire pounded the enemy ship, and battle reports indicated the Khajurahian was venting and likely had interior fires. Though the Rippler device slowed the torpedoes and rockets as they too raced toward the damaged ship, the enemy had stopped maneuvering. The *Chung Mu* reported that the enemy's engines appeared to be damaged. Captain Cole watched in near disbelief as the torpedoes and rockets closed the distance and began impacting all along the Khajurahian ship's hull. Light flared. And the enemy ship broke into pieces.

Captain Cole was only half-aware of the other action as the fight continued with the other two alien ships. The Khajurahians focused their effort on the *Fiske*, commanded by Captain Tricia Evens. The cruiser was taking a beating. But the *Avalanche* and *Natsek* were coming rapidly to the *Fiske's* aid. The *Avalanche* and *Natsek* were not normal cruisers. The *Natsek* was a battle cruiser and had all the firepower of the *Monarch* though its armor was thinner. This allowed it to travel at higher speeds than a battleship. The *Avalanche* was a heavy cruiser. Ships of its class were often given long-range patrols. They were fast and had a long range but were armored and armed sufficiently to take on most ships—at least long enough to escape. Once again the flare and scream of weapons fire and exchanged rockets ripped through space. Damage reports from the three closely engaged ships began coming into the command center. People were dead and dying.

Captain Cole turned his attention to the asteroid itself. Two of the human ships, the *Grampus* assault ship with its battalion of marines and the frigate *Ailanthus,* were approaching the slowly rotating rock. Their initial salvo of fire struck the damaged Khajurahian supply ship. The frigate moved in closely and poured its fire directly into the port side of the Khajurahian ship, and the enemy ship began to burn. A cheer erupted in the command center. The Khajurahian ship began limping out to space, trailing smoke and debris, as it was continually struck by fire from the *Ailanthus.* Admiral Oduya, from his flagship *Natsek*, ordered the *Ailanthus* to disengage and focus on supporting the invading marines.

The *Grampus* moved into orbit, and the command was given for the marines to disembark toward the asteroid. A fusillade of support fire flew before them, peppering the surface of the asteroid and smashing into the mining structure. There had been a lot of debate about that—shooting at Echo Mine—but it was only logical that the enemy would have occupied the mine. If General Gaspar's marines wished to land with minimal opposition, they had to put fire on it. Captain Cole hoped that any friendly peoples in the structure would avoid being killed by their rescuers.

One thousand combat marines in sixteen landing craft shot out of the *Grampus* toward the planet. Aboard each of these ships, Captain Cole knew, was a company's worth of marines and their equipment. They would be landing with Montgomery pulse tanks and E-670-D automated artillery. Combined with those heavy weapons were the JC dogs with their ARG-P5s, a plethora of Sentinels and Mark IIs. It was a heavy battalion. They moved rapidly and carried a mass of firepower. Their only weakness was sustainment. They kicked an enormous initial punch, but they were reliant on supply chains operated by the navy. That kept the marines operating on a short leash. But they were the perfect type of shock force for this operation. The immediate goal of the marines was securing the landing platform and pushing the Khajurahians back, allowing resupply ships to land.

"*Valor* is moving to intercept the damaged Khajurahian supply vessel," one of the staff told the admiral.

"Thank you," the admiral answered curtly. "Sensors, keep an eye out for a responding Khajurahian force. Let's keep paying attention to all of our battle space, ladies and gentlemen, so we don't get caught with our pants down."

There were salutes and murmured assent as the crew of the *Monarch* and the admiral's staff refocused on the whole battle.

"One of the enemy warships is making a break for it," someone yelled.

Captain Cole turned his eyes back to the ship-to-ship combat as the marines began landing on the surface of the asteroid. The *Natsek* and *Avalanche* were rushing behind a fleeing Khajurahian warship. The remaining Khajurahian warship was obviously too damaged to move, though it continued to fire at the human ships.

The *Alliance, Chung Mu,* and *Fiske* mauled the crippled alien ship. They had it surrounded, and though all three ships were sending the Khajurahians orders to surrender, the Khajurahian continued to feebly fire its weapons. It looked to Captain Cole as if the Khajurahian were picking on the *Fiske*, the smallest of the three human ships, in a bid to take at least one of the attackers down with them. It was brave. Brave and stupid.

It had become obvious to Captain Cole that the alien weapons and armor systems were not as powerful as the human's fleet. But their ships were agile and fast, as indicated by the inability of the *Natsek* and *Avalanche* to catch the fleeing Khajurahian warship. The Khajurahian was gaining space, and it had apparently noted the location of Admiral Molouf's blockade ships. It angled away from the *Scorpion* and *Lightning*. Having the advantageous vector and gaining speed, the alien continued to outdistance its pursuers. *Lightning* and *Scorpion* both launched numerous torpedoes and rockets at the Khajurahian ship, but the alien pilot managed to avoid each salvo.

It was at this point that Captain Cole realized that all four pursuing ships were allowing the alien to escape. They wanted the Khajurahian to get away. They must have hit it with a military pony—a computerized probe that had a brain just large enough to record its location before kicking back to the nearest message buoy and downloading its information for rapid transit back to the fleet admiral and Terra Corp. They were making it dramatic enough, but Captain Cole knew the ships could move faster—maybe not as fast as the Khajurahian but not as slowly as they were currently traveling.

The outgoing fire struck near enough to the alien to keep it honest, but to the captain's trained eye, the shots fell short or wide by design. It was a brilliant piece of military subterfuge, the captain thought.

Messages began flooding the command center. The marines had landed and were now in a deadly earnest contest with defending Khajurahian troops. Images of large, four-legged combat robots were filling the screen as the aliens deployed them in fairly large numbers against the marines. The robots were armed with dual pulsar weapons, had indirect fire capability, and were fairly heavily armored. However, the enemy had not dug in, and the firefight was conducted over the open space of Calico Flats. While not dug in, there were plenty of boulders and meteor craters in the area to make the fighting tough. It was a slugfest. Now the frigate *Ailanthus* joined the *Grampus* in providing fire support with aerial bombardments of smart munitions that took a heavy toll of the defenders. The Khajurahian line began to waver and fall back. The marines began taking significant fire from three alien gun emplacements on the summit of the cliffs that loomed above the plain. The three guns had interlocking fields of fire, and they effectively halted the marine's advance.

General Gaspar directed his fire support against the alien guns, yet they could not seem to knock them out of action. It appeared as if there was a force field of some type protecting the guns. The general therefore ordered in his reserves. A company of marines that had been hovering in low orbit above the battle now shot down through the dust toward the plateau. Their landing ships opened fire and raked the enemy guns, which, unfortunately for the Khajurahian, could not rotate a full 180 degrees. This design flaw created a dead zone or blind spot where the Khajurahian could not engage the marines. The landing craft hovered two hundred meters off the deck as marines began low-altitude jumps down to the surface. There they met head-on with a defending force, and a dirty battle erupted with Khajurahian and marine forces fighting at close range. From what Captain Cole was hearing, some of the combat was hand-to-hand.

The fight looked to be evenly balanced, and it was not clear who would win.

Then the *Monarch* detected a high-energy beam that burned across the space from Echo Mine's meteor defense system that was located on the edge of the bluff, a series of mirrors and lasers that were used to push asteroids left or right and thus out of a collision course with Echo Mine. The beam was wide, and it lit up the air as it careened into the enemy gun nearest to it. It smashed into the gun emplacement's shielding in a dance of rainbow fire and slowly beat its way inward toward the guns. Suddenly the gun emplacement's shield fell, and the beam burned through the emplacement's hard shell. The gun exploded in a tremendous display of pyrotechnics. Captain Cole wondered at the size of the explosion. Perhaps there was some type of munitions dump there as well.

The visible shockwave shook the plateau, and the marines both on the high ground and on Calico Flats below lurched forward. General Gaspar pressed the attack, as he felt they had reached a critical juncture in the battle. Soon the marines were advancing in all sectors, and the Khajurahian counterfire began to slack off until it was just a smattering of small-arms fire. The enemy's back was broken. The other two guns on the summit were taken, and the battle for the plateau abruptly ended. The first marine unit entered Echo Mine through a ragged hole in the main dome's side, and the fighting continued in the confined space of the mine itself. More marines followed as mop-up operations began. Soon medical transport ships were moving toward the asteroid as the butcher's bill was added and paid.

Admiral Mehra watched the battle unfold, ebb, and flow from his position next to Captain Cole. "Our ships are better than those of the Khajurahian," he said, thinking out loud. "Our armor and weapons are better—more effective. I would like a closer look at the robots that the Khajurahian are using for close fire support," he added.

Captain Cole agreed with the admiral. The Khajurahian robots were brutish machines and had given the marines a hell of a difficult time. And now reports of prisoners being taken were coming through the command net. Most of the prisoners were unconscious, had lost limbs, or were otherwise half-dead, but having them provided a great opportunity for learning about the Khajuraho, their civilization, and their industrial, scientific, and military abilities.

"Admiral," one of the tacticians monitoring the battle said. "Two of the enemy warships have been totally destroyed."

The admiral looked at the display. "Let's get wrecking and recovery crews to those hulks. I want to recover as much as we possibly can. Terra Corp, Syrch Corp, and Lin Corp are standing by to reconstruct the ships using what remains of them, and their computer technicians can capitalize on the remains of the Khajurahian computer and automated systems."

"Do you think there were any survivors?" Captain Cole interrupted the admiral's thoughts.

"What do you mean?"

"From the Geist Marines, sir," the captain replied. "And the staff of Echo Mine."

The admiral put a comforting hand on the captain's shoulder. "We'll find out soon enough, Captain. It looks like things are dying down. Take a squad of marines and a shuttle and go down to the asteroid. See if you can find any of them."

"Sir?"

"It's okay. Go on. You owe them that. And I owe you that opportunity."

"Yes, sir. And thank you."

The captain hurried out of the command center.

The admiral turned back to the tactical display. *Valor* had captured the enemy supply ship. The *Valor's* captain had sent his small contingent of marines on boarding lines to the hull of the Khajurahian ship. There had not been much resistance. They were now fighting desperately to keep the alien ship from exploding. It would be a great prize to capture the enemy ship intact.

Admiral Molouf had ended the façade of chasing the retreating Khajurahian warship and had returned to a defensive stance. Admiral Molouf reported that the enemy ship had been tagged and it was just a matter of time before they all found out where the enemy had run. All in all, it was a satisfactory outcome.

Fleet Admiral Mehra dictated his initial report and downloaded the battle sequence to a special military message pony. Soon the message pony was framing back to Callirrhoe Station.

The admiral knew it had been a great victory. The fleeing Khajurahian warship carried a message to its home world concerning the tenacity and strength of their new neighbors. The Khajurahian would not be so bold in the future. Nor, he knew, would they be so unprepared. As much as the humans had learned about the capacities and tactics of the Khajurahian, the aliens had learned a like amount about the humans. The next engagement, and the admiral believed this was just the first in a series of engagements, would not be so one-sided. The action on Echo Mine was the first clash in what the admiral believed would be a wide-ranging war. He hoped his nervous and sometimes delusional military, civilian, and corporate leaders would see it as clearly as the admiral did.

As the admiral managed the aftermath of the battle, he kept an eye on the vastness of space. Somewhere out there, a new enemy of infinite possibilities was waking up to the threat that humanity posed. It was unsettling.

The stale air was filled with the whiz of exchanged fire as the aliens poured into the open chamber. The marines and JC dogs met them with a rain of interlocking fire that chewed the aliens up. But the aliens maintained their momentum and pushed forward in a blare of exchanged laser, flechette, and mini-rocket fire. The ground shook with the impact of explosions, and the darkness was illuminated.

Alien robots clanged forward. Blood pumped, and hearts strained. The space between the two forces was awash in death, and in a killing frenzy, Sergeant Kade suddenly wondered if God had fled the battlefield in fear. The thought was as clear as a summer sky.

The civilians, all except for Anne Maria Noble, the former marine corporal who now fought from a foxhole on the left flank, had evacuated to the surface. With them went supplies and an unconscious Corporal Shea Alexander in a medically induced coma. Doctor McCall said the corporal was expected to recover, as long as she wasn't shot before then. They were prepared to blow the tunnel, and there were rough plans to run along the plateau toward the distant mountain line. But Kade doubted they would get that far. He felt the end coming. He wondered what it would feel like to die.

A salvo of fire danced along the walls of Sergeant Kade's fighting position. He ducked down and, holding his rifle blindly over his head, returned fire in the general direction of the enemy. They were close now. Kade could feel the line breaking, and suddenly he knew he had to get out of the foxhole into the trench. Forms moved, silhouetted in the darkness before his position, as the aliens moved like wraiths and demons in the strobe-like brilliance of explosions and weapons fire. It was surreal: the stocky aliens and their monstrous robots in their choreographed movement like still-frame photos flicking robotically across a computer monitor. The pressure of the battle was heavy. Sergeant Kade could feel the wave of the enemy's forces well up over the Geist Marines' defensive positions with tidal force.

Sergeant Kade slipped out of the back of the foxhole into the deep gray of night that was constantly shattered with the crash of lightning-like flashes, where the air danced with lasers and hummed with deadly projectiles.

"We can't hold," Sergeant Dixon's strained voice broke over the tactical net. Kade could hear a series of flechette bursts ripping from Dixon's KNR-FL.

"Fall back to the surface," Kade ordered as he mowed down a group of aliens that were rushing the trench line where he now stood. There were dozens of the creatures behind them, and with a final burst of fire, Kade beat a hasty retreat down the trench toward the central bunker.

All along the line, the aliens broke through. In the flashes of light that lit the dark, Kade could see them bounding over the tops of trenches and rushing toward the center of the defense. One of the alien robots crashed into the trench behind Kade where it seemed to be stuck. It whirled and buzzed as it struggled to extricate itself. There was no time to deal with it. Kade ran.

He spun through one of the ninety-degree turns that they had built into the trenches and ran headlong into four or five aliens who were hunkered down and shooting across the field of fire toward Alpha team. Kade bowled the first one over. The rest of them, stunned and surprised, turned inhuman faces toward him. In that second, Kade viciously attacked. He fired his rifle into the faceplates of two of the aliens and used his weight to carry two others to the ground. He beat mercilessly at the one trapped under his body and released his rifle, which was too large to effectively use in the tangle of arms and alien legs that filled the tight space. He pulled his pistol from his leg holster and fired desperately at the other alien who was scrambling back and firing at him. Kade felt something graze his shoulders with a thud, and sharp, burning pain coursed all along his back. He ignored it and sprung up and forward to grapple with the alien. Sergeant Kade locked hands to arms with the alien, and they fought roughly in the dark, the rest of the universe forgotten in the moment.

The thing was strong. Spindly and powerful arms tried to wrest Kade's pistol from his hands while one of the three-jointed legs hit Kade's right thigh and began putting enormous pressure on the muscle and bone. Kade could feel his leg stretching and the bone threatening to break. He stepped back and fell, clutching the alien closely to his chest. Using the momentum of the fall, he quickly pushed the alien up and over his head, throwing the creature over the corpses of its comrades. Whirling over, Kade fired rapidly at the alien as it struck the ground. Kade stumbled unsteadily to his feet, still firing at the now-unmoving alien and its comrades.

Kade's heart was pounding. Despite the explosions and chaos of interchanged weapons fire, the universe was ghastly silent. Kade could not hear, and his vision was narrow as he moved automatically into the open and began running toward the bunker, firing all around him into the milling mass of the melee. Figures rose around him. He fired, struck out, and bowled through the shapes that moved spectrally before and around him.

"Get down, Kade!" The voice rang over the tactical net, and without a hesitant thought, Kade dove. A flurry of fire cascaded over him like meteors burning across a night sky.

Kade crawled forward as quickly as he could. Before him he felt a space of air, and he tumbled over the edge of the last trench line before the bunker. The other marines were there in a defensive line firing wildly. As Kade watched, one of the marines collapsed as a bolt of fire ripped through his helmet and his head exploded in a burst of red and mash.

Sergeant Kade picked up the dead marine's rifle and squeezed the trigger at the first shape that moved across his field of vision. He realized he was firing a R-592, which meant the dead marine was Corporal Clancy Fox.

Damn.

The remaining three marines stepped back into the bunker and barred the door.

"Out! Out! Out!" Kade yelled as he sent a final round through the firing port.

The three of them dashed into the tunnel at the back and began running up toward the surface. They could feel the earth reverberate as the aliens attacked the bunker with heavy weapons. Sergeant Kade pushed the other two marines forward, and he fell back a few meters to give them covering fire if it came to that. The way was steep, and the pain in Kade's back was nearly unbearable. He fought to retain clear thoughts and suddenly came upon someone pulling a prone, unmoving figure upward in the dark.

"Help me!" The voice of Aaron Noble was desperate as he struggled to pull the body after him. "I can't leave her! Help me!" Aaron Noble looked as if he had been injured. He was half-dragging his right leg as he moved. It made it impossible for him to carry the body of his wife.

Sergeant Kade grabbed the body of Anne Maria Noble by the belt. Aaron Noble used both his hands to cup his wife under the shoulders, and the two of them began an awkward carry of the body toward the surface of the asteroid. Aaron was weeping and cursing as he stumbled along backward up the tunnel. It was a desperate effort, and it took several minutes to make it past the first turn. There Sergeant Kade found Sergeants Stratton and Dixon waiting breathlessly by the detonator.

"Come on!" Sergeant Dixon yelled.

Sergeant Kade and Aaron Noble carried the body past the two marines.

"Fire in the hole!" Sergeant Stratton cried. At that moment, he twisted the detonating device, and a series of rumbles cascaded along the tunnel where they had recently raced, and a shock wave blew into the rock walls, and the tunnel collapsed. The ground shook. The respirators in their spacesuits whirled at maximum as a mass of dust filled the air and billowed around and past them in the dark.

Sergeant Kade found himself face-first on the rocky floor. He felt a hand grab the back of his suit and pull him upward.

"Let's go!"

Kade scrambled up and frantically searched for the body of Anne Maria Noble, but he could not find it in the dark. Even his enhanced vision failed in the pebbled air, so he pushed forward. He decided he hated fighting underground and swore he would never do it again. A few hundred meters up the tunnel, he met up with Aaron Noble who was once again dragging his wife's body behind him.

"Dixon, Stratton!" Kade called. "Help Aaron with his wife."

Sergeant Dixon came back, his headlamp on infrared high. He bent down and hoisted Anne Maria up. Kade took physical control over Aaron Noble, slipped one of the man's arms over his shoulder to help him walk, and pulled him along up the long slope toward the uncertain surface. It was obvious to Kade that Aaron could not see at all in the smoky air. The man stumbled and floundered as Kade pulled him along.

It was a long and difficult climb, but the aliens had not managed to breach the collapsed tunnel. When a dim light appeared in the distance, all three marines picked up their pace in a bid to escape the tomblike walls of the mine. As the small group of survivors trudged the last few steps to the opening, Corporal Jehu Eyre appeared before them.

"Stay down," he warned as the Geist Marines and Aaron neared the tunnel's entrance. For the first time, Sergeant Kade felt the ground shake with the unmistakable feel of an aerial bombardment. "There's a hell of a fight going on out here," the corporal continued.

The marines emerged on the top of the cliff that overlooked the valley below and Echo Mine. They were in a semicircular pocket of heaped rock and sand that sheltered them from view. Behind them the small control building for the mirror array sat incongruously. Theresa Sloan and Doctor McCall were peering over the ridge of the protective pocket as above a marine landing craft roared by, and suddenly the sky was full of marines falling toward the surface under a steady stream of covering fire. The surviving Geist Marines joined Theresa and the doctor, leaving Aaron Noble clutching the body of his wife in the center of their small perimeter. A scatter of supplies and boxes were neatly piled nearby. None of the JC dogs had survived to carry the supplies. It occurred to Kade that they were therefore stuck, more or less, at this location.

The invading marines were fully engaged with the aliens. It was apparent to Kade that the marines were attacking three heavy gun emplacements along the ridgeline. Alien infantry poured out of crevasses in the earth to meet the marines in a sharp battle.

"Where is he going?" Corporal Eyre asked.

Sergeant Kade and the rest of the group turned to see what Corporal Eyre was looking at. Aaron Noble loped his way toward the small building and the mirror array. He was dragging his leg, but he somehow managed to keep going. Sergeant Kade was too tired to do anything about it.

"I don't know," Kade answered as he turned to watch the battle. Sergeant Kade enabled his personal beacon. He did not want the marine ships to mistake him for an enemy. He noticed the other Geist Marines follow his lead.

It was an even contest. The marines had close air support, but the aliens were holding their own with the combined use of attack robots and the heavier firepower of the three gun emplacements. Luckily for the marines' ships, the three powerful alien guns seemed unable to fully rotate upward. As long as the ships remained in a flight path above the emplacements, they were immune from the guns' fire. But that was not the case with the ground assault. The aliens rotated the guns toward the marines and were putting lethal fire on target. The battle surged back and forth. Soon, Sergeant Kade noticed that Corporal Eyre was firing his R-592. Really a sniper weapon, it was highly accurate with its smart munitions and long range. Kade considered telling the young corporal to stop firing as it might draw the enemy's attention but held back. The corporal was only doing what he was trained to do. And from what Sergeant Kade could see, the corporal was picking off aliens that appeared to be small-unit leaders. The other Geist Marines and he held their fire, content to let their brethren take the brunt of this attack.

A wave of heat and a citrus light washed over the huddled group. Alarmed, Kade rolled over and saw a brilliant sheet of light emanating from the mirror array toward the nearest enemy gun emplacement. The beam struck some type of force field, and energy rippled and flashed all along the gun position. The heat was intense, as it seemed to focus and adjust. The group of survivors shied away from it, crawling further away from the open mine shaft. Suddenly there was a huge concussion as the energy beam burst through the protective force field and the alien gun exploded in an aurora of colors. The beam then moved toward the next gun emplacement as the tide turned and the marines pushed forward. The aliens broke, and in a moment what had been a well-disciplined defense turned into a rout with small battles going on all over the plateau. Pockets of aliens were eliminated as the marines advanced. Sergeant Kade noticed the beam from the mirror array suddenly die as if it were an extinguished flame. Though it had not detonated the second enemy gun, it had damaged the weapons defenses, and a diving marine ship blasted the position to bits.

Kade heard Theresa cheer. He turned and saw Aaron Noble advance awkwardly from the small outbuilding to where his wife lay dead. Aaron sat down at the head of his wife and placed his hand on the top of her helmet. He stroked her silently.

It was only a little while longer before the marines had dealt with the enemy. The landscape was dotted with bodies and body parts. In the sepulchered silence that followed, Kade's group of survivors stood up and watched the marine landing force spread out and secure the area.

An uneasy feeling pricked at Sergeant Kade. He turned and saw Theresa Sloan looking at him. She was standing a little above him on the top of their protective pocket. Behind her, in the distant sky, Kade could see a multitude of asteroids staring silently down. The two of them stood there for a moment, their eyes locked. Then Theresa turned away, and Kade marched out to greet a marine lieutenant that was just cresting a small rise in front of the survivors.

"Master Sergeant Sayer Kade?" the lieutenant assumed. "How can I help you?"

Captain Cole stepped into the close confines of the landing craft. The airlock cycled, and he removed his helmet. It took a moment for the door to slide open, and he strode through the airlock and into the troop carrier area. His eyes were immediately drawn to the four Geist Marines and two civilians who were huddled on the long, bench-like acceleration couch. Not many had survived. The group was cupping steaming mugs of coffee in their hands and drinking silently. They looked like hell, and the smell rising from their bodies was palpable.

"Master Sergeant Kade," he said. "Sergeant Stratton. Sergeant Dixon. Corporal Eyre. I do not think I have had the pleasure of meeting you two," he added as his eyes swept across the dirty and smudged faces of Theresa Sloan and David McCall. "I take it the medical ship has the other civilian and Corporal Alexander?" When the group did not reply, the captain continued uneasily. "I'm sorry."

Sergeant Kade exchanged a look with his fellow Geist Marines. "Did you know?" he asked.

Captain Cole sighed and sat down opposite the group. He moved a tired hand over his face and took a deep breath. "No."

He looked at the Geist Marines, and they looked back at him. "Well," Kade offered. "You came back. That is something."

They sat for a long moment in silence. It was a wonder to finally be out of spacesuits. Though Kade could smell the pungent aroma rising from all of the survivors, the air seemed fresh and clean. The coffee was strong with a hint of chocolate and mint. And Theresa was leaning back against him. He could feel her body heat, warm and seductive. He looked at the captain, freshly bathed and all proper and prim, and though he felt he should be furious with the officer, Kade found he was not. After all, at the start of this adventure, Kade had told the *Ark Royal* to protect themselves. How could he now blame them for doing just that?

The captain stayed with them for their short flight back to the assault ship *Grampus*. There they showered, were issued new clothing, had a medical checkup, and were then ushered into a room where a tall, gaunt general named Gaspar waited to hear their debriefing. Kade and the others were grateful the debriefing was a short one. They were soon all asleep in private rooms offered by the ship's officers.

A few weeks later, Kade slipped onto the asteroid's landing field and boarded the *Arrow Hawk*. It was a luxury yacht used by Terra Corp's top administrator of Echo Mine. That man had died during the initial assault by the Khajuraho. Theresa had showed the ship to Kade on one of their long walks through the ruins of Echo Mine. Crews from Terra Corp had arrived and were beginning to get the mine up and running. It was, after all, a valuable jewel in their commercial operations. Two days ago, Corporal Shea Alexander opened her eyes only to find out she had been promoted to sergeant. Stratton, Dixon, and Eyre were making the rounds of all the ships, retelling their story and generally being welcomed as heroes. But Kade, after a formal dinner with the brass and a personal meeting with Fleet Admiral Mehra, preferred solitude. He had been drawn toward Theresa, and the two of them had wandered the open areas of the asteroid in subdued quiet. Kade found he was tired. He was worn out. And Theresa seemed to sense this and to be drawn by it.

Sitting in the pilot seat of the yacht, Kade heard a noise. He swiveled the black leather chair and found Theresa standing quietly behind him.

"I knew I would find you here," she said softly. She held a large duffle bag in her right hand. She was wearing a black pair of pants and a white shirt with flamboyant sleeves. The neckline was brocaded in a delicate, flowery pattern. Kade thought it was extremely feminine.

"You're stealing the ship, aren't you?" she asked. "You know it belongs to Terra Corp?"

Sergeant Kade smiled. "Are you going to stop me?"

Theresa moved forward and put the duffle bag down behind the pilot seat. She moved to the copilot seat and sank into it.

"No."

Kade found himself looking into Theresa's gray-green eyes. They reminded him of the shimmering surface of Lasslo Prime. Long ago, Kade had stood looking out at the water planet from the jump deck of the *Pintado*. The ship was there to fight a local uprising against the government of Earth. It was not the first taste of battle that was brought to mind by Theresa's eyes, but rather the way Lasslo Prime had glistened in the light of the yellow star, peaceful, seemingly content. It was as if the universe itself had held its collective breath and for one moment found within itself a contented soul. Kade knew a man could get lost in eyes like that.

Kade broke eye contact and shrugged.

"What's in the bag?" he asked into the uncomfortable silence.

"Oh, that?" Theresa reached back and popped the clasp open. She reached inside and pulled out a dark, clear crystal about the size of a volleyball.

"An insanity crystal?" The crystal was worth a fortune. "Where did you get that?"

Theresa smiled. Her voice was cheeky. "I like to think of it as a retirement present from our friends at Terra Corp."

"Oh," Kade murmured. "Really? A retirement gift?"

"Do you think you are the only one that can retire?" she asked.

"Well, it's not a true retirement," Kade offered. "It is more like a leave of absence. You can't retire from the Geist Marines."

They sat for a moment until Theresa laughed. The sound was as fresh as the sea. "Sayer Kade," she managed. "What am I going to do with you?"

"Well," he said. "I can think of a few things. But first things first."

"Hatches secured," Theresa said mischievously.

"Engines?"

"Hot."

"Systems?"

"Green."

"Theresa?"

"Yes?"

"Thank you for coming."

Theresa smiled.

Arrow Hawk rose from the surface of the asteroid and darted between the heavy cruiser *Scorpion* and its sister ship, the *Valor*. Below them, the twinkling green and blue lights of Echo Mine grew distant as Sayer Kade turned the *Arrow Hawk* out toward the stars. He no longer felt like he was running from bad memories. He no longer felt angry and alone.

As he throttled up and the frame drive jumped to life, Theresa reached out a steadying hand and wrapped it tightly in Kade's grip. For the first time in years, Sayer Kade felt like he had a real future. The universe was wide and free, and so was he.

REVENGE

At the end of the Second Trade War between the Earth, led by Terra Corporation, and the burgeoning corporate powers of Earth's early colonies, chief among them the Lin Corporation and its first truly powerful CEO Terrance Silva, Lin Corporation financed a raid on a refueling station in the Luyten system. A covert reprisal attack, launched by Terra Corporation the next standard year, produced one of the strangest and technologically enlightening episodes of the war. The attempted use of a prototype Frame Bomb led to the accidental discovery of early Ripplers. Sadly, its discovery was precipitated by … a mad man.

—*War Between The Suns: A History of War and Trade in the Early Expansion Period*, by Victor T. Dross

THE *REVENGE* decelerated slowly from the darkness of interstellar space as it left the heliopause and the first traces of solar wind registered on its sensors. The cylindrical tube that formed the bulk of the spacecraft rotated at nine hundred miles an hour, replicating the speed of the Earth's rotation at midlatitude. The centrifugal force it generated was sufficient to provide standard gravity of thirty-two feet per square inch in the interior of the craft. Now the computer strained as the ship slowed. The *Revenge* was slipping into the inner solar system at 18,600 miles per second. The computer calculated and adjusted spin. A constant series of fusion-produced propellant burst silently out of the secondary engine. It was an automated sequence—the spin and pull. And it went unremarked in Barnard's Star system.

Six light years from Earth, from Sol, through space so silently profound that the quiet of death was humbled besides it.

Two planets, at the size of two and three Earth masses respectively, hovered in the habitable zone of the system. They were double planets and orbited their common center of gravity, spinning like two dancers holding hands as they twirled, while the planets rotated about the red dwarf star. The twin planets were known as Van de Kamp's miracles. Both terrestrial planets with metallic cores, they were rich in canyons, mountains, and, along the equator of both planets, but particularly Dark Companion, active volcanoes. They were not supposed to exist. Yet early Earth probes had discovered them.

It was only a few centuries later that the first colony ships set forth, and now Dark Companion, the main planet named after de Kamp's book, was home of a thriving colony. The second, wetter planet, Makemake, named after an ancient Polynesian god, had vast oceans of water four times deeper than those of Earth. The star system was otherwise nearly empty. There was an asteroid belt at roughly seven astronomical units from Bernard's Star. And that was it.

These facts provided necessary astronomical information to the ship's computer as it adjusted its trajectory toward the twin planets. The ship continued to slow rapidly as its sensors conducted a multitude of passive signal searches in the system. It would not use active sensors until it was near the target. For now, it scanned, picked up radio and light messages that radiated out from the planets, and slipped ever closer.

Captain Lawson Cooper sipped a cup of reconstituted tea and watched the display screen. *Revenge* did not have any windows, as windows would reduce the efficacy and integrity of the ship. It was a warship, not a pleasure cruiser. Instead the sensor arrays produced composite real-time and computer-animated effects and displayed them on a large four-foot screen within the command room. Lawson noted the position of the double planets and adjusted some controls on his command console. He did not see any trace of other ships. He tuned the sensors to detect the rather noticeable radiation by-product of framing drives. But the sensors did not detect any of the residues left by the faster-than-light ships. Lawson suspected the telltale streaks of radiation were hidden behind the twirling masses of the asteroid belts along the main trade lane. It did not surprise him.

"Mary," he had named the computer Mary and changed its standard metallic voice to a smooth female one, "how long before we reach the asteroid belt?"

"Thirty-eight standard hours and twenty minutes," the computer's abnormally human voice replied.

"Full status?"

There were certain set verbal commands that prompted the computer to conduct preprogrammed subroutines.

"All ship functions are operating within normal parameters," the computer replied.

A section of the display screen split, and a graphic rendering of the *Revenge* appeared on a field of white. The Terra Corporation's TC monogram spun slowly in the lower left corner of the screen.

A rotating, cigar-shaped ship, poised between two elongated brackets that remained stationary to relative space, *Revenge* was sleek and minimal. It was a one-person attack ship, and that meant many lonely hours, days, and weeks as it moved in on its prey. Though Lawson's personality tested to the far side of introversion, nearly to the point of being autistic, even he found the weeks of isolation difficult. To escape the constant loneliness, Lawson had spent a whole week inside the virtual tank, floating naked in a bed of clear gel with wires and sensors attached to his body and his individually fitted vid-helm securely on his head. But even the virtual world games, computer stimulation of his body, and the near-real artificial intelligence of the computer could not make up for the lack of real life, real activity. It was almost enough to drive one insane.

Lawson was relieved to be active once again. His departure from Sol was unremarkable to the point of routine. While the war waged and ships darted through folded space at faster-than-light speeds, *Revenge* had slipped peacefully out of its moorings on Earth's moon. A black needle against the deep darkness of space, nearly invisible, *Revenge* crept out of Sol system and dipped into the vast, dark desert of interstellar space. Lawson's orders were to avoid the trade lanes, and that order had caused something of a dilemma. An unforeseen incident had pulled *Revenge* violently out of its journey.

Fifteen days into a twenty-four-day faster-than-light journey, the klaxon alarm sounded while Lawson was in his favorite v-world, an ancient war simulation where Lawson played a fighter pilot in the First Resource War. He had stumbled blindly out of the v-tank and fumbled barefooted to the command room. A dark planet—a rogue planet—was hurdling blindly through interstellar space. It was in *Revenge*'s flight trajectory. Unfortunately, the ship's sensors did not discover the rogue planet until *Revenge* crossed into its planetary well. One of the oddities of frame drives was its inability to function near objects of significant mass. The curvature of space near planets, a curve that resembled the depression a heavy bowling ball makes on a bed, disrupted the frame drive's ability to identify the natural rents in space through which faster-than-light spaceships travel. The phenomenon kept interstellar spacecraft from framing within an AU of a planetary body. Crossing the path with the unregistered rogue planet had jerked *Revenge* out of folded space like a baseball player snapping a line drive out of the air with a baseball glove. The sudden reintroduction of real space had subjected Lawson to a nasty dose of time dilation a la Albert Einstein. The rift had cost Lawson three months of his time while two and a half years passed in the outer universe.

Luckily for Lawson, he had strapped himself into the command chair through force of habit before the rogue planet's grip ripped *Revenge* back into real space. It was a violent reentry. Since *Revenge* was not moving kinetically through space, the ship began to tumble slowly as the gravitational pull of the dark planet took its inevitable hold on the ship. It took little effort to have the computer steady the ship and calculate a way around the rogue. However, it was much more time-consuming to fire up the fusion drive and push through the gravity well of the rogue planet. It was during this process that Lawson lost three months that, through the odd perversion of space and time, resulted in the two and a half years of time lost relative to Earth.

Even though the rogue planet had caused Lawson to lose so much relative time, the planet was an unexpectedly welcomed curiosity. Lawson had spent several weeks scanning the planet's surface and minimal atmosphere and running simulations on the planet's speed and course. The surface of the dark planet was potted with craters, some as large as skyscrapers. Lawson saw in them the signs of some ancient catastrophe that hurled the planet out of its home system into an endless voyage of perpetual night. And as *Revenge* adjusted and moved away from the rogue planet, Lawson, bored and sad to see the planet's virtual image fading away, launched a satellite probe. He knew it was a waste of a critical resource, but he did it anyway. The probe was programmed to scan the rogue planet for another twelve months before spinning back into deep space and framing back to Sol system where the technicians from Terra Corporation would examine the results in detail.

Who knew? Lawson thought. Maybe he would get a large finder's fee, or, in the least, the planet might be named after him.

That idea pleased Lawson. Lawson often felt he too had been cast into the void of space, darkly alone, bearing the scars of his past.

Luckily, besides that odd occurrence, interstellar space was unsurprisingly empty, and *Revenge*, once outside of the planetary well, had reengaged the framing drive and quickly completed its journey.

Two and a half years, he wondered. *Was the war still being waged?* Lawson watched the display screen as *Revenge* continued its entry into Bernard's Star system. The question was a problem.

With, *Revenge*'s target finally in view, Captain Lawson Cooper considered the situation. *Revenge* had stopped just outside the heliopause and was now using its less conspicuous fusion drive to close the thirty or so AU distance to the system's asteroid belt. He pressed a button on the command console, and a red line depicting *Revenge*'s approach to Van de Kamp's miracle planets appeared. His tea mug warm in his hands, Lawson's eyes moved purposefully over the display screen.

The trade war had been raging for several years when Lawson had departed on his solitary mission. It had not been going well for Terra Corp. If that trend had continued, there was no knowing what Lawson was actually facing. In that amount of time, the known universe could have ended, he thought to himself. And he would not have known it. It was as if he were outside of time, outside of reality, and now as *Revenge* entered Bernard's system, he was stepping back out of the looking glass into real time.

It was possible the war was over. It was possible Earth and Terra Corp had won. It was possible Earth had lost. And it was possible the war with Lin Corp and its lesser allies was still raging.

Lawson knew that now was the moment, confronted with these potential possibilities, that his resolve would be tested.

He rubbed tiredly at his eyes. Recently he had been seeing specs of shadows flickering at the edge of his vision. These dancing, floating specks always darted away when Lawson tried to look directly at them. A search in the computer's medical directories made Lawson think he might have some fluid in his eye or could, possibly, have damaged his retina while in the v-tank. It was not an uncommon v-tanking injury. Still, having shadows creeping at the edge of his vision was unsettling. He ignored them for now. He had other, more pressing things to worry about.

The *Revenge* carried with it a new and powerful prototype weapon of destruction. Based upon the principles of the framing drive, it folded space. But it also exerted an energy field that wrapped itself around an object so that when it folded space, it took that object with it. When launched at a planet—theoretically—it would grasp a huge section of the planet in its energy field and fold space, tearing a hole in the planet in a similar way as taking a bite out of an apple. One second the planet would be a natural sphere, and the next it would be ragged, off balance, torn and rendered. The loss would disrupt its natural rotation. The surface would be scoured clean by the resultant winds, its gravitational balance would be destroyed, and the planet would careen out of its orbit. Within a few hours, all unprotected life would be dead. The planet would be sterile, and, if calculations held rightly, it would be pulled into the star's gravitational well. The planet itself would crash into Bernard's Star.

The weapon had never been tried outside of a secret research facility on the Martian moon Phobos. The experiments carried out by the scientists were limited in scope. It would have been impossible to keep a full-scale test of such a weapon secret, so they had limited the tests to miniaturized and highly controlled experiments. Punching the results into a supercomputer, they extrapolated the results of the weapons now being carried by *Revenge*. The two bombs were untried. Nobody at Terra Corp was really sure the weapon would work. But the computer simulations of the bombs, Lawson considered, were quite convincing. He was convinced the planets would die.

Lawson took another sip of tea and stretched his legs. The idea of killing two planets' worth of people should bother him, he knew. But he had his reasons. A Lin Corp raider from Dark Companion had caught his wife's ship, *Symons's Dream*, as it refueled on Narious Station in the Luyten system. Cecilia had been a wonderful woman, full of energy and wit. And she had saved Lawson from the demons of his past. Lawson had felt as if no one in the world could love him. That his existence was an aberration, a mistake. Yet Cecilia had stolen in and shown him life. She had loved him for reasons he could not fathom, which amazed him and left him in wonder. And they had killed her. Killed everyone aboard *Symons's Dream* and Narious Station over a trade dispute. A trade dispute! Even after all this time, the fire of hatred flared in Lawson's blood, and for a moment tears filled his eyes.

Yes. Lawson had his reasons. He had chosen the name of his ship. He had volunteered for this mission. He wanted—he needed revenge.

Lawson continued to watch the display screen and fiddle with the controls. He reexamined his attack position and postulated scenarios both in his mind and on computer simulations. Still, even with all the change and the building pressure of the pending attack run, Lawson became fidgety.

Thirty-seven hours could be an eternity. Yet he refused to go back into the v-tank. Instead he went to the small gymnasium, channeling the growing stress in his body into a marathon workout. This left him exhausted and allowed him to get some sleep as, all the while, *Revenge* maneuvered undetected in Bernard's system. Lawson supplemented his activities with watching digital videos, checking the status of the journey, and playing computer games. And he filled the voided silence of his ship's passage with music that played incessantly from the ship's speakers.

The silence of *Revenge*'s passage and its machinations was unnerving. Unlike an air ship, one that plied passage through a planet's atmosphere, space travel was tomblike. The ship made no noise. There was no turbulence. Traveling in a spaceship with extended audio deprivation, Lawson knew from his training, enhanced the perception of isolation. That could be a problem. Early, extended forays into space travel and its inherent lack of natural sounds had led to anxiety, depression, and, in some extreme early cases, hallucinations. Scientific studies of sensory deprivation had revealed many negative side effects such as the seeing of faces and hearing of voices.

However, the most dangerous and common side effect was the conviction that an evil presence had materialized into the ship and was slowly consuming the crew's souls. In an altered mental state, the imagined evil force whispered and cajoled and bid crew members to utmost violence. The most serious incident in history happened to the first Mars exploration crew. Everyone knew about Dr. Werner. The voice he heard in the darkness, deep, seductive, bid him to kill the crew. He had used the only weapon available to him, a laser torch used for welding in deep space. The ship, *First Hope*, became a charnel house of blood, gore, and severed limbs. Mission Control had watched the monitoring screen helplessly as the maniacal doctor mercilessly tracked down and killed all seven of the other crew members. Eventually, Dr. Werner had overridden the computer's programs and crashed *First Hope* into Mar's moon Deimos. The doctor's demonic laughter was the last transmission from the doomed ship. It was childlike, hysteric, and held a tinge of glee.

It was the outcome of that first Mars mission that led to early developments of the v-tank. Over time, v-tanks had become more and more sophisticated until it could provide full sensory inclusion. Yet even that stimulation had its limitations. Simulative life often left the person in the tank feeling disconnected with other humans. The desire to be part of the living world could grow until it became too much. Too much v-tanking also led to psychotic episodes. It seemed people were fundamentally social creatures with a true need to interact with others and with their environment. The v-tank could not fool the body 100 percent. But it had allowed for extended, deep space travel. Luckily for spacefaring crews and public, the invention of the framing drive had cut the length of space travel to a few weeks or months between systems. V-tanks had become only another form of entertainment. But here, on *Revenge*, with its empty corridors and cryptic air, it was the breath of life.

Lawson knew he had tripped on the edge of sanity. Sometimes during the long flight, he had heard the sound of Cecilia weeping in the dark.

Thirty-six hours later, Lawson stood with his hands on his hips, his chest pounding from the long run he had just finished, watching as *Revenge* maneuvered through the asteroid belt. Lawson had always been fascinated by the solitary fragments of rock and ice. He shifted the view from composite to line of sight, focusing high-resolution cameras on the nearer asteroids as *Revenge* slipped between them. Like the Sol system, the asteroids of Bernard's Star numbered in the millions. They varied in size and shape from jagged shards to smooth boulders. Some were mere tens of meters across while others were vast dwarf planets that revolved around Bernard's Star at the edge of its occupied space.

Lawson selected a setting on the control panel, and small, white boxes appeared on the asteroids in view. The names or numbers of the asteroids were etched in the text boxes—Leviathan, Crandall's Cradle, and Rock Wall were some of the more colorful names that appeared. Others were numerically identified as B-XVI, B-XXI, or something similar.

Leviathan, a near dwarf planet, was composed of carbonaceous chondrite and had a small, desolate moon. It was a type of primitive asteroid thought to have formed early in the life of solar systems. It had a high proportion of water and likely had a vast collection of magnetite and olivine crystals. The surface of the leviathan was jet black. It seemed to absorb the dim red light of Bernard's Star as its pockmarked surface shifted in the perpetual void. It drew Lawson's curious attention for a moment. Yet it was the smaller asteroids and fist-size chunks of rock that held Lawson's attention. They were difficult to detect and had the potential of damaging *Revenge's* sensor arrays.

Lawson raised the ship's electromagnetic wave-shield, creating a type of pressure bubble around the ship. It was strong enough to catch and eject small objects, but anything larger than a motorcycle would get through the field with disastrous effect. This was the other problem with coming in the system from deep space. The space lanes had been cleared of much of the flotsam of the galaxy and were naturally kept away from larger space bodies that interrupted or confused framing drives. Sneaking into the system and flying the belt, while providing an unlikely attack vector, did require more attention. For the first time since the midflight planet, Lawson had to pay attention to the ship's position and help pilot.

"There is a potential for impact along the starboard side," the computer's feminine voice announced. "Adjusting thrust."

"Acknowledged," Lawson replied. "Display near objects," he commanded.

The view shifted showing a graphic image of *Revenge* floating in a sphere made of a striated series of expanding lines that indicated distances. Several red blips appeared within the graphical sphere showing the locations of near objects. T-lines, or lines of trajectory, blipped off and on from each dot, indicating the object's anticipated flight line. The object in question was about the size of a small terrestrial house and spun rapidly. The computer showed it was mostly dense metal, though one side of it had condensed ice on its surface. The text box near it indicated it had been given the designation of B-VII-D. As it spun, the ice occasionally caught and then reflected the light of Bernard's Star. The net effect was that the asteroid flashed off and on like an emergency beacon.

None of the other near objects seemed to threaten the ship.

"Adjusting along the vertical plane," the ship announced. Though he could not feel it, Lawson knew tiny thrusters were firing along *Revenge*'s relative-bottom, pushing *Revenge* relative-up. All direction in space was relative to one's own position. Lawson had long ago given up trying to truly grasp the concept of relative position. He just thought of up and down and let it rest at that.

"Acknowledged," he replied. "Center and zoom on B-VII-D. Notify when ship has cleared zone."

The screen adjusted its view once again. Lawson saw the ragged shape of B-VII-D as it hurled silently toward *Revenge*. As he watched, the asteroid slipped lower on the view screen.

"Adjust," he said, and the picture adjusted, placing the asteroid in center screen.

After a few tense minutes, the computer said, "Zone cleared." And Lawson knew the ship was out of immediate danger.

Lawson repeated this exercise time and again as *Revenge* wound its way through the asteroid belt. One of the problems with belts like this was that not all of the millions of asteroids had been identified and their orbits calculated. Several asteroids that appeared upon the screen were unknown, and the computer had to quickly calculate their position and trajectory relative to *Revenge* and then steer the ship around them. These massive calculations were made possible by metratronic computer chips that used the flow of light through their circuits instead of slower, electrical pulses. Since modern computers were self-enclosed systems that used nanorods of metamaterial, computers were no longer susceptible to the negative effects of radiation and electromagnetic forces. Computers had become as fast as light and could perform calculations that were fundamentally beyond the ability of man.

By the time *Revenge* had traversed the asteroid belt, Lawson was exhausted. His head ached. There were still four hours before *Revenge* would be nearing firing range, three AU from the planets. Lawson therefore made his way back to his stateroom, ordering the computer to wake him should it detect any ships transiting folded space. Lawson had to adjust his orders as the computer began informing him of the steady arrival of communication drones that popped in and out of real space at regular intervals. The drones emitted high-burst transmissions of millions of messages, images, and video to waiting communication buoys. These buoys, in turn, transmitted data to the drones in a rapid exchange before the drones once again left real space on their voyage to the next system. Lawson commanded the computer to ignore these communication drop spots and to limit its search for passenger-bearing ships. This adjusted order given, Lawson collapsed on his bed and fell into a deep slumber.

Something grim tugged at Lawson's mind as he spun in a void of sleep. He felt suspended at the edge of a gravitational whirlpool as below him a dark star swept all the matter of the universe into its hungry maw. Lawson knew that if he moved, he would cross the threshold of the Event Horizon and fall endlessly down into darkness. So he froze impenetrably still. Even his breathing was tight, shallow. Fear washed over him as he gazed with horror at the destructiveness below. Planets, even stars, were swept like chaff into the yearning darkness.

Suddenly, Lawson began to spin. He felt his head swimming as the galactic force whipped him around and around. Terrified, he clung to something he could not see, his breath raw, his heart pounding. Just before the fatal moment, when the pull of the dark star tickled his skin, he was suddenly motionless. He heard a voice crying in the dark. Sad. Empty and abandoned. It sounded as lonely as the void of space where there was nobody and no soul.

Lawson strained to hear it. But as it grew in volume, his curiosity turned once again to dread, and he clamped his hands over his ears in a vain attempt to keep the sound of weeping from resonating in his brain. He knew that voice. It was her voice. It was like an accusation, hot with despair. And he shrank from it. Yet it grew closer and closer, malevolent and vile, until Lawson was sure that a spectral hand would stretch through the darkness and grab hold of his leg, tear his eyes, and render his chest an open wound.

He jerked awake and sat roughly up, confusion muddling his mind. He was in total darkness, and for a moment he feared he had been swallowed by the black hole. But then he felt the reassuring comfort of his bed sheet, and his mind began to clear. He twisted and reached back to his pillow and pulled its comforting shape toward his chest, where he held it tightly for a minute. Fear still clung to him like mist and rain, but he forced it away. Just as he was about to command the computer to turn on the lights, Lawson heard a sound. A shuffle. It came from the foot of his bed. Lawson strained to see what it was, his ears piqued and senses taut.

And he heard Cecilia weeping—there in his room, in the quiet dark. She wept, and its sound was a torment.

"Lights!" he yelled, all the force of fear and dread causing his voice to crack and fray. The lights in the stateroom flickered and grew, and for a terrifying moment, Lawson expected to see his dead Cecilia staring accusingly at him from the foot of his bed. But when the lights rose, there was nobody there. His room was its normal, quiet self, bare of accoutrements and personal items. It was septic.

Lawson showered for a long while, letting the warmth of the recycled water mist about his body. He felt tension ease from his shoulders, and it was as if a weight were removed from inside his lungs. Refreshed, he padded toward the wardrobe and dressed in the white and blue uniform of an Earth naval officer. The uniform was designed to go under combat exo-armor. But he left his armor hanging on the wall and made his way to the galley. A cup of coffee and a dried snack pack in his hands, he slipped up the deck to the command center and sat heavily in the command chair.

"Status," he said.

"All systems are operating within normal parameters," Mary replied. For the first time, Lawson thought the voice of the computer sounded bored.

"Location?" he asked.

"The ship is approaching point three AU of the double planets. Estimated time of arrival is one hour and fifteen minutes."

"Any activity from either of the planets?" Lawson asked.

"Normal planet-to-planet travel. No increase in signaling. No apparent activation of defensive systems. Weather patterns on Makemake indicate a large storm system—"

"That's enough," Lawson barked. He was feeling a bit pensive. "No ship activity?"

"No ships have framed within system since we entered."

"And from the planets?"

"Normal planet-to-planet travel."

Lawson drank his coffee and ate his snack. The ship was quiet as it decelerated the final distance to its attack position.

It was almost time to use active sensors. The first order of business would be to signal the nearest public information buoy for an update on the status of the war. He would also look for updated mission orders. But his immediate need was to get properly dressed.

Lawson was not sure how long it would take before Dark Companion or Makemake discovered his presence, and it would not do to be caught in a fight outside of his armor. If the ship's hull were pierced and decompressed, he could, at least in theory, survive in his armor and continue to fight the ship. So he grudgingly got up and trudged back to his stateroom and struggled into the bulky suit.

By the time he returned to the command room, *Revenge* was completing final maneuvers. It had come to a complete stop and was now rotating 360 degrees lateral and twenty-five degrees vertical. Once the attack commenced, *Revenge* would be positioned for a hasty retreat into space. It was unlikely the planets would waste a Nebula torpedo on the small ship. Nebula torpedoes were large and expensive. They were built around a frame drive and skipped along in and out of real space at faster-than-light speeds. Falling back into real space just before it reached its target, the torpedo would detonate its nuclear warhead, vaporizing the ship in an instant. While it sounded like an easy thing to do, Nebula torpedoes often missed their target because their targets also had frame drives and jumped out of real space just before the explosion. However, *Revenge* was small and unassuming. It was more likely that conventional, real-space weapons would be fired at the retreating warship. After all, what danger could one tiny, lone ship truly pose? It was that kind of thinking that Lawson hoped would give him a chance to get away for the long voyage back to Earth. Six more months—he dreaded.

With his battle gear on and helmet secure, he sat uncomfortably in the command chair as the last technical requirements were completed. He ran diagnostics on his own torpedoes and armed their warheads. As he was finishing this task, the alarm klaxon sounded. At the same moment, Lawson thought he heard someone call his name. He turned awkwardly around and looked at the empty command room.

"Battle cruiser identified approaching Dark Companion," the computer announced. The screen switched to tactical display, and as Lawson turned back to the front of the room, he saw a red blip appear on the screen near the virtual planets. He knew that he had just minutes to react before the battle cruiser framed within attack distance.

"Incoming message, priority one," Mary announced.

What did that portend? A message from his own forces? Lawson considered.

"Where did that ship come from?" he asked the computer.

"It framed in just outside the double planet's flat spot," the computer answered.

"Damn!" The other ship was perfectly positioned between *Revenge* and the double planets.

"Play message," he ordered. Lawson felt something brush his right arm, and he jerked his head to the right, startled. There was nothing there. He should not be able to feel anything through his armor, so he ran a quick diagnostics on the suit but found nothing out of the ordinary.

"Scout ship *Revenge*, this is Commander Trillian Naismith of the battle cruiser *Firthjof*." The commander of the *Firthjof*'s voice was hurried yet firm. As he spoke, an image appeared in a call-out box on the forward display. Commander Naismith was ensconced in battle armor as well, indicating that he and his ship meant business and were prepared to fight. It looked like Lin Corp armor to Lawson.

"Captain Cooper," the commander continued. "You are ordered to stand down. Repeat. Stand down. The war has ended. We are at peace with the Earth. Please acknowledge."

"Mary, is that message coming through official naval code?" Lawson asked. He was slightly perplexed, as the commander of the other ship seemed to know the name of Lawson's ship. Where would that commander get such information?

"Affirmative," the computer answered.

But what the computer could not say or know was if the Earth naval forces had released that information to the *Firthjof* or if, having lost the war, the enemy had simply taken the code and stolen the name of *Revenge*. It could also be that the enemy had deciphered the code and was now using it to deceive Lawson.

"What type of ship is that?" he asked as he continued to prepare his torpedoes. He had decided to launch them in paired sequence. The first torpedo of each group held a conventional nuclear warhead. It would drop into the planet's atmosphere and detonate, clearing away defensive systems and disrupting communications. This would allow the second torpedo, with its devastating warhead, to track in undetected. Yet instead of firing his shot groups at both planets, he targeted both of them at Dark Companion. Since the enemy seemed to be ready for him, it increased his chance of taking out the main planet significantly. In addition, since they were double planets, the destruction of Dark Companion would cause a chain reaction to Makemake. He only had to hit Dark Companion to destroy both planets. That said, it was doubtful he would escape the battle cruiser.

"Admiral-class battle cruiser," the computer answered.

"Non-Earth ship?" *Great*, he thought. It would have to be admiral class.

"That is correct. The admiral-class battle cruiser is a heavy interstellar with reactive armor and second-generation frame drive. It's powered by a nuclear reactor and is armed with long-range energy weapons and multiple warheads and torpedoes. It has a crew of one hundred sailors and carries a company of space marines. First introduced in—"

"That's enough, Mary," Lawson said, cutting the computer's history lesson off. "Let me know the instant that ship begins to jump."

"Acknowledged."

"Reply message at my mark. Mark," Lawson said. "Commander Naismith, battle cruiser *Firthjof,* this is Captain Lawson Cooper, Earth naval forces, commanding attack ship *Revenge.* Transmit secondary command using alternate cryptographic code Delta, One, Eight. Repeat, Delta, One, Eight."

It was an old Earth code but one still used. Lawson figured that if peace had really broken out between the systems, the sharing of naval code would have been one of the first priorities. And he recalled a briefing from Colonel Fremantle that suggested this approach to claims of peace. It was basic. It was raw. But nobody in the long-ago briefing seemed to have a better suggestion.

"They are coming for you," a disembodied voice whispered at Lawson's shoulder. The voice was rasping, male, and sinister. Lawson barely heard it, and he quickly turned toward the sound only to find the command room empty. He was alone. Lawson shook his head to clear it.

"Mary," he asked, "did you register someone else speaking?"

"Clarify," the computer replied.

"Do you detect," Lawson stated, "any other life forms in *Revenge?* Were there any other voices in the command room?"

"Negative."

Lawson felt a twitch between his shoulder blades. He spun his chair around once and gave the empty room a thorough looking over, but he saw nothing out of the ordinary.

I need some coffee, he thought.

"Captain Lawson." Commander Naismith reappeared on the screen. "We are not familiar with that particular cryptographic code. A search of our databases does not register Delta, One, Eight. But we are broadcasting through the priority naval code. That code takes precedence. You are ordered to stand down, Captain. The war is over. Terra and Lin Corp have reached an agreement."

"How do I know you are telling me the truth?" Lawson responded as he continued to prepare to launch his attack.

"Check the communication buoys," the commander suggested. "We can wait."

The war is over? That can't be, he thought. It wasn't fair.

Lawson flicked off the sound to the communication system. "Have you scanned the communication buoys, Mary?"

"Affirmative."

Lawson waited an impatient moment. "Well? Any news of the status of the war?"

"They are coming for you," Mary replied. Her voice was slightly distorted.

Lawson felt a thump in his chest. "What did you say? Computer, what did you say?"

"A scan of the nearest civilian communication pod indicates that the war ended nearly one standard year ago," the computer answered.

Lawson closed his eyes. "No. Not that. What did you say before?"

"Affirmative."

"Mary? Did you just tell me that they were coming for me? They—who?" He opened his eyes again and caught a flicker of movement off to his right. He swung quickly around but didn't see anything there.

"Negative." There was silence in the ship.

"Mary, scan the next communication buoy and attempt to verify the end of the war." Lawson wondered if there was a computer glitch. He began running a diagnostics routine. If something were wrong, it would be a hell of a time for it.

Lawson kept an eye on the location of the *Firthjof* as he quickly worked. The warship was maintaining its current position between the *Revenge* and Dark Companion. Lawson knew there would be little chance to escape the admiral-class battle cruiser once he launched the attack. Even if Lawson scooted *Revenge* back into the asteroid belt, that would only buy him a little time. *Firthjof* would close the distance between the two ships rapidly, and *Revenge* would fall in easy range of the warship's energy weapons and torpedoes. He ran several possibilities in his head but always came to the same conclusion. The mission had just become a suicide run.

Still, he thought, what if the war was over? It had been two and a half years since he had left the Sol system. A lot could happen in that space of time. And even if the war was not over, nobody would blame him for surrendering the ship while under the unforgiving guns of the *Firthjof*. The *Revenge* was not much more than a living area wrapped around an engine with a handful of torpedoes, two untried weapons, and a small, defensive laser bank that was more of a placebo than a true weapon. *Revenge* had no chance against the greater Lin Corp ship. And did it matter that the war was over? Whose war? he wondered. Not his. Cecelia was dead.

Lawson stretched and began to contemplate his next move, but he found himself distracted by the computer's last message—the one that wasn't. *They are coming to get me? Who? The* Firthjof?

Cecelia died when they burned *Symons's Dream* out of existence. She died, and there was nothing left to bury.

Lawson finished the arming sequence. He was ready to fire.

How many people, he wondered, were living on Dark Companion and Makemake? There had to be several million on Dark Companion. It was a rich planet with at least two major cities. Makemake, though smaller, was a popular vacation planet with its miles of pristine coast and exotic fishing. Early colonists had transplanted an ecosystem of life into the vast oceans of Makemake. It was said that they even had whales. Lawson had always thought it would be nice to see a pod of whales. He had seen videos of the creatures, but they were ultra-protected on the Earth, and tourists were not allowed within a couple nautical miles of the creatures. But on Makemake, he had heard, you could hire a boat and sail right alongside massive pods of the creatures. A shame, that. Killing the whales. Well, Lawson decided, he just wouldn't think of that.

The people on both planets supported Lin Corp, enabled them. Their work had built the ship that destroyed Cecelia and bereft Lawson of the only person in the universe who had meant anything to him. They were guilty by association. It was their war.

Were there children too? Of course there would be, he knew. Was it right to kill the children of his enemies? Were they responsible for what had happened? The children had not built the ship that conducted the raid. They had not operated it. Lawson doubted the kids were even aware of the war—at least the true war. There would, of course, be propaganda from Lin Corp that placed all the blame for the war on Earth and Terra Corp. That was standard. But reality was a difficult thing for a child. To them the newscasts and video programs likely had the same meaning as cartoons or entertainment programs. They were innocents. Weren't they?

"Whose there?" he asked. He had heard the sound of weeping, soft, as if a woman were crying in a deep cave. He stood up and looked around the command room.

"Mary?"

"Yes, Captain?"

"Internal life scan," he ordered. "Is there any other life form on this ship?"

"Scanning."

Lawson walked around his command chair and cautiously made his way down the central hallway. He paused to take a side arm from the small armory. He looked in the workout room and his sleeping chamber. They were empty, silent. In the galley and the v-tank room, Lawson found nothing out of the ordinary.

As he was making his way back to the command room, the computer said, "Scan complete. Results negative."

"And the war, Mary? Did you confirm anything about the war?"

The computer did not answer.

"Mary?" He stepped into the command room once again. "Mary?" The computer did not answer. The air in the ship grew malignant, and a nimbus of dread flickered in the artificial light.

Lawson sat down and began looking at the results of his computer diagnostics. Everything appeared in order. "Mary? Respond."

When the computer spoke, her voice was oddly pliant. It held a different quality, as if another, deeper voice were mixed within it. It was almost an echo, metallic, and felt as if it were angry.

"Information on the second communication buoy is inconclusive. They are coming for you." The second phrase was almost subvocalized. Lawson was not sure if he had actually heard it.

"Repeat last," he commanded.

"The information is inconclusive," the computer replied. This time Mary's voice was clear, normal.

Lawson sat down once again. He shuddered, and a deep apprehension flooded over him.

There is nothing there, he thought. *I am alone.*

"Roll up the engine, Mary. Build up speed."

"Priority message from the *Firthjof*," the computer stated.

For the first time in his long journey, Lawson thought he felt the *Revenge* tremble.

"Maybe we'll buy a second or two. Display message," Lawson gritted.

A shadow moved.

"Captain Cooper, if you continue your provocative action, the *Firthjof* will have no choice but to destroy you. Please respond." Commander Naismith's tone was fierce.

"Firing one," Lawson said. A spit of nervous laughter erupted from his lips and sounded harshly in his helmet. "Tactical display!"

The *Revenge* eked forward, gaining speed as it moved away from the double planets. A single dot flared from the *Revenge* as the first torpedo spun toward Dark Companion and its brooding protector, the *Firthjof.* At first the torpedo moved sluggishly forward, but it gained speed rapidly. Suddenly its frame drive burst to life, and the torpedo raced toward Dark Companion. At this distance, it was still a six-minute flight.

"Battle cruiser weapons are hot," the computer warned, the computer's soft voice a staccato of frigid sound. It was as if she were dying.

"Firing two." Lawson pressed the launch key on the command console. The first of the prototype frame bombs shot out of the tube, luminous against the backdrop of space.

Lawson held his breath as the two blips moved precipitously toward Dark Companion. The *Firthjof* jumped to meet them. For a minute, Lawson thought the nuclear warhead in the first torpedo might get close enough to the battle cruiser to cause some damage. But before the weapon entered effective range, a sheer burst from the *Firthjof*'s forward guns sent a lethal sheet of energy at the torpedo. The torpedo detonated harmlessly, its warhead slagged before it could be activated.

The *Firthjof*'s energy weapons fired, and the second projectile, the one with the prototype frame bomb, convulsed and tumbled head over heel. It jarred off its planned course toward the *Firthjof*, which flicked as its frame drive came to life again, and the battle cruiser began to move rapidly to intercept the *Revenge*. *Firthjof* fired again, and the first frame bomb disintegrated uselessly.

The *Revenge* strained as its fusion drive poured ragged propellant into space. The strain eased suddenly as the frame drive took over, and *Revenge* started darting back toward interstellar space.

"They are coming for you," a desolate voice hissed out of the ship's speakers.

Lawson's head snapped around. The command room's lighting seemed to dim and took on a sickly green hue. The ship convulsed and rocked, and a shower of energy fired from the *Firthjof* embraced the exterior of the *Revenge* in a grotesque fire. Elongated shadows spread across the floor. The lights flickered. *Revenge* screamed as metal strained under the *Firthjof*'s initial attack. Lawson's helmeted head slammed forward into the command console, and for a moment he was stunned.

The *Firthjof* rapidly jumped forward. It was apparent that it would quickly overtake the smaller warship.

Lawson felt panic. He sat up and looked about. Lawson felt unseen eyes digging into the concave space between his shoulders, and, releasing his constraints, he leapt from the command chair and spun toward the stern of the ship. He realized his right hand was holding the handgrip of his pistol. He swung it up and before him wildly. The shadows danced and stretched monstrously. In the turbulent undulation, they began to disconnect themselves from the ground, the walls, and ceilings and crept nearer Lawson with a dread measure.

"Stay back!" he cried.

Cecilia wept.

The computer's infernal voice echoed and dripped as the alarm klaxon pulsed again and again.

Lawson fired. The sound was a cacophonous rage.

"You shouldn't have come," the computer's voice spit. It was distorted and held a squalid quality that grated on Lawson's nerves.

The shadows shifted in and out as the ship's lights glared, sputtered, failed, and then flashed back on in rapid succession. Lawson shrieked and covered his eyes with his arms to fend from their blasphemous approach. He feared they would stop him.

"No! They murdered her!" His tormented voice roused him to action. Lawson dashed to the command console and switched on the communication system. "Stay back!"

"Captain Cooper," the commander of the *Firthjof* responded. "You have unlawfully engaged us. Shut down your engine and prepare to be boarded."

"They murdered her! They murdered her!" Lawson screamed, and all the misery of his desolate soul crystalized in the air. But he was not screaming at the commander of the *Firthjof.*

Lawson fired rapidly around him. Again and again. Cecilia moaned, and the devil laughed.

The shadows surrounded Lawson and wrapped their hideous arms around his body as Lawson stood fixed in place. Ghostly fingers pried at his helmet, and Lawson dropped his gun and clung to the helmet's sides with all his might, straining to keep the shadows out. A tortuous cry cracked from his mouth. His arms ached, but his helmet turned, pulled, and slowly shook away from his head, exposing Lawson to the ship's pestilent air. Lawson flailed toward the command console.

"Firing three! Firing four!" A hideous yowl twisted from his throat as the shadows flowed into his opened battle armor and caressed his skin. In the infernal place where his heart beat, Lawson felt icy fingers marring his blood, tightening upon his desperate heart.

The *Firthjof* fired, and the third torpedo evaporated into dust. The battle cruiser was near now. It loomed over its prey and scented blood. *Revenge* shuddered and shook. In desperation, Lawson slapped at the detonation control.

They murdered Cecilia. They murdered her!

His face was twisted in horror and fury. And the universe froze.

At that moment, Cecelia's face coalesced out of the vapors and floated accusingly before Lawson. He could not breathe. The air in *Revenge* tasted of graveyards and putrid flesh. Time snapped and spun as darkness engulfed all.

Aboard the *Firthjof,* the crew lurched suddenly as the battle cruiser slammed into an invisible wall. The ship hung unmoving in space as if a giant galactic spider had spun an invisible web that had snared the ship in its unmeasured grasp. A ripple of energy spread out from the last frame bomb and held the *Firthjof* still. The battle cruiser fell out of its rhythm of framing into real space.

"Sensors on! Sensors on!" Commander Naismith barked. "All of them!"

"The engines are not working!" Someone yelled the obvious.

"Fire forward lasers!" Commander Naismith ordered. A burst of raw energy erupted from the *Firthjof*'s forward laser tubes toward *Revenge.*

On the tactical display, a flat-energy area surged erratically, holding the *Firthjof* firmly in its embrace. At the edge of the strange wave, a light burned, and the tiny warship *Revenge* vanished in dust and space.

"What the hell is happening?" Commander Naismith hissed.

"Whatever it is, sir," it was the voice of the *Firthjof*'s senior navigator, "it has incapacitated the frame drive. I think, though, I can move on traditional propulsion."

"The *Revenge*?" the commander asked.

"Destroyed, sir."

Commander Naismith turned and sat stoically in his chair. He took a considered breath. "Can you move us out of the range of this—this flat spot?"

"Yes, sir. Fusion drive coming on line now."

Commander Naismith watched as his ship started its way through the strange new energy field. It felt as if the *Firthjof* were maneuvering through a malaise. *What type of new weapon is this?* he wondered. He watched as a myriad of readings from the ship's sensors scrolled across the screen. *What has Terra Corp concocted?*

He began tapping a top-secret message to Lin Corporation. Whatever it was, Commander Naismith knew, it had just changed the rules of war.

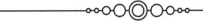

The universe rumbled, twisted and churned. In a far and unknown place among the stars, a sharp needle was born from a burning womb. The ship flicked into real space, cast into a star system unknown to man. Behind its protoplasmic wake, the prism of the universe shuddered, and a great rent in its heart closed forever. As the alien ship glinted in the bluish light of twin suns, a woman's gossamer voice wept in dire misery. The ship's engine blazed. Something sinister moved within the ship's pale air. The ship lurched and accelerated toward the speed of light. The ship had no windows. It made no sound. The endlessness of space held it in its embrace. Etched upon its hull, flashing in the primordial light, was one word: *Revenge*.

A LUCKY MAN

THE LAND rover stopped on the crest of a slight incline of desert sand. Haamar peered over the dash, wiped away grit with a yellow handkerchief, and focused through the glare of the noonday sun. A sea of sand stretched out as far as he could see. Rolling dunes accentuated the landscape with small outcroppings of sun-bleached rock scattered here and there like sentinels. The desert—known colloquially as the Great Desert—was by far the largest of the four major and seven minor deserts on the colony and shared the name of Haamar's adopted world, Telakia. Haamar and his wife, Yuyenda, had been driving through the Great Desert for four long days.

Haamar knew the desert landscape was changing. The signs were subtle. When he had first come to Telakia, the dunes of the Great Desert rolled unbroken through a no man's land. Yet here, within a one-day drive to the oasis city Umbaliya, the telltales of halfhearted, underfunded terraforming attempts could be seen. The dunes were smaller near the city and its overworked terraforming facilities. A great seam of twisting rock ledges was now clearly discernible in the day's heat.

The front of the land rover tipped forward as the little vehicle shimmied its way down the giving sand. Haamar turned the rover gently toward the ever-nearing jetties of rock. There, he knew, the vehicle would find better traction.

Haamar dimmed the windshield and stretched. He stuffed the grimy handkerchief back into the crevice beside his chair and checked the air filters. The light next to the toggle flashed orange to red and back again. He would have to change the filters soon. Yet even when the filters were new, the dust and sand managed to get into the little land rover, covering everything. It even got in the food. He sighed and admitted Yuyenda had been right. He should have spent the extra money and bought a rover with one of the new centrifugal filters. Those filters caught pollutants and sand and spun them into a trap that jettisoned them back outside. The centrifugal filters also sported an array of infrared lights that purified the air. And the salesman claimed they required almost no maintenance. But Haamar hated spending money, so he had bought the step-down model and shoved several tubular spare filters into one of the overhead compartments. Now, feeling the grime in his teeth and rubbing at irritated eyes, he wished he had listened to his wife.

The whine of the engine, driven at times by solar rays and at other times by a simple alcohol derivative fuel, A.D.L., pitched and groaned as the rover crested each small rise. Haamar felt a shift as the vehicle's tracks slipped before finding purchase once again. He jerked slightly in his safety harness.

Haamar preferred driving at night when the sun was down and the ground temperature dropped rapidly. Without the extra burden of keeping the vehicle cabin cool, the land rover ran solely on the weaker electrical engine. The electrical engine's soothing hum coupled with the blue-fringed light that floated ghostly over the nighttime desert. It was relaxing. Yet now, in the daytime sun, with the grind and the heat, Haamar felt tense. But Haamar knew there were worse things in the desert. Occasionally, massive sand storms blew in from the southeast with gale-force winds. They were monsters, rising suddenly like the hand of fate and crashing down in a choking darkness that swallowed the universe. He shuddered and hoped they could avoid the next storm.

He watched the sand as it streamed like mist across the rolling countryside, hearing its ceaseless scraping at the hull of the land rover, and dimmed the windshield a bit more, turning the glass into a darker, opaque brown to reflect the heat and brightness back into the desert waste. He had never grown quite used to the heat of midday. It didn't help that Yuyenda complained about the cooler temperature in the land rover, which Haamar kept at a high eighty.

Haamar felt sweat beading on his forehead and collecting on the back of his short-sleeved shirt.

The planet is just plain hot, Haamar thought. Maybe he would never get used to the heat.

He studied the interactive map that showed Umbaliya in relation to his current position. On the map, the city did not look that far away. He gazed through the windshield, hoping to catch a glimpse of the city. Outside, a distant pool of blue seemed to indicate a lake undulating in the heat of the horizon. But Haamar had learned that in the vastness of the Great Desert, both light and distances distorted. The lake was an illusion, a trick of the ever-oppressive heat reflecting off the sand. And Umbaliya remained hidden.

He sighed. There was still a ways to go. It was beginning to be a frustrating trip. And Umbaliya was only the halfway point. Far to the south, the capital city Kugadar lay at the edge of the desert. That was where he and Yuyenda were going. At the center of the capital's ringed-road system was the planet's only spaceport. The squat terminal building normally served the continental capitals, but it occasionally welcomed one of the more adventurous interstellar ships. And he and Yuyenda were going off world, to Sol, to Earth. It was the adventure of a lifetime.

Haamar fingered his bankcard absentmindedly. He looked back at the small bed tucked sparingly behind the driver's compartment at the sleeping form of his wife. He smiled as Yuyenda tossed slightly about before settling once again into deep slumber.

Squinting back into the sun, Haamar let his thoughts wander.

This first leg of their journey eventually led to the universally renowned College of the Mines in Colorado on Earth. The invitation had come from the college on a one-time grant from Terra Corporation. Terra Corporation was the largest and most successful corporation in the universe. They had been very gracious in their invitation. Once there, nestled in the Rocky Mountains, Haamar would present his findings.

He frowned, annoyed and feeling a bit guilty. It was as if his wife's work—her confirming, questioning, and encouraging—were not as equally important as his sudden inspiration. They should share the recognition. They were a team! Yet Yuyenda insisted upon giving Haamar the credit. It had been his hunch, she argued. His gut feeling led them down the exploratory path to a shocking discovery—a rich vein of ultra rare moissanite. A primary source for the high-quality carbon materials used to make spaceships and high-tech components, the moissanite vein ran through the heart of the Memphis Mountain range. It ran for miles. The find had catapulted the small mining company Haamar worked for to the forefront of space-based industrial production. And it had made Haamar and Yuyenda suddenly quite wealthy.

Haamar had lived on Telakia for over twelve years now, working for Zintas Mines. But his family originated on Centarus Five, an active and powerful planet known mostly for its textile works in Lunama Furs. His father and mother had worked their entire lives in the rich dirt of the New British Isles, harvesting an array of crops for local consumption. Not an exciting life. His parents had struggled to stay solvent while Haamar attended the university, diligently studying geological science. Instead of returning home afterwards, he broke away from the farm by taking a position with a company in the port city of Daleshire. Yet this did little to ease his desire to live a more adventurous life, and he found his way off world as an asteroid miner. That did not last long. It was a tough and thankless job.

By luck and by instinct, he eventually ended up on Telakia. Haamar found the planet culturally refreshing, spiritually renewing, and had discovered how to care for another human being. After all these years, the full depth of the planet and his wife often amazed him. They were full of constant surprises. Yuyenda, like Telakia, somehow remained as mysterious as the quiet, shifting sands of the desert.

A flashing light near the voltmeter gauge brought his thoughts back to the here and now. The light's warning reminded Haamar that the vehicle's battery cells had been damaged. He hoped he had enough A.D.L. fuel to make it to Umbaliya. He could not rely on the batteries or the electrical engine to get them through.

The land rover moved along the crest of a wind river, a slight depression carved out of the sand by wind and time. Haamar was careful not to slip the rover into the soft sand at the wind river's base. If the rover did, it would get mired. Instead, Haamar continued carefully along its edge where a line of rock provided a stable pathway. Known as ghost roads or bandit highways, the stone formations were the unofficial roads of the wastes.

Haamar would be grateful when they reached Umbaliya. He needed to replace their dwindling provisions, have maintenance on the rover, and relax. The city boasted many hotels and inns surrounded by a barrier wall and tall stonelike towers that radiated a force field that kept the worst the desert had to offer at bay. Perhaps there he would finally get the grit of sand out of his mouth and eyes.

"Is it my turn to drive yet?" Yuyenda's sweet voice floated sleepily from behind as she stirred, rolled over, and peered through the darkened cabin at her husband's form. "What time is it?"

Haamar glanced at the voltmeter gauge on the dashboard, trying to ignore the battery's warning light. The batteries were the first things he planned to have fixed in Umbaliya.

"Nearly noon," he replied. "You can sleep some more if you like, dear. I'm fine. Wide awake."

"No." She stretched with a warm purr. "I'm tired of sleeping. I'm tired of riding in this thing too. When do we reach the city?" She sat up, pulling the cover over her deeply tanned skin. She rested her head on the back of the driver's chair, her chin lightly touching Haamar's shoulder.

He smiled at her and looked at her as best he could, marveling at the slenderness of her nose and the quick smile on her lips. "A while yet. According to the GPS, we are still 250 miles away, but we're making good time and should arrive sometime early tomorrow morning—about eight hours." *If*, he thought, *the batteries hold out, we don't run out of A.D.L, and we can drive straight through the night.*

She nibbled playfully at his ear, kissing him lightly upon the neck. "Is it safe to put the autopilot on? It is our honeymoon, belated as it is. And it is so cold in these blankets." She laughed and reached over the chair, her hands caressing Haamar's chest.

"I think it's safe enough. We're on a ghost road and should stay on it for the next several hours. Let me punch the information in and all."

"You're so technically formal, Haamar. I'm going to have to break you of that habit, you know."

Haamar grinned sheepishly. "You've been trying that for years now. I'm surprised you haven't given up on me."

"I would have, if it wasn't so darn fun trying to convert you. After all, it's a wife's prerogative to change her husband. You were only half-civilized when I met you. And look at you now! You sometimes use full sentences and have even been known to clean up after yourself," she teased.

Haamar punched the autopilot, using his finger to sketch a route they were to follow to Umbaliya on the map that appeared on the heads-up display. The computer drew the corresponding route, and the driving wheel gave a slight roll as the autopilot took over. Haamar waited, impatiently ensuring the computer had been properly programmed. Yuyenda continued playing with his hair and lightly kissing the back of his neck. Finally, satisfied they would not run off course, Haamar swiveled the chair around. He passed his hand over Yuyenda's smooth skin and looked deep into her blue eyes. Slipping off his clothes, he crawled into the bed beside her, feeling the heat radiate off her body, excited yet calm as she quietly accepted him into her arms.

Haamar woke several hours later to the sound of a rising dust storm and an empty rumbling in his stomach. He knew Yuyenda was not in the bed the instant he awoke, and the smell of warming food wafting down from the galley told him where she was. He stretched lazily and popped his back by slinging his right leg, then his left, over the other and twisting his torso. Music filtered down from the galley, and he could see Yuyenda's shadowy form fluttering across the open stairway. The wind was already howling, low and soft but consistent. A tinge of fear crept through him, and he quickly rose.

Haamar glanced out the windshield. He plopped into the command chair, checking the radar and downloading information on the storm from the orbital weather stations.

He slowed the rover's speed. The sun was rapidly setting, and he flipped the headlamps on and took a quick positional reading. Confirming that the A.D.L. tanks were just under half-full, he decided to change the air filters. In a few minutes, he had pulled the long cylindrical tubes out of their recesses and replaced all four filters. That would help keep the worst of the sand out of the rover, he hoped. Haamar sat down again and quickly read through the weather report. It was not good. A haboob that stretched miles across a wide front was billowing down upon them. They did not have much time.

"Yuyenda!" he called. "We're in for it. Haboob," he added as he took advantage of the few moments of relative calm to triple check his position and program the autopilot. But the pilot relied too heavily upon the positioning satellites whose signals often grew too dim to detect in the heart of a storm. So he pulled out an old paper map and quickly marked their current location and the planned route to Umbaliya. Calculations rolling in his head, he sighed in relief. They had enough A.D.L. to get all the way to the city.

Now, he grumbled, if they could only manage to stay on course.

It was dangerous to lose oneself in the desert. If the elements didn't get you, then the bands of thieves would. Much like their nomadic ancestors on Earth roaming the vast lands between Russia's frontier with Afghanistan and India, the desert clans preyed on those unfortunate enough to fall within their grasps. And unfortunately, the Desert Mounted Police, DMPs, were undermanned and rarely captured or brought any of the bandits to trial. The bandits were therefore not discouraged. Additionally, the bandits were known to disable their victims' vehicles and communication equipment, giving the bandits time to get away.

Knowing this, Haamar had uncharacteristically installed a recycling plant on the rover. It had cost a pretty penny, but Haamar had been thirsty once. It had left an indelible mark on his consciousness. He had no intention of being a hapless victim of the bandits, stranded in the unforgiving desert, starved, burnt, and dead of dehydration. But the recycling plant relied on the batteries, and Haamar couldn't rely on his batteries. It was a lose-lose situation as far as he was concerned. It was best not to get lost. Best not to linger.

Haamar bent his mind in concentration, tracking the path of the storm. He didn't notice Yuyenda reappear, carrying a tray of soup and sandwiches, and seat herself in the codriver's seat.

"Is something the matter, Haamar?" Yuyenda said around a mouthful of grilled cheese.

"You should have woken me up," he answered a bit brusquely.

"You needed to get some sleep," she retorted defensively. "The storm is still a little ways off. You needed rest. And I was about to wake you up. If you'd take better care of yourself and stop pushing your body to the limit, I wouldn't have to worry about you getting sick all the time. Here," she announced, shoving a cup of soup into one of his hands and a plate of neatly sliced sandwiches onto his lap. "I made you something to eat."

Yuyenda's lips trembled as she picked up her sandwich and snapped off another bite of food. She chewed angrily, looking out into the building storm, away from Haamar.

"I'm sorry, honey. I didn't mean to snap at you. It's just that this is a really big storm, and the batteries might be dead for all we know. I'm afraid to stop the rover to check because we might never start it again. I just don't know enough about the damn things!"

He held his frustration in check and took a deep breath before continuing, looking at Yuyenda's averted head, yearning to touch her but knowing that would be the wrong thing to do.

"Look, I am sorry. I'm concerned, that's all. I really didn't mean to snap at you, and I don't drive myself that much anyway," he added. He had switched off the autopilot and was guiding the rover over the terrain. "I don't like being stranded—or the possibility of being stranded. And I don't want to get stuck and sit around waiting for the raiders to find us …" He sighed softly and looked down at the console, glancing at the map readout and their projected travel time to Umbaliya.

He took a steadying breath, adjusted the tray on his lap, and looked up. "Maybe I did need some sleep," he conceded, half-mumbling the words.

"Of course you needed the sleep," Yuyenda answered tartly, meeting Haamar's troubled gaze with a steady one of her own. "I was about to wake you, but I thought I would make you something to eat first. The storm hasn't progressed much yet, so I took a small risk. Better than having you drive us into an arroyo, don't you think? If you weren't so cranky and tired, you'd realize I did the right thing. It's going to take the both of us to navigate through this one. The weather stations all say it's a wallop of a storm, sweeping nearly the entire quadrant of the desert. They have issued warnings for all aircraft, which we should have taken in the first place, and they have warned the people of Umbaliya to stay indoors." Yuyenda huffed and stared out at the growing mass of sand swirling about the exterior of the land rover.

"I said I was sorry," Haamar said. And he was.

"I heard you. You can be so insensitive sometimes, but I forgive you." Her voice was suddenly light once again, the argument already forgotten. "Finish your food before it grows cold, and stop your scowling."

Haamar laughed and started in on his lunch. Yuyenda was a wonder.

Savoring the thick broth of the vegetable soup, Haamar kept his eyes divided between the console and the windshield. Haamar lightened the tinting on the glass and disengaged the outside ventilation system to prevent dust from fouling the air. Yuyenda flipped a switch above her seat, kicking the oxygen tanks on with a barely audible hiss as internal fans sifted the air in the rover. She adjusted the temperature downward and made sure a slight breeze blew upon Haamar's face. Outside the steady pelting of sand ricocheting off the rover's thin hull continued to increase as the vehicle's tracked wheels turned.

"Oh," Yuyenda said suddenly, pointing out of the windshield off to the vehicle's left. "Here it comes!"

Haamar peered out into the darkening sky. A huge cloud of brown dust that rose several miles into the atmosphere was plowing down upon them. Pushing outward like a nuclear mushroom cloud tilted on its side, the haboob devoured everything before it. Haamar tensed. The alarm klaxon sounded. He silenced it. Before he had time to do anything else, the storm swept over them. Visibility dropped to a few feet, and the engine strained. The wind pushed against the land rover, and the GPS signal winked out. They were now driving blindly. The trick, Haamar knew, was to keep the rover moving slowly enough that they could safely maneuver. It was up to the computer to guide the tiny vehicle, basing its trajectory on the last data downlinked from the GPS.

Haamar jotted down their current mileage on the edge of the paper map. He didn't want to trust his life to the computer with the batteries in an unknown state of worthiness. He would double-check the computer's work and physically plot their course. It was crude and involved a lot of guess work, but there was nothing for it.

Haamar glanced at his wife. He regretted snapping at her. But the sound of the sand clawing at the rover and the sharp, whipping wind made him nervous. He gritted his teeth and concentrated on driving. But when Yuyenda looked at him, he smiled apologetically. She glared back at him.

Haamar turned his attention to driving, feeling small but also feeling a little angry.

Yuyenda shifted in her chair. Her back was sore and stiff from sitting for so long. Haamar continued to focus on driving as she helped, adjusting controls and calling up helpful displays without being asked. They had spent a lot of time reconnoitering possible ore deposits for the company. Sharing in each other's presence on so many trips, they had mastered a routine.

Yuyenda understood Haamar's concern with the haboob, but she felt the risks were minimal. The vehicle was well designed for such storms. At worst, they would have to dig the rover out of a sand drift before they finished their journey to the spaceport at Kugadar. But she knew the storms made Haamar nervous. Her husband had grown up on an ocean world. The storms that hit the New British Isles were welcomed bearers of much-needed fresh water. Sure they had huge cyclones that swept in from the deep ocean, but the houses on the New British Isles were all made from reinforced plastacrete forms and could take a real beating. By contrast, the storms in the Great Desert were choking things. The sandstorms gunked up equipment, could suffocate people, and lasted for hours. The larger haboobs could burry a person in a few hours.

Yuyenda thought Haamar's fear of the great dust storms was derived from two things. Her husband was afraid of choking. It had something to do with a near-drowning accident when Haamar was a child. And the idea of being buried alive was common for miners.

Yuyenda and Haamar had lost more than one friend to the sudden collapse of mine shafts.

Yuyenda thought maybe it was a matter of comfort levels. She didn't think she would be very comfortable under torrential rains, with the threat of flash floods and tornadoes hovering around every water storm on the New British Isles. But those storms were everyday things for Haamar, a part of his childhood. He actually told her that he missed them! In the same way, Yuyenda did not fear the haboobs of the desert. They were as familiar as old friends—as long as you took the proper precautions. So she did not blame Haamar for his testiness. Even after all of these years, the haboobs were alien and frightening for her husband. Maybe she was being too hard on Haamar. She just wished he wouldn't get so snappy.

She looked at Haamar and sighed. The surrounding countryside was now black with flying sand. Yet he was hunched forward over the control wheel, peering out into the darkness as if he could actually see something. He could be so stubborn!

Yuyenda had enjoyed the time they spent together on this trip, but enough was simply enough. She felt restless. She wished she had forced Haamar to fly to Kugadar. The Terra Corporation had given them quite a subsidy. But Haamar wanted to drive. They could take their time, enjoy the trip, he had told her. However, Yuyenda dreaded the long voyage to Earth. Anything that dragged the trip out grated on her nerves.

Earth. They would be gone for two years. Two. The spaceship's communications blackout would be the worst. Yuyenda would miss her mother terribly. Yuyenda would be unable to talk to her mother at all until they reached their transition flight from Mars. Even then, it would only be through message drones and not person-to-person.

Her mother was not in good health and lived alone. Yuyenda's father died nearly four years ago of a stroke. Her sister, Tyena, and her older brother, Bachtuk, would check in on their mother daily. Still, Yuyenda worried. She felt like something dire was going to happen, and it gnawed at her. But what could Yuyenda do?

She fought back a tear and smiled weakly at Haamar, but he was too busy to notice. Yuyenda closed her eyes and gathered herself, telling herself again how important their discovery was to the planet. Haamar had worked brilliantly to uncover the moissanite vein. The vein had remained undiscovered due to a blanketing layer of lead-infused rock that otherwise shielded the metal from the ring of geological satellites orbiting the planet. Naturally occurring moissanite had only been found in asteroids and meteorites and in small veins on various planets in conjunction with ultramafic rocks. It was extremely valuable and rare.

Haamar's find was the first major find on any of the planets. Moissanite, rich in graphene, was in high demand by civilian and military industries. Its discovery promised to make Telakia a major producer of spaceships and all other advanced modern technological components and materials. Graphene metamaterials were widely used in space-going vessels, superconducting diodes, integrated circuits, transistors, thermal materials, bio equipment, high-capacity solar cells, and municipal water purification. Artificially creating industrial-quality graphene was expensive and required either growth of the valuable honeycomb crystal lattice from oxide reduction or from metal carbon smelts. Converting natural moissanite into graphene reduced production costs significantly. But none of that made Yuyenda feel any better. Dread and certainty. That is what she felt.

Gods, she prayed, she just wanted it over with. It was selfish of her, she knew. It was Haamar's big moment, but she just wanted to retire back to their little house and raise a family. Was it so wrong to want a small life? A normal life? She should be happy, she knew. Not only were they traveling to Sol, but they also shared a finder's fee of 15 percent—millions of credits, maybe billions.

Yet Haamar, Yuyenda giggled, was still concerned with nickels and dimes. Why fly when driving saved money? Haamar just didn't get it. They had been struggling with money for so long that he hadn't really absorbed the fact that their bank account was already racking up impressive totals. It would be difficult to break Haamar's old money-pinching ways, but money should be the least of Haamar's concerns.

He would simply have to change his mind about driving to the spaceport, she decided. Once they arrived in Umbaliya, Yuyenda intended to buy tickets and fly to Kugadar. While a drop in the bucket in terms of shortening the trip to Sol, it made her feel a little better. And, she thought, she wanted a bath. A real bath. Not a mist shower that left sand particles in her hair and kept her feeling as if she were not completely clean. A bath. Haamar just had to agree.

Yuyenda glanced slyly at Haamar, who was munching on the last of a sandwich, balancing it and a pen and map, plotting their progress.

"I'm going to play some music. Do you mind?" she said to break the silence. "Maybe I can find something that will blend with the rattling outside."

"Try the whale-song music. I like it a lot."

"You are a grim one, aren't you?" she replied, fishing through the list of music on the inboard computer. "I don't care for it much."

"Really? I thought you liked it."

"It's just that it sounds so lonely. I don't think I've ever heard anything that sounded so utterly lost. It makes me want to cry. Especially when they mix the sounds of the surf. I can't help feeling isolated, like I'm the one alone on the ocean, floating helplessly, waiting desperately for someone to notice me. Can't we listen to something a little more … bright?"

"I don't care," Haamar said with a brief smile, his thick eyebrows rising slightly, crinkles forming around his eyes. "I just thought the whale song would be soothing."

"How about this?" Yuyenda asked, punching up the booming sounds of an old classical piece. Clamoring drums and dashing cymbals built in great martial waves, adding to the natural sound of the storm with a shattering crash of syncopated thunder.

"Too loud," Haamar said, wincing at the volume.

"What!" Yuyenda yelled back.

"I said it's too loud!"

Yuyenda turned the music down a few notches. "What was that?" she teased.

"I said ..." Haamar sighed. "Never mind. That's fine now. What is it?"

"I'm not sure. I had the computer search its memory for some good storm music, punched in a few parameters, and this is what I came up with. Sounds nice, doesn't it? I think I'll mark the music file so we can listen to it again."

"Okay. Is it German?"

"Yes. Written by a soldier in the early twenty-second century, a gal by the name of Dietri Beck, just after the Second Resource War."

"Explains the military tones. Did she fight in the war?"

"Let's see," Yuyenda answered, accessing the history banks of the computer. "Dietri fought in the Ukraine and later in Turkey and Greece as part of the UN expeditionary force. This says she was awarded the German Cross at the battle of Istanbul and lost her right arm in Greece. She suffered from severe depression; her husband was killed during the war. Her only child went on to become a space pioneer. Still, she must have been very proud and self-assured."

"Why do you say that?"

"Listen to the power in the music. It is quite amazing. Only a strong woman could write music like this. Dietri, it says here, in a little blip of a quote, said that the music helped her contend with the loss of her husband, freeing her from the guilt she felt at having survived him. Gruesome, isn't it?"

"You've gotten into a mood, haven't you?" Haamar laughed. He leaned over and gave her a little kiss.

Yuyenda beamed. Little things mattered.

"Maybe we should rest a day or two at Umbaliya," Haamar continued. "We have plenty of time. And the rover needs repairs. And speaking of space pioneers, I'd like to see the museum at First Step. They are supposed to have the entire original landing site sealed up and give tours through the encased buildings. Can you imagine having to live all cramped up like that?"

Yuyenda chuckled and gestured to the enclosed cabin of the rover. "No. I couldn't imagine any such thing. I bet they had more room than this."

"I bet you're right at that," Haamar agreed. He reached out and squeezed Yuyenda's knee, leaving his hand there, enjoying the contact.

Yuyenda cupped her hand over Haamar's and turned the music up a little bit. Yuyenda stifled a bubble of laughter as Haamar winced slightly, mocking irritation.

She continued to smile long after, holding Haamar's hand as they wove their way slowly through the storm, the music rising in a brilliant crescendo and dying quickly to the hollow sound of wind blowing across a listless desert sky. It carried Yuyenda away, filling her full of an energy that had been lacking for the last several days and restoring her confidence in her mission to Earth. Her mother had said good-bye, making it perfectly clear that she expected her daughter to do no less than return with many tales and pictures of the mother planet. Instead of the chore the trip had seemed a few minutes ago, it now turned into an adventure, and she faced it with a realization of her place in history, her place in society, and with a joy in her relationship with Haamar that she had not felt so intensely for a while. She wanted to freeze the moment in time, holding Haamar's warm hand and listening to the fantastically powerful music of the long-dead woman.

Thank you, Dietri, she thought to herself. Settling back into her routine of checking the readouts and displaying the information Haamar needed to safely guide their rover through the sand storm, she relaxed in the cushions of her chair. Mechanically shifting through the reports, mentally plotting their progress, she looked forward to a friendly hotel, walks in the museum, and a deep and soothing bath in the bubbling waters of a refreshing tub.

Keeping one eye on the weather reports and the other on the terrain map, Haamar and Yuyenda drove steadily. The eye of the storm was out there, somewhere, the center of a huge mass of violent, boiling sand, an irresistible force of nature that had swallowed the sky.

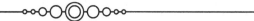

It was long past midnight before the storm abated. The land rover had crawled its way through the worst of it, making fifty miles before the sky abruptly cleared and the stars winked into the night as if by magic. A soft gloaming settled over the land from Lucia and Aula, the planet's two moons. Lucia was the larger of the two, and it hovered at the apex of its orbit. Aula, its little sister, sat quietly just below and to the east, glowing and free. Only the occasional gust of wind and clatter of sand was left of the haboob.

Exhausted, Haamar set the autopilot and stretched, extending his arms and arching his back. He could feel the strain of the past few hours. Yuyenda had nodded off some time ago, her head bobbing with the rover as it crested over a rise of ground. The vehicle swept down the steep bank.

Haamar turned the external fans back on, switched off the internal tanks, and took a deep breath of fresh air. Flipping his running lights back to normal, he spent a quiet moment before leaning over and lightly kissing his wife upon the forehead. She stirred a little, smiled, and murmured something he could not understand. Gently shaking her, Yuyenda woke up long enough to be led to the bed. Haamar tucked her in and sat beside her. She fell asleep instantly, leaving Haamar awake and studying her features.

Haamar was not a big man, but years of fieldwork left him lean and powerful. He was at his prime, a young thirty-five, trim and spry. But he was not particularly attractive. He thought of himself as middling at best. He did not have a chiseled face, but he did have good lines, and his eyebrows were naturally even—not too thin but not Neanderthal bushy either. He had a dimpled chin but lacked the ability to grow a full beard. Haamar had considered getting laser treatments to get rid of the small amount of facial hair that he did have, but he found he enjoyed the morning routine of shaving: the warm shaving cream, the sharp razor gliding over his skin, and the ritualistic cleaning of his skin when his pores were open. Yuyenda often teased him about his boyish beard, but Haamar had caught her watching him shave. There was something about it that she liked too.

He gently brushed a lock of hair from Yuyenda's forehead and wondered how he had been so lucky. Yuyenda had a lithe frame, sun-darkened skin, and deep brown hair. She was very beautiful.

Haamar had not been the only one interested in Yuyenda. When he had first met her, a wealthy landowner was pursuing her. Why she had chosen to forgo those riches for a rough life eking out a living in the dark mines of the planet, he didn't understand. What had she seen in the stumbling young asteroid miner with wanderlust in his eyes? Her father had frowned. Her mother sighed. And Haamar had done everything he could to woo this wonderful woman. Now, in the quiet of the little cabin, the tracks of the rover rumbling like an echo, he resisted an urge to touch her. It was not easy.

He hoped she would forgive him for taking her away from her family. Haamar knew it bothered her. She had never been off world before and had never been more than a few hundred miles from her home city. Unlike Haamar, who was light years from his family, Yuyenda clung fiercely to her home. She relied on her family to provide her warmth and comfort and a place in the universe.

It was a difficult chore for Yuyenda to tell her mother that they were leaving the planet for two years. He could see the shock and loss on her mother's face and hear the pain in Yuyenda's voice. Her mother masked her feelings quickly and tried her best to support the move. But Yuyenda, Haamar was sure, had seen it too. And it hurt her.

The two women supported each other in a way Haamar's own mother and father never sustained him. He was hard-pressed to understand it. It was not within Haamar's emotional experience. But he respected their relationship and didn't want to be responsible for causing a rift. Still, he was excited about the trip to Earth. Haamar had always wanted to see the pyramids of Egypt, the Coliseum, the Great Wall of China, Hadrian's Wall, London, New York, and a hundred other places he had read about with awe and wonder.

Haamar knew the trip, ultimately, was not necessary. But the invitation to present his findings to Terra Corp at the Colorado School of Mines, in person, had aroused Haamar's sense of adventure, and he needed, spiritually, to see the mother planet.

Haamar returned to the cockpit and settled in the driver's chair. They had entered an area where the ground was flat and even. The surface was hard and lacked the rolling dunes normally associated with the Great Desert. Here and there, sparse, prickly plants managed a harsh life. Haamar pushed the rover back to normal speed and bounded across the terrain, the city just a few hours away. Already he could see the signs of impending civilization. He passed a few scattered, deep wells and reservoirs, their stubby, circular tanks collecting water for the city population. Small mechanicals on rollers, their spidery arms moving over the exterior of the tanks, brushed away grime and performed basic maintenance. A few miles on, the rover slipped by a small desert house, its pink sandstone walls protected by the thin, shimmering amber light of its electromatic barrier.

It was difficult to keep his eyes open. He poured coffee and tapped his fingers and feet to music. Suddenly, he missed the sound of rain. Outside, the thin remnants of the sandstorm scraped against the vehicle like ghastly hands, and the land was a shimmering stretch of silence under dual alien moons.

Haamar watched the sun as it moved over the morning horizon, casting an array of colored light across the clear blue sky. A few hours later, the rover bounced down a rough slope, bringing it to the first of the mighty stone and metal towers that surrounded the outskirts of Umbaliya. The surface streets of Umbaliya were a maze of ramblings that had formed slowly over time, he knew. But here on the outskirts, a fifteen-foot wall encircled the city. Dotted here and there between sections of the wall were towers with radial arms protruding from them. The towers generated a force field that kept the worst of the desert storms at bay and stilled the air in the city, helping keep the amount of dust down. Haamar lurched the vehicle to a halt before the amber barrier and then began following the electromatic towers to the south, looking for a passage through the piles of sand that rested against the force field. Yuyenda, awakened by the rough bouncing, appeared over his shoulder and stared at the vast obstacle. She reached across to the command console and punched the communications button.

"Almost there?" she asked, scanning the band waves for news.

"They should have some mechanicals working through somewhere. See if you can raise the local DMP band and get some directions from their dispatcher about entrance into the city." Haamar felt exhausted.

"Ahead of you as always, dear," Yuyenda replied, the speakers crackling with the female voice of a DMP dispatcher.

"All ground vehicles seeking to leave or enter the city," the woman's staccato voice said, "must move to grid coordinate Alpha, Bravo, two-four-five, six-nine-one. Digger mechanicals have cleared through the sand along the outer corridor leading to the heart of the city. Again, all ground vehicles seeking to leave or enter the city must move through grid coordinates Alpha, Bravo, two-four-five, six-nine-one. Secondary openings will be reported on this waveband as they become available. Air travel from Tanta Airport has been delayed for flights leaving for cities in the north, with a projected two-hour delay due to the recent storm. All other flights in and out of the city are on schedule. Residents in the outer sections of the rift valley are advised—"

"I'll punch the grid into the navigation computer," Yuyenda said, switching the DMP report off and plopping into place beside

Haamar. "Do you want me to drive for a while? You've been in that seat for nearly thirty-six hours straight."

"Yeah. I suppose I could use a break."

"Tired?"

"Yes, exhausted and a little stiff. I think I'll take a shower and grab something to eat. Do you want anything?" Haamar stood and shuffled behind the driver's seat as Yuyenda took his place, pulling the seat a little closer to the console so her feet could reach the pedals.

"I could use something hot to drink."

"Gun Powder tea?" Haamar grinned.

"Why," Yuyenda mocked with a flourish, "how did you ever guess? And my good man," she added, "a few cookies would do nicely. I especially enjoy the chocolate chip ones, warmed—the ones with a slight minty taste."

"A slight minty taste? Your wish is my command," Haamar returned. He bowed as best he could in the cramped cabin. "Will that be all, my lady?"

"No. You may kiss me now."

Haamar lightly kissed his wife before trundling off to the closet-sized shower, stripping, and letting the hot, misting water waft over his back. As Yuyenda guided the rover around the protective electromatic field, Haamar dressed, went upstairs to the galley, prepared two cups of hot tea, warmed cookies, and microwaved a single serving of thick vegetable stew. He rejoined his wife as the rover neared the coordinates provided by the DMP.

Haamar ate his soup as Yuyenda snacked on her cookies and merged the vehicle with the steady flow of traffic moving into Umbaliya. She drove between two of the electromatic towers and onto a slowly widening thoroughfare, abruptly leaving the desert behind. Large transport vehicles dominated the roadway, bringing fresh produce in from the surrounding hydro farms.

The squat buildings of Umbaliya belied their true size. The visible parts of the buildings were just the tops of larger superstructures. To avoid the heat of the day, the buildings dove deep underground. Protected from the elements, the denizens of Umbaliya moved contentedly in giant underground plazas that served as social hubs. Still there was a fair amount of traffic on the upper roadways. Yuyenda masterfully handled the rover around slower-moving vehicles, looking for the Capstone Inn where they had made reservations. Conveniently located near the airport, the hotel was well known to the traveling business community. They had chosen it due to its proximity to both the airport and the museum of First Step.

Yuyenda wound the rover through circuitous roads with the help of the GPS. The trip didn't take long. Before Haamar knew it, they were pulling into the parking elevator, which clicked and hummed as it took the rover below ground to the parking garage.

"Oh, we're here," Yuyenda said, stepping out of the rover with a suitcase in both hands. Haamar followed behind her as she walked through the automatic doors of the inn and into the main lobby. "Isn't it beautiful? I'm going to enjoy a long rest here."

"It is nice," Haamar conceded. "But maybe we should splurge a little. Why don't we see if we can get one of the best rooms in the house?" he added. He was cheap, but he enjoyed spoiling Yuyenda when he could. "After all, it is our belated honeymoon."

"Our second honeymoon," Yuyenda playfully reminded him. "Our first one was in pit number 352. I think you found a small vein of quartz that brought us our first little bonus."

"And we celebrated with a takeout Korean dinner, as I recall," Haamar laughed, remembering the petty amount that find had netted them. They moved toward the smiling man behind the check-in counter. "There went our entire bonus! And we didn't even get to bed for another two days because of our work schedule."

Yuyenda giggled and placed the suitcases down before the counter. "You grew very impatient," she whispered back.

"Mays I helps ya?" the desk clerk asked. His voice rasped in his throat with a strong local accent.

"Yes. We have a reservation for two days, but my husband has decided to ask for one of your better rooms and for two extra days. We decided to take a small break from the driving and to stay and see some of the city's sites. Will that be a problem?" Yuyenda asked.

"Four days?" The clerk punched some numbers into the computer and smiled. "Nots a problem. Ya want a suite wits what conveniences? Our embassy suites haves severals luxury areas, includings a wets bar, dual bath with hots tubs, fully stocked kitchens, and an emperor-sizes bed."

Haamar handed his credit voucher to the man.

The clerk gracefully took the voucher card and ran it through his computer. "Yes, heres you are. The embassy suites?" the clerk asked.

"That will be fine." Haamar's voice was a bit husky. He'd forgotten to ask the price.

The clerk graciously produced a printed copy of the charges, which he handed to Haamar. Haamar tried not to wince. He swallowed hard, put on his best smile, and slowly nodded at the clerk. Yuyenda looked at him with concern, silently asking him if it was really all that much.

"We can afford it now," Haamar said to her. "We might as well get used to it."

"Please," the clerk said, indicating the hand scanner.

Haamar placed his hand on the scanner to verify his identity. Yuyenda placed her arm about him and leaned affectionately against his shoulder, and he slipped his arm about her waist and gave it a slight squeeze.

Haamar felt Yuyenda stiffen. She had seen the bill.

See? he told himself. He wasn't the only penny pincher in the family. "Four nights will be nice," he said to mollify her.

"Everythings is in order, sir." The credit voucher worked, and a receipt was printed. "Checkout is at noons. I will haves ya baggage taken to ya suites. Is there anythings else I can do for ya?"

"Actually there is," Haamar responded. "I need to have some repairs done to our land rover. Could you suggest an able mechanic?"

"I will call one and haves ya vehicle pickeds up. All I needs is ya registrations number. Will ya use the same credit voucher?"

"Yes, and that will be fine. It's the air filter and the batteries," Haamar added. "The batteries do not seem to be holding their charge. But I would appreciate a call before any work is done."

"I will haves it so. Lady, please place ya hands on the scanner for identifications purposes. It will allows ya access to ya room. I all ready haves the gentleman's."

Yuyenda complied and then followed Haamar out into the central lobby, abnormally lush with vegetation. The sounds of birdsong softly played from discretely placed speakers. From the lobby, they could see the wide-open central area of the hotel. Around the centerpiece of an oval pool were game tables, vending machines, exercise and dining areas. Conference rooms lined the far side of the circular room where a few parties of business people relaxed in dark suits, drinking coffee and listening to a lecturer. There were several people in the pool splashing about. The recycled water looked cool and inviting. Two children climbed in and out of the water, chasing one another. The older boy leapt into the pool with a loud, laughing splash as his little sister suddenly stopped at the edge. Realizing how deep the pool was on that end, the little girl was afraid of following. Their mother called watchfully from the adjoining hot tub, telling Mary to remain in the shallow end, and slightly admonishing Eric for luring his sister toward the deeper water.

Leaving the lobby area behind, Haamar and Yuyenda took the elevator up to their floor and located their suite.

Their rooms were extravagant. Three video visions, one theater-sized, two wet bars, a double shower, hot tub, two guest bedrooms and baths, plus a master bedroom that Haamar suspected made most middle-income houses seem small. He felt a pang of guilt at having such a lavish place to stay. Haamar knew that most engineers spent the majority of their time in tiny, carved-out hollows of earth. If they were lucky, they had a video vision in a cramped commons area. But the feeling died away as Haamar realized that he and

Yuyenda had lived that way for years. It was good to spoil oneself every now and again.

Haamar explored the kitchen with Yuyenda. Finding the pantry stocked with canned and bottled goods, he opened the refrigerator and discovered twelve fresh roses and a chilled bottle of champagne.

"Compliments of the house," he said, reading the card and handing the flowers to his wife. "That was nice of them. The roses smell good too.

"Let's save the champagne for later," Haamar managed. He suddenly felt a little dizzy. He was dead on his feet. "I think I'm going to take a nap and then figure out how to get reservations for the museum. If you don't mind," Haamar added. "I haven't been so worn out for a long time."

"Maybe we should reconsider driving all the way to Kugadar," Yuyenda suggested. "We'll both be exhausted if we have to drive another seven hundred miles through the desert. It took us three days to get this far and will probably take us another three or four before we reach Kugadar. You know the sands get worse from here."

"You think we should fly?"

"Why not? Driving across the planet was a lovely idea, but the reality has left something to be desired."

"And what about the rover? We can't just leave it here for two years."

"Well," Yuyenda answered, thinking. "We could ship it back home, or have someone fly here and drive it back."

"I don't know. I'm beginning to think I'd hate to drive more, but that is a lot to ask of someone. It might be easier just to sell the thing." Haamar sighed and walked into the master bedroom, plopping down on the huge bed. Yuyenda followed. "Can we discuss it in a few hours? My mind isn't clear right now. I think my body is shutting down."

"I really think flying would be best," Yuyenda added, helping Haamar off with his shoes. "But we can talk about that later. Is there anything special you wanted done to the rover? I mean, besides the batteries?"

"Yeah," Haamar replied, his voice drowsy and drifting. "A general checkup, I suppose. And anything else you can think of."

Haamar crawled up to the top of the bed. He struggled halfway under the comforter and wrapped his arms around one of the pillows, curling up like a child. He had reached the end of his endurance, and his energy slipped rapidly away.

"Should I have it painted orange?" Yuyenda asked. "Maybe have a blue cow painted on the side of it?"

"What?"

"A blue cow."

"A blue what?"

"Cow, sweetheart."

"Okay. If you want. I guess. What's a cow?"

"Good night, Haamar." Yuyenda smiled, tucking blankets up around her husband's chin. "I love you."

"Love you too, funny bunny."

Yuyenda lay down besides Haamar but didn't fall asleep. Instead she listened to Haamar's heavy breathing, the relaxed intake of breath and the tired exhaling of warm air. Occasionally Haamar made a deep half-groaning sound, which Yuyenda knew he did when thoroughly exhausted. If she wasn't so uncomfortable driving, she berated herself, then he wouldn't be as tired as he was. There were just some things she didn't like doing, and driving across the wild desert, especially in the rift valley where pockets of soft sand could quickly swallow a vehicle, was one of those things.

After Haamar began to snore softly, Yuyenda crept out of bed and called the museum and made their reservation, making sure they had tickets for the cyber-space tour, knowing Haamar would enjoy the surrealistic romp through the original landing site. She located an American restaurant and made sure it took walk-ins.

Haamar would wake famished. Then she sat in the lush cushions of the couch, the theater-sized video vision turned on low.

Yuyenda's mind drifted back to the children they had seen playing in the hotel's pool. They could afford a family now too. But she didn't know how to broach the subject with her husband. He had always reacted defensively whenever they had discussed children of their own, and she could not understand why. After ten years together, she still wondered about the man. He was afraid of the attention children demanded and shied away from the subject as quickly as he could. Haamar had always used their lack of money as an excuse before, but she realized it was something deeper. Yuyenda knew enough of his childhood to know it had been an unloving one, and he was a gentle man at heart, fearing to make the same mistakes his working parents had. She had tried to subtly change his views on children, and though she had chipped away at the wall he had erected, she was afraid Haamar would never be comfortable with the idea. Maybe if she stopped her medication and let nature take its course, then she could simply tell him she had forgotten.

No. She couldn't do that. She did not want to spend the rest of her life knowing she had lied to him, and more than anything, she wanted Haamar to want children, to want to have children with her.

Yuyenda could almost feel a child, like a ghost walking besides her, her tiny hand held warmly, and Yuyenda bit back a lonely tear. Haamar could be so difficult at times, but she loved him. Why couldn't he see that she wanted a child? Yuyenda had been dropping hints for half a year. Maybe he was just unaware. Haamar was not the best person at taking hints. If Yuyenda were a little more direct? A lot more direct? She decided to breach the subject with him soon, though she was still afraid of doing so.

Yuyenda stared at the show playing on the video vision. She didn't recognize it, but she rarely watched. Still, she stared at it and let her mind drift.

Yuyenda groaned when the videophone rang. She flailed at the communication button on the end table, finally activating the viewer. It showed a rough young man with dark eyes and crooked eyebrows, wearing a gray suit and a quick smile.

"Yuyenda Ransan?"

"Yes. Who are you?" Yuyenda replied to the pleasant voice, wiping the red from her eyes.

"I'm sorry if I woke you," the young man said, noticing Yuyenda's tousled hair.

"Who did you say you were?" Yuyenda repeated. "I don't think I heard you."

"Sorry again. My name is Paul Harlamor. I work for the investigative department of the DMP."

"A cop?"

"Yes, sort of. I don't do the regular patrols. Like I said, I'm in the investigative department."

"Can I help you with something?"

"Well, just answering the videophone has helped me. We've had a missing persons report on you and your husband, Haamar, since early last week. Apparently you missed your flight off world, and your corporation, the Zintas Mines, was worried." He paused for a second before continuing. "Is everything all right with you and your husband?"

"Fine," Yuyenda replied, confused slightly. "You say that Zintas was worried? That's novel. But my husband changed our flight a month ago. We decided to drive to Kugadar. You know, see the sights before leaving? Anyway, we're fine. Is there anything else, Mr. Harlamor?"

"No. I'll let Zintas know. These sorts of mishaps occur all the time. Should I tell them you plan to continue driving?"

"We haven't decided yet," Yuyenda answered. "It's a long way to Kugadar, and we might just fly the rest of the way. But what does it matter?"

"It doesn't. I just thought you might want to let them know what you two were planning. That way they won't keep calling me and asking if I've found you yet. Could your verify your license plate number for me?"

"Excuse me?"

"Your plate number," he repeated patiently.

"I suppose so. Can you wait a moment?"

"Sure."

Yuyenda flipped the mute button, leaving the young man waiting as she browsed through her purse looking for the rover's registration number. Why he needed it, she didn't know. But she dug the slip of paper out and headed back to the videophone, her feet slipping through the thick carpeting.

"I found it," she said, punching the speaker button once again. "Are you ready?"

"Yes. Go ahead."

"Okay. The number is, five, five, four, three, six, nine, two." Yuyenda looked at the young man as he scribbled the number on a piece of paper. "Got it?"

"Yes. Thank you. It matches what we have on file here."

"Why did you need it then?"

"When we couldn't locate you, we started looking for your vehicle. Your being in the desert explains why we couldn't find it. Normally the traffic control cameras would have captured your plate's image—we could have tracked you down that way. Anyway, we always do a follow-through. This is just one of those steps I have to do to make my boss happy. Standard verification for the closing report."

"Oh."

"I don't want to take up any more of your time, Mrs. Ransan. I'm sorry I had to bother you. You look tired."

"I am. You know how long drives suck the energy right out of you. So how did you find us?" Yuyenda added in sudden curiosity.

"Find you?"

"Yes, just now. How did you know where to call?"

"Ah, that was simple. As soon as you ran your credit voucher, our systems alerted. Then when you both scanned your hands, I knew we had you. Quite simple, really."

"A little creepy too," Yuyenda replied.

The man laughed lightly. "I suppose it is," he said. "It can be very helpful though. And I am glad to find you both on the end of the video. Mr. Ransan is there too, isn't he?"

"Yes—what? Why are you glad I answered the videophone?"

"We do have a criminal class, Mrs. Ransan. When nobody heard from you for a couple days ... well ... we feared the worst."

"Oh," she conceded. "Well, thank you for checking up on us, and give my regards to Henry."

"Henry?"

"From Zintas. He's the one who filed the missing persons isn't he?"

"Oh, yes. Henry." Paul smiled broadly and glanced down. "It took me a moment to place the first name. I'll be sure to let Mr. Gustoff know. Thank you, Mrs. Ransan. Have a safe journey. Good-bye."

"Good-bye." Yuyenda hung up the videophone. The young man's face faded away. "Strange conversation," she said to herself.

It's good of old Henry to worry about us though, she thought. She made a mental note to call him later and let him know, personally, that they were all right. She berated Haamar for not telling Henry they had canceled the flight. Haamar had promised he would. No wonder Henry was so concerned. It must have seemed like they had simply vanished, an easy thing to do on a desert world.

She lay back on the couch, telling herself she had to call her mother too. Yet her eyes were heavy.

The video vision splashed its way through an advertisement before returning to an old movie, an ancient black-and-white film about a group of crazy old ladies who had hidden a dead man under a window seat of some sort. Yuyenda watched, half-asleep, at the frantic pacing of the young actor, a handsome man, dark haired, angular, and energetic. She wondered what his name was and thought dreamily about the two children she had seen playing by the pool. With a sigh, a jerk, and a start, she finally eased into sleep, while a chubby man in the movie yelled something about Panama ... wherever that was.

The artificial glow of underground lights illuminated the white plastered walls of the First Step museum. A small but steady throng of tourists meandered along the many displays depicting the evolution of human life on Telakia. Split into four main levels, the walking journey through Telakian history cumulated at the replicated site of the first human settlement on the planet. The original landing site was actually a few kilometers outside of Umbaliya. A small obelisk marked its spot. But they had moved some of the few remaining artifacts here, to First Step.

Preserved in airless vaults of Plexiglas, the original domed living quarters of the founding fathers and mothers lay like a pharaoh's tombs. It had been designed to withstand harsh conditions, and, after considerable restoration efforts, it had regained its original metallic luster. Outside of the dome, the curators had placed an abundance of ancient, bulky electronic equipment and workstations. Replicas of settlers in original protective garb stood before worktables and terminals. In another exhibit, figures sat unmoving over dinners, hunched together in tight groups around small plastic tables, or lounging by the famous blue gardens. The medical center, with its neat array of specialized tools and the replicated agriculture dome with living plants, was of great interest to Haamar. But the small schoolrooms used by the first native Telakians made Yuyenda feel softly sad.

Yet Yuyenda's spirits revived in the replica of the landing craft, *Homestead*. Haamar and Yuyenda climbed their way through the ship, the many onboard screens playing simulations of what the original pilots would have seen as they maneuvered their way down to the planet. They looked at the uncomfortable seats the colonists used when descending to Telakia. Yuyenda imagine the colonists holding hands, each thinking silent thoughts about an uncertain future.

After the museum, Haamar and Yuyenda shared a quick lunch at the First Step Saloon, watched a movie on the first years of the colony, and shared a malt—rounding out a lazy day. Later they headed back to their rooms for a short rest before exploring the labyrinthine realm of Umbaliya.

The city had grown from the first tentative tunnels of the original colony into a medium-sized metropolis known for its tourist attractions. The largest attraction was the miles of corridors and vaulted ceilings that connected the city. Great thoroughfares wove their way through the rock, supported by huge columns of granite and marble, smoothed by automated machines that moved like giant spiders across the walls, clearing debris and patching holes. Railed byways dove through tunnels burnt out of the living rock by powerful lasers. Some tunnels rose to the surface like whales breaching a wave, while others meandered slowly upward toward the waiting sun. Each passage carried passengers and goods. The city was thriving, teeming with life. Having worked underground in rough caverns and deep mines, Haamar and Yuyenda marveled at the sheer scope and beauty of Umbaliya.

Innovative structural designs met the challenge of underground life too. Open buildings with terraces, shopping squares, and individual homes were all designed to provide the illusion of wide-open spaces, while retaining an amazing amount of resilience and strength. Art and buildings alike were resplendent with calm earth tones. The calming colors created a balance between the blazing desert above and the layers of eternal rock below. Yuyenda and Haamar found that Umbaliya, known as the Oasis City, lived up to its hype. They roamed the shops and the avenues, enjoying the quiet pulse of the city, genuinely happy.

"When we get back to the room," Yuyenda said as they walked down one of the side streets, "I want to call Henry."

"Gustoff?"

"Yes. Oh I didn't tell you, did I?" Yuyenda replied. "Henry apparently called the DMP and reported us missing. Didn't you tell him we had changed our minds about flying?"

"Of course I did. The DMP? I'm sorry, honey, but you've lost me."

"Last night after you fell asleep, I got this phone call from some investigator at the DMP," she started, her voice quizzical. "He said they had been searching for us for several days. Henry, it seems, was worried when we missed our flight to Kugadar and reported us missing."

"But I told Henry about our plans," Haamar said. "Not even the old man could be that forgetful. We must have talked about it for over a week! Are you sure they were looking for us?"

"No," she quipped. "They just called me because I'm so attractive. It happens all the time."

"Are you sure it was Henry?"

"That's what the man said."

"Strange."

"Strange or not, I'd like to call Henry and let him know we're all right. The DMP can be so impersonal, and I would rather talk to him anyway. I have a question for him." Yuyenda stopped and looked in the window display of a flower shop. The flowers were exotic and bright. Some looked as frail as raindrops while others stood as straight and strong as a steel pole. She pointed at one of the more fantastic flowers, a phantasmagorical thing that swayed beneath its sun lamp. A placard below it read "Make-Make Singing Betty."

"Question?" Haamar interjected.

"Oh, yes," she answered. "I was going to ask him if he could arrange to have the rover picked up after we fly to Kugadar."

Haamar smiled as he took Yuyenda by the elbow and started walking down the yellow sidewalk. Turning left, he saw the movie theater the concierge had recommended.

"I didn't know we had decided to fly to Kugadar," he said.

"That's what we talked about. Remember? Besides," she added, "I'm tired of riding in that thing. I want to get this trip over with as soon as possible. Or do you want to drive all the way to Earth? It feels like that's what we're doing."

"That would be a long trip." Haamar laughed. "Have you made the flight tickets yet?" he asked, shaking his head in resignation.

"What's so funny? Of course I haven't. Stop looking at me that way," she murmured.

"I don't know how you do it."

"Do what?" She batted her eyelashes again.

"Now you're getting carried away. I concede. You win. To be honest, I'm kind of burnt out on driving too." He paused in thought. "The DMPs? You don't think they called your family and told them we were missing, do you? I'd hate to think of the commotion that would cause. I'm surprised they just didn't call us on our car phone. As a matter of fact, you've talked to your mother since we've left, haven't you?"

"A little fixated? All right, I'll bite. But I don't get it."

"Well, it seems to me," Haamar said, "they would have called her. She would have told them we were driving to Kugadar, wouldn't she? In the least, she would have told you about any call from the DMP. It just doesn't make any sense. Why wouldn't they call her? Or call us?"

"Maybe they don't have our phone number."

"Very funny. And how did they know where we were staying?"

"I asked that too." Yuyenda tapped Haamar on the chest with a finger. "Through our credit voucher and," she grabbed his hand in hers, "our bio data. The officer said as soon as we checked into the hotel—bam! His computer got an alarm. Then, I suppose, he just traced us here. Simple."

"I suppose so—two for the next showing of *Mars Unconquered*," he told the sales attendant. The movie starred Slate Stone and Liquin Rhodes. It was a romantic action thriller.

"But we should call your mother," Haamar added as they moved into the theater. "Snack?" he asked her.

"No, dear. I am fine."

They sat down near the center of the theater, two rows behind a balding man and a group of four children.

"Call Henry and mother," Yuyenda acknowledged. In a whisper and pointing at the children who were squirming in their seats, she added, "I hope they calm down some." But she smiled at the boys, her eyes twinkling. "That poor man. It must be his wife's night off."

Haamar glanced at the children. "Must be," he replied.

The movie dealt with the early settlement of Mars. Earth had almost exhausted its resources, creating pressure from its large population. At the critical moment, the discovery of Gravity Well Generators made travel in the solar system feasible. The heroine was an attractive oriental woman who was torn between a nascent corporation and the corporation's leader, the male protagonist and love interest. It was a racy movie that overemphasized the tragedy of the character's relationship, but Yuyenda enjoyed the human aspect, though she found the movie a bit violent. Afterward, they both decided it was a decent movie, but in no way would it win an Oscar.

It was late in the evening when they boarded the public transport back to their hotel. The lights of the city were amber, Umbaliya's way of replicating the drowsy effects of the setting sun. The lights gradually shifted from yellow, to amber, to a deepening purple, reversing itself when morning came. It was strangely beautiful. The mellow light merged softly with darkening shadows at the edges of caverns and tunnels. It looked like the afterglow of a meteoric fall. But Yuyenda knew that some sections of the city never slept, their lights remaining bright and sure, where revelers danced and played thirty-six hours a day. Yuyenda was grateful for the city designers for having the foresight to provide both options to the denizens of the city. She preferred the colors and shadows of the slowly darkening lights.

The transport's electric engine hummed as it moved up the tracks toward the center of the city, picking up speed as it neared the steep rise from level three to level two. The sudden upsurge and rush of air caused Haamar's stomach to quiver, and he giggled softly. Yuyenda felt a bit queasy but smiled at Haamar, hanging on to his arm for support. Soon the transport leveled out and stopped at the off-loading platform. Yuyenda guided Haamar through the crowd, down the ramp, and they sauntered the short distance back to their hotel.

"Ya vehicles is ready, sir," the pretty, female desk attendant said to them as they walked in the entranceway. She smiled at Haamar's surprised expression and explained. "The day clerks tolds me ya hads ya vehicles getting serviced. He pointeds ya out when we changed shifts earlier. I haves the bill for ya's."

Yuyenda stepped forward and took the slip of paper from the attendant, thanking her with a nod of her head and glancing at the total. She winced slightly but handed it to Haamar, who peeked at it and slipped it in his pocket.

"The batteries needed to be replaced," he said. "Twenty batteries cost a lot."

"We should have sold the thing. Somebody would have bought it," Yuyenda replied. "I thought they were supposed to call you before fixing anything."

"They were. Maybe they left a message on our phone." Haamar looked past Yuyenda at the attendant, meeting her dark eyes with a quizzical smile. "Do we have any messages?"

"Yes, sirs. Ya can hear them from the vid-phone in ya rooms. If yas likes, I can call it ups here?" The woman's voice twinkled.

"No thank you," Yuyenda said politely but sternly. "We'll wait until we get to *our room*. Good night." She took Haamar's hand in hers.

"Good nights," the young woman replied cordially.

"Thank you," Haamar answered, following his wife out of the lobby.

"She's too young for you," Yuyenda said as they made their way to the elevators. "She wouldn't appreciate you at all."

"What are you talking about?" Haamar pushed the elevator button and waited for the door to open. "She was just being friendly."

"Exactly," Yuyenda stated. "Good nights!" she mimicked. "Thank you! Oh," she added, "you're impossible."

"Good grief, honey."

"You just never know what's going on around you. That woman was interested in you, and you didn't even know it. But then you never know it, do you? It's hard to believe that you can be so blind all the time. How in the world did I ever get you?"

"Persistence?"

"Persistence! I had to beat you over the head with a club. How can you miss so much?" Yuyenda shook her head in amazement. She had to protect Haamar in some ways. He was an intelligent man but lacked an understanding of anything not technical or controlled. The basic human drives often left him baffled and confused. Most of the time, she enjoyed it, but not now, not on her belated honeymoon.

"I don't know what to say." Haamar shrugged and put his arm around Yuyenda's waist. "What do you want to do tomorrow? I would like to have a look at the tunneling facilities here. See what type of equipment they use and how they plan and dig new tunnels. They're supposed to be digging a deep shaft somewhere that will be part of a lower section. Did you know they have at least a mile between levels? Can you imagine the cost?"

"You want to see how they mine the rock?" she said in disbelief.

"Yes," Haamar answered. "Did you see those columns? Not the dreary support beams of the mineshafts. They look solid too. Maybe we could adapt their designs to our work. Who knows? Think of the possibilities!"

"Possibilities? You didn't even like spending the money it cost to rent our room, and as much as you tried to be nonchalant about our repair bill on the rover, I know it bothered you. Make mine shafts … pretty? You're crazy.

"Oh!" She stopped in the hallway and turned accusingly toward Haamar. "You just changed the subject!"

Haamar grinned and squeezed Yuyenda warmly. "In Xanadu did Kubla Khan, a stately pleasure-dome decree." He kissed Yuyenda on the cheek and held her tightly. He held her for a long moment before allowing her to slide from him, looking at her for a troubled moment.

"Is something wrong, dear?" Yuyenda asked quietly.

"No. No. Well, yes. I don't know," he admitted. "Something I can't put my finger on. It's nothing. It's just … I don't know."

Yuyenda leaned into Haamar's chest, resting her head there. "I'm sorry. I didn't mean to accuse you of anything."

"That's okay. If you didn't get jealous, I would think you didn't care."

"Are you sure you are okay, Haamar?"

"Yes. I think so." He stumbled for the words. "I just suddenly feel a certain amount of dread for some reason. I guess this trip to Earth has got me thinking about things. That must be it. I'm going to miss Telakia. I'm going to miss spending long hours working in our stifling office doing those little things I never thought much about. It's all going to change, you know. I know that's a good thing, but I can't help feeling a little sad at losing it. It was, after all, our home. And I was very happy with what we had. I know it wasn't much, but I never needed much.

"At the same time, I want to move on. I want to see the old planet, walk around on green grass, and see the high mountains of our forefathers. I feel connected in some primordial way to Earth. I want this, and I don't want to lose what we have."

Yuyenda giggled, regretting it the instant she did. Haamar was having trouble with leaving too. She never would have expected it from him. He always seemed so self-assured and directed. It was a relief to find that he was, after all, as fond of their life as she was.

"You've been reading history again, haven't you? I can always tell. You get moody." She smiled at him, feeling protective. "We'll be fine. I'll miss our home too, but this is what we've both been working for over the last seven years. It's the chance we've always wanted. We can see the universe together, get out from under our debts, and give something back to the community. We'll be able to do so much now. I am so proud of you. You barely even realize what it is you've done. Do you? Do you know that you've changed the course of life for everyone on this planet?"

"They would have figured it out sooner or later," Haamar countered quietly. "Hey! Isn't that the argument I made to you about visiting Earth?"

Yuyenda laughed. "Noticed that? And I wouldn't be so sure, Haamar, about the moissanite. Nobody even thought to look. No one but you."

"Well, I had a lot of help. You did most of the real work. I just plotted things into the computer and made some educated guesses."

"You invented the phone for these people, Haamar. I just ran the wire. I am so proud of you. I look at you and wonder how you, that little man I met who seemed to fall out of the stars and into my life, could have done this thing. This is one of the richest worlds in the universe now. I'm a little overwhelmed by it all. And we will come home, Haamar. I promise you that."

"Thanks, honey. I don't know what's gotten a hold of me." He turned and led Yuyenda to their suite. Haamar reached out and touched Yuyenda's shoulder, stopping her silently.

"I've been thinking," Haamar said. "I've been thinking," he repeated as he pulled Yuyenda close. Yuyenda shuffled awkwardly forward.

Yuyenda pushed back so she could see his face.

"What is it?" she asked softly. They were standing in the empty hallway of the hotel a few feet from their door. The clean lines of the wall led back toward the elevator and the ice and vending machines.

Haamar brushed his lips against Yuyenda's. "I've been having this dream," he said, his voice serious and low but soft and unsure. "Over and over again … you know? The dream is always the same. Always. A little dark-haired girl is running through a field of white, and I am calling to her. 'Ona! Ona!' And she is laughing."

He shifted his eyes shyly away from Yuyenda and dropped his head forward. "She is wearing some type of dress—purple I think—with a … with a flower or something on the front. And when she reaches me, the girl throws her arms around my legs in a giant hug. But that is not the startling part," he continued as Yuyenda tried to pull his head gently up again. His head slowly rotated, and suddenly Yuyenda was looking into brown eyes. They were clear, bright, and so deep that they seemed to go on forever.

"She was our daughter, Yuyenda. Our daughter." He paused. "I don't understand it. I don't know why. But over and over for a couple months, that little girl runs laughing across a white field in my dreams, and I call to her. And when she looks up at me, I find it hard to breathe. Her eyes, sweetheart, they are so blue. They are … your eyes."

Haamar ran his hand quietly over the small of Yuyenda's back. Yuyenda melted forward into his arms, and for a moment the two of them stood quietly entwined.

"Surprised you with that," he said softly. "Didn't I?"

"Make love to me," she whispered in his ear. She felt weak and strong at the same time, and an overwhelming love coursed through her in a dizzying manner. She clung to Haamar and felt a need for him, for his touch, for this strange display of bravery—he was terrified of being a father. Yet he stood, childlike himself, telling her about their child. Their child! And he even knew their daughter's name.

Yuyenda took his right hand in hers and turned, this time pulling him forward toward their door. Haamar followed. Yuyenda pressed her finger on the door lock, and the door clicked open. The room beyond the hallway was dark yet full of possibilities. As she guided Haamar into the murky room, she closed the door behind them and paused for a moment for a long kiss. She had never wanted to make love to her husband so much in her life. The thrill of the future burned within her as she turned and began leading Haamar to the bedroom.

A shape moved on the far side of the room. Out of the shadowed, cold darkness, a man slipped into a dim sliver of light. Shadow line crossed his roughened face. For a moment, Yuyenda and Haamar stood stunned.

The man fired, and Yuyenda collapsed to the ground, her hand torn out of Haamar's grip. The smell of burning ozone filled the sharp air, and then a light vomited from the man's gun, and Haamar fell besides her. Haamar lay still, just out of Yuyenda's reach.

Haamar ... Yuyenda's last frantic thought slipped through her mind. And in the span of a heartbeat, the universe went forever dark.

The air was cool in Henry Gustoff's office. Henry liked to keep the temperature low, and the air conditioner worked overtime to meet the energy demands placed on the system. Outside of his closed office door, the open area Henry thought of as the bullpen housed over twenty cubicles where the everyday operations of Zintas Mines were conducted in a perpetual routine. But here, in his lush office with its mahogany desk, matching wall-length bookcase, and tall, wide windows, was the type of luxury reserved for the executive class. Henry reveled in it. He had finally broken the glass ceiling of upper management and moved into the powerful world of boardroom deals and sweeping visions. It had been a difficult climb through the ranks, but the hard work had paid off. He leaned back in his chair and kicked his feet up on his desk.

Henry's desk computer, leather writing pad, and wireless keyboard were neatly arranged next to the photo of his two children, a boy and girl. Both kids had graduated from secondary school and were off in college. A photo of his wife, a soft woman with delicate features and the echo of crow's feet near her eyes, hovered behind the photos of the kids. He had a happy family. Henry himself was middle-aged, with the sharp features of a former star athlete. His shoulders and arms were still robust, but a small paunch showed slightly under his buttoned shirt. Gray mingled with the rich brown of his hair, giving him, he thought, a distinguished look. Though married, Henry knew women found him attractive. He carried himself with an ease of confidence and swagger that belonged to a powerful man.

Yet a twinge of guilt nagged him. In the corporate world, he knew, sometimes you had to do unpleasant things.

Henry had fired people, destroyed careers, and—when necessary—stretched or simply lied about his achievements, all in a never-ending quest to climb the corporate ladder. When the parent company, the Militan Corporation, requested his presence at a hurried meeting with Zintas' core leaders a few months ago, it had been his chance to reach the next rung. But he had not expected the meeting to go the way it had. They had assigned him one of the most unpleasant tasks in his storied career. Henry Gustoff had been ordered to oversee a special mission. He had been ordered to kill someone—and not only someone but two people with whom he had a long, personal relationship.

Haamar and Yuyenda Ransan were scientists in the exploratory division of Zintas Mine. They were meek, honest, and hardworking. But their discovery of moissanite running through the Memphis range had changed everything. Zintas had suddenly moved from a minor supporting role of Militan's operations to a leading one. But the executives of both Militan and Zintas were concerned about the bottom line and the loss of profits, partly in the shape of a finder's fee—an archaic paragraph in Haamar Ransan's employment contract that had, by accident, been overlooked when the company began removing the clause from other contracts. It had been a costly mistake. If it had ended there, Henry thought, they still might have worked something out. Contracts can be rewritten—even after the fact. But then Haamar had accepted the invitation to visit Earth. And the invitation came from Terra Corporation. Terra Corp!

Terra Corp was the largest and most powerful corporation in the human universe. It was a major competitor with Militan. There was a long history of dirty business, politics, and murder between the two organizations. Henry thought of it as laissez-faire economics with guns. In the world of the corporations, unbridled competition was organic, natural.

The Ransans' acceptance of the invitation did not go unnoticed. No. In fact, Henry realized as the meeting had progressed, the chief executive officer of Militan positively sat up and screamed! Henry grimaced at the memory.

"See this!" Tonya Livingston hissed, slamming newsprint on the boardroom table. She looked sharp in a slim skirt and fitted blouse. "What type of operation is Zintas running anyhow? Well, I'll tell you … ladies and gentlemen," she brayed, sneering. "Terra isn't going to get away with it. No! Not by a long shot. Do you hear me?"

And the boardroom sounded like a graveyard at the end of a rainy day. Then the CEO had wheeled upon him and fixed Henry with deadly eyes. The fingers of her right hand held like a pointed spear, she jabbed it at Henry to emphasize her words.

"Henry," her voice changed, becoming serpent soft and just as deadly. "Henry. I think we must take special action. I think we must … remove this new threat. Do you love your family, Henry? Do you? And wouldn't you like to see your children graduate from college and get good jobs with the corporation?" She smiled. But the threat was there. "Here, dear Henry, is the very thing that will destroy us all. Terra Corp. Bloodsucking Terra! They will worm their way into Telakia and rip our good fortune from us. And that fool of a man that Zintas hired—Ransan! He has no idea how he is being manipulated. A brilliant fool."

"A fool," echoed Karsten Neumann, the weak CEO of Zintas Mines and Livingston's puppet. He bobbed his head like a Catholic priest giving a benediction.

Henry remembered the sinking feeling that grew as CEO Livingston continued to extoll the vices of Terra Corp and the danger she saw in having Haamar Ransan fall into their sphere of influence. The man was becoming a worldwide hero on Telakia, and that—ladies and gentlemen—gave Ransan power. Power and money and Terra Corporation. And that was unacceptable. Something had to be done!

And then Tonya Livingston had put her slender arms about Henry's shoulders and whispered in her purring voice, "The price of membership to the board, dear Henry, has always been blood." Henry had looked into the Militan Corporation's chief executive officer's eyes and saw within them a final certainty. Her short, dark hair had brushed the side of his neck as the CEO laughed, sweet, high—the chittering sound of a flirtatious schoolgirl.

He had, at first, refused. The Ransans were good people. Surely they could be reasoned with, and if not that, threatened. There were legal if unethical ways for the corporation to retain the finder's fee without having to resort to such a drastic measure. And Henry knew Haamar. The machinations of Terra Corporation and the threat it posed to Militan and Zintas would never occur to the eccentric geologist. Perhaps the board could explain it to Haamar. But Henry's ideas and pleas fell on deaf ears.

"But the Ransans?" he had said slowly, his voice full of regret.

"The Ransans." CEO Livingston sighed into the crisp office air. She twirled her body away from him, her hand lingering on his shoulders in a long caress. She walked the short distance back to the head of the conference room table and sat down, her fingers steepled before her, her head slightly bent down, her green eyes turned up and staring.

"Yes, well," Henry stammered. "I suppose there is nothing else to be done?"

They had smiled. All of them. All the men and women in their designer suits and four-hundred-credit haircuts. To his dismay, Henry found himself smiling too. How easy it had been, once the decision had been reached. In truth, it was like any other decision he had ever made—just words—words that quickly faded in the bright light of the boardroom. But in his heart, Henry knew those insidious words lived on like a specter, a slavering ghoul waiting for the moment of realization.

Henry found the follow-on instructions similarly easy. It had not taken much: access to personnel files, a little conversation here and there, the dark shadow of the enforcer's voice dimly received via a secure call, and the deed was set in motion. Yet the chase had been nerve-racking. The Ransans had purchased a land rover for their trip and driven it right off the lot and into the Great Desert. Caught off guard, the enforcer lost them for a while. But the two surfaced in Umbaliya. The enforcer boarded a private flight to the city. Yet something had gone wrong. Haamar had some defect of physiology, and the enforcer had not bothered to ensure Haamar had died.

To Henry's great dismay, the first responders found that Haamar had survived.

Henry had rushed to the hospital and did everything he could to make sure Haamar was comfortable. What else could Henry do? How would it look if he didn't rush to Haamar's side?

When Henry first saw Haamar unconscious, strung up on the medical tubes and machines that moved blood and air and kept him struggling against death, Henry had felt the full import of those tiny boardroom words. And he had prayed: prayed for forgiveness, prayed for Haamar to recover, prayed for Haamar to die, and prayed for blissful forgetfulness.

Now he sighed and looked out his bright windows at the row of mountains that spun off toward the horizon on his left and right. The Zintas Mines headquarters building was shaped like a half moon and stood on a promontory of red rock overlooking part of the Memphis range. Off in the distance, he could make out the growing depths of the Great Desert basin. It was a harsh planet. And it made Henry feel sad.

Henry had to steel himself, he knew. He had to maintain the appearance of deep concern for Haamar. But he also had to make it plainly known that his full loyalty lay with the corporation. It was terrifying. Haamar was in the press. His story had gone interplanetary. That, no doubt, was a maneuver by Terra Corp. The dynamics had therefore changed. Henry did not know how to solve the problem. It was clear something had to be done, but how, with the worlds watching? Henry was too new to this level of corporate intrigue to have the experience needed to figure it out. He decided, therefore, to follow the CEO's instructions. Yes, he vowed. He would follow the CEO's instructions very, very carefully.

He looked nervously at the pictures of his wife and kids. Henry would toe the line. He was, after all, a corporate man.

A metallic bird chirped. Again. Again. A rhythmic, invasive pattern, it tugged at the blanket of oblivion insistently. Awareness. A hint of light. Suddenly, the undistinguished gray turned into something, and the world took form. Haamar burst from an encompassing nothingness like a drowning man finally breaking the surface of the ocean's vast waves to take one, all-defining breath.

I am. I am. I am Haamar.

Self-awareness reborn sharpened the haze, and in that moment Haamar's eyes flickered open, and sound rushed into his ears.

"He's awake." A young woman in a white medical coat leaned forward and passed a light across Haamar's blurry eyes. "Doctor Andrews," she said to someone outside of Haamar's limited field of vision, "the patient is awake."

The woman moved back, and another woman, older with lines around the corners of her eyes, moved into view. She passed a medical device over Haamar's chest and studied the small readout on the device's screen. She then looked behind her at a larger device that was measuring Haamar's vital signs. The doctor murmured something before turning back and smiling broadly at her patient.

"Mr. Ransan." The doctor's voice was light and airy. "Can you hear me? Do you understand me?"

Haamar tried to answer, but his throat was raw, and the effort caused considerable pain. He blinked his eyes several times and managed to nod his head.

"Good. That is wonderful. You gave us quite a scare, Mr. Ransan. You are going to sleep again." She made a small gesture to the first woman. There was a shuffling sound, and a machine chirped.

"You are going to be okay, Mr. Ransan. But we are keeping you in a medically induced coma for a few more days. We only woke you because we needed to do a test on your brain function."

Haamar tried to move, but his body felt weighted and dead. He had a hard time understanding the meaning behind the woman's words. He had to focus.

"No," the doctor said, putting a restraining hand on Haamar's shoulder. "Lie easy. Relax. You are a lucky man, Mr. Ransan. Very lucky indeed."

The sound of the doctor's voice began to drift as the drugs hit Haamar's system. He closed his eyes and fought against the urge to sleep, straining to hear what the two women were saying.

"It is a very strange case," the senior doctor said to her pupil as they finished reviewing the medical readouts. "Dextrocardia—misalignment of this patient's heart from the left side to the right side—quite uncommon. And furthermore, most uncommon to not have had it corrected at birth. I can understand the reluctance," the doctor continued. "Normal blood flow. No abnormal arrhythmia."

"Yes, but dextrocardia situs inversus totalis?" the younger doctor asked. "And fully functioning? That has to be most rare."

"Not as rare as you would think," Doctor Andrews replied in an instructive voice. "One in twelve thousand or so. Mr. Ransan, though, is a special case."

"How so?"

"None of the normal disorders associated with dextrocardia. No bronchial, esophageal, or cardiovascular disorders. However," the doctor added, "I do believe that he may be infertile. But that is fairly minor and can be compensated for. Kartagener syndrome—known for abnormalities of cilia in the respiratory tract and on sperm. In our patient's case, it only affects his sperm."

"He can still have children?"

"Of course," Doctor Andrews added. "It is a minor procedure. Of course we would have to run a full diagnostics on the sperm before implantation to ensure there are no abnormalities passed to the fetus. But we can splice in corrective gene patterns if necessary."

The younger doctor paused in the hallway. "Does he know?"

"About his condition? Most definitely. It is possible he does not know about his infertility." Doctor Andrews paused in thought. "Best we let him heal from his wounds before we bring that subject up. Especially considering the circumstances."

"His wife?"

"Yes. Sad. But I have seen so many senseless and sad things in my days. However, in Mr. Ransan's case, dextrocardia saved his life. If his heart had been in the correct location …"

"The gunfire would have struck his heart," the younger doctor finished.

"Yes, well, it is good to see his new lungs growing strong. And his ribs are healing nicely. Brain readouts are normal as well. I do believe, given time, Mr. Ransan will make a full recovery."

The younger doctor pursed her lips and in a surge of emotion asked, "Do the police know why? Why his wife was killed and Mr. Ransan was shot?"

"The human capacity for violence is amazing," Dr. Andrews replied. She took a final reading and made a note on her digital pad, annotating Haamar's record. "Once I did an autopsy on a victim— stabbed to death by his drunken brother. Why? Over the last piece of pizza. And the other brother, the murderer, hadn't even realized, in his drunken state, that he had killed his brother. He had sat back down and finished the pizza, talking to his dead brother as if the corpse could hear. What fools people are," she added with a shake of her head. "What masters of the senseless. But that isn't our problem. We just fix them as best we can. Let the police handle the why.

"We have other patients to see. Mr. Ransan is progressing nicely. Coming, Doctor? And, please, tell me about this next patient."

"Yes, Doctor Andrews," the younger woman answered. She hurried to catch up to the older physician, who had stepped into the hall.

Haamar fought for consciousness as long as he could.

Yuyenda. Yuyenda is dead.

A hole opened in his soul. He wanted to curse and cry. But the medication stole in, and Haamar slept.

He did not dream. All he had was silence.

What did Haamar feel as he struggled to put one foot before the other? Was it anger? Was it despair? Desperation? His soul twisted and turned as it fell into the funneled void of this indefinable thing that had swallowed him. Yuyenda was dead. She was dead.

Sometimes his mind played tricks on him. He could hear Yuyenda coming down the hall, the sound of her footfall sharp and clear. Haamar could swear Yuyenda was about to step into the hospital room. He would turn and stare at the door, expecting to see Yuyenda's lithe form, her mischievous smile, to feel the air move with each of her subtle breaths. But she never appeared. And in that moment of depleted expectation, he suffered the news all over again. It raked at him. Again and again, in the silence of his heart, he wept. It was too much.

But outside, Haamar was a stone.

He pushed the thought aside, cursed, and struggled to walk the few steps across the room. Gripping the metal poles of the parallel bars, he struggled to move his legs, but he stumbled. Haamar fell forward, but helping hands reached out and caught him, softening the blow of his forearms on the hard metal rods.

"That was much better," Peter Bayof, Haamar's physical therapist, said as he helped Haamar back to the wheelchair. Peter Bayof was friendly, overly full of energy and enthusiasm, and had a clean soul. Haamar could not help but like the man.

"How much longer?" Haamar asked as he settled weakly in the wheelchair.

"Today or in general? Um … today? About twenty minutes, I think. In general," Bayof replied, "you are recovering quickly, Mr. Ransan." Bayof helped Haamar lift his legs and put them in the footplate of the wheelchair. The wheelchair was not automated; that was part of the treatment too, intended to get Haamar to use and rebuild atrophied muscles. "I think you will be heading home in a couple of weeks, a month at most."

Haamar looked awkwardly over his shoulder at the therapist who had shifted behind him and was pushing the wheelchair back to the start of the parallel bars. "A month? That quickly?"

"The human body is a remarkable thing, Mr. Ransan. You will be jogging easily by the time you leave us. You know you are only here this long because of your lungs. I know this hurts you," he indicated the parallel bars and the other workout equipment in the therapy room, "but it is really your new lung function that we are keeping close tabs on. We did not have adequate time to grow them. They are still forming. All this—well," he shrugged, "we could do all this on an outpatient basis. But let's take advantage of the extra time we have. I'll have you in tip-top shape in no time at all."

"I know," Haamar said, passing his hand unconsciously across his chest. "I feel like I am always out of breath. It doesn't hurt exactly, but sometimes it does feel like I am drowning." He smiled and then frowned. "Give me a minute, would you, Peter? And then we'll try again?"

"Sure, Mr. Ransan," Bayof said, stepping in front of Haamar and looking down on him. "It has been a rough session today. Why don't we take ten minutes and then we will get back to it."

"Thank you."

"Ten minutes," Bayof admonished. Then he smiled, excused himself, and left Haamar alone.

It was an odd concept to get his mind wrapped around, Haamar thought as he rested and caught his breath. A new set of lungs. Haamar had read about the technology before, but he had never thought he would be one of the people benefiting from it. Dr. Andrews had used an extracellular matrix seeded with Haamar's blood. His blood cells were stripped of their biological identities and placed within the matrix. Given new biological cues, his blood had formed new cells that eventually became lungs. In addition, while the opportunity had presented itself, the doctors had given Haamar's abnormally placed heart an upgrade with new arteries and veins tailor-made for his body. The new arteries were actually better than the originals. They were made of cells that were more disease and blockage resistant. The doctors told Haamar that his "accident" likely led to an increase in his life span now that he had a tune-up. They were trying to put a silver lining on the situation. And the science behind it was a welcome distraction that naturally appealed to Haamar's disposition. It was science like this, Haamar knew, that had led to repairing spinal cord injuries, regeneration of limbs, and fairly much ended the aftereffects of physical injury.

Yet in Haamar's case, his lungs had been rushed and were not fully formed when they implanted them in his body. In the third week of Haamar's medically induced coma, his original lungs had started to fail. Even with the help of machines, the battered lungs just couldn't keep operating. So with little choice, the surgical team had opened Haamar up and implanted the new lungs even though they would have preferred to wait two more weeks for them to mature in the nutrient bath. And the lungs still had a little growing to do. So Haamar had found himself trapped in the hospital. He went through his painful daily rehabilitative routine. And everything looked fine.

Fine. Nothing was truly fine, he knew. Yuyenda was gone, and he didn't understand why. In quiet moments like these, Haamar tried to make sense of it all. Why would someone break into their hotel room and wait for them to return, simply to rob them of their meager amount of money and a trinket of jewelry? It nagged at him.

He remembered Yuyenda telling him about a strange call from the police, but records indicated that Yuyenda had accepted no incoming calls. There had been no calls to or from their hotel room at all. But that was a blatant alteration of records. Yuyenda would not have lied about the call. Who had called her? Was it really the DMP? Could it have been the killer? And what was all that about Henry Gustoff and Zintas Mines? What had Yuyenda said? That Henry was looking for them? These questions stirred dark thoughts and suspicions.

Could it be that Henry had something to do with his wife's death? The idea was boggling. Haamar knew Henry. They were old friends. The idea that Henry could be involved sat wrong in the pit of Haamar's stomach. And when Haamar had woken from his coma, he had found out what lengths Henry and Zintas Mines had taken to ensure Haamar had received the best medical care. If Henry and Zintas Mines had wanted Haamar dead, then why would they then work so hard to save him? You couldn't fake the ashen look that Henry wore each time he visited. It couldn't be Henry or Zintas, Haamar concluded. But it also wasn't a simple robbery. But who did that leave?

An answer had formed slowly over a couple of days of contemplation.

The parent company for Zintas Mines was Militan Corporation. With no direct heirs, his 15 percent finder's fee would revert back to Zintas Mines and, through them, to Militan Corp. Yet doubts still lingered.

Zintas and Militan Corp would not be directly involved in something like this. Would they? It made no sense. While everyone knew corporations were mostly concerned with the bottom line, some were worse than others. Militan Corp was well respected by the citizens of Telakia and had a good intergalactic reputation. It was not Militan's style to murder someone. Like their historic hero, the East India Company of the long-defunct British Empire, they too had overlain their own version of civic and military governance over the worlds that they controlled. The executives at Militan felt responsible for the people on their corporate worlds. They had a moral and ethical compass. But that did not mean Militan Corp moved with impunity. Local politics and larger economic and treaty obligations tied them into the darker side of modern times. And Militan's recent partnering with Syrch Corporation left them exposed, Haamar thought, to that darker side. Syrch Corporation employed brutal tactics.

Headquartered on Papen's World, Syrch Corp was one of the "big three" corporations specializing in intergalactic shipbuilding and space construction. Syrch Corp was starved for raw materials and was trying to improve its reputation. It was no big stretch to understand why Militan Corp, with its mines and low-orbit processing factories, had aligned with Syrch Corp. Well, that is what Syrch Corp called it. In fact, Syrch had bought a commanding share of Militan stock. Syrch owned Militan, and Militan owned Zintas. It was a good deal for Syrch Corp. Militan, with its good-guy attitude and profitable mining operations, fit the right bill in terms of production and public relations. Now that moissanite had been added to the mix, it was a match made in heaven. So who lost?

Was it just the money? Could Haamar's share in the profits be that significant?

That thought made Haamar's heart skip a beat. Maybe Syrch Corp was behind his wife's murder. Could that be? Haamar had never had direct dealings with any of the executives in the big corporations. The executives, everyone knew, were part businessmen and women, and part thug. Never cross a corporation. You would suddenly find yourself in prison or worse. That was the general philosophy of average people.

The more he thought about it, the more convinced Haamar became that Syrch Corp had ordered his and Yuyenda's death. Even if Militan Corp had been told about the hit, a small corporation like that could never stand up to one of the big three. Object too much, and you may just become part of the project. No. Militan Corporation, Haamar told himself, didn't have the expertise or gumption to do such a thing. No. But they also didn't have the ability to resist a powerful force like Syrch Corp. Who knew what that type of pressure might bring? What would he do if one of the Syrch goons threatened him or his family? Would Haamar turn a blind eye and wash his hands of the matter if he were in Zintas' or Militan's shoes? Where does morality end when fear and desperation reigns? It was Syrch, he thought bitterly—Syrch with its history of blatant violations of interstellar laws and its boundless assets.

But how to prove it? How could he expose Syrch Corp for what they were, murderers and thugs? It gave him something to think about at night. And as Haamar waited to resume the agony of rehabilitation, the question continued to revolve in his mind. How? How? How? And what would Haamar do when he found the proof he needed?

It was no fun being yelled at. No fun being threatened. But the worst thing in the universe was to be calmly thrashed by Militan's CEO Tonya Livingston. Paul Thorne, aka Paul Harlamor, aka DMP Investigator Harlamor, walked out of the meeting with a bead of sweat sitting at the small of his back. He stopped for a moment to grab a paper cup and pour a drink of fresh water from the cooler. Paul looked much younger than he actually was, with a baby face and creamy skin. Crooked eyebrows gave him a look that was less than divine but kept the women staring. He smiled warmly at a pretty woman in a cubical. She smiled uncertainly back.

Crumpling the cup and throwing it in the waste bin, Paul looked back at the closed door to Livingston's office. Her title and name were printed boldly on a brass placard in the upper center of the wooden door. Paul adjusted his tie. He looked around at the working people in their everyday routine, sitting blissfully in their cubicles, secure in the knowledge that they worked for Militan Corporation and that this, the desert world of Telakia, was their world. They were at the top of this world's corporate food chain. It was a lush and pampered life. But there were bigger fish in the universe, and one of them had just parked their massive presence on Paul's chest.

Syrch Corp was not happy.

It was never a good thing to know too much about the jobs Paul was given. The orders were always simple and direct but also vague. He never knew why. He never asked. Livingston said break someone's legs, kill someone, and Paul put on his game face, and the job was done. It was an uncomplicated relationship that he worked hard to maintain. But what Livingston had just done was change that formula, and it made Paul wonder if his lifeline had just been chopped off at the end. The CEO had all but told Paul that he was the fall guy. If the Ransan mess was not cleaned up, and quickly, she would throw Paul to the wolves.

Those wolves were mean, large, traveled in packs, and enjoyed killing.

The Militan Corp enforcer took a deep breath and moved away from the CEO's office, down the rows of cubicles and out of the glass doors into the foyer where the elevators and bathrooms were located. The foyer was empty. Paul pushed the elevator button and then thought better of it. As the elevator rose to the twentieth floor, Paul followed the exit signs to the stairwell and began trekking down the concrete steps. Elevators could fall. And Paul was a careful man. It was this penchant for self-preservation that had allowed him to flourish as the corporation's favorite enforcer and helped explain his long career. Paranoia and the ability to keep his mouth shut, those were his true attributes. Any mutt could pull a trigger. And he had met his share of mutts over the years. They came and went and ended up in trash heaps with their brains blown out or their bodies chopped up and used as plant fertilizer. Yet Paul had survived. That was what he was good at.

Syrch Corp! Shit! Shit!

Sometimes, as a professional it was good to have a recognizable name. At other times, being recognized was not so great. Livingston had dropped the dime on Paul to Syrch, and the big boys and gals had their expectations. From what little Paul could tell, Syrch had big plans that revolved around moissanite, and they felt that their arch nemesis, Terra Corp, the mother of all monstrous corporations, was trying to muscle in on Syrch's lunch. Where did that leave Paul? Right in the middle of the universe's two most ruthless organizations with a target the size of the sun emblazoned on his forehead. That's where! What ever happened to the good ol' days when he would do his little job and slip off to a long vacation in the gambling halls on Lucia? Gods, he grumbled, he was in an undeniable mess, and this time it looked like he could not redeem himself.

Paul, feeling a bit winded, finally reached the ground floor and was about to step through the back emergency exit when a feeling crept over him. He glanced up, and sure enough, there was a CCTV camera pointed his way. He grimaced, his hand hovering an inch before the door's push bar. Rotating one-eighty, the enforcer stepped out of the stairwell and into the main lobby. Three guards in pressed blue and white uniforms watched him as Paul left the building and stood in the bright heat of the Telakian sun. He turned left and walked several blocks. Paul crossed the street three times, dodging through traffic, trying to see if he was being tailed. But he didn't see anyone. That was a good sign. Maybe he still had a bit of magic and luck left over.

The enforcer almost never took the subway. Those few times he had visited Militan's headquarters building, he had flagged down a random cab that he rode to a predetermined location. There he would take another cab to where he had stashed his motorbike—a thing he had stolen years ago and for which he had purchased some very expensive license plates under someone else's name. But today he stepped on the escalator and into the cool tunnel of the subway. Being unpredictable was part of his security measures. He stepped on a half-empty car and rattled along on it for several stops, carefully watching the other passengers. He remained on the car to the end of the line and was relieved to see that nobody who had entered when he had remained on the train with him.

Rambling up the stairs, Paul made his way to where he had stashed his motorbike. At the last moment, he stopped and stared at it. How safe was it, really? But he loved the bike …

Hell, he could get a new one. Pulling the collar of his suit up, the enforcer waved down a cab.

"Astaire's," he told the driver. "On 151st Street, northwest. Number ten." It was not his apartment, but it was within a mile of it. He would walk the rest of the way.

A while later, Paul stepped into his cool apartment, locked the door behind him, set the alarm, and plopped down on his couch. Only then did he remove his gun from his shoulder rig and place it on the coffee table. A half-full glass of bourbon was sitting there. He had left it there earlier. He picked it up and sipped it. It was warm. *Damn.*

How was he going to extricate himself from this mess? Obviously he had to erase Ransan. But how? When? The press hounded the man.

Paul noticed a light blink on his communication pad and picked up the clear cube and unfolded it until it was a six-by-twelve screen, the thickness that of a sheet of paper. He punched in his password and swore. A coded message. With an unsteady hand, he scanned his iris. A message block opened up, and a shadowed form gave the enforcer his marching orders.

Paul Thorne listened quietly and finished the warm bourbon. He wished he had thought of adding a few ice cubes to it.

Oh, he thought as he listened to his instructions. *That's it then. A blood bath.*

A long time was spent in the hospital, working with Peter Bayof and Doctor Andrews. Haamar steadily improved, and after being prodded and probed more than he cared to remember, Haamar was released. He stepped into the crisp air of a bright day four months after having been rushed into ICU. He found a car and driver waiting for him. He put his plastic bag of personal items in the vehicle's trunk, including the invitation to dinner that Peter had given to him. Peter and his husband had a small flat in the center of town, and apparently, Haamar had become quite a local celebrity. The news journalists had sensationalized the murder of his wife. A newly minted multimillionaire's wife is found murdered while her husband survives—it was the stuff of tabloid nirvana. Luckily the pauper press, as Haamar referred to them, were not present at his discharge and Haamar quietly got into the car, which lifted and moved away toward his and Yuyenda's tiny home.

Haamar dreaded arriving. There he would have to face a lifetime with Yuyenda. He would see her in the post-modern furniture, with its clean lines and rich upholstery. She would be in the porcelain dishes, the artwork on the walls, and in the colorful, hand-woven comforter with its purple flowers that adorned their bed. And her cramped closet with her clothing—the photos of her—the thought of dealing with it threatened to overwhelm him. Yet he knew he had to come to terms with her passing and find some type of peace.

Haamar sat back and tried to relax. The buildings moved by in a menagerie of blurred shapes and pastel colors. Here in the high mountains, where Haamar lived, the rust color of dust that was the hallmark of Telakia was replaced by sweeps of trees, brush, and flowers. In a few hundred years, maybe they would make some headway on terraforming the deserts. But until then, the thin strips of mountains offered the only planetary relief from high temperatures and the furnace winds of the planet. This thought skimmed across Haamar's mind and vanished just as quickly. The vehicle moved through a driving circle on the last leg of its journey.

Haamar turned to say something to Yuyenda. The words caught in his throat. He leaned his head against the warm glass and closed his eyes. After a while, he felt the vehicle stop, and Haamar straightened up. The driver opened the door, and Haamar stepped out onto the peppered brick driveway of his home. The three-dome structure was just as he remembered it. Nothing had changed. Yet everything had changed.

Haamar smiled at the driver and shuffled up the flight of stairs to his front door. His small bag of personal items in one hand, he passed the other over the locking mechanism, and the door chimed and swung inward. The house with its kitchen dome, living room dome, and bedroom dome was whitewashed and clean.

"Welcome home, Mr. Ransan," the soothing voice of his home computer system purred. "I hope you had a good day."

A good day? Haamar notice his legs were shaking. He stood in the doorway and glanced into his little, empty house. Haamar wondered if it were so wrong to commit suicide. Then it would all end, and, perhaps, if the petty priests with their withering eyes and endless haranguing about sin and heaven were correct, he could see his wife again. Just one more moment with her to tell her he loved her, to say good-bye. That would be worth an eternity in hell.

The old clock ticked on the wall. Air churned as the air conditioner kicked on. A bird sang a little trill, and Haamar, alone at last with his grief, closed the door, fell upon his couch, and wept.

It was not until the next morning that he stirred, worn but feeling somehow refreshed. It was if a great, emotional damn had burst. What was left was a horrid mess, but the pressure that had steadily grown over the past few months had eased. Haamar could function, he discovered. He found himself slowly going through the closet and putting Yuyenda's clothing into bags for—what? He was not sure what he would do with them. But dealing with her clothing was therapeutic too. He felt close to her, and good memories swarmed out of her closet and surrounded him with her voice and laughter. It was a languid process with many stops and bouts of mourning, but like the uncontrolled weeping, the process made Haamar feel somehow better. In the end, Haamar stacked bags of clothing in his vehicle and donated them to charity at the local drop. There were a few items he could not bear to part with. These he hung back up gently.

While out, he bought supplies and wandered around an old-fashioned bookstore. He was restless. But after settling again into the house, Haamar found it gave him comfort.

Much later in the week, Haamar discovered the strength to visit Yuyenda's mother, sister, and brother. It was an uncomfortable meeting. Haamar was haunted with a feeling of guilt. He told Tyena and Bachtuk that he felt like he should have been able to do something to save Yuyenda. He should have shielded her with his body, pushed her to the floor, anything but stand there dumbly as she was shot down. A man is supposed to protect his wife. What type of a man fails at it so miserably? And he could not remember much either. It rubbed at him. A man in the shadows, a grimace, and a flash of light—the memory was as vague and shifting as shapes in clouds. And them came the moment of ultimate truth. Haamar faultingly told Tyena and Bachtuk that he and Yuyenda had just decided to have children. He burst into a moment of tears as he told them that he had betrayed Yuyenda. He had let her down, kept her from being a mother. And it was all because he had been afraid! He had thought they had all the time in the world. Haamar didn't realize how quickly it could all change. In the end, there had been no time. No time at all.

They reassured him, and Tyena gave Haamar a hug. She whispered to him, and his eyes became glassy, and he stared at his shoes. Was that even possible? He looked at her, and Tyena smiled back. Her face was sad.

Haamar's darkened house, and the voice of his home computer welcomed him once again. He sat dejectedly on the couch with an open soda in front of him. The video-vision was on, but the sound was muted. A soft shadow of colored light danced from the large screen, and outside the sun was down. Everything was hushed. The universe twirled, and a thousand worlds drifted through eons of space. Yet Haamar felt alone in a teeming universe. For a man's life is but a reflection of his senses. The universe existed—Haamar theorized—only because he existed. And because he existed, Yuyenda still lived. She lived in his heart.

Drowsing, Haamar noticed a small, white envelope sitting on the coffee table. It was square, and there was no writing on it. It looked to him like an invitation. But how had it come to be on the coffee table? Haamar sat up.

"Lights on," he said, and the computer raised the lighting in the room.

Haamar fingered the envelope silently. It was sealed. He opened it and stared for a moment at the small scratch of paper that was inside. Pulling it out, he noticed that printed on the paper, in standard script, was a singular message. Haamar turned pale, and the lonely peace of the night was banished.

It is not over.

Four words. Four obscene little words. And Haamar knew what it was to be afraid.

It is not so easy for an honest person to buy a gun. That was doubly so on a law-enriched world such as Telakia. Only the police and military were legally permitted to have them, and though everyone knew that the criminal class trafficked in weapons and used them on a routine basis, that did not mean they were readily available. You would have to know a criminal to know where to buy a gun. For Haamar, who had never even crossed the road outside of a crosswalk, it seemed an impossible task. Where did one go? How was the subject raised with a perfect stranger? How did you know the stranger was not a police detective or a corporate snitch? In the end, Haamar had taken an odd tact. He had skimmed through the news reports until he found a story on the arrest of Dashiell Thompson. The report said

Thompson was arrested on suspicion of the murder of one Balzac Godshock, a popular local businessman. There were rumored reports that Thompson had been an enforcer for the Gianolla crime family. But for some reason, the mafia had not provided Thompson with a high-paid lawyer. One reporter suggested that Thompson had acted on his own because of the victim's alleged romantic involvement with Thompson's wife. Unfortunately for Thompson, his actions had brought the Gianolla family into the spotlight and put them under tightening pressure from the authorities. The Gianollas did not like the attention. They were keeping a low profile and had left Dashiell Thompson in the lurch.

Haamar hired an attorney, and a deal was struck. Thompson would answer Haamar's confidential question in exchange for Thompson's legal fees. The question Haamar had asked was, where can I purchase a gun?

The answer brought Haamar to the Newlings district in the seedy part of the planet's capital, Kugadar. The sky was dark, and the flicker of streetlights illuminated the road in long shadowed strips while the sound of police sirens routinely plied the night's air. It was muggy and hot, and Haamar wiped a bead of perspiration from his forehead as he set the rental car alarm. He looked to his left and right, but the street was empty. Only the forlorn buildings in their squalid misery and a trickle of water from a nearby building's leaky central line welcomed him.

"Five ninety-one Wallace," he mumbled to himself.

It was a tall building of concrete, with dirty windows and a set of double parawood doors. There were discarded hypodermic needles and a variety of debris strewn about the sickly lawn and entranceway. A fat man, apparently oblivious to the world, hunched with his back against the wall near the door. A paper sack with a bottle top sticking out of it was clutched in his left hand. His right hand was hidden in the folds of a double-breasted, tweed Ulster coat that had seen better days. The fat man looked like he was sleeping.

Haamar paused and fought against a sudden desire to turn back. He was out of his element, and though he was determined, a flush of fear wafted through him. He had to push himself to walk the five steps to the decrepit front door. On the left, almost directly above the sleeping fat man, was a metallic register with a small, touch-screen display. Haamar dialed up room 421 and waited as the intercom rang. The noise disturbed the fat man who moaned a fetid smell of alcohol and piss into the air. Haamar covered his nose and mouth at the sickly smell.

"What do ya want?" a voice emanated from the register. Haamar looked at the face that appeared in the touch screen. It was thin, and the eyes were sunken and hollow. The man was bald, and his face weathered and aged beyond the youthful sound of his voice.

"Mr. Sidney Blithe? I am Haamar Ransan. A friend sent me," Haamar replied. He had to bend down a bit to see into the screen.

The bald man's face screwed up in concentration, and he looked behind him for a moment as if checking to see that nobody else was around. "I've seen ya on the news, Mr. Ransan. Come on up."

The image faded away, and the door buzzed. Haamar walked into the dimly lit foyer of the apartment building and located the bank of four elevators. Soon he was standing outside the lackluster door of apartment 421. Haamar was sweating with nerves, and he steadied himself as he pushed the door buzzer.

"Ya alone?" the voice of the bald man came clearly through a little speaker on the side of the door.

"Of course," Haamar ventured. He shifted his weight and looked down the long, empty hallway. The carpet was worn, and the walls tinged with years of grime.

The door opened, and the bald man, a middle-aged white man in an old T-shirt, motioned Haamar into the apartment. The man took a moment to scan the hallway before closing the door and turning his rather small frame toward Haamar.

"This isn't any jiz, is it?" the man asked. His rat-like eyes sized Haamar up as he moved Haamar back into the lightly furnished living room by a hand gesture.

"Excuse me?" Haamar asked.

"Ya, know, entrapment. Here, stands still," Blithe answered, pulling a small rectangular box from the back pocket of his well-worn jeans. "I'm ganna scan ya."

"What?"

"Scan ya. Ya know, for bugs, vids—that type o stuff. I knows Dashiell set this up, but I have no idea what type o' fucked-up Juice those bastards in the force have been feeding him. And ya. I don't know ya, mister.

"But what I hear ain't all that good. It ain't all that bad either. You the guy that discovered some ultra-rich vein of rock became an overnight multimillionaire?"

"Yes."

"Yeah. And ya wife? I heard that too." He passed the scanner over Haamar, following the contours of Haamar's body.

"Are you satisfied?" Haamar said stiffly, indicating the device in Blithe's hand.

"I s'pose," the man replied. "Sits down, Mr. Ransan. Ya bring the stuff?"

"Yes." Haamar assumed the man was referring to the money.

"Great. Be rights back." Blithe disappeared into the other room.

Haamar waited patiently for the man to return. He looked around the dirty and worn apartment, wondering how long it had been since Blithe had cleaned. The kitchenette was stacked with dirty dishes and used boxes from various takeout foods. The small, counter-high table was cluttered with debris and cups, and its surface was stained. Between Haamar and the room into which Blithe had disappeared was a small, rectangular living room with an old couch of synthetic leather that was torn and oddly patched. The rug was a thin, shivering thing that might have once been white but was now a dirty beige. On the glass-top coffee table were a pile of papers, old dishes, and what looked to Haamar like some type of digital assistant pad. A blue, pinstriped platform recliner, faded and torn, stood a little off to the end of the sofa under a dim, bronze floor lamp, its lampshade smudged as if someone had wiped a cloth of tea across its surface. The air was fetid and reminded Haamar of damp earth and rotting vegetation. Haamar thought about sitting on the sofa but, after looking at it dubiously for a moment, decided he would just stand.

"Ya knows how to use this thing?" Blithe asked as he stepped back in the room and handed Ransan a small plastic box. The box had a handle and two clasps. Blithe handed the box to Haamar.

Haamar opened the box and looked inside. A small, silver and blue handgun sat neatly in cut-to-shape protective foam. There were two rectangular magazines in the box as well. The magazines were dull tan, and Haamar could see they were loaded.

"Nice little job, the Malcolm Mauser," Blithe said, obviously proud of himself. "Ya indicated to Mr. Thompson that ya were a bit new to using one o' these things."

"Yes, a bit."

"Take it out. It ain't loaded and won't bite ya."

Haamar took the pistol in his hands. It was light. The frame was smooth and cool to the touch.

"Double action, flechette—older I know—but it is a sweet little weapon, easy to use, almost no kick. Ya knows what double action is?"

Haamar admitted, "No. Not really."

The man smiled, and Haamar noticed Blithe was in need of a good orthopedist. "After ya pulls the trigger the first time," Blithe explained, "the gun becomes easier to fire. There's less trigger pull. That lets ya shoot faster, and with that baby there are a whopping fifty rounds per magazine. Knows how to load it?"

"It's not loaded?" Haamar hadn't even thought that it might not be loaded.

"Now would I be givings ya a loaded weapon?" Blithe admonished. "Here. I'll give ya a quick lesson—don't worry, it won't cost ya none. But first …" He let the words trail off expectantly.

Haamar stood for a moment wondering what the bald man was asking before it dawned on him.

"Oh." Haamar took an envelope out of his breast pocket and handed it to the other man.

"It's all here?" Blithe asked, pushing the envelope into his back pants pocket.

"You can count it."

"No need. Any friend of Dashiell's a friend o' mine. Now here, let me shows ya how to load it. Ya got to seats the magazine, see? Gives it a little tug to make sure it is seated. Then rack it. By that I means pull back on this here slide and let it snap forward." The gun clacked as the first round was loaded. "Now it ain't got no safety, man. Ya knows what I mean? Good. Just pull the trigger, and you're in business.

"Now to unload it, just press this button on the side o' the gun and, see, the magazine just falls out. Rack it. Did ya see that flechette eject? It's lying on the ground. Good. Now to reload, slap in the other magazine, rack it, and you're back in business. Understand, boss? Good. Now here, let me unload it once again—not that I don't trust ya—and I'll hand it back."

Blithe handed the pistol back to Haamar, who took it uncomfortably and put it back into its box.

"The detectors at the airport won't spot the thing?" Haamar asked.

"No. It ain't got no metal at all, boss. Looks like it—all pretty and sleek—but ain't no system at the airport, short of eyes on—if you get me—will find that thing. That is my personal guarantee."

Haamar didn't give much stock in the man's guarantee, but Haamar knew how badly the killer Dashiell Thompson needed his legal fees paid. And that gave Haamar a sense of confidence in what this strange, dirty man was saying.

"What ya goings to do with that thing?" the man asked. "No. No-no ... wait." He held up a deferring hand. "I don't wants to know. I don't wants to know anything else. Once we are done with this little transaction, we are done. Got it?" Blithe half-spit. "Ya go your way. I'll go mine."

"That's how I want it," Haamar said. "Are we done then?"

Blithe passed a hand over his bald head and smiled. "Yeah, we're all done, boss. But ya let Mr. Thompson knows I done ya real good, right? That is one mean son o' a mother ... Ya knows what I mean, right?"

"I think so," Haamar said as he followed Blithe to the door.

"Good. Ya remember that, boss. He is the real deal. He'd kills his own mother for a few credits. And ya don't wants no man like that breathing down ya neck. Ya and he have a deal, and I'm sure ya'll respect that. Knows what I mean?"

"Yes," Haamar replied, stepping out once again into the lonesome hallway. "Good-bye, Mr. Blithe," he said.

"Good-bye, Mr. Ransan."

Haamar left the bald man standing in his doorway and slipped back out of the building and into his waiting rental car. He dropped the pistol case on the passenger-side seat and began driving his way back out of the city. It was still dark. The heat was bearable. As he turned onto the major thoroughfare toward the airport, Haamar wondered what it was he was actually doing. *Yuyenda*, he thought, *would be ashamed of me.* But he had spent many hours thinking about this, about the cryptic note. Haamar had no intention of using the weapon, but he needed protection, and he needed to show Henry that he meant business.

Henry Gustoff knew something. Haamar could feel it. The man had become evasive and shuffled his feet uncomfortably whenever Haamar was around. Oh, he was friendly enough, but it was a type of overt friendliness that convinced Haamar that Henry was dirty. At the least, Henry knew something and was trying his best not to tell Haamar. At the worst, Henry was intimately involved. But

Haamar found that difficult to believe. He knew Henry. It was more likely Henry had gotten in over his head and had stumbled upon something. The other man did have access to Zintas Mines' records and computer system. Maybe he had seen something there that caused him to suspect either Militan or Syrch were involved in Yuyenda's death. Now Henry was just afraid. Haamar could understand that. The man had a family to protect. But, one way or the other, Henry was going to come clean.

Haamar didn't want to use the weapon. All he wanted was justice. Justice and some type of final peace. But if he had to, he could scare Henry with the gun, and, who knows, Haamar might need a weapon to protect himself.

The drive to the airport was uneventful, and though Haamar felt nervous checking the gun with his baggage, Blithe had been true to his word. Nobody seemed to notice the weapon. Still, Haamar's nerves were shot by the time he sat back into the lush cushion of his seat and accepted a drink of red wine from the slim stewardess. She smiled, and he returned the smile reflexively. As the door closed and the engines roared to life, Haamar closed his eyes and tried to relax. Haamar was a peaceful man. He had never hurt anyone. But on the flight back home, Haamar could not stop daydreaming of shooting the angular face of Yuyenda's killer.

It's all fantasy, he told himself. But the daydream ran endlessly across his mind and always ended with Haamar being mortally wounded. As he imagined his death, he also imagined Yuyenda's ghost greeting him as he crossed to the other side.

Yet the rational part of his mind clung to the belief that the gun was just insurance. He couldn't shoot a man, could he?

The thought tickled his mind as the aircraft soared over the barren landscape, darting toward the horizon and the towering peak of Mount Kiskadare.

No. He wanted justice. Justice for Yuyenda. Nothing more.

But in the quiet space between reason and romance, Haamar could not stop daydreaming about blood.

"Henry."

"Haamar! How are you? You look great. Thank you for coming at such short notice. Please, please sit down."

"Thank you."

Henry Gustoff sat down in his plush chair, the deep rich mahogany desk a protective barrier before him. Haamar sat opposite him in one of the two black, leather arm chairs.

Haamar wore an ivory colored, linen, two-buttoned suit, a light blue dress shirt that was un-tucked, and an open collar. His shoes were sparkling brown leather with a pointed toe. A single, brass buckle took the place of shoelaces. Silver, rectangular cufflinks and the edge of a watch were just visible on his left arm; the sleeves of his suit jacket were pulled slightly back.

Haamar sat for a quiet moment. He felt like he had gained a sharper edge, but he was not looking forward to this discussion.

"Haamar, are you sure you are all right? Forgive me," Henry added, "but you seem a little tense. Have you gotten any sleep? You have dark hollows under your eyes. Would you like something to drink, maybe? Some water perhaps?"

"No thank you, Henry. I guess I am a little tense," he conceded. "It's been a tough time."

The two men sat in silence for a moment. Henry glanced back and forth between Haamar and the cheerful photos of his family that sat upon his desk.

"I'm really sorry, Haamar," Henry said sadly, uncomfortably. "I wanted to see you earlier," he added, "but I have been very busy. There are contracts to write, negotiations to hold, and plans to be implemented. It has all been very fracturing. I wish there was something more I could do. I just …"

"I know, and believe me, I appreciate all you have done for me, Henry. I never did thank you properly for all the time and energy you spent at the hospital after ... well, you know."

"I am doing better, though." Haamar smiled. "Truly. I've got the house cleaned out—mostly—and put some things in storage. Doctor Andrews says I'm physically recovered, but she does worry about my mental state."

"And?"

"Not to worry, Henry." Haamar laughed softly and sat back into his chair. "I'm as fine as I expect one can be. But ... well ... Henry ..."

"What's on your mind, Haamar?"

"I know you asked me here to discuss something important, Henry. But I just have to talk to you about something. Do you mind?"

"That's okay, Haamar. My business can wait just a few minutes more. What is it?"

"The night before Yuyenda was ... The night before Yuyenda was murdered, she took a vid-call from the DMP."

"And?"

"We were going to call you the next day, Henry. Only ... well, anyway, the DMP officer said that Zintas Mines had put out a missing persons report on both of us and that this report came from you. Did you report us missing, Henry?"

Henry sat for a quiet few seconds.

"I don't recall having filed a missing persons report, Haamar. Maybe someone in HR was using my name," he suggested. "Maybe such notifications have somehow made it into company policy or something. But I don't know why anyone would have called the DMP. We all knew where you and Yuyenda were going. But I can call Jill and ask her."

"So you didn't file a report?"

"No. Why do you ask?" Henry began rearranging the items on his desk.

"I was remembering," Haamar explained. "Yuyenda and I were going to call you in the morning—you know? On that day. Did I say that already? I guess I did. Well, maybe it wasn't the DMP, after all, that called. That's what I've been thinking. Maybe ... please don't prejudge this, Henry. Maybe someone in Syrch Corporation ordered ... you know ... a hit."

"A hit?" Henry's voice was small. "You mean ... You mean a murder? You think someone in Syrch Corp ordered your wife's murder?"

"Not just hers but mine too."

"That is a pretty serious charge, Haamar. What makes you think that?"

Haamar looked off through the office's windows for a moment. "Nothing else makes sense, Henry. And ever since Zintas and Militan got involved with Syrch—you know things have changed. Syrch uses heavy-handed tactics, Henry. They strip whole planets bare. It is all in the name of profits too. You know that. Hell, everyone knows that. They are ruthless.

"No, wait, Henry. Listen to me."

Henry leaned carefully back and put down the stone drink coaster he had been experimentally shifting around the desk's surface.

"Seriously, Henry. You know I have a large financial stake in the moissanite. It doesn't mean that much to me, but that is a potential fortune in profits that Syrch may very well want back. And with Yuyenda and me gone? It would go straight back to them."

"Then there is the note."

"Note? What note?"

Haamar fished into his pocket and took out the little note that he had found in his home. He unfolded it. "It is not over," he read it out loud.

"What isn't over?" Henry asked.

"It's a warning, Henry. Someone slipped this into my house to warn me."

"Warn you? Warn you about what? Syrch Corp? Does it say anything else?"

"No," Haamar admitted.

"Then you are extrapolating."

Haamar looked at the tiny slip of paper absently and then carefully folded it and put it back in his suit pocket.

"Haamar," Henry started, his voice soft, "let's think about this. You think Syrch murdered your wife, right? But that would mean that Militan was in on it too, and as far as I know, they've never done anything along those lines. I just can't believe Militan would do something like that—or Zintas Mines for that matter."

"I find that hard to believe too, Henry. But there would be no reason for Syrch to tell Militan. No reason at all," Haamar emphasized. "They would want to keep it quiet.

"I've thought about this for a long time, Henry. Telakia is a Militan Corporate world, but they don't have the type of clout needed to conduct murder. They couldn't pull enough strings, and someone would talk. And if Militan was involved, and that were discovered, the whole planet would turn on them. It would be a mess.

"No," Haamar said. "Militan couldn't take the risk. But one of the big three? And it's Syrch, Henry. Not Terra or Lin, but Syrch! The more I think about it, Henry, the more I ask, why not? Why wouldn't they? And I can't find a good answer."

"Haamar."

"And even if Militan Corp found out," Haamar added with a flourish of his hand, "I bet Militan executives wouldn't complain. No. They would happily claim my finder's percentage. I doubt Militan would even press for a deep investigation." Haamar felt sick. A great weight rested on his heart. "And the police don't seem to be doing a very robust job either, Henry. The only reason anyone has done anything is because you seem to be pushing it."

Henry stood up and came around the desk. He rested against the desk's edge and looked Haamar in the eyes. "I just don't see Syrch

Corp doing that, Haamar. I grant that Syrch may have something to gain, but you were already getting lots of press. It would be extremely risky, I think, for them to do something so blatant. And on Telakia? It's not one of their home worlds. Sure they have influence here, but, Haamar, seriously." He took a deep breath. "Have you … have you talked to anyone else about this idea of yours?"

"No," Haamar sighed, "not yet. I wanted to get your feedback first."

"Gods and planets, Haamar." Henry ran his hand through his hair. "I am not sure what to say. Anything is possible, I suppose. But murder? Syrch makes tons of money, and your finder's fee may be a lot for you and me, but for one of the big three? It must be a drop in the proverbial bucket. You think they'd risk it when they already have Militan and Zintas in their pocket and a nice spike in profits and material?"

"Henry," Haamar responded, "do you think Yuyenda was killed for a few credits and some cheap jewelry? Come on!" Haamar had to forcibly lower his voice. "It can't be a coincidence. I just don't buy it."

The two men remained silent for a moment, Henry leaning on the desk with one hand across his chest and the other cupping his chin, and Haamar looking wistfully out of the large bay windows.

Henry sighed. "I'll tell you what, Haamar. Before you go off and spin everybody up, let me snoop around some. Maybe I can turn something up. If they did this, there would have to be some type of record, right? At least some type of money exchange or something?"

"I suppose." A deep resonance filled Haamar's voice. "We've been friends a long time, Henry. Don't you think …" Haamar said, "there is more going on here than is observable on the surface? And you know something, Henry. I think you already have seen something that indicates Syrch or Militan, or both, are up to no good." Haamar sat forward toward Henry. "We've been friends a long time, Henry. Tell me if you know anything."

Henry's mouth twitched. "I … think," he began slowly, "that you have been through a lot. More than most people. And … I think that I am your friend, Haamar. I am Yuyenda's friend as well. If I had any reason to suspect anyone, I would have gone straight to the authorities. I know that you are hurting, Haamar, but now is the time to hold on to your friends, not obliquely accuse them. Frankly, I'm shocked and disappointed, Haamar. But I understand, I think.

"It's a nightmare. And you want answers. I can't explain the note, and I admit that is a bit odd. But maybe there is no sense in Yuyenda's death, Haamar. Did you consider that? Did you? Maybe this is just what it appears to be, a random criminal act. A horrid act. But not one that has anything to do with anything else."

Haamar ducked his head and stared at the floor. "Perhaps you are right, Henry. But ... why now? Why did it happen now? And then there is the strange phone call that Yuyenda took. It all seems to point to something else. And why are you acting so uncomfortable and strange, Henry? You haven't been the same since I got back, and you always seem to be walking on eggshells."

Henry smiled sadly. "I was nervous," he admitted. "That's all. I don't know what to say or do. Yuyenda's death didn't just affect you, Haamar. We were all impacted by it. I don't know what to say to make it better. I don't know anyone who has been murdered before."

Henry had moved closer and put a comforting hand on Haamar's shoulder.

"Maybe. But I have to know," Haamar said softly. It was so soft that Henry was not sure he had heard him.

"What was that?"

"I have to know that it wasn't anything more, Henry. I have to know that she wasn't murdered because of those damn rocks. And I intend to find out."

"How? How are you going to find anything out?" Henry withdrew his hand.

"I was thinking of hiring an off-world private investigation service, Henry. You know? Maybe someone aligned with Terra Corp? I'm sure they wouldn't mind digging up some dirt on the competition."

Henry staggered back, and the blood drained from his face.

"That sounds both extreme and dangerous," Henry managed. "Look, I know you are upset, and you have every right to be. But mull this over for a while longer before you do anything. Let me ask around on the QT. I'll put some pressure on the police and get them to give us a briefing on the status of the case. Let's see what that turns up before you start pissing off a major corporation like Syrch, Haamar." Henry wiped his forehead. "Don't be rash. Just stop for a moment and take it a little slowly. Please."

Haamar put his head in his hands and for a moment stared at the top of his knees.

"All right, Henry. I'll wait a bit and see what you can turn up."

"Thanks for waiting to see me before you did anything, Haamar. I appreciate your trust," Henry said as he moved back behind his desk and sat down heavily. He looked absently at a sheet of paper sitting on his desk.

Henry's videophone rang, and Henry jumped.

"Scared the dickens out of me," Henry laughed. "It's a private call. Do you mind?"

"No. No. Go ahead." Haamar stood up and walked to the back of the office where Henry kept a stock of cold drinks. He poured himself some water and waited patiently.

"Yes. Yes. I see. No," Henry was saying. He had a phone set held up to his ear. "I don't think that will be necessary. Why ... why, yes. Yes. I think that is an excellent idea. Yes. Right away. And you have arranged it already? Good. That is fantastic." His voice flooded with relief. "I do appreciate the situation and your faith. Of course, lunch next week? That would be fine. Thank you. Thank you very much." Henry disconnected the call.

"I am sorry for the interruption," Henry said.

Haamar walked back to the chair and settled in once again, a glass of water and ice held in his hand.

"Haamar," Henry said seriously, "I want you to meet someone. He works in the security department and is a really good man. I wouldn't know where to begin looking into your fears, but he would. I trust him."

"Do you think that is wise?"

"I'm not an investigator, Henry. I don't even have an idea of how to go about looking into it. He will know. Mind if I call him?"

"You may not know this, Haamar," Henry said as he picked up a pen and twirled it nervously between his fingers, "but Militan is pretty hot on this whole thing. They want to find this person as much as Zintas and you do. Militan wants to set an example. You know," Henry paused, "it is odd. That is why I asked you for this meeting. I wanted you to talk to the security guy. I was going to have him put some pressure on the police—you know, push them along some. I thought it would be better if he had a chance to hear the story directly from you. Can I bring him in?"

Haamar shrugged. "Sure, Henry. Why not? If you think it will help."

"Great. Hold on. Margery?" Henry pressed the intercom and called his secretary.

"Yes, Mr. Gustoff?"

"Please send in Mr. Harlamor. Mr. Ransan will see him now."

"Yes, sir. I will let him know."

"So," Henry said, "have you decided if you are still going to Earth? It might be nice to get away for a little while."

"I haven't really thought about it, Henry."

"Go see the sights. I took my family there once, a long time ago. We were in the old world—as they call it—Europe. It was very mild and very pleasant. It might do you a world of good."

"It might."

"I have half a mind to go back to Earth myself. There is this zoo in Japan where they have wooly mammoths. Do you know what they are?"

"No. Japan?"

"It was an industrial island nation. It is not in Europe. It's—that doesn't matter. They managed to clone some mammoths, an extinct species—kind of a huge, hairy rat. I don't know the details on how they did it, but now they have quite a group of them, I'm told. I think it would be neat to see an extinct species come back to life. Don't you? It's believed humans drove the mammoth to extinction through extensive hunting, but …"

The office door slid open, and a tall, dark man entered the room. His face was chiseled. He wore a tight, black leather jacket and deep blue dress pants. Haamar froze in his chair. He had seen that face before. It was the face he saw every night as he relived the death of his wife. He gasped.

"Henry, run!" Haamar shouted. Haamar was up and running toward the back of the room. He had no conscious memory of moving, but he quickly found himself hugging the far wall. There was no exit there. He turned.

Henry was standing behind the desk, his face a mask of regret.

Haamar and Henry exchanged eye contact, and in that moment, Haamar understood. It was plainly written on the executive's face.

"My God, Henry!" Haamar's desperate voice was an accusation.

Haamar frantically fumbled for the small gun he had in his pocket, but his hands had lost their agility. He looked up and saw the other man, the murderer, advance two steps in the room. The door closed. The man held a pistol of some type in his right hand. It had a straight barrel with a bulb on the end of it. The man fired, calmly, deliberately, and Haamar felt the impact of the first round in his right shoulder. The second round took him in the belly, and the third in his right thigh. As if in liquid time, Haamar felt his body folding under him. His mind was not clear. He realized he had finally pulled his pistol from his pocket, but instead of aiming it at the man shooting at him, Haamar found his wavering arm extended with the gun pointed toward Henry. But Haamar could not steady his arm. His body was not his own. Haamar tumbled forward to the floor.

Paul Thorne, aka Paul Harlamor, quickly crossed the room and kicked the extended weapon out of the dying man's hands. Haamar turned stricken eyes up to him. Haamar struggled to breathe. Henry Gustoff had not moved.

"You got away from me once, Mr. Ransan," Paul said politely. "I won't make that mistake again."

"Yuyenda ..." Haamar's voice was feeble and desperate.

Paul paused. "Do you believe in God, Mr. Ransan?" he asked.

Haamar looked at the assassin through teary, drooping eyes. "Yuyenda."

"Yes, Mr. Ransan," Paul said. "That's better. Hold onto her a while longer. Think of her. It won't be long now."

Haamar turned inward. He saw Yuyenda as he had seen her on the very first day they had met. The sun caught her delicate features in the early afternoon. She turned toward the sound of his voice as he put his book down and stood up to introduce himself. She was beautiful. As she turned, her dark hair flowed, and she brushed it nonchalantly back and smiled. Her eyes sparkled, and warmth blossomed across her face.

"Yuyenda. Yuyenda," he weakly called. She was so beautiful. Haamar felt so lucky.

Paul Harlamor shot the geologist once in the center of the head. Haamar's skull exploded behind him, and a red spray of blood spat upon the back wall. For good measures, and just to be doubly sure, Paul shot Haamar two final times in both sides of his chest. He then turned to Henry Gustoff.

"Oh, Gods," Henry said as he slid into his desk chair. "I didn't think you were going to do it here." His voice was shaking. He glanced at the photos of his wife and children.

Paul sat down in the seat recently vacated by Haamar. He crossed his legs and rested his weapon across one knee. "It's a messy thing, ending a life, Mr. Gustoff. But I had to tie up loose ends."

"But here? In my office!" Henry's voice surged in anger.

"Why not? Is there a better place to die?"

"Damn it, man! He was a ... a ..."

"What?" Nasty sarcasm suddenly filled Paul's voice. "Was he a friend of yours?"

Henry forgot to breathe. "Yes. He was a friend of mine. What have I done?" He put his head in his hands and shook. "It was necessary. Wasn't it?"

"Necessary?" Paul replied. "Necessary, yes." He wiped his nose with his free hand and looked hard at Henry. "Yes. It was. I am glad you see it that way. Sometimes unpleasant things are … necessary."

Henry looked at Paul quizzically. There was something in the enforcer's voice.

Paul fired his weapon. The first round caught Henry Gustoff in the forehead. The back of Henry's chair was a sudden crimson, and his body listed forward, a look of surprise etched upon Henry's face. Paul stood up and put two more rounds in Henry's body. It took some effort not to continue shooting the despicable man. But Paul was a professional. He stopped.

Pressing a button on his watch, Paul sent a coded message back to Tonya Livingston, CEO of Militan Corporation. It told her the job was done. There were no loose ends. *Well*, he thought, *almost none.*

This was the moment he dreaded. Two ends tied but one left open—him. He was the only thread left, and it was not beyond his employer to have hired someone to kill Paul as soon as he stepped out the door. So Paul approached the door with a wary stride and stood to one side as it opened, his weapon held at the ready. The body of Henry's strangled secretary was already cooling on the floor in the outer room. Another loose end. Life was full of them. But there was no one else around.

Paul was always careful. He was bound to Militan. He had been for a while, having come in as an independent operator a few years back. He had consciously built up a reputation of a man to be trusted, a man who would die before divulging any secrets. So far he had earned Livingston's trust. The CEO had never found anything in all her snooping that tied Paul or Militan Corp back to any of the jobs he had been commissioned to do. That was his saving grace. It had kept him alive up until now. But with the press and the amount of cash on the line ... Well, Paul held no delusions. So he slipped his weapon into his pocket but kept his hand on it as he cautiously made his way to the nearest stairwell. A few minutes later, he was out of the building and on his way.

The sun was shining, and he needed a stiff drink.

Tyena Totske rocked silently in the wooden rocker. Sleeping in her arms, wrapped protectively in a soft pink blanket, a baby slumbered. Ona. They had named her Ona Yuyenda Ransan. The peaceful child was one of the wealthiest people in the universe. Born from an egg harvested from her dead mother and a genetically-infused sperm donated by her father, the girl wiggled as she nestled closer to Tyena's breast. Oh, they had to splice in a few gene modifications, but the child was 90 percent Yuyenda's and Haamar's. It had been Haamar's way of trying to hold on to a part of the wife he loved so dearly. Now Ona was the sole heir to her dead parents' fortune.

"Are you all right?" the gruff voice came from a dangerous man. Tyena was glad to have the former enforcer for the Gianolla crime family, Dashiell Thompson. For some reason, he had offered his services to protect Ona. He said he owed a debt to Haamar.

Tyena had not asked.

And Thompson had been good to his word. They were safe. They were protected.

"Yes, thank you," she answered.

As Tyena rocked the dark-haired baby, her heart beat heavily in her chest. Tyena would give all of the money away just so Yuyenda and Haamar could see their child. But Tyena knew Ona would never be alone. Yuyenda and Haamar would have found comfort in that. Tyena loved the child and would try her best to live up to Haamar's wishes. He had spelled them out in a newly minted will and testament. Tears formed at the corner of her eyes.

It was not fair. How could life be so unfair?

The sun shown through the window and bathed the two of them in its light. Feeling the heat of the sun, the child opened her eyes. They were sky blue.

Outside, the wide expanse of the Memphis Mountains spread forth in all their glory under the alien sky. In the distance, the great depths of the Telakian desert pulsed to the beat of eternal winds. Much nearer, on the paths and crags of the mountains, tall, genetically modified pine and spruce trees shimmered in the breeze as far, far above, starships moved with tiny purpose in a boundless universe.

A SEASON FOR KILLING

The First Resource War, as it is now called, fought primarily between the Chinese and what would become the North American Union, was brutal and ushered in 138 years of conflict. It was only after Earth Twilight and the invention of Gravity Well Generators in 2175 that the resources of the Sole system alleviated the crisis and gave humankind its first outposts on the moon and Mars. Yet the terrible years of the war, the stark privations and suffering, also had an empowering effect upon humanity. The aforementioned Gravity Well Generators that allowed for transport of material into earth orbit, a heretofore financially infeasible obstacle, are perhaps the best-known instance of technological innovation during the time of the two resource wars. What is not well known is that the First Resource War led to a discovery that would forever change humanity's place in the universe.

Mistakenly ascribed to Lachi Bhuta—who theorized that massed objects could be moved over large distances through taking advantage of naturally occurring folds in the fabric of space—Lachi Bhuta did not invent the Insanity Crystal. The inventor of the Insanity Crystal grew up in what was the United States before Lachi

Bhuta was born, during the blood-washed years of the First Resource War. Though never recognizing the value of the little crystal she invented as part of her master's thesis at the newly constituted University of Antarctica, the accomplishment, coupled to Lachi Bhuta's theoretical work on the nature of space, enabled Er Qin, the founder of Lin Corporation, to invent the first frame drive in 2215.

The most curious thing about the inventor of the Insanity Crystal is that she almost never had the opportunity to make her discovery. These were desperate times, and everything, humanity's very survival, hung in the balance.

—Professor Albinus Frej Boyson, *Crisis Point: Humanity's Brush with Extinction*

THERE WAS something different in the sky. A streak of soft velvet-red cloud, backlit against a deepening night, portended something new and dangerous. When Jordan looked at the meandering clouds, she felt a dead chill and deep foreboding. The wind blew gently yet cold from the north, and even that seemed to spread a bone-aching dread. It was all wrong. *They should have been here by now,* she thought. She brushed a lock of brown hair behind her ear and headed back toward her apartment. The apartment stood in what had been a nicer area of the city, but that was before the war and the bombings. Now the streets were strewn with a jumble of rubble, scorch marks, and jagged scars.

There had been nothing substantial to eat for a while. What she wouldn't give for a pizza—a real pizza with thick, chewy crust and gobs of cheese! She shouldn't think of it, Jordan knew. Thinking of what used to be just made her hungry. Hungry and sad. She looked over her shoulder again, hoping to see the small airplane flying just above the building line. The buildings toward the center of the city were pockmarked with holes and broken glass. The taller buildings had been some of the first hit by cruise missiles and what her father had called low-level orbital ordinance. Those had been the horrible days: the noise like thunder, the blinding lights, the ground shaking, and the air filled with a deep, choking dust that coated everyone and everything. Her friend Joetta had died the first night. Her building had been one of the first ones hit.

Jordan tried to forget. But her thoughts flittered back against her will to Joetta's last birthday party. It seemed like a century ago. They had stayed up all night and watched movies and talked. Gods, that girl could talk! Joetta had been so excited about a book that was supposed to be made into a movie. And she had been so, so funny. Jordan didn't think she had ever laughed so hard or so long. It had just been the best day—the absolute best.

Jordan felt the gravel and grime shuffle beneath her sneakers as she stepped over a small line of rubble and slipped down an alley between two husks of buildings. The shadows were long and heavy and seemed to move beside her. Normally she didn't mind this particular route back home. It was off the main drag with its lumbering citizens who moved so quietly that at times Jordan wondered if they were dead. Dead. Joetta was dead. So were Lolly and Francesca. The little annoying boy with the big eyes and runny nose—he was dead too. Mrs. Roberts and Mr. Hubbard with his cracked tooth. Those had been the bad days, Jordan told herself. This was now, and she was alive. That is what mattered. That and her dog, Sachi. They were okay. They were okay.

Where did that dog go?

Walking out of the shadows, Jordan turned west toward the setting sun and scrambled over piles of rock and debris, expertly avoiding the sharp pieces of building and protruding rods of rebar. The rebar was particularly dangerous, especially when it was dark. Jordan had seen a couple people impale themselves on the jutting shafts, and she had seen a few dead bodies hanging from their terrible grip. She walked up the center of the roadway, which had been cleared by the survivors by hand, past the old, burnt-out medical clinic and comic book store, and then left, off the road, up a small flight of steps. She entered the courtyard of the apartment complex, a group of four buildings nestled around the common play area and the now dried and dirty swimming pool. Jordan could hear a baby crying, and she thought she could hear the whimpering of some older kids. Their little community of survivors would have realized that Jordan's father and the other foraging party members had not returned. Another hungry night. Another hope dashed.

"No sign?" A gruff voice protruded into Jordan's thoughts. She jumped and looked up to where a dark figure stood unmoving in an alcove of the nearest apartment building.

"Mr. Waara? Is that you?" Jordan said. Her heart was in her chest.

"Yeah, kid," he replied. He stepped out into the meager light. He wore a long, dark coat. His left hand was in one of the pockets, and he cupped a cigarette in his right hand. He took a long draw on the cigarette, and his face was lit ruby red from the burning end of the tobacco rod. It wasn't until he shifted and the front of his coat opened momentarily that Jordan saw the small, snub-nose assault rifle tucked neatly against his body.

"I didn't see any sign of them," Jordan admitted. She looked back the way she had come. "Do you think they are okay?"

Mr. Waara shrugged. "Maybe, kid. They were going out quite a ways this time. That little executive airplane ... Well, you know."

Jordan did know. It was a Maverick Astro bizjet. It was an advanced model and ran on some type of special biofuel. That made it reliable but slow. And it meant that the normal fossil fuels that were still relatively easy to find would not work in it. The bizjet's advantage was its ability to lift and land horizontally. It did not require a runway. This had been the last planned trip of the bizjet. It had just enough fuel for one more foraging trip.

"Do you think they found anything?" Jordan asked.

"You know I hope so, kid." Mr. Waara replied. "If not, there will be a lot of hunger, and some people won't make it."

"But Mr. Andrews said it was the best bet, didn't he? And he used to be in the military, and then he worked at the dam. He should know. Shouldn't he?"

Mr. Waara looked at Jordan for a moment, took a puff of his cigarette, and said, "He would know. Andrews—he's a good guy. If he says there was a FEMA underground storage area near the dam, then it's there. It's there. It has to be." Mr. Waara turned and looked up at the third story of the building just across the quad. Jordan knew Mr. Waara was looking at his apartment where his wife and two teenaged children were getting ready for the long night.

"Will we get raided, Mr. Waara?" Jordan asked as the man turned toward a sound that shuffled from behind him. "Do you think we'll get raided?" Jordan was afraid of the raiders. Each little community in the city had reverted into defensive tribes. They protected their meager supplies and had recently started raiding each other's stores in what Jordan's father said was a final act of mad desperation. It had led to a loss of life, and now Jordan's little community posted guard.

The tough man grinned with a swagger. "Not tonight, I don't think. We gave the last group a licking two nights ago, and they'll be going after easier prey for a while. Have you packed?"

"Yes, sir."

"Good," he said. "Either way, we head out in a day or two. We can't stay here. Not any longer. The city is full of starving people. We have to get out into the country where we can forage—get into the farmland. It's a rough life. Ain't it, kid?"

Jordan heard the tenor of his voice. He was thinking of his family again. She nodded her head.

"You better get back home, Jordan. Get some sleep. It will be a long day tomorrow. If your father and the rest get back, we'll let you know. Don't worry too much about," he motioned at the night, "them. Lots could have happened. It probably got too dark, or maybe they were loading the plane or ran out of fuel and are hoofing it back. They know what they're doing."

"Okay, Mr. Waara. Will you … You be careful tonight, okay?"

The man laughed, took a drag of his cigarette, and looked out into the night. "Hey, kid," he added as Jordan started making her way to her apartment. "Keep that puppy close, understand?"

"Sachi?"

"I thought so." He smiled. "Been worried?"

Jordan nodded.

"Sachi came back a little before you did, kid."

Jordan's face lit up. "He sometimes drives me crazy!"

Mr. Waara chuckled, soft and warm. "Yep," Mr. Waara leaned closer to Jordan, "he's a good dog, but you've got good reason to worry about him. These are desperate times. And some people … well … let's just say they wouldn't mind a Sachi sandwich. Okay? Keep him close and safe."

Jordan didn't know what to say. She hadn't thought that anyone would hurt Sachi. Were they that hungry?

"Run along."

Jordan walked and then ran the rest of the way to the stairs that led to the fourth floor. She pressed hard up the stairs and was out of breath when she arrived at the closed door to the apartment. She threw the door open, and soft candlelight meandered out of the doorway into the hall. Her older cousin, Dyson, turned to look at her as Jordan rushed past him and collapsed in front of a medium-sized dog. Sachi was a Berger Picard with a mix of light brown, gray, gold, and black bedraggled fur. Stubborn as an ox and strong for his size, Sachi leapt into her arms, his tail wagging. He was glad she was home.

Jordan held Sachi tightly, and the tears she had held back came flooding out. What if her father didn't come back? What if he was dead? An ache spread out of her chest through her body, and as much as she tried to hold it in, she was soon sobbing uncontrollably.

Dyson knelt down beside Jordan and Sachi and wrapped them both in a deep hug. "It will be all right, Jordan. It will be all right."

How could Dyson say that? It wasn't all right! Joetta was dead. Her mother was lost in the war, and her father was missing. Jordan sobbed. Nothing would ever be right again.

Laura Mathis shifted uncomfortably in the command chair. How long had she been stuck in the command module flying the drone over Washington, DC? She flexed her fingers and felt the early pang of arthritis in the joints of her hands. Her eyes flicked at the radar and then back to the live video feed. She adjusted the drone's trim and moved the rudder pedals slightly with her right foot and let the drone roll toward the Atlantic. She was piloting one of the new Falcon Interceptors with its ultra advanced particle-beam weapon, the Hersh 53. The weapon had been in development when the war started. Famine in Africa had led to a mass exodus into Europe. The Europeans had pushed back, and fighting had erupted up and down the Gulf of Lyon and all along southern France, eastern Spain, and western Italy. That exodus precipitated a run on commodities as people began to panic. Inflation became hyper as, domino like, the pressure of the last few decades overflowed into sudden shortages. Governments began conserving resources that led to new shortages, and when these became critical, it resulted in new fighting. Like a flash fire, waves of violence spread out of Africa into Europe and from there to Russia and Russian Asia. But it was when the mega populated states of China and India felt dire shortages that the conventional war had begun. The international systems of trade, commerce, and financing collapsed, and soon even the closest allies found themselves at odds as the crisis deepened.

God! Her back hurt. She tried to stretch, but the latest cyber attack had meant that the drone pilots had to maintain manual control of the drone fleet. The computer hack had resulted in the ships turning their weapons on the city. It had been nearly twenty minutes before the military was able to isolate the attack and counter-punch, and another ten minutes or so before the drones had been returned to air force control.

Laura flexed her right foot anyway, slowly sending her drone into a controlled roll as it flew over Bear Island, northwest of the capital. She watched the video feed as the drone slowly rotated along its axis. She was bringing the drone back to the makeshift landing strip in Rock Creek Park. It needed fuel and some minor repairs.

Soon they would move most of the drones down south along the Texas border. Laura wondered if she would have to go too. There had been another heavy attack a few days ago. A mass of Wuhezhi, low-quality local troops impressed by the Chinese as fodder to weaken the American battle lines, had poured into Mexico City. There had been intense fighting.

The Chinese northern advance up from the Panama Canal toward Guatemala was ponderous and slow but irresistible. They had begun impressing locals into massed fighting groups, which they flung without concern at the united armies of Mexico, the United States, and Canada. Other freedom fighters comprised of refugees from South American countries still friendly with the United States fought alongside the allies too. But the Chinese armies were now strongly entrenched in South America. A juggernaut, it was only a matter of time before they arrived at the border of the United States. When that happened, Laura thought, all bets were off. President Anderson would have to use the nuclear arsenal.

And that—Laura shuddered—represented the end.

Laura did her best to stretch and watched the clock. Finally, she banked the drone toward the landing strip and began the slow descent toward the field. In the old days, she would have punched the engines and swooped for a landing, but the new antiaircraft batteries were automated, robotic. The reaction time of people had proven too long to be effective against the latest generation of unmanned attack vehicles and cruise missiles. Though the robotic defenses were more capable of defending the skies, they were still full of irritating glitches. They were programmed to fire on anything that made a rapid descent. So she looped the drone north toward Rock Creek Park, impatient but maintaining her self-control.

Easy, she thought. *Just a little more time.*

"Officer Mathis?" A shadow fell across her back and darkened her flight console.

"Yes … Hold on, please. I'm landing. Give me a second."

It took a few more minutes before Laura got the drone on the ground. She took her headset off, wiped the sweat from her forehead, and slowly stood up, feeling stiff and achy all over.

"You have a recreational, lighter-than-air and rotorcraft license. Is that correct?" It was Captain Allyn Toriksen. The captain had been a member of the civil air patrol back before the war. Before that, he had been a crew chief on a military helicopter. Captain Toriksen had joined the police force after serving eight years in the army. His background had made him an obvious choice for the newly established Civilian Defensive Force. The CDF comprised of mostly middle-aged, technically skilled citizens who could operate the mass of semi-automated defensive systems, freeing younger men and women for more active combat rolls.

"Yes, sir. I used to fly balloons and," she looked at her command station, "I'm qualified for rotary."

"We need someone to take over piloting our aeroship, *Defender One.*"

"The blimp, sir?"

Toriksen frowned. "The captain, unfortunately, had a heart attack last night. Do you know Captain Fleming? No? Good guy. Sad. Well," he shifted his weight from one leg to the other, "we need someone to take his place, and you seem to fit the bill. Interested?"

"*Defender One* … It's a huge ship."

"Class five," Captain Toriksen agreed, "almost a four-hundred-ton payload and the size of a football field. She's a real beast."

Laura knew there were six sister ships to the *Defender One.* They were spread across the forty-eight states and were a critical part of the air defenses. Slow and ponderous, they made up for their lack of speed with the incredible lift and storage capacity.

"You would help monitor our region. It's an important job, Officer Mathis. And this time, the *Defender One* will be fitted with cellular communications gear that will restore much of the region's cellular network. We'll finally reestablish communications with most of the civilians in our region."

"It's a sitting duck," Laura said softly, thinking about how easy it would be to shoot one of the slow super blimps out of the sky.

"Four fighter drones, launched right from the *Defender's* bay and a slew of auto-cannon and other defensive systems—we haven't lost one yet." Captain Toriksen sighed tiredly.

"Can I think about it a bit?" Laura asked. Her mind was a bit dull from the long shift. It was, she thought, the worst time to make a decision like this one.

"Sure," the captain replied. "Why don't you sleep on it? Give me an answer tomorrow."

Laura brushed her hair out of her eyes. Her bangs were longer than she liked them, but it was so hard to find a decent hairdresser nowadays. She smiled in response.

"Great," Captain Toriksen said. "Get some rest, Officer Mathis. The *Defender One* will be on the ground tonight for refitting, supplies, and crew change. If you decide to take the job, just come to the Army-Navy Country Club in the morning. That is where she'll be resting. It'll leave at eleven sharp."

"Yeah, okay." She yawned. "Is that all?"

"Yep. See you in the morning?"

Laura laughed. "Probably," she admitted. "Let's at least pretend I am going to think about it."

"Goodnight, Officer."

"Goodnight, sir."

Laura took her leave, her feet clanking down the metal stairway of the underground bunker as she headed toward the showers. She had wanted to get into the air again, flying for real instead of spending her days piloting drones from deep inside the damp and stale command base. But a super blimp? Was she even qualified? Her mind was too numb to think about it. She needed some food and sleep. Laura pushed the offer to the back of her mind and trundled into the locker room. Soon, showered and dressed, she meandered to the cafeteria for a quick feed before making her way to her tiny room, setting the alarm, and falling into an exhausted sleep.

Laura dreamt of a clear sky and soft clouds turning slowly in the dying light of a red sunset. Far below, smoke billowed from a thousand buildings as the capital burned.

Jordan pushed Sachi's wet nose away from her face. The dog was whining.

"Leave me be," Jordan said, shoving the dog away. But Sachi was insistent and began tugging on her arm and yapping softly.

"What is it?" Jordan snapped. And then the smell of smoke registered in her sleepy mind. She darted awake.

"Sachi? Dyson!" she cried.

There was a thin layer of smoke in her bedroom. Jordan sat up and brushed her brown hair away from her face. Sachi had jumped into her bed and was trying to nervously lick her.

"I got it. I'm up. What's going on?" Jordan quickly pulled on a pair of jeans and slipped into her sneakers. Outside she heard a burst of gunfire.

"Come on, Sachi!" she called as she darted to her doorway, grabbing her emergency backpack and slinging it over her shoulder. She knelt down and began fastening Sachi's backpack on too. While she fumbled the dog's backpack into place, Jordan called to her cousin, "Dyson? Dyson!"

There was more shooting outside. This time the weapons fire rose sharply and thrummed heavily. Keeping away from the windows as best as she could, Jordan scooted across the living room. Her Marlin 336XLR was by the apartment door. It was an older, lever-action rifle, but her father said it was tough and reliable. She reached up for it, pulling it from the wall mount, and tucked it under her right arm, cycling the action to put a round into the chamber. Flinging the sling over her head, she pulled Sachi close and whispered in his ears.

"We're going to be okay, boy. We have to get out of here. The smoke is getting worse. I wonder," she added in frustration, "where Dyson went. His pack is still here."

Jordan took a deep breath and tried to remember the evacuation plan. But her mind was full of fog. It was difficult to focus. Kneeling, holding her rifle pointed generally to her front, she turned the handle of the apartment door and slowly cracked it open. Peeking out, the hallway was dark and empty. A thickening layer of smoke twirled above her on the ceiling. The smoke moved and twisted as if it were alive. A thinner layer of smoke hung throughout the hall. Jordan knew they didn't have much time.

Crouching, she said, "Come on, Sachi," and began a low shuffle toward the stairwell. As she moved, she pounded on closed doors and called out to her neighbors about the fire, but nobody answered her calls. Torn between staying in the smoke-filled hallway and finding the stairwell, she stopped and turned back.

"Fire!" she yelled as loudly as she could. Taking a deep breath to yell again, Jordan suddenly gagged as smoke poured into her lungs, thick and roiling. She fell to her knees, coughing horribly, her eyes watering and half-blind. Jordan took a desperate breath of air from lower to the floor. Sachi was tugging on her arm and whining. Jordan fell backward and slowly rolled over to her hands and knees. Her lungs were burning. Looking up, Jordan found Sachi's eyes level with hers. The dog licked her and made a darting motion toward the stairs. Sachi went a few feet ahead and then came back to Jordan and licked her again.

Jordan tried to say something, but the words caught, and she coughed chokingly. Instead, Jordan crawled along on her hands and knees toward the stairwell. Sachi bounded back and forth before her, leading Jordan down the hall. When they finally reached the fire door, Jordan felt upward for the door release and gave it a good shove. The door opened with a rush of cooler and fresher air. Jordan tumbled into the stairwell, Sachi already moving ahead and down toward the exit. When Sachi arrived at the next landing, the dog barked several times. Jordan took a few deep breaths and then pulled herself to her feet using the banister. Moving slowly, Jordan took a tentative step and then another as she followed Sachi down into the darkness.

By the time she reached the ground floor, Jordan's mind had begun working again. The air in the stairwell smelled of smoke and ash, but it was clear and easy to breathe. Standing before the door that led to the outside, Jordan knelt and put a protective, restraining hand on Sachi.

"Quiet now, boy," she warned.

She tightened her grip on Sachi and slowly pushed the door open. She could hear people calling and the sharp report and counter-report of gunfire. Light—yellow, orange, and white—flickered against the ground, creating elongated shadows that danced ominously. But the way seemed clear.

"The bridge, Sachi," she said. "We're going to the bridge."

Jordan could see the corner of the nearest building. She knew if she could put the building between herself and the center of the quad, she could slip, unseen, into a slope in the ground that was lined by an old chain-link fence. She could follow the fence into the park near the creek.

Follow the creek, she thought, *and that will lead to the bridge.*

"Come on," she whispered. And with that, she stood up and trotted toward the next building, looking around desperately for raiders or, hopefully, for friends from her community.

Jordan ducked behind the corner of the building and stopped to peer back toward the center of the quad. Shadows of men moved chaotically here and there. The lower floor of her building was burning, and occasional gunfire erupted from the rooftops of several of the apartments. The raiders returned fire, but they seemed more interested in looting than in fighting. Many of the shadows dashed out of the quad, their arms loaded with plunder. Jordan watched for a few moments, hoping to see a friendly face materialize out of the night. Instead she saw what she thought was a body lying facedown by one of the bushes that hemmed in the playground. An arm was outstretched to the body's side. Jordan thought she saw the remnants of a burning cigarette clutched in the corpse's hand.

Just then a group of men walked into the firelight, their weapons and bodies silhouetted against the buildings. One of them pointed upward. His companions fired a few rounds at the indicated location. The men began to talk, but Jordan could not understand them. It became obvious to her that the man who had pointed was the leader as he barked some type of orders and the others moved off to obey.

Before Jordan realized what she was doing, she raised her rifle to her shoulder and placed the darkened sight against the center of the silhouetted leader. A calm determination overcame her, and her breathing slowed, deepened, but she could not pull the trigger. The smell of burning wood assailed her nose. She lowered her rifle.

I'm sorry, Mr. Waara. I am sorry I couldn't help you.

Jordan ducked behind the building and ran toward the chain-linked fence and the walking path. Sachi led the way, a bundle of energy scouting ahead as behind them shouting echoed, smoke rolled, and the only home Jordan had ever known seemed to scream as it burned.

Dyson, where are you?

Jordan hit the shadowed path and ran. Her backpack jumped and rumbled against her shoulders. Trees in the park that followed the stream swayed in the breeze, their leaves fluttering like the voices of the dead.

Dyson. Daddy, Jordan thought desperately. *Where are you?*

Sachi moved. Jordan shifted, feeling the hard ground beneath her, the sound of the running stream bubbling nearby. Jordan moved closer to her dog, the chill of the early morning and dampness of dew making her shiver. Sachi, as if sensing her need, huddled closer, half-draping himself against Jordan.

The night after fleeing the fire was a blur of dark shadows. Jordan had run along the walking path through the park, under the tall trees and their evil whispers, through a city injured and torn. Jordan was not sure how long she had wandered, half-dazed, fearful of being followed. Each night-sound had sent tendrils of panic through her until finally, exhausted, she had crawled up a small embankment and nestled down beneath a huddle of bushes. Hidden from the ghosts that chased her, she had held Sachi and wept until falling suddenly into an empty sleep. Now, groggy and staring at a day turned pale, she held Sachi for his warmth and tried to collect herself.

Had she walked past the bridge? The thought was disturbing. The evacuation plan was for everyone to meet up beneath the bridge at the far side of the park. But she couldn't recall having seen it. Dyson had walked her to the site during the daylight, but at night the world took on a strange aspect that confused and left Jordan feeling lost and desperate. What would she do now? Should she go back?

Jordan sat up and looked around her. She was beneath the arching branches of a bright-colored row of bushes and trees. A few feet from rich grass that was sprinkled with yellow wildflowers, Jordan could see the tops of various trees running off to the north and east. The sound of running water floated on the breeze to the accompanying chirping and twirling of birds greeting the day. Barely visible between the trees were houses of red brick. They were the smaller types of houses found at the edge of the city and near suburbs.

Jordan found it strangely silent. She stood up and stretched. Sachi slunk out of their sleeping place, bending his two front feet down and arching his back upward before shaking vigorously. He yawned and spent a few seconds licking and chewing his right rear leg, then sat on his haunches, looking at Jordan expectantly.

"Come on, Sachi," Jordan said, slinging her backpack onto her shoulders and turning toward the sound of the water. She picked up her rifle and held it loosely in her right hand. "Let's get a drink and figure out what to do."

Jordan pushed in through the foliage and was soon standing on the shallow, sandy shore of a narrow creek that followed the tree lines north and east. She sat next to the water and fumbled through her backpack, looking for her water purifier.

"Sachi, don't," she said as the dog began to lap at the water. "Just wait a minute." But the dog ignored her protestations and continued to lap at the water.

"Okay, but don't blame me if you get sick."

Jordan found the cylindrical device she had been seeking and spent a few minutes plugging the intake and output hoses into their correct slots, unwrapping the carbon filter, and arranging her water bladder in such a way that it would not spill filtered water over the ground. When Jordan's father had showed her how to use the filter, she had thought it was fun. But she realized now, pumping the small handle to force water from the intake hose through the filtering system, how difficult it would be to fill up her entire water bladder. Her arm was soon tired. She decided to stop, rest a bit, and eat a little breakfast.

She called Sachi, who plodded over and nuzzled her.

"Hungry, boy?" She had forgotten to take Sachi's pack off of the dog the night before. She reached beneath his belly and unhooked the strap and removed the pack. "Feel better, Sachi? You've got some food in here. Not much though," she warned. "Dad said it was a little over sixty miles to the dam. An hour in a car, but he said it might take as much as six or seven days to reach it on foot. And," she looked at the bag of dried kibble she pulled from Sachi's pack, "we don't have a whole lot."

There was a cloth bowl in Sachi's pack too. Jordan unpacked it, opened it, and put about a cup of dried food into the bowl. She then rummaged through her pack and found a little dried beef jerky and trail mix. She gave Sachi some jerky and ate a few handfuls of the trail mix and two pieces of jerky. Sachi crunched his kibble and then lay down next to Jordan as she repacked everything. Jordan pulled a clear plastic bag from the top zippered compartment of her backpack and took her father's hand-drawn map out and unfolded it.

"Dad said to follow the second eastern fork," Jordan considered aloud, though Sachi seemed unimpressed. "But is this the second fork or should we go further upstream? It doesn't look wide enough to be the fork he was talking about. Do you know, boy? No. Um … you're no help, are you?" She scratched Sachi behind the ear.

"Well, the rest of the group will follow the stream too. Maybe they are still coming up this way." Jordan looked back in the direction they had come, hoping to see some sign of the rest of her little community. "Wait for them? We can meet them here, or," she pointed at the map with a small twig at a junction of roadway and the stream that was off to the east, "we can meet them here at the next rendezvous point. It's a couple miles from here. Then we go up here, boy, toward the open farmland until we find this little river. Dad said the river leads to the dam—like a highway. Do you think Dad is waiting there for us? That would make sense. He knew we were moving out in a couple of days, and maybe, maybe it would have been too hard to bring supplies back to the apartment. Maybe he is getting our camp near the dam put together. What do you think, Sachi?"

Sachi looked at her and tilted his head to the left and back to the right as if he were trying to puzzle out what Jordan had been saying.

"If this is the branch we want," Jordan continued, "then we must have walked right under the bridge last night and just missed it. Can you miss a bridge? I wish Dyson were here," she said, exasperated. "He would know."

Jordan sat quietly for a few moments. A low embankment followed the split of the stream to the north and east, rising between four and six feet above where Jordan and Sachi sat. She could not see what was beyond the little ridge, but it looked as if the trees might thin out on the higher piece of land.

"Come on, Sachi. Let's go take a look over there and see what we can see. Then we will decide."

Jordan stood up, shoved the map back into her pack, and, leaving the backpacks behind but taking her rifle, she and Sachi splashed across the stream and up the small embankment. It took her a couple of minutes to find a place where she could scramble up the side. Standing on the embankment's edge, she looked back down at their two packs and cursed in her head. She should have hidden them before climbing up the embankment. She stood still for a moment looking at the trees, the apparently empty houses that were tucked here and there, and listened. The day sounded peaceful.

"Come on, Sachi. They'll be fine for a little bit. It doesn't look too far to the edge of the tree line."

Jordan led off through the brush. Sachi soon overtook her and darted ahead. The dog stayed within sight as Jordan stepped on sticks that cracked and broke with every other step.

So much for moving quietly, she thought.

Jordan slowed down and tried her best to sneak forward. People were not as friendly as they had once been. She didn't want to stumble into someone dangerous.

"Sachi!" she whispered loudly as the dog suddenly disappeared beyond the tree line. "Sachi!" But the dog did not turn back.

Hurrying a little, Jordan came to the edge and knelt down by a large tree of some type, peering out into a sports complex. There were bleachers arranged around an oblong running track that surrounded a soccer field. A small outbuilding on the far side and a few wooden pavilions with picnic tables complemented the field. The area was overgrown with lush grass.

She looked for Sachi but couldn't see the dog. Standing, Jordan scanned the area and finally breathed a sigh of relief when she saw Sachi's tail wagging just above the top of the grass.

Jordan didn't see anything in the field. It was probably safe to wait on the embankment for the rest of her group. But she wanted to be on this side of the creek, on the high ground, where Jordan could see more clearly. She was about to call out to Sachi when she saw the dog's tail suddenly go stiff and still. Sachi's low growl carried softly across the field.

Jordan took a step into the grass. "Sachi?"

She heard her dog growl again.

"Coming, boy!" she called, darting out of the tree line. Though she could not see what the dog was growling at, she could tell that he had frozen in place.

Catching up to him, Jordan reached a hand down and pet Sachi quickly on his forward shoulder and back. "What is it?" she started. But then the words caught in her throat.

"Jesus!" She raised her rifle to her shoulder, placing the butt stock firmly into her shoulder socket. "Come on, Sachi!" She reached down with her left hand and began pulling the dog backward. "Come on! Damn you, Sachi. Let's get out of here!"

Sachi, his ears down tightly against his head, looked confused but followed Jordan.

Jordan took three or four steps backward and then turned and walked, and then ran, back to the tree line.

"Oh my God. Oh my God!" she exclaimed as she hurried into the trees. Making sure Sachi was behind her, Jordan jumped down the embankment, falling face-first onto soft earth. She bounded up and quickly splashed across the stream and threw herself down by her backpack.

"Sachi!" she snapped. The dog came to her, and she quickly strapped his pack onto his back. Capping her water bladder and stuffing it and the filter into her backpack, she added, "We're leaving."

Jordan looked to the north and shook her head. "Not that way." Turning east, she walked up a sandbar along the edge of the water, looking nervously back over her shoulder. "Come on, Sachi. Let's go."

Sachi trotted up the water and took the lead. He stopped and put his snout near the water's muddy edge and took a few deep, short breaths through his nose. Then without a look back, Sachi continued up the creek branch with Jordan trudging behind.

Jordan hurried. The field had been an immense, open-aired mass grave. The dead were tangled together in various poses and stages of decomposition. Jordan wiped her eyes and tried not to think about it. But the image of bodies, rotting in the peaceful morning air, followed her. Tears slid down her cheeks as she shouldered her pack higher on her shoulders.

Run, she thought. *Run. And never look back.*

The air was crisp, and Laura could see for miles. *Defender One* was a fine ship. Lighter than air, *Defender One* moved easily as it circled high above Washington, DC, riding the waves of wind as smoothly as any ship that sailed a peaceful ocean. At twelve thousand feet, the ship dipped in and out of clouds as they shifted in great swaths of billowing white across the sky. Six propellers, each eighteen feet in diameter, spun nearly soundlessly as *Defender One* continued to increase altitude.

The aeroship was capable of ascending to nearly sixty thousand feet where it could float in the stratosphere for months on end, monitoring the northeastern United States with its newest generation of Doppler radar, a separate laser-based radar system, and a plethora of other sensors. Commander Reiner, the overall commander of *Defender One*, had ordered Laura to take the ship to thirty thousand feet where it would begin a long, slow patrol. Laura was happy to get the ship higher, safe from small arms and shoulder-fired rockets.

The war was coming home.

Defender One was stuffed full of supplies and held a significant number of weapons and munitions. But the ship's main job was to identify incoming enemy aircraft, drones, and missiles and direct ground-based systems to engage them. Resupply was its secondary mission. *Defender One* had been ordered to refrain from directly shooting down incoming hostiles for as long as possible. Made from a thin polymer that had the tensile strength of steel, the ship was nevertheless masked from most radar. Firing *Defender One's* weapons would surely reveal the ship's location, drawing fire. And that, Laura reasoned, was something she would prefer not to happen. She knew the ship was made out of a new high-tech material, and Commander Reiner had said the ship could take a couple hits, but thirty thousand feet was a long way up. Laura did not want to be the first lighter-than-air ship to test the resilience of its hull under fire.

Laura recalled the last briefing. Commander Reiner stood stalk-still. His voice low and soft, Laura had strained to hear him. The gathered military leaders on *Defender One* sat like tombstones in a tired graveyard as the commander explained the situation. President Anderson had made a decision. The fight for Mexico City was too costly. Wuhezhi soldiers had pressed the allied forces, and if reports were to be believed, tens of thousands of allied soldiers were dead. Mexico City itself was a ruin, bombarded by air, laced with lasers; the city had burned, and civilians had died in massive waves. The president had decided not to allow the Chinese regulars to join the battle. Laredo, Del Rio, and El Paso were just some of the American cities that would meet the same fate as Mexico City if the bulk of the Chinese army pushed through. No. The president had given the order. The Chinese would be stopped in Chiapas, the southernmost region of Mexico.

While the allies could not defeat the Chinese in a one-on-one engagement, the allies could make the Chinese bleed and rethink the invasion of the New World. The general plan, Laura had been briefed, was to draw the Chinese into the Central Depression, an area in the center of the state of Chiapas, which was bordered by the Sierra Madre de Chiapas Mountains. Once the bulk of the Chinese army was located in the depression, the allies would unleash nuclear strikes in depth. It was the military's plan to destroy the bulk of the Chinese invading army as they were penned in the depression, pepper Chinese supply lines back to the Panama Canal, and use surface nuclear strikes along the main sailing routes in the Pacific Ocean between China and South America. The allies hoped to thereby destroy the Chinese Third People's Fleet as it escorted enemy ships near the North and South American continents. At the same time, the allies would cordon off the northern approaches to the North America with warships, mobile launchers, and multiple concentrations of air defensive systems. Laura and everyone else knew that the Chinese would not take nuclear strikes without a retaliatory response. That was what *Defender One* was bracing for—a desperate defense against a retaliatory nuclear strike.

But for now the sky was crisp. Laura piloted *Defender One* slowly upward in a spiral climb. Below her, farmland stretched out between networks of roads that from this high up gave the illusion of careful functionality. Laura knew, however, that much of the countryside was infested with bands of criminals and upstart potentates who were trying to carve out kingdoms from what they assumed was a failed United States. Yet the Civilian Defensive Force was on the move too. Soon the CDF would break out from its strongholds into the countryside where the CDF would reestablish federal control.

If, Laura thought, anyone on the planet survived the next seventy-two hours.

Seventy-two hours. Laura flipped a switch in the cockpit and turned a few dials. Her hands shook. *We could all be dead in seventy-two hours.*

The farmhouse looked tiny and distant in the hazy dusk of the evening. Old roof tiles, stained and cracked, clung desperately to the peaked roof. Smoke slipped out of the brick chimney, and light flickered out of one of the four windows that Jordan could see. The light wavered. Jordan thought it looked like candlelight. On the wooden porch, with its faded paint, a porch swing and rocker with tired pillows moved ever so slightly in the breeze. The movement gave the impression that ghosts were sitting on the porch, watching as the sun sank into the horizon. But it was the tantalizing aroma of food wafting through the air that caught and held Jordan spellbound.

Sachi whined.

"I know, boy. I'm hungry too."

Jordan shifted and briefly raised her body up above the long waving grass in the hopes of getting a better view of the farmhouse. There was an old beater pickup truck parked in the driveway. It was rusted red. Off to the far left, some large farm equipment sat in the overgrown grass near a chicken coup. Jordan was not sure what the machines were designed to do, but they looked old too.

Maybe the owners would be friendly. Maybe they wouldn't mind giving her just a little bit of food.

Jordan looked at Sachi. She could tell her dog wanted to run to the house but was resisting the urge, barely. Jordan reached a restraining hand out and grabbed Sachi's collar, holding tight.

"Let's watch for a little while, Sachi. Come on. I've got a little more to eat. It'll get us through tonight."

Jordan thought Sachi looked disappointed, but the dog relaxed as Jordan got out the last of his kibble and fed it to him before sharing her meager meal with the dog. The two of them nestled under a low-hanging tree at the edge of the overgrown field of grass and, watching the farmhouse and listening to the buzz of insects, began their vigil.

Jordan picked absently at Sachi's fur. The dog was matted, with brambles twisted and tightly packed within layers of his long fur. Jordan wished she had thought to pack a pair of scissors. There was no way she was going to get all the knots out. But Sachi seemed content to let her work away at the mess, occasionally licking Jordan's face. Sachi's ears flicked back and forth as he listened to the night, and if Jordan had not been so hungry and frightened, she might have enjoyed the soft evening.

A week on the move—Jordan and Sachi had crept along the creek away from the city, all the while hoping to come across Dyson or someone else from their group. Winding along the sandy creek bed, Jordan had not seen anyone. She had been grateful for the lack of contact at first. But as time crept on and her supplies dwindled, she had grown more desperate. Having slipped through a drainage pipe under a highway, she moved away from the creek and up a long, slow slope where grass moved in the sunshine's breeze. At the top of the rise, Jordan saw the deep valley beyond. It was dotted with farm fields, orderly patches, and circles where crops had once grown. Now the fields were fallow, and from where she and Sachi stood, the houses all looked distant and empty. Off to Jordan's right, she could see where the creek continued to cut a scar across the valley's floor. A growth of trees followed the creek bed, which in turn was followed by an old, dirt and gravel road. Here and there, light reflected off of small, teardrop-shaped ponds where livestock had once bathed in the heat of the day. It was picturesque and peaceful, but Jordan did not see any movement. None at all. And a flutter of concern tripped through her belly. It was as if all the life had been sucked out of the universe, and she and Sachi were the last living souls.

Jordan and Sachi had moved down into the valley and began following the dirt road where walking was easier. Since it followed the creek, there was a ready supply of water. They explored the houses they passed and occasionally found a can of fruit or beans or tuna, but for the most part, the houses were picked clean of food. Repositories of dust and old memories, the houses were forlornly cast across the countryside like ancient standing stones. The houses seemed dead and lifeless to Jordan, and if need had not forced her to search their abandoned husks, she would have avoided them.

It had been Sachi who alerted Jordan to this house. They had been walking along the dirt road, Jordan humming a tune aimlessly, when Sachi suddenly stopped. The dog's ears perked up, and his body went rigid. Jordan stopped too, trusting Sachi's higher senses of smell and hearing. She watched as the dog tilted his head to the left and right, putting his long snout high into the air and taking short, quick breaths through his nose. Sachi looked at Jordan, and she replied silently with a nod of her head. Released, the dog darted forward with Jordan trundling after.

The smell of cooking food assailed Jordan. She reached for Sachi and stopped the dog from moving closer to the farmhouse that was barely visible behind a small bump in the ground, along a northern fork in the dirt road. Caution led Jordan to pull Sachi back toward the more protective undergrowth of the creek, which they skirted until they flanked the farmhouse. Now the two of them sat in the growing gloom as night settled and muffled sounds of talking and dishes clacking together seeped out of the house into the dark.

The air was cool, and Jordan thought it might rain later. She wished she could make a fire but didn't dare. Instead she pulled out her poncho and draped it over her body as she and Sachi settled down. Above, the moon was in three quarters, its light soft as stars flickered and the long streak of the Milky Way meandered across the sky.

Caution, Jordan thought. They needed to be patient. Watch. Watch. Maybe they would find help here.

Hopeful and feeling the pull of sleep, Jordan moved closer to Sachi. She could feel the dog's warmth. She pulled her rifle to her. The night drifted along, and finally Jordan fell into a deep and blissful sleep.

Jordan awoke with a jolt. She heard a sharp blow followed by a faint cry.

"Sachi!" she whispered. Sachi had stood, and Jordan grabbed him and pulled him back down.

Jordan blinked several times and looked out across the grass. The house was bathed in a long steak of colored sunlight. A woman stood, angry and gaunt, her hand raised high, ready to strike out at a cowering little boy. The boy could not have been more than five years old. An older child, a girl of seven or eight, moved between the boy and the snarling woman.

"Pick it up!" The woman's voice was a harsh whip. "Pick it up, you dirty ... rotten ... good-for-nothing ... brat!"

"It was an accident!" The little girl's voice was frail but determined.

The woman's hand came down with a flash, full across the girl's face with a loud slap that reverberated across the ground. The girl fell, crying out.

"Mary! Mary!" the boy shouted through his own tears as he fell down on her and tried to shield her from the solid kick that followed the blow.

"You are such dirty, ungrateful brats!" the woman hissed. She pointed a long finger at a jug and a white dish that lay scattered on the ground before the porch. "Pick those up. Pick them up!"

Two older boys stepped through the doorway. They were grinning. Their eyes were wild. Tousled hair the same dark shade as the woman's framed faces that were brutal. Sharp eyes and wicked smiles. One of them lurched forward threateningly at the little boy and the girl. The boy cried out, and both of the older children laughed, unmerciful and full of glee.

"Ha! See that, David?" The older boy on the right called out. "Is wittle Woby don'in ta cry agin?" He laughed.

"Go on!" the other older boy, David, added cruelly. "You heard what Mother said. Get to work!"

The little boy, Robby, slowly got up, letting Mary rise too. Robby was shaking. Mary held a hand to her reddened face, trying unsuccessfully to choke back tears.

"David, Keith," the woman snapped, "don't you have chores to get done? Go check the traps near the cedar field." She reached out her hand and gently stroked the two of them on their heads. The woman glanced at the sky where clouds moved. She harrumphed as if satisfied. The woman looked at her two boys. "I want the traps checked before you go lollygagging around today. And bring in a stack of wood for the fire."

"Yes, Mum," the two boys answered in unison.

The boys hesitated for a moment before disappearing briefly into the farmhouse. They reappeared carrying rifles in the crooks of their arms. Robby and Mary were picking up the jug and dish. The boys walked menacingly toward the two, and at the last moment the larger of the boys, Keith, pushed Mary. Mary stumbled backward but managed to keep her feet. The boys laughed before walking off to the right, where they disappeared behind the house.

The woman sniffed loudly and faded back into the house, slamming the door behind her.

"Come on, Robby," the little girl said. She rubbed at her face and forced herself to stop crying.

"I didn't mean to drop it," Robby said.

"I know. Are you okay?"

Robby nodded, and Mary gave him a long hug.

"I want Mommy," Robby cried.

"I know."

"I want Mommy!" he insisted.

Mary held Robby out at arm's length and looked steadily in his eyes. "Mommy's dead, Robby. She's dead."

"I don't want her to be dead!"

Mary held the boy again. "I know. But I'm here, Robby. I'm here."

Robby cried, and Mary squeezed him reassuringly. "Come on, Robby. We need to get the water from the pump and feed the chickens. Mrs. Rawlings will be angry if we don't get our chores done. Come on. You like feeding the chickens."

Jordan watched the two shuffle to the left side of the house. Jordan could see bruises on both of their faces. Robby had a deep purpled bruise peeking out of the short-sleeved T-shirt he wore. The children were disheveled and dirty.

Sachi growled.

"Shhh, Sachi," Jordan warned. She had to think. "Keep quiet."

The first drone appeared on the Doppler radar as the sun peaked its amber light across the horizon. The sky was sharp between mounds of billowing clouds that meandered in clumps of frothy white. At first Laura did not understand the alarm that beeped insistently in her headphones. Then the voice of a ground-based targeting center radio operator shocked her mind into clarity.

"All stations, this is Golf One Lima. Target acquired."

"Golf One Lima, this is Golf Six Tango, we have target lock. Request permission to engage."

There was a small pause. Laura found she was holding her breath.

"Affirmative, Golf Six Tango. This is Golf One Lima. You are cleared to engage the target."

Somewhere far below *Defender One*, Golf Six Tango fired a laser-guided missile at the enemy drone. Laura watched the missile's signature moving rapidly toward the drone on her display. The missile divided into four distinct parts, each of which honed in on the drone with deadly accuracy. The drone must have detected the attack, for it suddenly changed its trajectory, flashing upward at an angle that would have killed a human pilot.

"Counter fire," Golf Six Tango announced. One of the missile streaks on Laura's screen vanished, but three others continued their hot pursuit. "Golf One Lima, this is Golf Six Tango, over."

"Go for One Lima," the ground station replied.

"Golf One Lima, we have video confirmation. The target appears to be a Zhanshi Five." The intercepting missiles began a counter dance as the Zhanshi Five drone initiated elaborate evasive maneuvers.

Laura typed the name of the enemy drone into her computer. A quick review of the information revealed that the Zhanshi was a midranged drone. It was an older model that could be fitted with offensive payloads or as a scout.

"Incoming?" The tall, lean figure of Commander Reiner suddenly towered over Laura. She had not heard *Defender One's* commander enter the cockpit.

Laura glanced back at her radar screen just in time to see the Zhanshi drone's signature flick out of existence. "Midranged drone, sir," she replied.

Commander Reiner hunched down and looked out of the forward window at the serene sky. "What do you think?"

"I could climb," Laura suggested. She dreaded being on the receiving end of an attack and knew that the higher in the air *Defender One* was, the more time they would have to maneuver. But, she also knew, the farther they had to fall.

"Do you think it's premature?" the commander replied.

"I've never been in combat before," Laura responded.

"No," the commander considered, "you're right. Let's go to sixty thousand." Commander Reiner reached around Laura and flipped a toggle on the console. In the tight space, Laura could smell the deep musk of his cologne. "Battle stations. Battle stations," his voice was even and calm. "This is the commander. All personnel to their battle stations. High-altitude jump gear for all personnel. We're still good, people. Incoming drone."

"Sir." Laura pointed at her monitor as several new signatures appeared.

The commander glanced at the blips that snaked across the screen. "Correction, incoming drones, weapons tight. Weapons tight. We are not to engage. We are not to engage. Passive monitoring only."

They all knew the orders. *Defender One* was the eyes and ears for the ground-based stations.

"Slow climb, Officer Mathis," the commander added after breaking off the in-ship announcement. "Nice and easy. It is no time to panic."

"Yes, sir," Laura replied. Her tongue felt thick and swollen. "Slow climb." She adjusted the flaps, and the giant aeroship caught the air and began spiraling higher. It was hard not to stare at the monitor and its blossoming number of radar signatures that slashed across the screen. The incoming enemy drones were met by a like number of antiaircraft missiles and lifting drone-interceptors. The radio crackled with battle reports. Laura noticed the battle was happening far away at the edge of northern Maryland. That meant they were safe—for now.

"Sir?"

"Yes?" The commander seemed distracted as he watched the battle through *Defender One's* sensors.

"This doesn't seem right," Laura confessed. "Look at all of them."

"No, Officer Mathis, it does not seem right to me either. There are too many." Commander Reiner flipped the intercom back on. "All unit commanders to the tactical command post," he announced. "All unit commanders to the tactical command post." He put a hand on Laura's shoulder. "We'll be monitoring from the TCP. Your copilot will be here soon. Can you handle it by yourself for a few more minutes?"

"Yes, sir." Laura pointed at the Doppler screen. A jagged line marked the boundary between the North American continent and the Atlantic Ocean. "Sir?"

"Yes?" The commander had turned to go, but he stopped.

"That first drone was a midranged one," Laura said. "Where did it come from?" She indicated the open ocean.

The commander smiled and shook his head. "Good question, Officer Mathis. I expect we will find out soon enough. Keep her steady as she goes."

"Steady as she goes, sir."

Commander Reiner stepped out of the cockpit and disappeared into the heart of the aeroship. Laura continued to steer *Defender One* higher into the sky. She tried to block out the rapid reports that burst over the radio as the battle to the east continued to grow in intensity. She concentrated on flying. But this eventuality—attacking drones—had not been part of the briefing. The fighting was supposed to be in Mexico, not along the eastern shore.

Below, ground-based positions raged.

Laura saw that there was no counter fire rising up from the Atlantic.

Where was the navy?

The Atlantic fleet had been hovering near Washington, DC, for several months, but suddenly, when it seemed they were needed, they were nowhere to be seen. What were they waiting for? Why weren't they engaging? It was then that Laura noticed that the navy ships had turned their transponders off. Not a single ship, fighter plane, or submarine showed up on her tactical screen. It was as if they had all suddenly vanished. What the hell was going on?

As Laura flew *Defender One* through the crystal blue sky, she heard the first report of enemy bombings. People along the coast were dying. But what did it mean?

Sachi slipped through the grass, Jordan quietly on his heals. The sun had fully risen, and the sky was a deep azure. Clouds floated here and there, long curling things that changed their shapes as they were blown quietly by the wind. Jordan and Sachi moved to the left of the farmhouse, keeping to the tall grass, maneuvering to the fenced chicken yard and its two-story, beaten and worn chicken coup. Jordan froze for a moment as the two kids, the younger girl named Mary and the boy named Robby, rattled a bucket as they walked slowly through a throng of gathered chickens. Robby was taking handfuls of feed from the bucket and scattering it on the ground where the hungry chickens rushed to feast. Now that Jordan was closer, she saw how ragged the children were; obviously drawn and malnourished, dirt clung to their faces, arms, and hands, and their clothing was ripped and torn—threadbare. They were focused on the chickens at their feet and did not notice as Sachi and Jordan stalked forward.

"The chickens are hungry," Mary said. She held the heavy bucket with two hands, at an awkward angle, as Robby reached in, took another handful of feed, and scattered it on the ground. "Throw some over there, Robby," Mary suggested, "by the door to the coup. Those little ones aren't getting anything to eat."

"Okay." Robby threw a handful toward the smaller chickens that had been pushed out of the main group.

"Let's check for eggs, Robby."

"Can I get them?" Robby asked.

Mary smiled and tousled her brother's hair. "Sure. Just be careful not to break any. Mrs. Rawlings wouldn't like that."

"I'll be careful."

Jordan watched, her hand resting lightly on Sachi's shoulder, as the two younger children put the feed pail away and got a small, wicker basket that was layered with straw. They walked to the edge of the chicken coup, and Mary, arms crossed and a smile on her bruised face, watched as Robby entered the coup and began searching for eggs. The boy squealed when he found an egg and proudly displayed it to Mary. Mary dutifully put it into the wicker basket.

Jordan watched and considered the situation. The kids were obviously abused. Some of the bruising Jordan could see looked half-healed, while some seemed cruelly fresh. Jordan didn't want to get entangled in whatever was going on here, but the deplorable state of the two younger kids tugged at her heart. She felt like she had to do something, but she was not sure what. Did she think she could take the kids with her? Jordan was half-starved herself. How would she feed Mary and Robby when she couldn't even feed Sachi? And Jordan felt no match for the adult Mrs. Rawlings and her two brutish boys. Jordan doubted they would let the two younger children go. They may even try to imprison Jordan for slave labor—or worse. She couldn't get involved, could she?

Perhaps Jordan and the kids could sneak off to where her father waited, she hoped, at the old FEMA emergency supply depot. Jordan did not think she was too far away from the dam: one, perhaps two days. There would be food enough for all of them at the supply depot. If Jordan's calculations were correct. If she hadn't made a mistake somewhere along the way and mistakenly taken the wrong path.

Doubt plagued her. For the last two days, Jordan had felt a rising desperation. She was not panicked, but the sharp edges of uncertainty, hunger, and fatigue were taking their toll. Jordan had studied the map every day, but she could not shake the nagging feeling that she had followed the wrong creek, that she was hopelessly lost. If she didn't find the dam in two days, Jordan had planned to turn back, retrace her steps, and hope to find other survivors from the attack at the apartment complex. How would she feed two additional mouths for another week or more? But Jordan couldn't just abandon Mary and Robby to the sharp, mean woman who was now hidden somewhere in the farmhouse. Could she? Nobody deserved to be beaten.

Jordan's mother had gone to war to protect people, Jordan knew. And her father had flown off on the under-fueled jet in the hopes of helping people. Could Jordan do any less? If Jordan didn't help these two kids, what would happen to them? Would they end up dead? Jordan shuddered as the image of the field of dead by the creek on her first day of travel flickered into her mind's eye. *If good people sit idly as evil deeds are done*, her father had told Jordan once, *then evil wins*. Jordan had to do something.

Determined, Jordan stood slowly up, the grass swaying at her knees. She was just beyond the chicken yard. "Excuse me," she said in what she hoped was a nonthreatening voice.

Mary jumped at the sound and spun around to stare open-mouthed at Jordan. Robby clung to Mary's leg and half-hid behind his older sister.

Jordan smiled and said, "Hi. I'm Jordan. And this is my dog, Sachi. Don't be afraid. We won't hurt you."

"What are you doing here?" Mary whispered. She looked over her shoulder at the farmhouse. "You have to go. Mrs. Rawlings … You have to go."

"Please." Jordan slowly put her rifle on the ground at her feet and held her open hands where they could be easily seen. "We just need a little food to get us through the next couple days. Sachi and I don't mean any harm."

"Robby, stop pulling!" Mary pushed at Robby, and the boy stopped trying to pull his sister backward. "You don't understand," Mary warned. "If Mrs. Rawlings sees you, it will be really, really bad."

"Look," Jordan took a half step forward, "I saw her hit you. And," Jordan pointed at Mary's face and Robby's arm, "it doesn't look like the first time. It isn't right. Is she your mother?"

"No." Mary was sullen.

Jordan looked at the two children quietly for a moment. "You don't have to stay here," Jordan offered. "If we can get some food, you can both come with me to find my father. He's really nice. He'll take care of us. He isn't that far away. Really."

Mary walked over to the closed gate, Robby trailing after, and glanced at the farmhouse. "We can't. If we're caught … Please, you need to leave before she sees you. You don't understand. She'll hurt you and punish us."

Jordan walked up to the gate and stood in front of the children. "Mary, is that your name?"

The younger girl did not answer. Mary stood chewing at her lip and looking back and forth between Jordan, Sachi, and the menacing door of the farmhouse.

"You don't like it here, do you? How long before … Mrs. Rawlings seriously hurts you or Robby? How long are you going to be a punching bag?" Jordan softened her voice. "Look, I know you don't know me. But anything has to be better than this. Let me help you."

"You don't really want to help. You just want some food," Mary retorted, though there was no conviction in her voice.

"I would like one of those chickens," Jordan admitted.

Mary quickly turned and put her hands over Robby's ears. "Shh …" she said.

Robby pushed at Mary's hands and stomped his foot. "I want to hear!" he demanded. "Is she going to kill one of our chickens?" Robby asked. He looked around at the scraggly birds as they pecked at the ground. Robby rubbed his eyes.

"Hush, now, Robby," Mary said. "Nobody is killing nothing." Mary sighed and turned back to Jordan. "We just can't go. She'll catch us. They'll …" And her lips began to quiver.

"Can I pet the doggy?" Robby asked. He looked up at his sister and then over at Jordan.

"Sure you can," Jordan replied. She took a knee and wrapped restraining arms around Sachi. "Sure, Robby. But we have to open and close the gate quickly. Sachi is excited about the chickens."

"He likes chickens?"

Jordan smiled. "Yes. He is a good dog, but he does like chicken. Come on," Jordan encouraged. "Sachi won't bite."

Jordan waited patiently as Mary opened the gate and both kids scooted out, closing the gate carefully behind. Robby rushed over to Sachi, ignoring his sister's worried grab at his arm, and tumbled into the dog at a rush. Jordan suppressed a giggle and held Sachi close. "Now, Sachi, be good."

Sachi looked questioningly at Jordan as the little boy roughly pet him.

"He smells," Robby announced.

"Yes." Jordan laughed. "He needs a bath." She eyed Mary as the younger girl slowly stepped up and touched Sachi. Sachi pushed his head into the girl's hand and suddenly licked her fingers. Mary pulled her hand back but then reached out again and pet the dog.

"He likes you," Jordan said.

"Does he like me too?" Robby asked.

"Of course. Sachi loves everyone."

Robby shrieked and laughed as Sachi ducked his head forward and began licking the boy's face. "Ah!" Robby exclaimed. "That feels funny!" Robby looped his arms around Sachi's neck and gave the dog a giant hug. Sachi's tongue lapped at the boy all the while.

Suddenly Sachi came to attention and turned his head toward the farmhouse. Jordan had heard it too, the unmistakable clanking of wood against wood as the screen door opened and shut. Mary followed Jordan's eyes and took a frightened breath. Mrs. Rawlings, a shotgun held at the ready in her arms, came striding across the yard toward them.

Jordan realized that she had left her own weapon a few paces behind her. She had not wanted the kids to be frightened by it. Jordan stood slowly up as Mrs. Rawlings came to a halt about ten feet away, the shotgun pointed directly at Jordan. Sachi growled. Robby, taken aback, realized something was happening and turned to see what Jordan and Mary were looking at. When he saw Mrs. Rawlings, gaunt and gray, standing like an apocalyptic devil in the worn grass, Robby began to cry. Jordan's heart grew hard as she stood, keeping a grip on Sachi, to face the older woman.

Mary and Robby moved a little away from Jordan, Robby crying all the time, Mary cringing with each word Mrs. Rawlings said.

"Who the hell are you?" Mrs. Rawlings's voice was bitter venom. "Mary, Robby, git back away from that garl. Hear me?" She snapped. "Well now," her eyes flashed, "what *do* we have here?"

Defender One flew silently through the air as Laura shifted in her seat. Her copilot, a balding, freckled-faced man in his early fifties, adjusted his glasses and flipped a few toggle switches above the command console. He was a nice enough man, though he tended to eat too much garlic. Laura could smell it seeping out of his pores, under a mask of deodorant and cheap cologne. His uniform shirt, bright white with a buttoned-down front, was rumpled.

"Another sortie," he said, his voice a little higher than one would expect from a man his age.

A flurry of activity on the tactical display rippled across the east coasts of Maryland and the District of Columbia. The incoming enemy drones, bombers, and fighters scurried across the screen. Beneath each aircraft, a digital number indicated their altitude. The fighters flew above the bombers, and the drones were on low-altitude vectors. Sandwiched in between, bombers flew in tight formations that reminded Laura of ducks flying south for the winter. As Laura expected, an answering salvo of ground fire, intercepting drones, and antiaircraft missiles rose to meet the Chinese threat. So far, *Defender One* had remained off of Chinese radar, the ship's instruments providing the overview that was necessary for defending forces. But Laura wondered how long that would last.

"Do our countermeasures appear less … robust to you, Fred?" Laura asked.

"I think most of our firepower was moved down south into Texas in anticipation of the battle there. And the units here must be taking losses. So, yeah, I think you're right."

Laura turned a worried eye toward the coastline. She reached to the screen and pinched it, centering the display on the Chines naval craft and zooming. The computer registered naval gunfire as the flotilla hovered off the coast. A quarter of a mile closer to the coast, a large number of smaller craft were chugging toward the shore.

Laura felt a bead of sweat sting her eyes. "How long before those ships get to shore?" she asked.

Fred shrugged. "An hour, maybe. Just before sunset."

"Then what?"

"Well," Fred considered, "I imagine they will go back and get more soldiers. You have to count on at least three waves of invaders. They will probably land all through the night."

"You don't think we'll stop them?"

"From landing? No. Too many of them. They'll get on shore due to sheer weight of numbers if nothing else. But we have a good chance of kicking them back into the surf. We've got units moving up too. It's going to be a bloody mess."

"Only a chance of stopping them?"

Fred took a deep breath and let it out slowly. "Well, the Chinese must have a plan. And they wouldn't be doing this if they didn't expect to be successful. Then there is the fact that most of our fighting forces are way down south. I think it could go either way."

The Atlantic and Pacific Oceans had been the best defensive barriers in the history of human civilization, but steady technological innovation from the nineteenth century onward slowly chipped away at their vast distances. The lonely waters of the Pacific and the frigid depths of the Atlantic had slowly become the world's greatest superhighways. And the Chinese navy and army were using them to great advantage.

Invaded. The idea sent chills through Laura.

The United States mainland had been invaded only once since the formation of the country. The British sacked the American capital in 1814. The Library of Congress, Capitol building, and the original presidential house were put to the torch. President Madison and the rest of government had fled into Maryland. But the British attack had been a retaliatory raid, and the British quickly withdrew. The next closest thing to an invasion was the Japanese attack on Alaska's Aleutian Islands during the Second World War. The Japanese hoped to disrupt American supply lines into the Pacific by controlling the Aleutians' vital shipping and air lanes. Neither army intended to push into the interior of the great nation. That would have been suicide. An invasion of the continental United States would take an incredible amount of manpower and supplies. Both Great Britain and Japan had lacked the capacity. But by 2040, China had an estimated eleven billion people and half of the world's manufacturing might. If the Chinese only sent a billion soldiers to the United States, that would be double America's population. How could America withstand such an onslaught?

And it looked to Laura like the Chinese were coming to stay.

Several hundred landing craft moved toward the coast. Behind them, a continuous stream of battle craft provided supporting fires, while at least three aircraft carriers launched midranged bombers and drones at the American defenders. Long-range, stratospheric bombers joined the attack from hidden South American bases, raining bombs in series over the apparent landing site, the capital, and other targets of tactical interest. Smoke bloomed as cities burned. But the Americans were giving it back, shooting down Chinese aircraft and sinking several enemy vessels. But as brave as the defenders were, the twirl of Chinese ships of the line seemed unaffected and unimpeded.

Laura watched the display with growing trepidation as the battle flowed toward dusk and the landing craft drew nearer to the coast. A feeling of helplessness flooded through her as the moon peaked its way into a clear and darkening sky.

Where the hell was the navy? Why weren't they engaging the enemy flotilla? Had they all been destroyed? Surely Laura would have heard of any such battle. But there had been no such reports. The army and air force, alone, defended against the invaders. The navy had simply vanished. But to where? Why? It made no sense. It was criminal! Criminal!

United States Army units moved hurriedly into the anticipated enemy landing zones as Laura whispered a prayer. *God, they've got to hold them. Hold them. Please, let them hold the lines.*

But the Chinese landing craft kissed the shore, and their troops began pushing inland. Tanks, robot drones, mobile artillery units, and countless scores of infantry poured into an infernal of defensive fire. Laura heard the battle raging over the radio, watched concussive waives of bombs and tracer fire dancing in the gathering night, adjusted the flight controls, and wiped tears from her eyes.

The Chinese invasion force advanced as America bled.

The army just has to hold. They just have to.

Jordan shuffled her feet and held tightly on to Sachi's collar as her dog growled threateningly. Mrs. Rawlings pointed the shotgun at the dog. Jordan stepped between them and hurriedly told Sachi to be quiet. Mary stood wide-eyed, grasping her brother's hand as Robby tried his best to hide behind his older sister, whimpering all the while. The two kids were off to Jordan's left. They had shuffled halfway between Jordan and Mrs. Rawlings, where they stood uncertainly. Terrified.

"You best hold onto that dog, honey. If it takes one step toward me, I'll blast that dog of yours to hell."

The woman was a bully, preying on those around her to feed her own lust for power and authority. Mrs. Rawlings was the worst type of human being. Cruelty and stupidity combined, Jordan's father had warned, made for the most dangerous of persons.

Jordan did not doubt Mrs. Rawlings would kill Sachi if given any reason. Even without a clear reason, Jordan suspected, Mrs. Rawlings might shoot. But Mrs. Rawlings was hesitant. Jordan could see her attempting to glance around the area to see if there were any other strangers nearby.

Jordan kept one hand on Sachi and the other before her, palm open. She took a slow step backward, trying to get back to the spot where her rifle lay hidden in the high grass.

"That wouldn't be very wise," Jordan said. She tried to speak confidently, dismissingly.

Mrs. Rawlings raised the shotgun to her shoulder. "What do you mean?"

"Oh, just that my brother and cousin probably have you in the sights of their scopes at this very second. You didn't think I would come toward a strange house without some type of cover, did you? And Dyson is an expert shot. He served in the army." Jordan told the lie easily. "And before the war, he was an avid hunter." That part was true.

Jordan turned her head back to the brush line south of the house where she and Sachi had camped last night. The terrain followed the creek east where a high bluff rose out of the surrounding valley floor.

Mrs. Rawlings followed Jordan's look and stared for a moment at the trees at the far side of the high-grass lawn. "How do I know yer not lying?"

"Keep pointing that thing at me, and you'll find out," Jordan challenged.

Mrs. Rawlings slowly lowered the shotgun but kept it pointing generally in Jordan's direction. At this range, Jordan knew, the woman did not have to aim. Most people loaded buckshot into shotguns. When fired, the pellets spread out in a conical pattern that expanded as the lead pellets sped away from the gun. Everything in the cone got hit. That is why people liked shotguns. They didn't require much skill. Point and shoot.

"What do you want?" Mrs. Rawlings drawled.

"I came to see if you would sell some food. We're interested in buying a couple of chickens. I've got some money."

Mrs. Rawlings cackled. "Money? Money has no use. Do you have anything to trade? Salt? Alcohol? Gasoline?"

"Um …" Jordan continued to move slowly toward her rifle. She tried to hide her intent by tugging on Sachi. It made Sachi nervous, but there was nothing she could do about it. He would just have to suffer the indignity. "Not with me. My father and the group have some of those things. We came across a rural gas station a while back that still had fuel in the tanks. We might be able to trade. How much gas for three chickens?"

"Three?" the woman considered. "Twenty gallons each. For the power generator."

"That is a lot for a chicken," Jordan replied. She had stopped walking and stood firmly on the top of her rifle. She could feel its solid form beneath her shoes. But how to reach it? "Would you consider fifteen? Fifteen gallons of gasoline sounds more reasonable to me."

"No. I don't need the gasoline. It'd be nice, but it ain't necessary. That is my offer."

"Well, I will have to ask my father," Jordan replied. She turned and waved at her imaginary brother and cousin. "Letting them know everything is fine," she explained.

Mrs. Rawlings looked at the wood line. Jordan took the opportunity to kneel down, and, pulling Sachi close and turning him a bit, Jordan used the dog to shield her other hand from view. With her left hand, she reached down and felt for the rifle, pulling it up and resting it across her knees.

Mrs. Rawlings's eyes darted back to Jordan. "What are you doing?" she snapped. The shotgun swung ominously in her hands.

At that moment, Jordan fumbled the rifle and reflexively released Sachi as she scrambled to grab the rifle with her right hand. Freed, Sachi darted forward toward the two kids. Mrs. Rawlings raised the shotgun and brought it to bear on Sachi.

"No!" Jordan yelled. She rotated the repeating rifle in her right hand, cocking it is a fluid moment, and brought it to her shoulder.

Seeing the movement, Mrs. Rawlings swung the shotgun toward Jordan, ignoring the dog. A wicked look crossed her face, and her eyes narrowed. But Jordan fired first, the sound a whip crack in the air. Mrs. Rawlings fell, the shotgun going off in a concussive blast. Jordan heard the supersonic rip of eight lead pellets zip harmlessly high in the air. Jordan ducked instinctively, and the kids screamed. Mrs. Rawlings grunted, and Jordan could see the woman trying to charge the shotgun as she lay on her back.

"Don't." Jordan stepped forward. Her weapon was centered on the older woman. But something wild had come over Mrs. Rawlings. Her features were feral. Straining, Mrs. Rawlings managed to charge the action. "Don't," Jordan repeated.

Mrs. Rawlings screamed and swung the barrel at Jordan. Jordan fired. The bullet entered Mrs. Rawlings skull just below her left eye socket and blew the back of her head and brains into the scraggly grass. The shotgun tumbled harmlessly. Mrs. Rawlings's body jerked twice, and air hissed out of her lungs. The woman stared, unseeing, at the sky.

Jordan approached the body cautiously, giving Mrs. Rawlings a kick with her foot. Jordan felt ill.

A cry came from far away, along with the crack of bullets that jabbed through the air high above Jordan. Jordan looked toward the sound of the cry and saw the two older boys, David and Keith, rushing across a far meadow. They stopped, and both sent two or three rounds cascading through the air. They were wild shots and cleanly missed Jordan and the kids. Sachi barked and jumped.

"Come on!" Jordan pushed at Mary and grabbed Robby in an awkward, one-handed embrace. Carrying the little boy, Jordan yelled, "Sachi! Come on!" And she darted clumsily toward the relative safety of the woods. Mary followed, crouching as she moved. The two boys continued their pursuit, firing as they dashed back to the farmhouse.

Jordan, Sachi, and the kids reached the concealment of the wood. Pushing into the protective covering, Jordan put Robby on the ground and turned just in time to see David and Keith stop at the unmoving form of their mother. David threw his weapon angrily on the ground as Keith fell upon his mother's body and sobbed. David picked up his weapon and fired several rounds in frustration in Jordan's direction. They ricocheted through the trees.

"We have to go," Jordan said at the two smaller kids. "Mary," she reached out and shook the older girl. "Mary, come on! Get Robby and let's go."

Mary looked at Jordan. Confusion and shock registered on her face.

"You can't go back," Jordan said. "If they catch us, they'll kill us. Come on, Mary! Robby! Let's go."

"Where?" Mary managed.

"Up," Jordan replied. "We go up the bluff. It will be safer up there."

Jordan put Sachi's backpack on the dog. Swinging her backpack over her left shoulder, she began to move.

Sachi leaped forward, down a ripple in the ground, through the trees, toward the creek. The three kids followed, splashing across the cool waters as behind them Jordan could hear one of the boys yelling.

"We'll kill you! We'll fuck'n kill you! We'll kill you!"

The ground rose at a slight angle as Jordan, Mary, and Robby followed Sachi out of the creek into a thicker area of woods. They had been walking for a while. The noonday sun flickered through the swaying treetops, casting shadows, as a cooling breeze blew at them steadily from the northeast. Autumn had arrived. The first hints of fall colors—star-orange, yellows, and bright, blighted greens—rustled in the air.

The children were moving too slowly for Jordan's liking. Robby was trying as best he could, but his little legs seemed to churn four times faster than he actually moved. Jordan tried to push the siblings to go faster. But it was no use. They could only travel so quickly. Jordan knew that David and Keith were hunting them. And the older boys would be moving much more rapidly. Even if the boys had stopped to bury their mother, it was only a matter of time before they caught up. Jordan didn't think she could win that fight. She was outgunned and hampered with the two kids. But she could not leave Mary and Robby behind. That, she knew, would be as good as shooting them herself. As Jordan and the kids walked up the long slope toward the bluff, Sachi's feet padding through dry leaves, Jordan could almost feel crosshairs on her back. Every few steps, Jordan looked over her shoulder, but she saw no sign of their pursuers.

Mary looked at Jordan. She had been quiet all morning. Anger and fear mingled with shock and confusion flowed over the contours of her face. Robby seemed a little bit better. He trudged forward without an apparent care in the world, the events of the day already fading into the strange dreamlike mind of the extremely young.

He had found a small stick somewhere, which he swished back and forth as he walked. Robby would occasionally reach out and grab at Sachi's tangled fur. Sachi would duck his head and dart forward out of Robby's reach.

"It's okay, Sachi," Jordan told her dog. "Go on ahead, boy. We'll follow."

Sachi looked at Jordan for a few seconds, understanding and possibly relief reflected in his eyes, before lunging ahead. Jordan smiled.

"Where are we going?" Mary finally asked.

Without stopping, Jordan answered. "My father said there is an old FEMA storage facility by a dam. He and my family are there waiting for me. We got separated. You don't know what FEMA is, do you?" Jordan noticed the lack of comprehension on Mary's face.

"No."

"It is an old stockpile of supplies and stuff," Jordan explained. "The government kept it close to Washington, DC, after the waters started to rise. My dad said they were worried about hurricanes and stuff. That means," Jordan continued, "there is lots of food there. Anything you could want."

"Pizza?" Mary asked sarcastically.

"I like pizza," Robby agreed.

"I guess so," Jordan said. She really hadn't thought about it that much. Her father said there was food, and that had been enough for Jordan. "My dad's waiting there for me," Jordan added, a bit of hope in her voice. "Sachi and I have been traveling to meet him for a while. He shouldn't be that far away."

"My mom is dead," Mary said. "She got sick."

The pronouncement caught Jordan by surprise. "And your dad?"

Mary shrugged.

"Daddy ran away," Robby replied. "Well, he did!" Robby said when Mary gave him a hard look. "Mommy said he got scared and wasn't much of a man."

"Robby."

"That's what Mommy said! He got scared 'cause he couldn't find a job, and so he went looking for one after I was born. Mommy said he might come back some day. Do you think he might? I've never met him. Why couldn't he find a job, Mary? Why?"

"I don't know."

"Do you think he found one? What type of job would he do?"

"I don't know, Robby."

"Did you kill Mrs. Rawlings?" Robby asked Jordan.

Jordan swallowed. "Yes."

"She was mean," Robby said. He swished his stick back and forth and furrowed his brow. "She hit me. Mommy never hit me," he mumbled.

"That's good then, right? Your mother loved you?" Jordan said as she scanned ahead where Sachi had disappeared into the brush. She could still hear him sloshing through the underbrush, but she didn't like it when she couldn't see him.

"Yeah … Where is your mommy?" Robby asked.

Jordan felt her chest clench. "She's a soldier. She's fighting in the war."

"War? What war? Mary, will you have to fight in a war?"

"I'm too young, silly."

"I have to use the potty," Robby announced, stopping.

"You have to do what?" Jordan said.

"I have to use the potty!"

"Number one or number two?" Mary said. Robby held up one tiny finger. Mary seemed relieved. "Okay. Well, why don't you pee on that tree?"

"Pee on a tree?" Robby laughed.

"Why not? Jordan's dog pees on trees. Why can't you?"

"That's funny," Robby replied.

Mary helped her brother pull down his pants, and Robby began urinating on the tree. Jordan felt a blush of embarrassment and turned to look the other way while Robby asked a series of questions. Did the tree like getting peed on? Did ants live on trees?

Did she think there were any monkeys in the woods, because he liked monkeys? He used to have a stuffed monkey, but he lost it. Did she think they would find Mr. Monkey again? How about apples? Apples grow on trees. Did Jordan like apples? Could Sachi climb trees? Jordan answered each question as best she could.

Robby finished, and Mary helped him with his pants. Sachi had come looping back and started to sniff the tree. He lifted a leg and urinated on the tree too. Robby laughed.

"He peed where I did!" Robby squealed.

"Sachi …" Jordan admonished. "Get out of that."

Sachi looked at Jordan, unconcerned, and trotted off again.

"Come on, you two," Jordan said. "We have a long way to go. We have to get to the top of that bluff."

"I'm tired," Robby complained. "And hungry. I'm hungry, Mary."

Mary looked at Jordan. Jordan frowned and shook her head.

"Maybe we can eat when we get to the top of the hill, Robby." Mary suggested.

"Pizza?"

"I don't … Pizza? No," Mary said. "I don't think there will be pizza at the top of the hill."

"But you never know, do you, Mary? Mommy said, 'Never say never.'"

"Never say never, Robby."

"Come on. Sachi is waiting. Look," Jordan announced.

They all looked up the rise to see Sachi, a tangle of marbled fur and large, brown eyes, looking expectantly down on the group.

"Coming, Sachi!" Robby yelled, food forgotten for a while.

The three children began making their way through the woods. Above them, the trees whispered in the breeze. Jordan adjusted her pack and walked slowly behind Mary and Robby as they struggled up the hill. At this rate, it would take them several hours to reach the relative safety at the top of the bluff. Jordan hoped the two kids would have the energy to climb it.

Jordan looked behind her, stopping for a moment as her eyes slid back along their route of travel. The woods looked quiet and peaceful. Birds chirped, and insects hummed. She saw no sign of David or Keith. But Jordan knew they were there. Somewhere.

Easily catching up to the other children, Jordan's thoughts turned to her father. She felt desperate to see him. Tired, footsore, and down to her last provisions, a wave of despair shivered through her. She had to be strong. Strong for Sachi. Strong for the kids. But being strong all the time was so hard. Jordan wondered if her father ever felt this way. He had never shown any fear or doubt. He always knew what to say to make Jordan feel safe. Would Jordan ever see him again? Would he ever wrap his arms around her in one of his giant hugs? Would she see Dyson or anyone from their neighborhood?

Jordan wiped a quiet tear from her cheek.

Would she even survive the day?

Defender One rocked and shook as the shock waves from near hits reverberated through the air. The gargantuan lighter-than-air ship had launched its four defensive drones, though only three of the spear-shaped craft still flew above *Defender One* in defensive over-watch positions. The fourth drone had flamed out after being hit by some type of invisible energy weapon that clipped it near the fuselage and sent the craft twirling through the deepening evening, where it disappeared in a fiery impact far, far below.

Laura cursed. *Defender One* didn't bob and weave but rather floated and … floated. Staying at their current position was a type of suicide. The only thing keeping the ship in the air were the layers of air-defense rings that spun outward from the capital into Maryland and Virginia. The flack, drones, antimissile missiles, rail guns, and dwindling number of fighter aircraft caused attrition to the incoming attacks targeting *Defender One*. It also helped that the hull of the aeroship was covered with a polymer that had certain radar-absorbing properties, making targeting *Defender One* much more difficult. Yet it was only a matter of time before something got through. Already, Chinese landing craft were hitting the beaches as the sun sunk behind the western horizon. The Chinese destroyers and cruisers were peppering the beaches with fire as aircraft and drones from the three supporting aircraft carriers provided close air support. The long-range bombers, launched from land bases somewhere in South America, had returned as well. They struck deep, cutting off roadways and pockmarking airports. The tide of the battle was turning against the Americans. Laura could feel it in the rattle and rage of the fire coming her way, in the shrill sounds of American radio communications, and by the mechanical way the tactical display showed the steady Chinese advance in pictographic symbols. In the distance, Laura could see tracer fire skipping into the sky. The massed fire seemed centered about Washington, DC. But from Laura's vantage point, it didn't seem to be doing significant damage to the enemy air strikes.

"They're getting close," Fred, Laura's copilot, said through a clenched jaw. *Defender One* bucked and jumped, one of its defending Gatling guns having detonated an incoming missile just a couple hundred feet away from the bulky aircraft. The explosion was briefly blinding.

"Jesus!" Laura agreed. She looked at the Doppler and for the hundredth time in the last hour wished she had declined to serve aboard the aeroship.

Laura nearly jumped out of her skin when the voice of Commander Reiner seemed to materialize behind her.

"Get her on the ground," the commander said, his voice tense.

The ship rattled and jostled. Laura turned her head and saw Commander Reiner looming behind her, his left hand holding the back of her seat. His face was apprehensive as he tried to keep on his feet.

"What?" Laura loudly asked. With all the weapon systems on *Defender One* firing and the incoming, it was difficult to hear.

Commander Reiner pointed his index finger downward and yelled, "Get the ship on the ground, Officer Mathis! Get her on the ground, now!"

Laura nodded and began a slow descent—a long, arching drop.

"No!" the commander yelled. "They're going to nuke the Chinese, Officer Mathis. Do you understand what that means? They're going to nuke 'em! We need to get on the ground now, or we'll be blown out of the sky!" The commander reached to the control console and punched the intercom. "All hands, all hands, this is the commander. Move to evacuation stations. Move to evacuation stations! Prepare to abandon ship!"

"Oh, shit," Laura swore as it dawned on her what was happening. The kinetic energy in a nuclear shock wave would rip *Defender One* to shreds. And if they somehow managed to avoid that, the ionizing gamma radiation would fry them all in just a few seconds.

"We need to put some ground between us and the sea," the commander continued. "Find us some place behind a hill or ridge or something. Do you understand? Officer Mathis, do you understand?"

Laura's mind was numb. The commander shook her shoulders. Laura looked at the tall man's eyes and slowly nodded.

"How much time?" Laura asked.

"Ten, maybe fifteen minutes. Get us down, now!"

"Strap in, Commander," Laura warned. "Fred, we'll drop to the west." Laura was already flipping toggles and sounded the emergency klaxon. "Let the crew know when we hit twenty thousand," Laura said as she depressed the flight controls and *Defender One* dipped nose-first toward the ground. Laura knew the crew could jump at twenty thousand and hit the ground within five minutes. That would give them a better chance of survival.

"Commander," Laura shouted. But when she turned to look at the man, he was already stumbling his way out of the cockpit down the stairs. "Fred, we can't just let this thing drop out of the sky. It's packed full."

"What? Yeah. Big explosion. I know. But we can't get it on the ground in fifteen minutes."

"We can get it on the ground," Laura said. "It just won't be pretty. We'll level her out, and you and I will jump from three hundred."

"Three hundred feet?" Fred exclaimed. "That is calling it awfully close, don't you think? Two-fifty is the safety margin. Anything after that is ... base jumping."

"The ship will kill anyone who is near it when it hits," Laura argued. "We can't push the crew out at twenty only to land this fireball on top of them. Let the crew jump, and we'll steer the ship away from them, farther west. And I can't do it by myself. Fred? Fred?"

Laura and Fred looked at each other. *Defender One* continued to shimmy as it dove to the ground. The escorting drones dipped their winds and looped in behind the aeroship. The sky continued to be pockmarked with flashes of incoming fire. Finally, Fred nodded.

"It's a hell of a thing," Fred said.

"Yes. Yes it is," Laura agreed. "We're at a forty-five-degree bank. Increasing to fifty."

"Fifty thousand and dropping," Fred said.

"Come on, come on, come on!" Laura yelled. She was straining at the controls. Had the nukes been launched yet?

"Forty thousand, Laura!" Fred hit a switch, and the jump lights turned amber.

Defender One plummeted. The air outside the hull screamed. In two minutes, the aeroship dropped another twenty thousand feet, and Fred hit the jump lights again, turning them green. "Abandon ship! Abandon ship!" Fred yelled into the intercom.

All across the ship, exterior doors opened, and the crew began bailing out into the dark sky. They zipped away into the rushing air and fell far below the aeroship. Laura and Fred struggled to move *Defender One* further west of the escaping crew, angling the ship to an area in Maryland where the terrain was a series of rolling hills and flat land. Laura aimed for an area of country where there were not any major cities. *Defender One* continued to trail bodies as the crew abandoned ship. At ten thousand feet, Laura grunted as she and Fred pulled back on the controls and tried to level the ship out, hoping to soften its landing.

"Five thousand!" Fred warned.

"Get ready!"

"Two thousand! One!"

Laura quickly punched a series of commands into the navigation computer and then hit the autopilot. *Defender One's* programming took over, and the ship screeched as the computer tried desperately to stem the ship's descent. Alarms blared, and red warning lights flashed all along the control console. Laura was pressed into the straps of her chair as the g-forces became nearly unbearable.

"Eject! Eject! Eject!" Laura yelled.

There was a loud hiss and explosion as Fred's ejection seat activated, shooting the copilot out of *Defender One* into the night's sky. Laura struggled to reach her ejection switch, and finally punching it, she was thrown clear of the ship as it turned, leveled, and then crashed with a blinding flash and roar into the ground. Parachute deployed, Laura floated down in the cool air as below the farmland burned.

Laura could see the shadows of trees below. The trees grew in long spiraling arms that ran along a low bluff. Steering the parachute as best she could, Laura prepared to land. She wanted to be as close to the trees as humanly possible. From there, she could run and jump down the protective side of the bluff. How much time did she have left? How much time had they spent crashing *Defender One* into the countryside?

The Chinese pressed their attack. The air was alive with death as their army swarmed ashore.

Laura struck the ground with a grunt, was dragged several feet by her parachute, and then came to rest in the high grass. Stunned for a moment, she lay there gathering herself, testing her body to see if anything was broken. Behind her, *Defender One* fluttered and burned. Laura slapped at the release mechanism on the straps that held her in her ejection seat and pushed away, collapsing on the ground.

Laura looked up at the surrounding terrain and pulled herself to her feet.

The nukes, Laura thought. *Oh, God, the nukes!*

Laura ran.

The bullet struck with a resounding clack and zing just above Jordan's head. She ducked instinctively and grabbed Mary by the shoulder, turning the younger girl to face her.

"Take Robby and keep going," Jordan said in a rush. "Carry him if you have to. Go to the top of the bluff and wait for me. But if I don't come soon, then keep going that way." Jordan pointed east. "Do you understand?"

"What are you going to do?" Mary asked. She could hear David and Keith's taunting calls.

"I'll slow them down," Jordan replied. She hit the quick release on her backpack and took a second to take Sachi's pack off. The cumbersome weight would only be a disadvantage. "Take Robby and go!"

Mary took little Robby's hand. "Let's go, Robby. Come on! You can do it."

"I'm tired!" he cried.

Mary reached down and awkwardly picked the child up. She could not carry her brother for very long. Taking a deep breath, she pushed up the steep incline, using trees as handholds, her feet turned flatly against the grade to give her better traction.

Jordan watched her and Robby disappear into the dark underbrush before scrambling horizontally across the face of the hill, down into a divot that crawled its way from the summit down to the creek below. Using it to mask her movement, Jordan ran lightly,

Sachi following, and then popped up about two hundred meters from where she had left Mary and Robby.

David and Keith continued to shoot wildly. Their jeering cries echoed in the valley.

"Sachi, here," Jordan ordered. She found what she had been looking for—a deadfall tree about eight inches around with a myriad of spindly branches. The end of the tree was still attached by a shard of wood and bark to the tree trunk, creating a protective pocket. Jordan crawled under the branches and lay prone, her rifle only slightly sticking out along the side of the trunk. Sachi pushed his way in too, and Jordan pulled the dog to the ground.

"Stay," she commanded.

Jordan did her best to calm her breathing. Though she could not see the boys below her, the scrunching of leaves, occasional shot, and constant threatening calls and hooting gave Jordan a good idea of their positions. Jordan hoped to catch the silhouette of the boys as they neared the base of the hill where she could get a good shot.

"We're coming for you … Wo … Wo … Wobby!" One of them yelled.

"I'm going to rip your head off!" followed the other boy.

Jordan saw a slow ripple of movement. She blinked and strained in the evening haze, wondering if she had imagined it. But then she saw it again. Two shadowy figures, about thirty feet from each other, were slowly making their way to the hill. The closer they came, the easier it was for Jordan to see them. The boy on the far side was moving from tree to tree, careful to put as much cover between him and where he thought Jordan and the kids were located. The other boy was not so astute. He took the most direct and open path forward, his rifle held in a low ready position. He almost looked, to Jordan, as if he were lazily hunting pheasant and not people.

Jordan waited patiently as the boys moved, hoping they would drift back together. But the two kept their distances. Still, Jordan was on their left flank and had a 30 percent angle of aim at the nearest boy. Neither of them looked in Jordan's direction. They focused on the slope to their front. Jordan attempted to put the closer boy in her sights, but she could not get a sight picture. It was too dark. Instead she shifted the rifle a little high, aiming over the barrel, and lined the top of the barrel with the boy's head. She suspected the round would drop lower than her point of aim, so she shifted it again until she was looking over the barrel at the boy's chin. She squeezed the trigger, and the boy fell.

"David!" Keith yelled.

Keith returned fire. Several rounds kicked in the dirt in front of Jordan or thwacked into the deadfall tree. Sachi leaped up and dashed off into the woods.

"Sachi, no!" Jordan cried, but it was too late. The dog disappeared into the dark.

Jordan tried to see what the other boy, Keith, was doing. But when she peaked around the corner of the log, three well-aimed shots cracked into the tree trunk, throwing bits of bark and wood and lead. Jordan hurriedly scuttled backward and started crawling her way back to the divot, which she hoped to use to maneuver up the hill without exposing herself. Rolling into the divot, Jordan risked a peak over a lip of ground to spot Keith. Jordan could see David, still lying where he had fallen. But Keith had vanished.

"Damn," she murmured. She looked desperately for Sachi with no luck. Afraid Keith might have gone after the smaller kids, Jordan cursed. *That dog*! She had to move.

In a low, crouching jog, Jordan swung around to her right, up the hill, hoping to come in on the kids in an advantageous position should Keith appear. Jordan tried to move as quietly as she could, but the undergrowth seemed to actively oppose her. Hit across the face by stinging branches, tripped up by clumps of vine and thorny plants, she pushed herself bodily forward, ripping through the underbrush when it got in her way. Finally, she hit an open seam that led back to her left. She darted forward as quickly as she dare.

Jordan was just a few feet from the very top of the bluff. She could see the edge sticking out in the sky above her like an umbrella.

If it was as steep as this all the way around, Jordan reasoned, then the kids would not have been able to climb it. They would be stuck somewhere down along the length of the bluff.

Jordan almost didn't see them. She was just about to hurry past them when Mary called out. "Jordan? Is that you?"

"Mary? Robby? Are you both okay?"

"I couldn't get up the hill," Robby complained.

"It's okay," Jordan reassured them. "Give me your hand. We'll go back this way. I think we can get to the top back along the way I came."

"Where is Sachi?" Mary asked. She and Robby emerged from a small depression in the side of the bluff. Robby took Jordan's outstretched hand.

"He's okay—just being Sachi. Come on, we have to go quickly. We're almost there."

Robby slipped, and Jordan grabbed him before he could tumble down the hill. "Quiet now," she added.

Guiding the exhausted little boy through the dark wood was not easy. He was slow, stumbled and slid, and whimpered incessantly. Jordan considered picking Robby up, but she didn't think she could carry him and her rifle while maintaining her balance on the steep terrain. So she did the best she could. Occasionally Jordan could feel Mary grab hold of her shirt for balance. In this manner, the three of them skirted back the way Jordan had come. Jordan looked for an opening to the top of the bluff with no luck. They had gone several hundred feet when the terrain forced them to move down a little, Jordan dragging a hand against the steep hillside, pebbles and dirt rolling beneath her feet. She was just gathering herself when Jordan heard the distinct sound of a breaking twig. Jordan froze.

A shadow stepped out of the trees.

Keith pointed his rifle at Jordan and snarled, "You bitch!"

Time dilated and stretched. Jordan saw the rifle slowly rise to Keith's shoulder as suddenly the sky above exploded and screeched. The sound of tearing metal ripped through the night as a fireball flashed orange-red into the sky. The ground shook and trembled, and a blur leaped out of the dark. Sachi bit Keith on his firing arm, deflecting Keith's aim. The rifle cracked.

"Sachi!" Jordan yelled. Her voice seemed distant.

Sachi grabbed the boy by his leg and, growling furiously, pulled Keith down the side of the bluff. Keith struggled, slid down, and punched at the dog with the butt of his weapon.

"Sachi!" Jordan jumped forward to help the dog, but she was too late. Keith desperately rotated his rifle and shot Sachi in the head. The dog yelped and fell back, letting go of Keith's leg and slipping away into the underbrush.

Keith wheeled, snarled, and gained his feet. He pointed his rifle at Jordan's chest. Jordan could see the anger on Keith's face. But as much as she tried, she couldn't move. She was frozen in place.

"Die, bitch!"

Someone screamed, and a body flew over the bluff and slammed into Keith, sending him careening backward. His rifle fired in the air then flew out of his hands as Keith, tangled with the newcomer, landed on his back. The stranger rolled past him and hit a nearby tree with a tremendous crash. As if released from a spell, Jordan dashed forward and struck Keith with her weapon. Again and again and again as the boy feebly tried to block the blows. A noise was coming from Jordan's mouth, incoherent, full of rage. She shifted her rifle into a baseball bat hold and swung with all her might at Keith's skull. The thick thud of a hammer on meat reverberated in the night as blood covered Keith's face.

"No, no!" the boy cried. Jordan swung again, the rifle crossways, breaking Keith's jaw in one mighty crack.

Dropping the rifle, Jordan fell on the boy. How her knife got in her hand, Jordan could not say. But she ripped at Keith, plunging the knife into his chest and neck rapidly.

"What the hell?" A woman's voice rose, confused, from the tree into which the stranger had slammed.

Jordan threw her knife away and scrambled on her hands and knees through the underbrush, frantically searching for her dog.

"Sachi! Sachi! Sachi!"

Jordan felt wet fur and wrapped her arms around her dog. She could feel Sachi breathing, but it was ragged and weak. Sachi met Jordan's eyes. Then he suddenly stopped breathing.

"Sachi! No. No. No. No!"

Hands reached out of the dark and pulled at Jordan. She fought back, but the grip tightened.

"Stop fighting!" Laura yelled. She pulled the girl away from the dead dog and up the slope. "Lie down!" Laura pushed the stunned kids down and, forcibly shoving Jordan beneath her, pressed the kids into the hard earth. She lay on top of the three kids and held them.

Night turned to day. A series of suns exploded across the horizon, and a vicious wind grew from the east. It howled and roared. Trees bent westward in supplication. In the high atmosphere, an undulating wave of color, like some bizarre elongated rainbow, rolled as energy-infused particles danced through the stratosphere. Unlike the soft beauty of the northern lights, the colors churned angrily. The ground reverberated with wounds that, though distant, sounded like the hollow, deep thrumming of kettledrums. A mighty, thunderous sound echoed across the sky. It sounded as if the world had split open. When the terrible rumble passed, the whole world was silent. And then darkness returned with blinding surety.

Laura pulled herself up, surprised to be alive. She blinked and tried to focus her eyes. Finally, some of her night vision returned. Below her were three kids: an older kid of maybe eleven or twelve who was weeping, a younger girl of seven or eight who clung desperately to the third child—not much more than a baby, a little boy.

"It's all right," Laura breathed. "It's all right. We're alive. And I've got you."

It wasn't much of a university. The interconnected domes of the old research station were laid out in concentric circles on the coast near Halley Town. The waters of the Weddell Sea churned, deep and ice blue. The University of Antarctica was not much more than a dozen or so domes by a small runway. A newer dome was under construction. Larger than the rest, it was to house the main archives and library. Construction cranes rose into the crisp sky of the short summer as men in hard hats moved here and there between stacked supplies, shipping containers, and heavy equipment. Jordan had plans to take a boat ride with her friends into Ronne Bay, the bay formed out of the retreating ice shelf of the same name. Tonight she had a flight back to North America. In a few days, it would be ten years. Jordan had no intention of missing the anniversary of Sachi's death. But first she had to pass her final lab exam.

Jordan stared at the small, clear container in her hand and frowned. It wasn't much of an experiment. She hoped Professor Grastorf would give her a break. Jordan needed a C to pass the course. But her experiment into icosahedral quasicrystals left a lot to be desired. The crystals she had grown were about the size of a half peanut and were highly unstable. Jordan had spent too much time on them following a hunch on crystal formation that she hoped would prove to be a new type of superconductor. And the crystals did conduct electricity. The crystals just did not do so in any recognizable manner. That is, if they didn't … well, she wasn't sure what they did! Vanish? Dissolve?

Oh, Jordan wailed, the professor was going to hate it. She wasn't going to get a passing grade, and then it would be another year working on a new thesis for her master's degree!

Jordan sighed and stepped into the lab. She had two hours before the professor and a couple of his colleagues arrived—Jordan's master's advisory board members. Jordan began setting up her equipment: the electromagnetic containment field, the protective sphere where the harness for the crystal would be suspended, the minute wires that held the harness in place, the laser that would shoot power into the crystal, the mass spectrometer, and the high-speed cameras. Everything had to be just right.

"Miss Mackley." The deep, rich voice of Professor Grastorf broke Jordan's concentration.

"Oh, Professor, I didn't hear you enter." Jordan turned around from her bulbous contraption to see Professors Jerry Grastorf, Kimberly Pike, and Alen Zagami arrayed by the door to the laboratory.

"Are you ready, Miss Mackley?" Professor Pike asked. She was the youngest of the three professors, with a full head of curled, blond hair and sharp blue eyes. Jordan knew Professor Pike was much more likely to be forgiving when it came to scientific application. The University of Antarctica was primarily a research institution that prided itself on the application of science to earth's problems. Professor Pike would probably appreciate Jordan's experiment based solely upon the science of it—even if it was inconclusive and created more questions than answers.

"Yes, Professor. I'm ready."

"Have you managed to adjust for your instability issues?" Professor Zagami asked. He was a tall, thin man with a beaked nose that supported thick glasses. He apparently had some type of eye issue that could not be corrected with laser surgery. Jordan had heard the professor had been offered a new, cybernetic implant that would replace the natural lenses in his eyes, but the professor had opted for the bulky glasses instead.

"Um … well … sort of …" Jordan admitted. "Theoretically, the crystal form should be more stable. I think the growing process is still imperfect. The lattice structures become more solid over time, but I suspect that the forces of gravity are having a limiting effect upon them."

"Can you elaborate a little?" Professor Grastorf came closer to survey Jordan's contraption.

"The crystalline structures are fragile when forming. It is one of the reasons why I can't seem to grow them any larger than half a centimeter. The walls of the lattice collapse in on themselves as if they are unable to sustain their own weight."

"One of the reasons?" Professor Pike asked.

"Yes. One of them."

"What are the other reasons?" the professor prompted.

Jordan smiled, feeling a little queasy. "They seem to be inherently unstable. That," she indicated the containment field and the crystalline containment globe where the harness was suspended, "is why these precautions are necessary."

"Is it dangerous?" Professor Grastorf asked.

"To be completely honest, Professor, I am not sure." Jordan reached into the pocket of her lab coat and pulled out a handful of sliced metal. "Parts of harnesses," she said, pointing at the heart of her contraption. "They are mostly nickel—not too strong. But every now and again, when I introduce power to the crystal, there is some type of force that is released that slices through the harness. It's a shearing force and appears to have an elliptical striking arc. When it happened the first time, it cut through the harness and a pencil I had been holding by the edge of the crystal for measurement purposes. The pencil gave scale for the camera.

"Since then I've taken care to keep away from the crystals when adding power. It seems that the shearing force only reaches out six inches past the center of the crystal. The protective sphere is twice that distance from the crystal."

"I see," Professor Grastorf replied with a frown. "Well, let's get copies of your final thesis, and then you can walk us through the experiment."

"There is something else ... something new and unexpected," Jordan added. "I've added a section to the end of my thesis paper. It is a phenomenon that only started happening recently, and I wasn't sure what to make of it. But now I can replicate the phenomenon pretty regularly."

"What type of phenomenon, Miss Mackley?" Professor Zagami said as he took a copy of the paper, which Jordan had dug out of her backpack, handing a copy to each of the professors.

"That's why the mass spectrometer," Jordan replied. "I'm measuring the crystal's mass. Really, to be honest, the mass of everything within the protective sphere. Because ..." She took a deep breath. Jordan knew how silly her next statement would sound. "The mass appears to change."

"What?" Professor Grastorf sounded bemused and irritated at the same time. "The mass is changing? I had assumed the protective sphere isolated the experiment."

"It is fully enclosed and surrounded by the electromagnetic field."

"Then explain yourself."

"Please, Professor, let me demonstrate it. I have the mass spectrometer set up and the high-speed camera. Before I tell you what my conclusions are, I'd like you to observe the crystal in action. That way I can't predispose you to any conclusion."

"By all means, Miss Mackley. Let's proceed then," Professor Grastorf said.

Jordan passed protective eyewear to each of the professors and took a gulp of air. She moved off to the side of her device to give the professors an unfettered view of the experiment and did a final check on her equipment. Satisfied, she took a long pincer with a rubberized tip out from the table and gingerly reached into the box where the crystals sat. Drawing one of the crystals out, she carefully moved it into place, suspending it in the harness so that its triangular ends pointed straight up and down. The crystal hovered between the nickel and a small electromagnetic field as if it were floating is space. The crystal centered itself in the suspending ring of the harness where it twinkled in the room's light.

Jordan let out a tense breath as the crystal settled. That was a good sign. It was not uncommon for the crystals to dissolve during the setting process.

"Okay. I'm switching on the containment field and isolating the crystal." Jordan punched a button and twisted a knob on power lines that ran from her contraption to the power outlet. "Now to get a mass reading," she added.

It took a few moments before the mass spectrometer had measured the mass and component parts of all items within the sphere.

"Are you satisfied with the reading, Professor Grastorf? Professors Pike, Zagami?"

"You're doing fine," Professor Pike said with a smile. The woman adjusted her protective eyewear. "Your crystal seems to have settled in the field. You have improved its structures."

"Yes, Professor. Thank you for your suggestions. They were very helpful." Jordan pointed to a monitor that was connected to the mass spectrometer. It showed a graph with various lines that reflected the makeup of all the material in the protective sphere. "You'll note the reading," Jordan said. "Now, we'll just turn on the laser and introduce energy into the system. I am shooting it right at the heart of the crystalline structure. Ready? Okay. Here goes …"

Jordan turned the laser on and slowly began increasing the amount of power flowing to the crystal. "Here I'm going to demonstrate the shear," she said. "A minute flux in the intensity of the laser will cause …"

The crystal flashed, and suddenly the harness was sliced into multiple jagged pieces that fluttered to the bottom of the protective sphere. At the same time, the crystal itself disintegrated into a fine powder that also settled on the bottom of the sphere.

"Interesting," was all Professor Grastorf said. He flipped through Jordan's thesis and stopped, examining something.

"You'll note the mass in the sphere has not changed." Jordan indicated the reading on the monitor.

"As expected," Professor Grastorf replied.

"Yes, yes. But, here, let me get ready for the next test. It will just take a couple minutes. Then I'll show you this new effect."

Jordan spent several minutes cleaning out the sphere and setting up the next iteration of the experiment. While she worked, the three professors chatted about her thesis and flipped through the revised pages. Jordan tried not to listen to them as they dissected her paper. It was difficult. Her whole future depended on their awarding her the master's degree.

"Okay. I am all ready. See the mass readings? Take a close note."

"Go ahead, dear," Professor Pike said.

"Here goes." Jordan swallowed hard and once again turned the laser on, slowly increasing its power. But instead of creating a low flux in power beamed at the harnessed crystal, she suddenly drove the power high. There was a flash and pop, and where before the crystal had sat within the protective sphere, suspended in the harness, there was nothing.

Professor Grastorf stepped forward, consternation clearly on his aged face. "Where did it go, Miss Mackley?"

"I don't know," Jordan answered. "And look at the mass reading now. The mass of the crystal is missing. It's gone."

"That's not possible," Professor Grastorf retorted. "You did something wrong. Play back the high-speed camera."

Jordan did so. The ultra high-frame camera captured the crystal's disappearance. One moment it was suspended in the harness, and the next instant, it was simply gone. At the same instant, the mass in the protective sphere dropped by the weight of the crystal.

"That doesn't make any sense," the professor said. Professor Grastorf turned to his colleagues. "Does that make any sense to you?"

"Something has to be wrong with the isolation field," Professor Zagami agreed. "You can change the form of an object, but you can't destroy mass. It should be there. Somewhere."

"It's not," Jordan claimed. "I've done this experiment a couple hundred times, and the mass is always less. I can't explain it, but the crystal isn't here anymore."

"Where is it then?" Professor Pike asked.

"I'm not certain," Jordan admitted. "But I have a theory."

"Is that why you've made a last minute change to the title of your thesis?"

Jordan nodded. "Conjunction of Dark Matter, Icosahedral Quasicrystal Lattice and the Nature of Space"—yes. It is the only thing that made sense to me. The crystal has the ability to capture dark matter. And when the two forces collide, matter and dark matter, they cancel each other out. The crystal vanishes. It is unmade—well, that is my theory at least. Needs a lot of work …"

Jordan looked at the three professors. She knew the experiment was not the best. It had no practical value. And her theory about what had happened to the crystal was, well, a little crazy.

"I am a little disappointed in you, Miss Mackley." Professor Grastorf stood back from the experiment with a sigh. "The University of Antarctica is a research university, but we pride ourselves on the practical application of science. The crystal you've developed is highly unstable and … dare I say … dangerous? I don't think your crystal is worthy of a degree."

"It is an insane little crystal," Professor Pike agreed. "But surely Miss Mackley's work in crystalline structure growth is worthy of the university, Professor Grastorf." Professor Pike ran a hand through her blond hair and smiled. "That work has great potential."

"I agree," Professor Zagami added. "This … insanity crystal … is a curiosity at best. You allowed it to distract you, Miss Mackley. And though I agree with Professor Grastorf that the crystal you are focused on is not worthy of a degree, we should not ignore the advance crystalline work represented in your paper. I think the process you use could be expanded commercially and improve the quality of current generation superconducting crystals."

Jordan felt a roll of failure and elation and hope. Maybe she had not blown it after all.

"Professor Grastorf?" she asked. Professor Grastorf was the chair of her thesis committee. His would be the deciding voice.

"Yes," the professor considered aloud. "The value of your research is in crystal construction. Your conclusions, however, are a little fantastic. But we can't ignore the rest of the work. It has merit.

Will you commit to a rewrite that emphasizes the growing process over the dark matter theory?"

"Yes, Professor. If you all think that is for the best."

"Then, Miss Mackley, send us the rewrite after the summer break, and we will welcome you into the doctorate program. Congratulations."

Jordan beamed. "Thank you, Professor Grastorf—Professors Pike, Zagami. Thank you so very much!"

"I expect the revised paper promptly after the break, young lady. Promptly."

"Yes, sir."

"I have some other meetings now," Professor Grastorf said. "Are you coming along?" the professor said to his colleagues.

"You two go ahead," Professor Pike replied. "I will help our newest graduate dismantle her experiment."

"As you wish. Miss Mackley, Professor Pike, good day."

Professors Grastorf and Zagami turned and left the laboratory. It had been no more than an hour since they had arrived.

Jordan sighed. "Thank you, Professor Pike. I thought I had blown it."

"This is a most curious little crystal you created, Jordan. I've never seen or heard of anything like it. But Professor Grastorf is a stickler, and he lacks vision."

"Professor!"

Professor Pike laughed. Her voice sounded like wind tickling ice crystals. "Well, he is! You did good work. Really. I am proud of you."

"Thank you, Professor. That means a lot."

After the lab was cleaned and the experiment mothballed, Jordan raced back to her living quarters to finish packing. After such a stressful day, she needed to relax with a boat ride on Ronne Bay before flying back home. As she finished packing and then took a transport to the port in Halley Town, Jordan let her mind drift and flutter over her thesis paper.

"The Insanity Crystal: Icosahedral Quasicrystal Lattice Growth and Advanced Crystalline Design." Jordan thought the new name had a little more zing. There was something about it that resonated. And she had passed, barely. After the break, she would formally enter the doctorate program. She couldn't wait to tell her father and stepmother. They would be so happy for her.

Jordan rolled over onto her back by the little grave overlooking the steep bluff. Laying once more by Sachi's side, Jordan watched as the moon rose, full and bright against a darkened sky. On her way here, Jordan had stopped and visited her father, who still lived by the old FEMA storage facility just three miles from where Jordan relaxed. It was now called Sunstep and sported a small community of nearly thirty thousand people. Jordan had been shocked at how old and frail her father appeared. But he had Jordan's stepmother, her adopted brother Robert, and Jordan's other adopted sibling, Mary, to keep him company. Robert was starting high school, while Mary was just finishing her senior year. Next year, Mary intended to follow Jordan to the University of Antarctica. The woman who had stumbled onto the kids during that last night, Laura Mathis, was a leading member of the Civilian Defensive Force and was in charge of the fifth district along the east coast. They were still close friends. And luckily everyone was healthy.

Many people suffered various cancers due to the use of tactical nuclear weapons in the Battle of Washington. Of course, nobody traveled anywhere near Washington, DC, anymore. It was part of a vast area left abandoned to radiation, the encroaching ocean, and a developing wilderness. Consequently, the capital of the North American Union, encompassing the old nations of Canada, Mexico, and the United States, was now firmly established in Kansas City. The military alliance of the war had evolved into a single government due to the Chinese nuclear counterstrike. Limited though the strike was, the three nations of North America could not handle the amount of damage on their own. As for the Chinese, their forces destroyed, they abandoned the Americas and faded back into the Far East. The war had precipitated social upheaval that marked the end to China's militaristic ambitions.

Jordan ran her hand through her brown hair and stared up at the stars. "Someday, Sachi," she said. "Someday we'll live up there. Wouldn't that be nice? What do you think is up there? Do you think we'll find extraterrestrial life?" She paused. "You know, I passed my exam. I got my master's. Isn't that great? I'll start the doctorate program next year ... God, I miss you."

Jordan smiled sadly and rolled over in her sleeping bag. Fresh flowers covered the grave, and the tiny marker she had placed a few years ago was damp with the evening dew. Reaching out one hand, Jordan draped it across Sachi's grave.

"You saved my life, boy. I love you, Sachi. I love you. You're the best thing that ever happened to me."

Closing her eyes, Jordan silently mourned. The wind danced, and the moon shone bright. And there was not one cloud in the deep, wondrous sky.

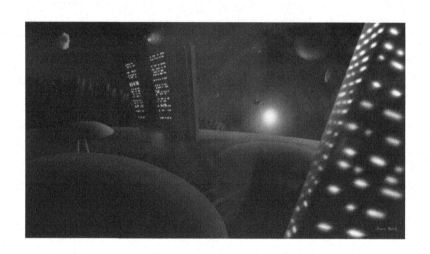

Appendix

ALIENS AND ALIEN RACES

humans. Bipeds originally from the Terra or Sol system.

Khajuraho. An alien race first discovered in the Selee system. They are slightly shorter than humans, stocky, and powerful nitrogen breathers.

Technoprey. A destructive alien life form that lives in the gaseous clouds of a gas giant. The Technoprey swarm every forty thousand years and attack any source of artificial energy (i.e., technology).

CORPORATIONS

Lin Corp. One of the big three corporations. Lin Corp was established by Er Quin on the planet Mars. It later relocated to Romeo, second planet in the Lingmi system. Lin is the most environmentally conscious of the big three corporations.

Militan Corporation. A mining corporation that is a subsidiary of Syrch Corp. ("A Lucky Man")

Terra Corp. One the largest of the big three corporations. Terra Corp was the first modern corporation that tied together Sole system's economy under their umbrella. Terra Corp is the largest and most powerful of the three big corporations.

Syrch Corp. One of the largest of the three big corporations. Syrch Corp is the most greedy and least environmentally conscious of the three corporations.

Zintas Mines. A mining company on the planet Telakia. Located in the Memphis Mountain range, the company is a subsidiary of the Militan Corp. ("A Lucky Man")

MILITARY UNITS

Civilian Defensive Force. A quasi military/police force in North America during the First Resource War. ("A Season for Killing")

Defenders Division. Terra Corp's military headquarters. The Defender's Division is located in the Oort cloud of Sol on Callirrhoe Station. ("Threshold")

Geist Marines. Highly specialized, augmented marines nominally controlled by the government of Earth but in reality controlled by Terra Corp. There are not many Geist Marines, as augmenting the marines is astronomically expensive. They are the special forces of Terra Corp's naval and marine space service. ("Threshold")

Wuhezhi. Low-quality, South American troops, impressed by the Chinese during the First Resource War to fight in North and South America. ("A Season for Killing")

PLACES

Echo Mine. A Terra Corp asteroid mining facility in the Selee system. It has five domes and two control towers known as Alpha and Bravo. ("Threshold")

Calico Flats. The large, open flat land is the location of the landing platform and Echo Mine. ("Threshold")

Callirrhoe Station. Terra Corp has its premier naval base located in the Sole system, in the Oort cloud, on the dwarf planet 90377 Sedna. ("Threshold")

Kugadar. The capital city of the planet Telakia, located at the southern edge of the Great Desert. It is the location for the planet's only spaceport. ("A Lucky Man")

Narious Station. A refueling station owned by Terra Corp in the Luyten system where the ship *Symons's Dream* was destroyed. ("Revenge")

Umbaliya. Known as the oasis city, Umbaliya is located in the near center of the Great Desert on the planet Telakia. The city is mostly underground. ("A Lucky Man")

University of Antarctica. A prestigious university located near Halley Town, near the Weedell Sea, in Antarctica.

PEOPLE

Aaron Nobel. Employee of Terra Corp on Echo Mine. He is a machine operator and married to Anne Nobel. ("Threshold")

Admiral Molouf. An admiral from Lin Corp sent to assist Terra Corp with the return mission to Echo Mine. ("Threshold")

Admiral Oduya. An admiral from Syrch Corp sent to assist Terra Corp with the return mission to Eco Mine. ("Threshold")

Ambassador Weir. A political person from Earth sent with the Terra Corp Navy to attempt a political solution regarding Echo Mine. ("Threshold")

Anne Nobel. Employee of Terra Corp on Echo Mine and is married to Aaron Nobel. She is a former Terra Corp Marine, Fifth Corps, and carries a personal pulse gun. ("Threshold")

Barlow. An ensign on the *Ark Royal*. ("Threshold")

Captain Allyn Toriksen. A captain in the Civilian Defensive Force during the First Resource War. ("A Season for Killing")

Captain Jimmy X. Fleet Admiral Mehra's aide-de-camp. ("Threshold")

Captain Donovan Cole. Captain of the *Ark Royal*. ("Threshold")

Captain Lawson Cooper. Mad pilot of *Revenge*. The ship carried an early frame bomb and was launched in a reprisal against Lin Corp. ("Revenge")

Cecilia Cooper. The deceased wife of Captain Lawson Cooper. She was killed by a Lin Corp attack on the ship *Symons's Dream*. ("Revenge")

Commander Trillian Naismith. Commander of the battle cruiser *Firthjof*. ("Revenge")

Commander Ryan Reiner. The overall commander of the aeroship *Defender One* during the First Resource War. ("A Season for Killing")

Corporal Clancy Fox. A Geist Marine. Carries a Ram 592, sniper rifle. ("Threshold")

Corporal Fergus Yeaw. A Geist Marine. ("Threshold")

Corporal Jehu Eyre. A Geist Marine. Carries a Ram 592, sniper rifle. ("Threshold")

Corporal Mardick: A Geist Marine. ("Threshold")

Corporal Ryes. A Geist Marine who carries a KNR-FL assault rifle. ("Threshold")

Corporal Shea Alexander. A corporal in the Geist Marines. She carries a KNR-FL assault rifle. ("Threshold")

David McCall. Employee of Terra Corp on Echo Mine. He is Echo Mine's medical doctor. ("Threshold")

David Rawlings. A cruel boy during the First Resource War. ("A Season for Killing")

Dashiell Thompson. A thug for the Gionolla crime family on Telakia. Arrested for the murder of Balzac Godshock. Becomes the protector of the infant Ona Yuyenda Ransan. ("A Lucky Man")

Dietri Beck. A soldier during the Second Resource War who went on to be a music composer in the classical style.

Dr. Werner. The doctor was a member of the first Mars exploration. He went insane and killed everyone else on the ship *First Hope*. The crazed doctor eventually crashed *First Hope* into the Marian moon Deimos. ("Revenge")

Ensign Pennington. She is an ensign on the *Ark Royal* and runs the tactical station. ("Threshold")

Ensign Redman Naidoo. Ensign Naidoo is a young, tactical officer aboard the *Ark Royal*. ("Threshold")

Fleet Admiral Rakesh Mehra. Commanding admiral of Terra Corp's navy. His headquarters is on Callirrhoe Station. ("Threshold")

Fred. The copilot of the *Defender One* during the First Resource War. ("A Season for Killing")

General Grant Gaspar. A roughneck, Terra Corp Marine general. ("Threshold")

Haamar Ransan. A geologist who works for Zintas Mine, in the exploratory division, on the desert planet Telakia. Husband to Yuyenda Ransan. ("A Lucky Man")

Henry Gustoff. An executive for Zintas Mines on the planet Telakia. ("A Lucky Man")

Jema Rawlings. A cruel woman during the First Resource War. Mother to David and Keith Rawlings. Slaver of Mary and Robby. ("A Season for Killing")

Jordan Mackley. Inventor of the Insanity Crystal. A survivor of the First Resource War. ("A Season for Killing")

Junior Lieutenant Kapana. JL Kapana was an amateur singer and thespian from Eibsee Major 95128. He is the communication and sensors officer aboard the *Ark Royal*. ("Threshold")

Karsten Neumann. The weak CEO of Zintas Mines. ("A Lucky Man")

Keith Rawlings. A cruel boy during the First Resource War. ("A Season for Killing")

Laura Mathis. An officer of the Civilian Defensive Force (CDF) and pilot of the aeroship *Defender One*. ("A Season for Killing")

Lieutenant Colette Giggatelli. She is the flight control officer on the *Ark Royal*. ("Threshold")

Lieutenant Commander Kory Spade. Second in command of the *Ark Royal*. ("Threshold")

Lieutenant Crispin Leforce. An officer aboard the *Ark Royal*. ("Threshold")

Mary. The computer for the ship *Revenge*. ("Revenge")

Master Sergeant Sayer Kade. A grizzled veteran of the Geist Marines, he has been physically enhanced and is superhuman. ("Threshold")

Paul Thorne. AKA Paul Harlamor. An enforcer for Militan Corp. ("A Lucky Man")

Professor Jerry Grastorf. The master's thesis chair for Jordan Makley at the University of Antarctica. ("A Season for Killing")

Professor Kimberly Pike. The master's thesis committee member for Jordan Makley at the University of Antarctica. ("A Season for Killing")

Professor Alen Zagami. The master's thesis committee member for Jordan Makley at the University of Antarctica. ("A Season for Killing")

Sachi. Jordan Mackley's Berger Picard breed of dog. ("A Season for Killing")

Sergeant Eric Stratton. A Geist Marine who lost his vocal cords on Aldor Prime. He has a cybernetic right forearm. ("Threshold")

Sergeant Steven Dixon. A Geist Marine. ("Threshold")

Sidney Blithe. A small-time crook on the planet Telakia. Lives in the rundown Newlings District of the capital city Kugadar. ("A Lucky Man")

Terrence Silva. The first CEO of Lin Corporation. She led a trade war with early earth colonies against Earth and Terra Corporation. ("Revenge")

Theresa Sloan. She is the comely, blond, forty-something foreman of Echo Mine and works for Terra Corp. ("Threshold")

Tonya Livingston. Chief executive officer of Militan Corp. ("A Lucky Man")

Tyena Totske. Sister of Yuyenda Ransan. Resides on Telakia and is the stepmother to Ona Yuyenda Ransan. ("A Lucky Man")

Vice Admiral Mathew Crow. An admiral assigned by Terra Corp to the Battle Task Force against the Khajuraho. ("Threshold")

Yuyenda Ransan. A geologist who works for Zintas Mines, in the exploratory division, on Telakia. Wife of Haamar Ransan. ("A Lucky Man")

STAR SHIPS

Ark Royal. The Terra Corp cruiser captained by Captain Cole. ("Threshold")

Arrow Hawk. A Terra Corp luxury yacht used by the administrator of Echo Mine. ("Threshold")

Defender One. A huge aeroship flown by Officer Laura Mathis during the First Resource War. ("A Season for Killing")

First Hope. The name of the first ship sent to Mars. The journey ended in tragedy as Dr. Werner, suffering from hallucinations, slaughtered the crew. ("Revenge")

Firthjof. An admiral-class battle cruiser captained by Trillian Naismith. It is a Lin Corp ship. ("Revenge")

Pintado. A Terra Corp jump ship.

Revenge. A stealth ship sent from Lin Corp in the First Trade War against Terra Corp in a retaliatory attack in the Barnard's Star system. ("Revenge")

Symons's Dream. The ship that was destroyed as it refueled on Narious Station in the Luyten system. ("Revenge")

Battle Task Force ("Threshold")

Strike Ship Group

Monarch. A capital-class battleship, it is the flagship of Fleet Admiral Mehra of Terra Corp.

Avenger. A heavy cruiser.

Eos. A heavy cruiser.

Nornen. A destroyer.

Rover. A destroyer.

Skipjack. A frigate.

Warbler. A heavy assault ship.

Blockade Group

Scorpion. A heavy cruiser. It is the flagship for Admiral Molouf. Lin Corp.

Valor. A cruiser. Lin Corp.

Lightning. A destroyer. Lin Corp.

Attack Group

Natsek. State-of-the art heavy battle cruiser. The flagship for Admiral Oduya. Syrch Corp.

Chung Mu. A destroyer. Syrch Corp.

Avalanche. A heavy cruiser. Terra Corp.

Alliance. A destroyer. Terra Corp.

Fiske. A cruiser. Terra Corp.

Asteroid Assault Group

Ailanthus. A frigate. Terra Corp.

Grampus. An assault ship. Terra Corp.

SYSTEMS AND PLANETS

90377 Sedna. A trans-Neptunian object (dwarf planet) in the Sol system, in the Oort cloud, where Terra Corp has its premier naval base, Callirrhoe Station. The dwarf planet has three moons: Cynthia, Selene, and Diana. ("Threshold")

Aldor Prime. A small system controlled by Terra Corp in the Aldor system. It is the location of a small but dirty little turf war between Terra and Syrch. ("Threshold")

Bernard's Star. A system six light-years from earth. It has a red dwarf star and twin planets known as Van De Kamp's miracles: Dark Companion and Makemake. ("Revenge")

Dark Companion. The planet is three times the size of Earth, is known for its volcanoes, and is located in Barnard's Star system. It is one of two planets in a rare phenomenon where two planets of near equal mass orbit each other and share an orbit around the system's star. Its companion planet is called Makemake. ("Revenge")

Lasslo Prime. The main, watery planet in the Lasslo system where a small rebellion against Terra Corp was put down. ("Threshold")

Luyten. The location of the fueling station Narious where the ship *Symons's Dream* was destroyed. ("Revenge")

Makemake. The planet is two times the size of Earth, has vast oceans four times deeper than those on Earth, and is located in Barnard's Star system. It is one of two planets in a rare phenomenon where two planets of near equal mass orbit each other and share an orbit around the system's star. Its companion planet is called Dark Companion. ("Revenge")

Centarus Five. A water world of many islands to include the New British Isles. They export textiles and Lunama Fur. Their main water-port city is Daleshire. ("A Lucky Man")

Selee system. Location of Echo Mine.

Sol. The humans' home system with its planet Earth.

Telakia. A desert world known for its abundance of moissanite. Its capital city is Kugadar at the southern end of the Great Desert. It is a Syrch Corp world. ("A Lucky Man")

TECHNOLOGY

communication drones. Drone ships that used framing drives to pass information between systems by emitting high-burst transmissions to communication buoys.

communication buoys. The backbone for interstellar communication. Drones framed into a system in designated drop spots where they exchanged information with communication buoys. They drones then framed to the next system and repeated the process.

electromagnetic wave-shield. An early form of protective shield for interstellar ships, the EWS creates a pocket of protective energy around a ship. ("Revenge")

frame drive. The engine that allows for interstellar space travel and is powered by insanity crystals.

insanity crystals. Crystals that allow for framing and are the backbone technology for interstellar space travel.

Juice. A drink of tiny nubots, little nucleic acid robots generated in septic free-fall laboratories. They rebuild muscle tissue, bones, and eyes and enhance their functions. Lin and Terra Corp make the most effective Juice. High-end Juice is very, very expensive. ("Threshold")

kirlov radiation. Radiation caused by use of an insanity crystal when a ship's shields displace objects at the destination point of a frame drive jump. It is recognizable as a faint glow around ships that are framing through space.

v-tanks. Full-body tanks that isolate the body and create sensations to make virtual worlds nearly realistic. They were developed for early space travel to keep people stimulated on the long journeys, but after the invention of the frame drive, they were used mostly for entertainment purposes. Too much "v-tanking" is known to create psychotic episodes. ("Revenge")

TERMINOLOGY

drop spots. The location within a given system where communication buoys are posted. There were kept clear so communication drones could quickly frame in and out of a system, exchanging information.

flat spots. Artificial gravity wells created by Ripplers that, when detonated, make it impossible for ships and weapons within their reach to use their frame drives. ("Revenge")

folded space. Framing drives use the folds in space to "jump" a ship between folds. This allows interstellar ships to traverse the stars.

heavies. A term used to refer to physically powerful men and women who specialize in the use of force. Often used when talking about Geist Marines. ("Threshold")

junked-up. A derogatory term used to describe people who have used too much nano augmentation on their bodies. ("Threshold")

metratronic computer chips. Computer chips that use the flow of light through their circuits instead of slower, electrical pulses. ("Revenge")

T-lines. Lines of trajectory for objects (ships, missiles, drones) moving through space. ("Threshold")

WEAPONS AND GEAR

ARG-L35s. Ship-based argon lasers.

combat packs. Transport devices dropped from low orbit that contain large pieces of equipment like Scouts, Mark IIs, and so on.

E-670-D automated artillery. Robotic artillery used by Terra Corp Marines.

IR-10 actuators. Remote-controlled devices that when activated ignite whatever explosives are attached to them.

jump chute. A rectangular, near full-body device that allows for low orbital jumps for troops. Colloquially called JCs. Once on the ground, they provide tactical logistic support by carrying gear and have small-caliber automatic weapons, ARG-P5 (argon-based pulse weapon). In that configuration, they are normally referred to as Dogs.

K-90s. A ship-based weapons system.

KNR flechette rifles. High-capacity rifles that fire iron needles at ultra-high velocity with very little recoil and provide significant firepower.

Malcolm Mouser. A double-action flechette pistol with no metal that is difficult to screen for—favored by criminals and assassins.

Mark IIs. A particular type of robotic Scout favored by Geist Marines. They resemble spiders and are capable of providing close air support.

Montgomery pulse tanks. Pulse-laser, heavy tanks used by Terra Corp Marines.

Nebula torpedoes. Torpedoes that used frame drives, dropping into normal space just before hitting their target.

pony. Also known as a "military pony," it is a tracking device that latches onto an enemy ship and periodically drops off ponies that frame back to friendly forces and provide location intelligence.

Ram 592s. Sniper rifles with laser-guided smart munitions. They fire supersonic munitions that adjust their flight trajectory as they go and almost never miss. They are precision weapons and do not carry many rounds.

Ripplers. Space mines that cause disruptions in the fabric of space. They create a gravity well that replicates the wells of large celestial bodies, like planets, which prevent frame drives from functioning. They catch enemy ships and torpedoes and force them to use in-system engines, slowing their movement. The artificial wells are known as flat spots.

Scouts. Robotic battle units that specialize as remote, advance scouts.

sheet lasers. Lasers with a broad breadth that are used to counter mass orbital jumps by hostile infantry.

Sentinels. Robotic battle units that specialize in defensive actions.

tungsten pole. A cylindrical device that replicates the impact of a large meteorite on a planet or moon, causing an explosion similar to a nuclear one without any radiation. It relies on kinetic energy.

Zhanshi Five. A midranged Chinese drone during the First Resource War. ("A Season for Killing")

Dryden Sci/Fi Universe Time Line (V 2.0)

2035   Primer Epoque begins.

2037–2054 First Resource War, also known as the Extermination War. Nuclear and chemical weapon exchanges leaves much of North America and Eurasia depopulated. Some land areas remain uninhabitable for centuries. Establishment of the North American Union, the immediate precursor to the more formalized New American Federation.

2053   Events of "A Season for Killing" take place—the Battle of Washington.

2056   Qin, the first permanent lunar colony, founded by Chinese.

2063   Dr. Jordan Mackley, the inventor of the insanity crystal, finishes her master's thesis at the newly constituted University of Antarctica. Entitled "The Insanity Crystal: Icosahedral Quasicrystal Lattice Growth and Advanced Crystalline Design," Dr. Mackley never realizes the significance of her discovery. ("A Season for Killing")

2089   First attempted manned mission to Mars ends tragically when Dr. Adelchi Werner goes insane aboard the ship *First Hope*, killing the crew and crashing the ship into Mar's moon Deimos. ("Revenge")

2099   First successful manned Mars landing, China.

2106	First manned Venus landing, New American Federation.
2110	First Mars colony, International Space Association.
2108–2117	Second Resource War. Chinese moon base Qin destroyed. Rebuilt, named "Er Qin."
2118–2175	Period of global depression following Second Resource War. Referred to as Earth Twilight because Earth's resources past peak.
2175	The dawn of regular spaceflight. Gravity well generators invented, making ground-based space launches inexpensive and providing shipboard gravity for long-distance space flight. Trade across planets within the solar system commercially feasible for the first time.
2180–2210	Period of rapid expansion within the solar system. Venus colony in 2184; Europa colony 2188; Jupiter Cloud colony in 2210; may asteroids settled.
2184	University of Antarctica grad student Lachmi Dryden publishes doctoral thesis titled "The Effects of Natural State Frame Fluctuations on Massed Objects," which outlines the principles for moving an object from one point in space to another without passing through the points in between, effectively allowing faster than light travel without violating e=mc2. The paper receives little attention.
2208	Events of "Star Dust" take place.

2211   Er Qin (precursor to Lin Corp) purchases a majority of Mars, Venus, and several asteroids and becomes the first extra-terran mega corp.

2212   Terra Corp formed. Terra Corp consolidates the majority of Terra's (Earth's) economy, with Europa colony, Mercury Base, the Jupiter Cloud colony, and several asteroids. Earth is effectively one economy.

2215   Er Qin tests PTB 94, a prototype framing drive, based on the synthesis of Dr. Jordan Mackley and Dr. Lachmi Dryden's research. While the engine's failure is visible across the solar system, results indicate that the device jumped between points 2.3 light seconds apart before destroying itself. Media popularizes the term "insanity crystal," invented by Dr. Jordan Mackley 152 years ago.

2216–2223 Terra Corp and Er Qin (precursor to Lin Corp) race to develop stable framing drives. Both claim success in 2223.

2219   First contact is established between researches at the University of Antarctica and Cetaceans. Over time, the bond between Cetaceans and the UoA leads to the building of a secret research station at Lake Vostok, Antarctica. Genetic modification of Cetaceans results in the Ile Soltaire.

2240   Captain Othall of Er Qin (precursor to Lin Corp) successfully pilots the *Hai ou (Sea gull)* from Mars to Earth and back using the framing drive. While his average frame-to-frame jump is only 3.6 light seconds, he completes the journey in eighty-four hours, hundreds of times faster than conventional ships.

2243	Threat of war forces Er Qin off of the moon. They reorganize on Mars as Lin Corp.
2247	Undersea Ocean on Europa reached for the first time. Intense pressure and extreme temperatures slow exploration.
2250–2296	First Trade War. Intense competition between Terra Corp and Lin Corp occasionally boils over to open combat.
2253	First space flight by a Cetacean. A bottlenose dolphin named Hides-in-Ferns secretly pilots a University of Antarctica craft to Earth's moon and back.
2297	Lin Corp stuns the solar system by announcing that it has colonized fourth planet in Proxima Centari system and has explored three other systems. They reveal a secret base on "First Stone," a hundred-kilometer-wide object in the Oort cloud from which they have built and launched ships capable of travels at speeds up to one light-year per five hundred hours.
2298	Without warning, the humans and cetaceans of Lake Vostok, now referring to themselves as Ile Soltaire, leave Earth in a ship of their own design.
2301	Terra Corp establishes its primary space naval base, Callirrhoe Station in the Oort cloud, on the dwarf planet 90377 Sedna.

2305	Theiana Mason born in the city of New Paris on Mars, to Derrik Markowitz and Patricia Mason. Markowitz is a hydroponics engineer. Mason is a classical musician. Theiana is trained as a musician. However, she is captivated by the discovery of life on Ninus 7 and enters the Sea of Tranquility University on the moon as a biologist with a specialization in exobiology.
2315	Lin Corp announces the discovery of a life-bearing planet in the Ninus system. There have been three previous life-bearing planets found. Ninus 7 is the first bearing complex multicellular life.
2317	Terra Corp announces colonization of Tennus Star system.
2320–2329	Second Trade War. A series of nuclear "accidents" on Mars, Earth, and the Ingus asteroid result in Lin Corp relocating to newly colonized Romeo system. This change gives Terra Corp control of the Sol system.
2325	Tennus system declares independence from Terra Corp; Parmer system is charted by upstart Pim Corp.
2328	First contact with the Europan, which resides beneath the frozen oceans on Europa. The Europan is the first clearly sentient exo-species.
2331	Events of "Revenge" take place.
2338	League of Planets formed. League of Planets is a loose confederation of planets that join together to resist the ever-increasing power of the mega-corporations.

2341	Contact lost with colony Olive i-4. An investigation reveals that a mutated Terran Flu virus, usually carried by canines, infected the local environment. The virus infected all organisms on the planet, destroying the ecosystem.
2341	Theiana Mason and others form the Interspecies Defense Fund (IDF). The IDF establish protocols for the identification and protection of life-bearing worlds.
2341	Facing hostile takeover by Lin, Pim corporation dissolves itself, giving the League of Planets full control of the Parmer system. They rename the second planet in the system League Prime.
2346	The League of Planets launches a series of deep-space exploration craft. Among them is the legendary *Duster*.
2355	Syrch Corporation is founded on Papen's World. Civil war breaks out between the independent Federation and Consortium planets.
2358	Lin Corp charters the Genrith system.
2360	Events of "Alder's World" take place.
2370	First sighting of an Ile Soltaire spaceship in deep space.
2375	Events of "A Lucky Man" take place.
2380	The Interspecies Defense Fund (IDF) adopts "The Charter," allowing for the use of violence to protect alien species.

2385	Events of "The Eclipsing of Sirus C" take place.
2387	End of the civil war between the Federation and Consortium with a Federation victory.
2398	The first recorded attack on corporate interests by Theiana Mason's ship, *The Moth*.
2404	Ile Soltaire ship orbits League Prime and issues a short statement declaring thousands of star systems toward galactic center off-limits to all humans.
2414	Syrch Corp secretly begins the development of a ring world around Skeelar's Star, at the edge of Ile Soltaire's no-fly zone.
2435	Events of "Threshold" take place.
2503	Start of Big Damn Dryden Role-Playing Game. Events of "Skye Goddesses of Dryden" take place.
2700–2720	The Battle for Sol. Events of "Rise of the Europan" take place. The Europan takes control of the Sol system.
2720	End of the Primer Epoque. Beginning of the Belle Epoque.
BE 20,000	Events of "Demon's Eyes" and "A Matter of Trust" take place.
BE 40,000	Technoprey awake and begin their destructive swarm. End of the Belle Epoque. Beginning of Codex 2.0.

Printed in the United States
By Bookmasters